MARVEL-VERSE

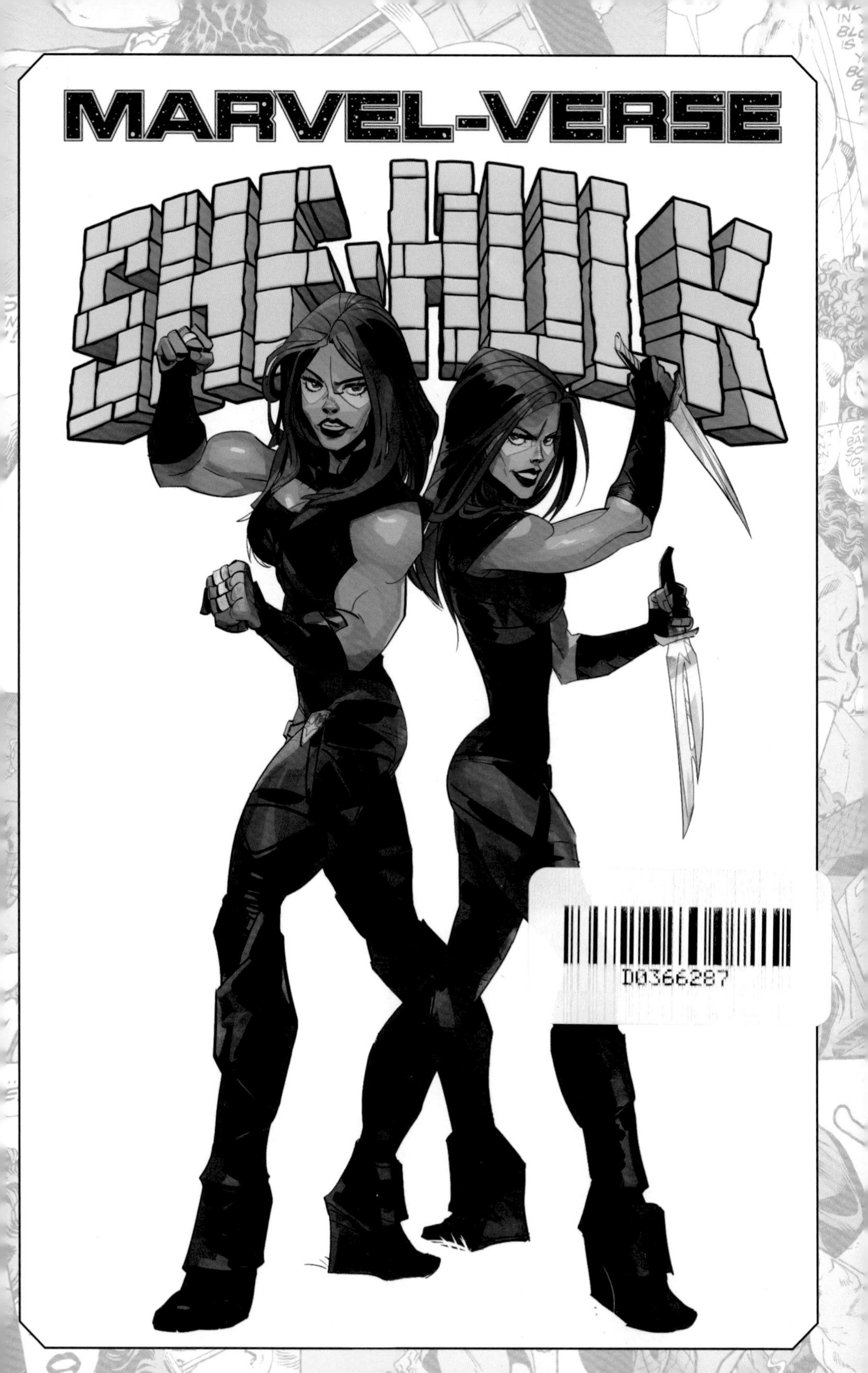
SHE-HULK

MARVEL-VERSE

SAVAGE SHE-HULK #1

WRITER: **STAN LEE**
PENCILER: **JOHN BUSCEMA**
INKER: **CHIC STONE**
LETTERER: **JOE ROSEN**
EDITOR: **JIM SHOOTER**

SENSATIONAL SHE-HULK #4

WRITER & PENCILER: **JOHN BYRNE**
INKER: **BOB WIACEK**
COLORIST: **GLYNIS OLIVER**
LETTERER: **JIM NOVAK**
ASSISTANT EDITOR: **JAMES DIGIOVANNA**
EDITOR: **BOBBIE CHASE**

MARVEL-VERSE: SHE-HULK. Contains material originally published in magazine form as SAVAGE SHE-HULK (1980) #1, SENSATIONAL SHE-HULK (1989) #4, AVENGING SPIDER-MAN (2011) #7, GUARDIANS TEAM-UP (2015) #4 and KING-SIZE SPIDER-MAN SUMMER SPECIAL (2008) #1. First printing 2021. ISBN 978-1-302-93083-7. Published by MARVEL WORLDWIDE, INC., a subsidiary of MARVEL ENTERTAINMENT, LLC. OFFICE OF PUBLICATION: 1290 Avenue of the Americas, New York, NY 10104. © 2021 MARVEL. No similarity between any of the names, characters, persons, and/or institutions in this magazine with those of any living or dead person or institution is intended, and any such similarity which may exist is purely coincidental. **Printed in Canada.** KEVIN FEIGE, Chief Creative Officer; DAN BUCKLEY, President, Marvel Entertainment; JOE QUESADA, EVP & Creative Director; DAVID BOGART, Associate Publisher & SVP of Talent Affairs; TOM BREVOORT, VP, Executive Editor; NICK LOWE, Executive Editor, VP of Content, Digital Publishing; DAVID GABRIEL, VP of Print & Digital Publishing; JEFF YOUNGQUIST, VP of Production & Special Projects; ALEX MORALES, Director of Publishing Operations; DAN EDINGTON, Managing Editor; RICKEY PURDIN, Director of Talent Relations; JENNIFER GRÜNWALD, Senior Editor, Special Projects; SUSAN CRESPI, Production Manager; STAN LEE, Chairman Emeritus. For information regarding advertising in Marvel Comics or on Marvel.com, please contact Vit DeBellis, Custom Solutions & Integrated Advertising Manager, at vdebellis@marvel.com. For Marvel subscription inquiries, please call 888-511-5480. **Manufactured between 5/21/2021 and 6/22/2021 by SOLISCO PRINTERS, SCOTT, QC, CANADA.**

10 9 8 7 6 5 4 3 2 1

KING-SIZE SPIDER-MAN SUMMER SPECIAL #1

WRITER: **PAUL TOBIN**
ARTIST, COLORIST & LETTERER: **COLLEEN COOVER**
COVER ART: **OLIVIER COIPEL, MARK MORALES & JUSTIN PONSOR**
CONSULTING EDITOR: **MARK PANICCIA**
EDITOR: **NATHAN COSBY**

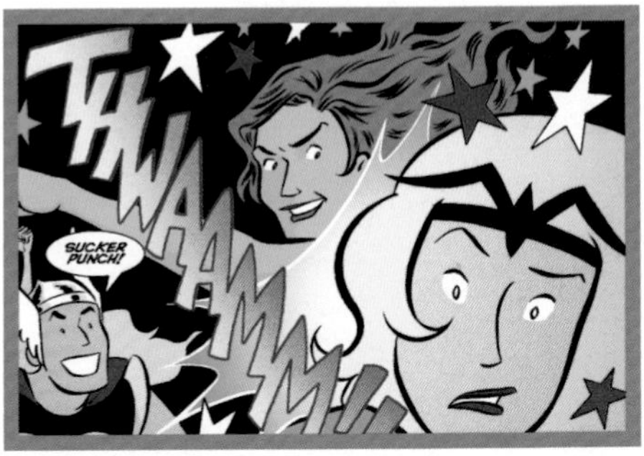
SUCKER PUNCH!

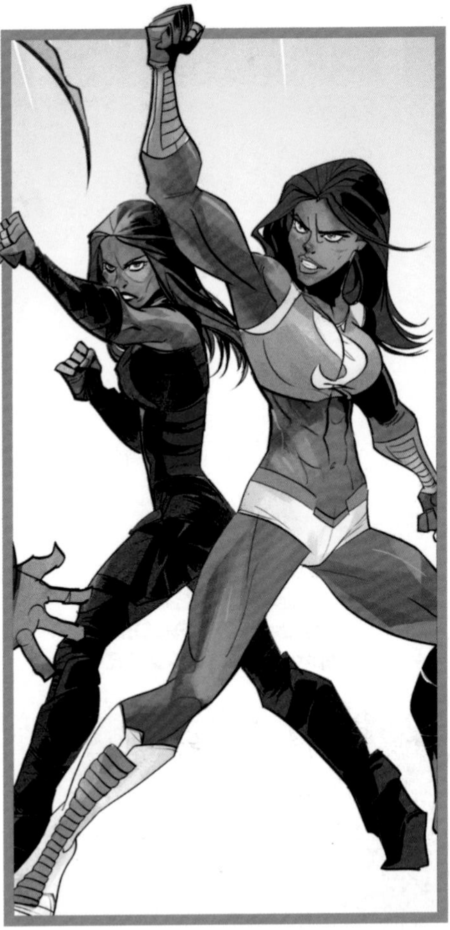

AVENGING SPIDER-MAN #7

WRITER: **KATHRYN IMMONEN**
PENCILER: **STUART IMMONEN**
INKER: **WADE VON GRAWBADGER**
COLORIST: **MATT HOLLINGSWORTH**
LETTERER: **VC's JOE CARAMAGNA**
COVER ART: **STUART IMMONEN, WADE VON GRAWBADGER & MATT HOLLINGSWORTH**
ASSISTANT EDITOR: **ELLIE PYLE**
EDITOR: **STEPHEN WACKER**
EXECUTIVE EDITOR: **TOM BREVOORT**

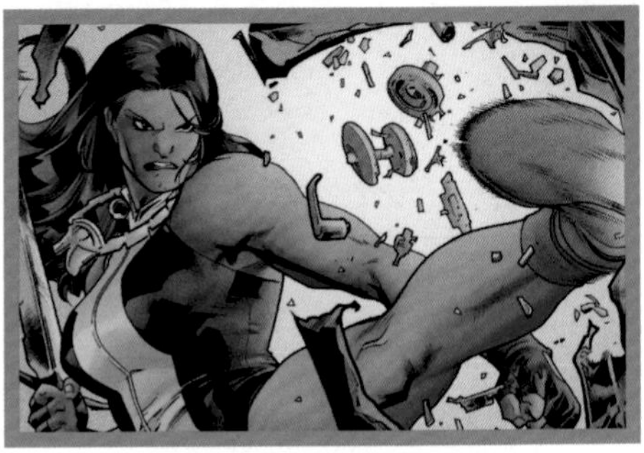

GUARDIANS TEAM-UP #4

WRITER: **JOHN LAYMAN**
ARTIST & COLORIST: **OTTO SCHMIDT**
LETTERER: **VC's CORY PETIT**
COVER ART: **OTTO SCHMIDT**
ASSISTANT EDITOR: **XANDER JAROWEY**
EDITOR: **KATIE KUBERT**
GROUP EDITOR: **MIKE MARTS**

COLLECTION EDITOR: **JENNIFER GRÜNWALD** ASSISTANT EDITOR: **DANIEL KIRCHHOFFER** ASSISTANT MANAGING EDITOR: **MAIA LOY**
ASSISTANT MANAGING EDITOR: **LISA MONTALBANO** ASSOCIATE MANAGER, DIGITAL ASSETS: **JOE HOCHSTEIN**
MASTERWORKS EDITOR: **CORY SEDLMEIER** VP PRODUCTION & SPECIAL PROJECTS: **JEFF YOUNGQUIST**
RESEARCH: **JESS HARROLD** BOOK DESIGNERS: **STACIE ZUCKER & ADAM DEL RE** WITH **JAY BOWEN**
SVP PRINT, SALES & MARKETING: **DAVID GABRIEL** EDITOR IN CHIEF: **C.B. CEBULSKI**

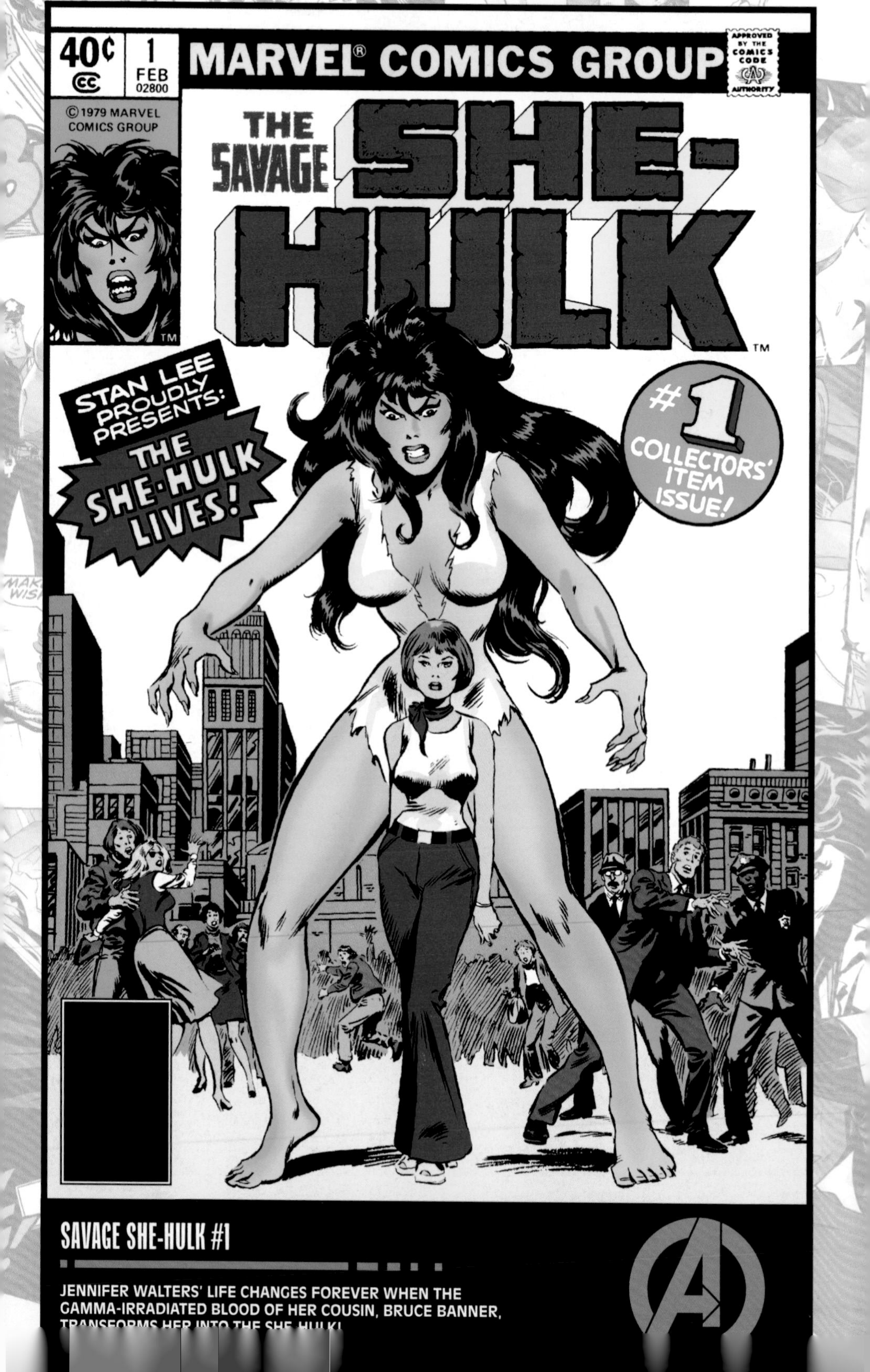
40¢
1
FEB
02800
MARVEL® COMICS GROUP
© 1979 MARVEL COMICS GROUP
THE SAVAGE SHE-HULK
STAN LEE PROUDLY PRESENTS:
THE SHE-HULK LIVES!
#1
COLLECTORS' ITEM ISSUE!

SAVAGE SHE-HULK #1

JENNIFER WALTERS' LIFE CHANGES FOREVER WHEN THE GAMMA-IRRADIATED BLOOD OF HER COUSIN, BRUCE BANNER, TRANSFORMS HER INTO THE SHE-HULK!

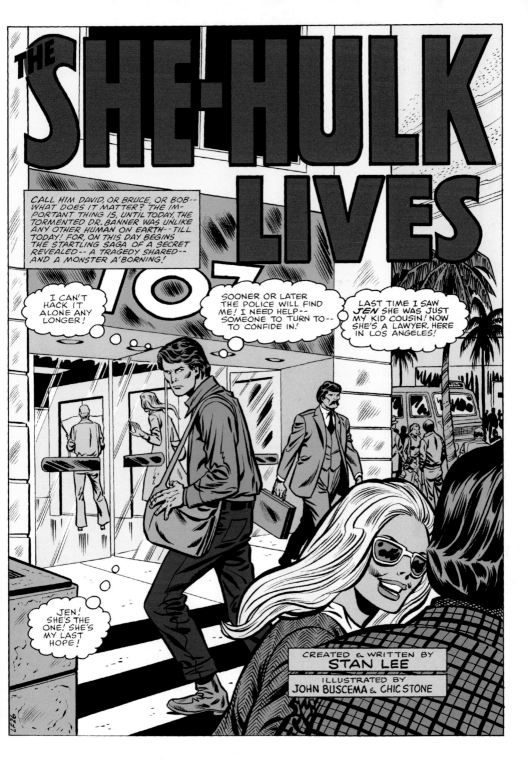

THE SHE-HULK LIVES

CALL HIM DAVID, OR BRUCE, OR BOB-- WHAT DOES IT MATTER? THE IMPORTANT THING IS, UNTIL TODAY, THE TORMENTED DR. BANNER WAS UNLIKE ANY OTHER HUMAN ON EARTH-- TILL TODAY! FOR, ON THIS DAY BEGINS THE STARTLING SAGA OF A SECRET REVEALED-- A TRAGEDY SHARED-- AND A MONSTER A'BORNING!

I CAN'T HACK IT ALONE ANY LONGER!

SOONER OR LATER THE POLICE WILL FIND ME! I NEED HELP-- SOMEONE TO TURN TO-- TO CONFIDE IN!

LAST TIME I SAW *JEN* SHE WAS JUST MY KID COUSIN! NOW SHE'S A LAWYER, HERE IN LOS ANGELES!

JEN! SHE'S THE ONE! SHE'S MY LAST HOPE!

CREATED & WRITTEN BY
STAN LEE

ILLUSTRATED BY
JOHN BUSCEMA & CHIC STONE

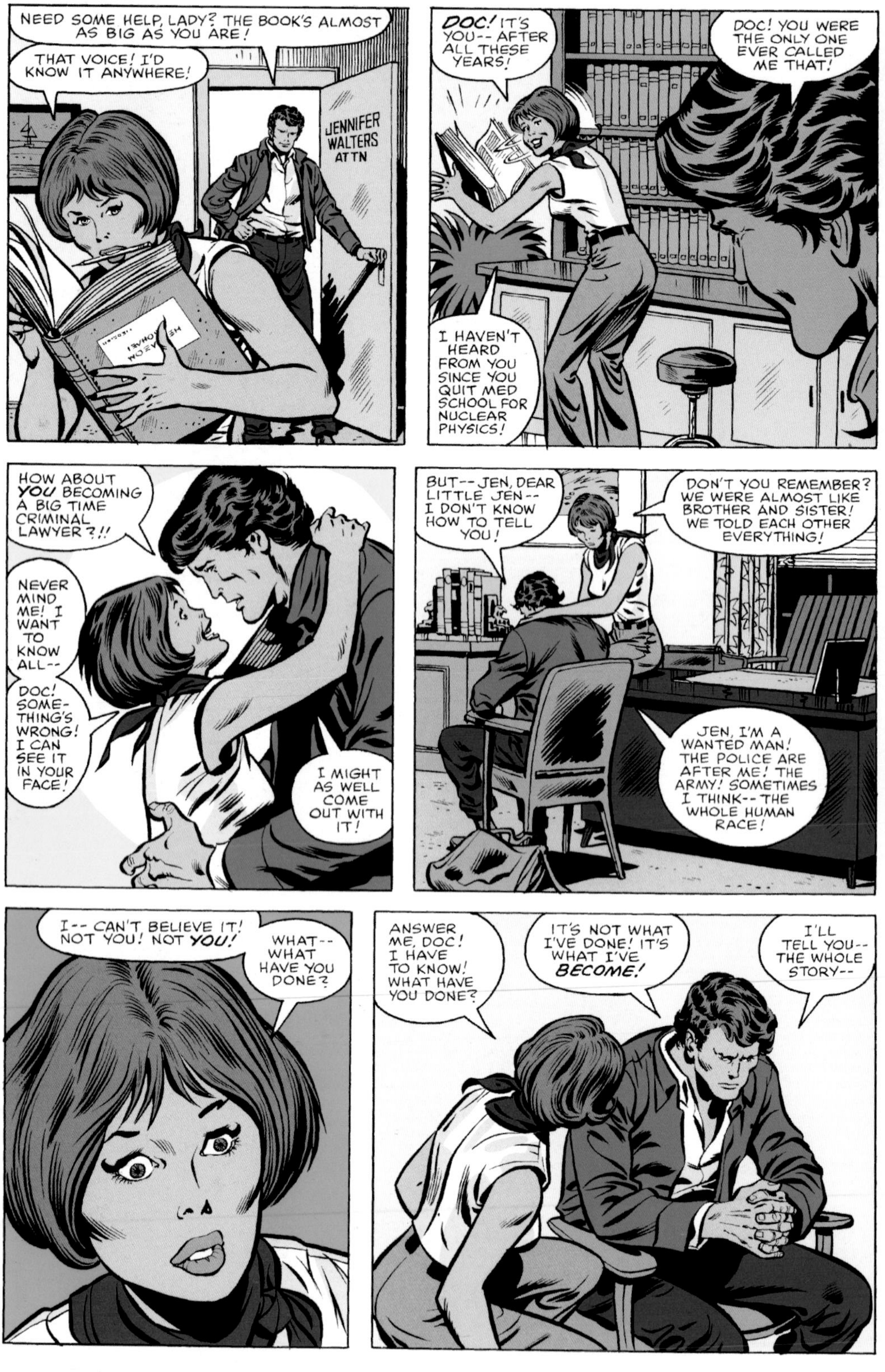
NEED SOME HELP, LADY? THE BOOK'S ALMOST AS BIG AS YOU ARE!
THAT VOICE! I'D KNOW IT ANYWHERE!
JENNIFER WALTERS ATTN
DOC! IT'S YOU-- AFTER ALL THESE YEARS!
DOC! YOU WERE THE ONLY ONE EVER CALLED ME THAT!
I HAVEN'T HEARD FROM YOU SINCE YOU QUIT MED SCHOOL FOR NUCLEAR PHYSICS!
HOW ABOUT YOU BECOMING A BIG TIME CRIMINAL LAWYER?!!
NEVER MIND ME! I WANT TO KNOW ALL--
DOC! SOMETHING'S WRONG! I CAN SEE IT IN YOUR FACE!
I MIGHT AS WELL COME OUT WITH IT!
BUT--JEN, DEAR LITTLE JEN-- I DON'T KNOW HOW TO TELL YOU!
DON'T YOU REMEMBER? WE WERE ALMOST LIKE BROTHER AND SISTER! WE TOLD EACH OTHER EVERYTHING!
JEN, I'M A WANTED MAN! THE POLICE ARE AFTER ME! THE ARMY! SOMETIMES I THINK-- THE WHOLE HUMAN RACE!
I-- CAN'T BELIEVE IT! NOT YOU! NOT YOU!
WHAT-- WHAT HAVE YOU DONE?
ANSWER ME, DOC! I HAVE TO KNOW! WHAT HAVE YOU DONE?
IT'S NOT WHAT I'VE DONE! IT'S WHAT I'VE BECOME!
I'LL TELL YOU-- THE WHOLE STORY--

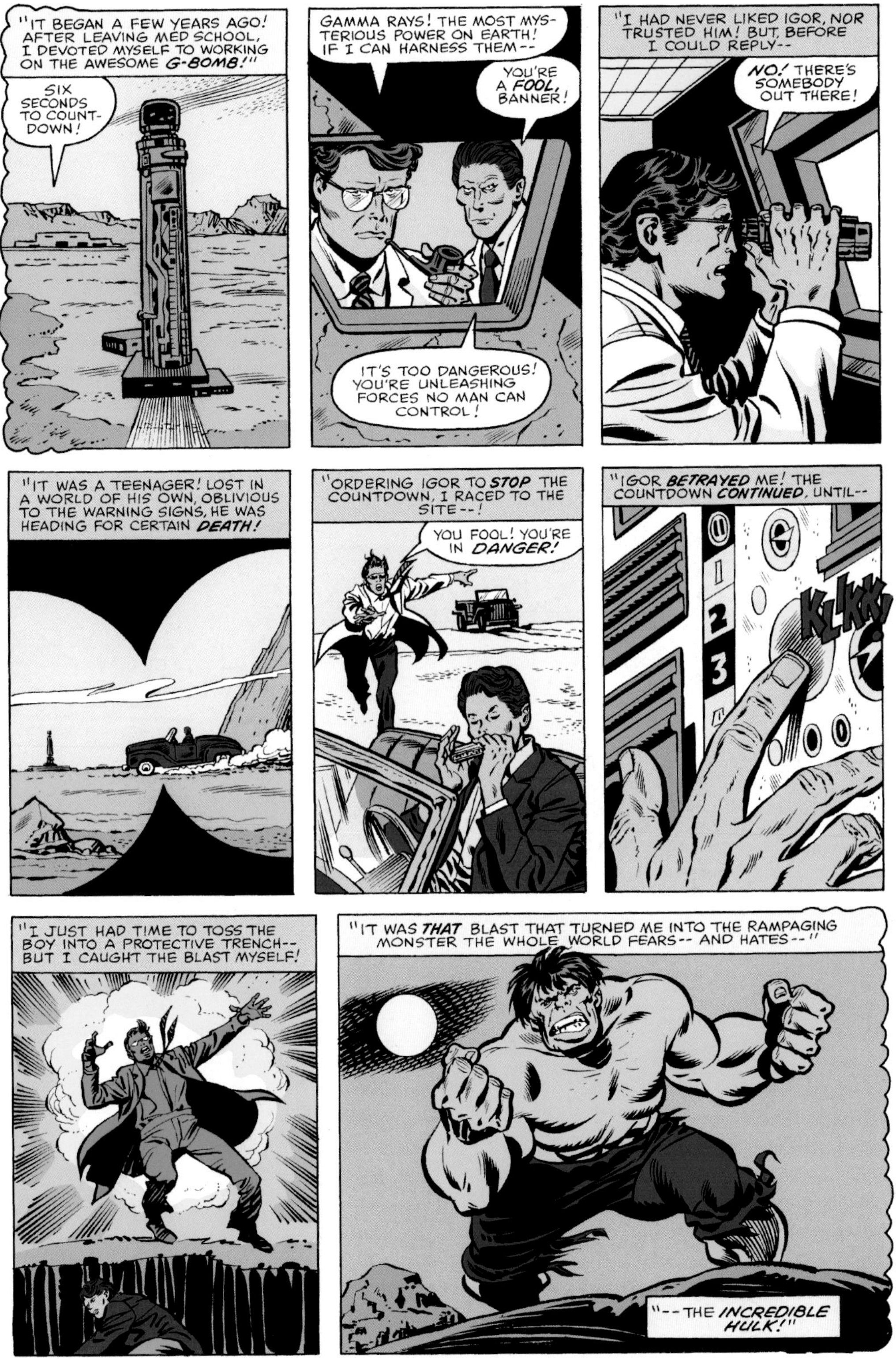
"IT BEGAN A FEW YEARS AGO! AFTER LEAVING MED SCHOOL, I DEVOTED MYSELF TO WORKING ON THE AWESOME G-BOMB!"
SIX SECONDS TO COUNT-DOWN!
GAMMA RAYS! THE MOST MYS-TERIOUS POWER ON EARTH! IF I CAN HARNESS THEM--
YOU'RE A FOOL, BANNER!
IT'S TOO DANGEROUS! YOU'RE UNLEASHING FORCES NO MAN CAN CONTROL!
"I HAD NEVER LIKED IGOR, NOR TRUSTED HIM! BUT, BEFORE I COULD REPLY--
NO! THERE'S SOMEBODY OUT THERE!
"IT WAS A TEENAGER! LOST IN A WORLD OF HIS OWN, OBLIVIOUS TO THE WARNING SIGNS, HE WAS HEADING FOR CERTAIN DEATH!
"ORDERING IGOR TO STOP THE COUNTDOWN, I RACED TO THE SITE--!
YOU FOOL! YOU'RE IN DANGER!
"IGOR BETRAYED ME! THE COUNTDOWN CONTINUED, UNTIL--
KLIKK!
"I JUST HAD TIME TO TOSS THE BOY INTO A PROTECTIVE TRENCH-- BUT I CAUGHT THE BLAST MYSELF!
"IT WAS THAT BLAST THAT TURNED ME INTO THE RAMPAGING MONSTER THE WHOLE WORLD FEARS-- AND HATES--"
"--THE INCREDIBLE HULK!"

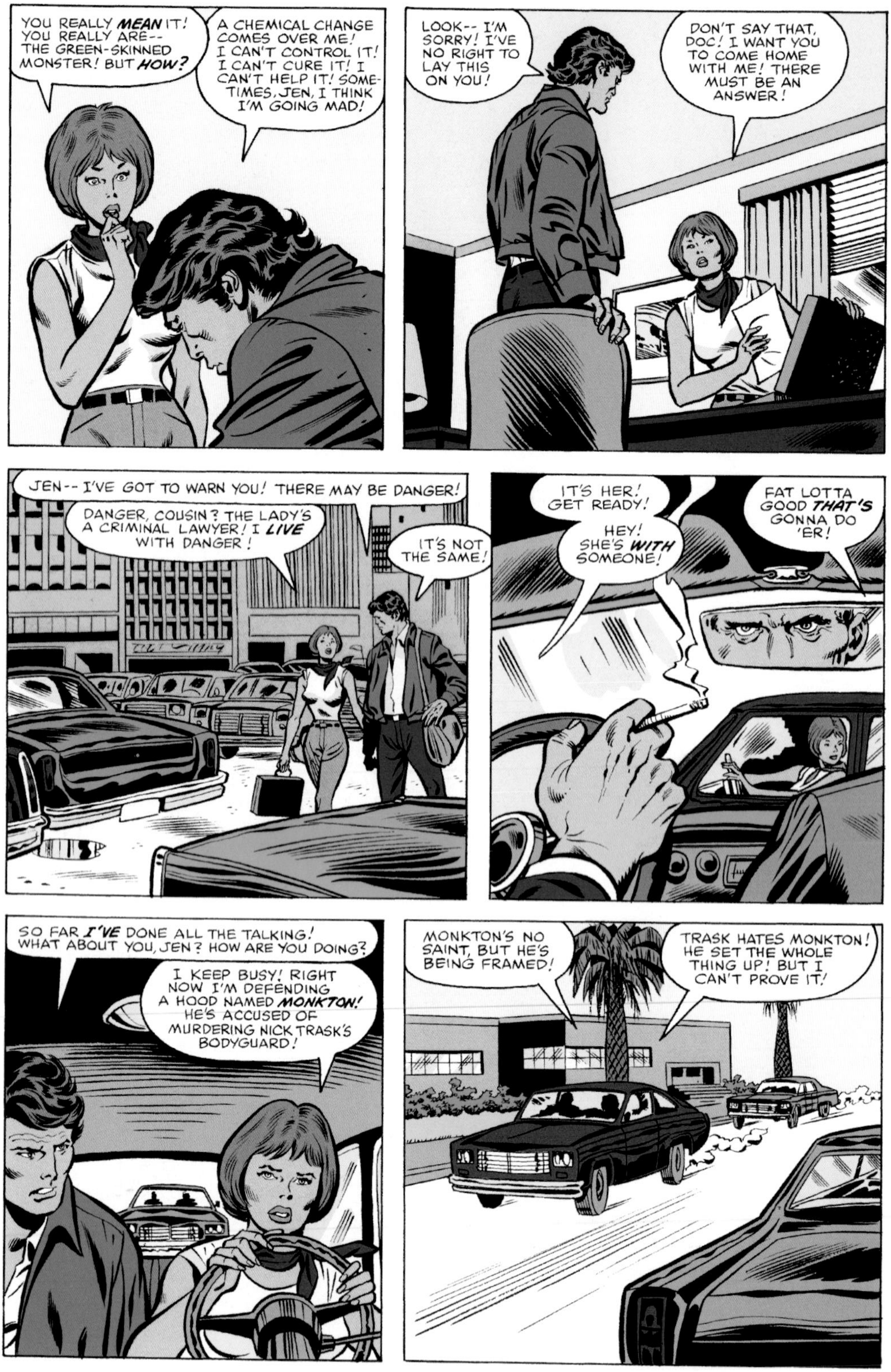

YOU REALLY MEAN IT! YOU REALLY ARE-- THE GREEN-SKINNED MONSTER! BUT HOW?
A CHEMICAL CHANGE COMES OVER ME! I CAN'T CONTROL IT! I CAN'T CURE IT! I CAN'T HELP IT! SOMETIMES, JEN, I THINK I'M GOING MAD!
LOOK-- I'M SORRY! I'VE NO RIGHT TO LAY THIS ON YOU!
DON'T SAY THAT, DOC! I WANT YOU TO COME HOME WITH ME! THERE MUST BE AN ANSWER!
JEN-- I'VE GOT TO WARN YOU! THERE MAY BE DANGER!
DANGER, COUSIN? THE LADY'S A CRIMINAL LAWYER! I LIVE WITH DANGER!
IT'S NOT THE SAME!
IT'S HER! GET READY!
HEY! SHE'S WITH SOMEONE!
FAT LOTTA GOOD THAT'S GONNA DO 'ER!
SO FAR I'VE DONE ALL THE TALKING! WHAT ABOUT YOU, JEN? HOW ARE YOU DOING?
I KEEP BUSY! RIGHT NOW I'M DEFENDING A HOOD NAMED MONKTON! HE'S ACCUSED OF MURDERING NICK TRASK'S BODYGUARD!
MONKTON'S NO SAINT, BUT HE'S BEING FRAMED!
TRASK HATES MONKTON! HE SET THE WHOLE THING UP! BUT I CAN'T PROVE IT!

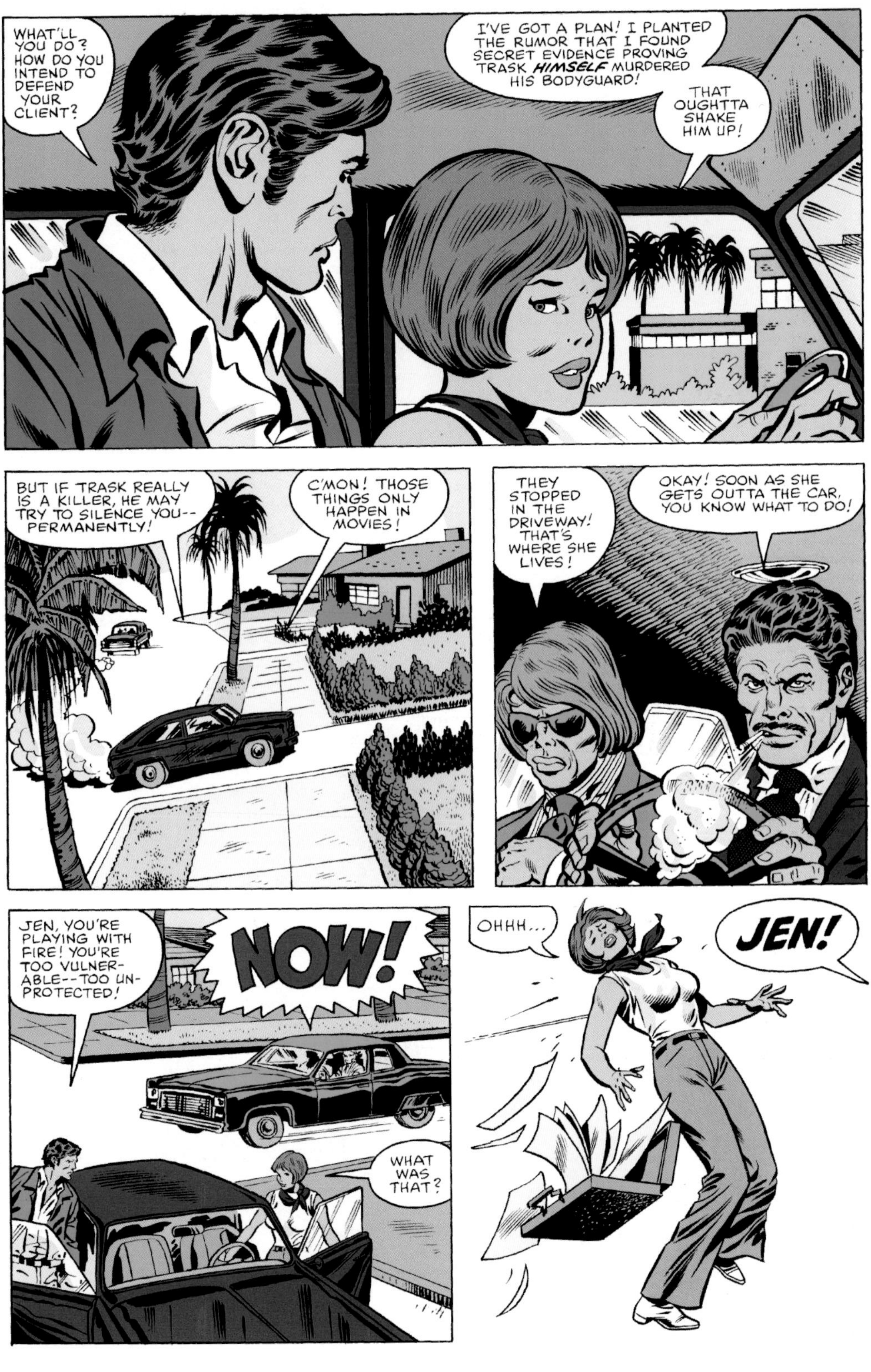
WHAT'LL YOU DO? HOW DO YOU INTEND TO DEFEND YOUR CLIENT?
I'VE GOT A PLAN! I PLANTED THE RUMOR THAT I FOUND SECRET EVIDENCE PROVING TRASK *HIMSELF* MURDERED HIS BODYGUARD!
THAT OUGHTTA SHAKE HIM UP!
BUT IF TRASK REALLY IS A KILLER, HE MAY TRY TO SILENCE YOU--PERMANENTLY!
C'MON! THOSE THINGS ONLY HAPPEN IN MOVIES!
THEY STOPPED IN THE DRIVEWAY! THAT'S WHERE SHE LIVES!
OKAY! SOON AS SHE GETS OUTTA THE CAR, YOU KNOW WHAT TO DO!
JEN, YOU'RE PLAYING WITH FIRE! YOU'RE TOO VULNERABLE--TOO UNPROTECTED!
NOW!
WHAT WAS THAT?
OHHH...
JEN!

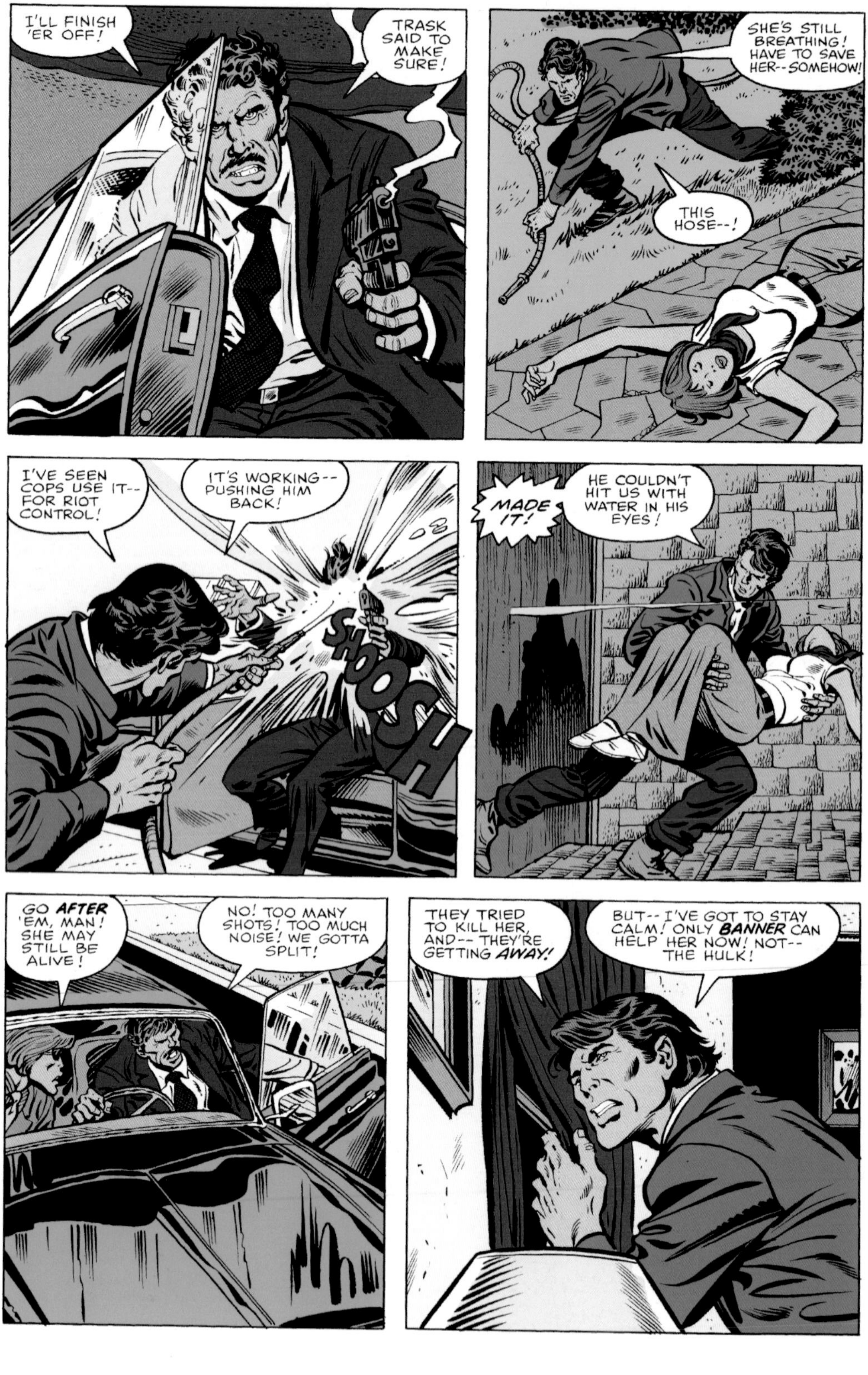
I'LL FINISH 'ER OFF!
TRASK SAID TO MAKE SURE!
SHE'S STILL BREATHING! HAVE TO SAVE HER--SOMEHOW!
THIS HOSE--!
I'VE SEEN COPS USE IT-- FOR RIOT CONTROL!
IT'S WORKING-- PUSHING HIM BACK!
SHOOSH
MADE IT!
HE COULDN'T HIT US WITH WATER IN HIS EYES!
GO **AFTER** 'EM, MAN! SHE MAY STILL BE ALIVE!
NO! TOO MANY SHOTS! TOO MUCH NOISE! WE GOTTA SPLIT!
THEY TRIED TO KILL HER, AND-- THEY'RE GETTING **AWAY!**
BUT-- I'VE GOT TO STAY CALM! ONLY **BANNER** CAN HELP HER NOW! NOT-- THE HULK!

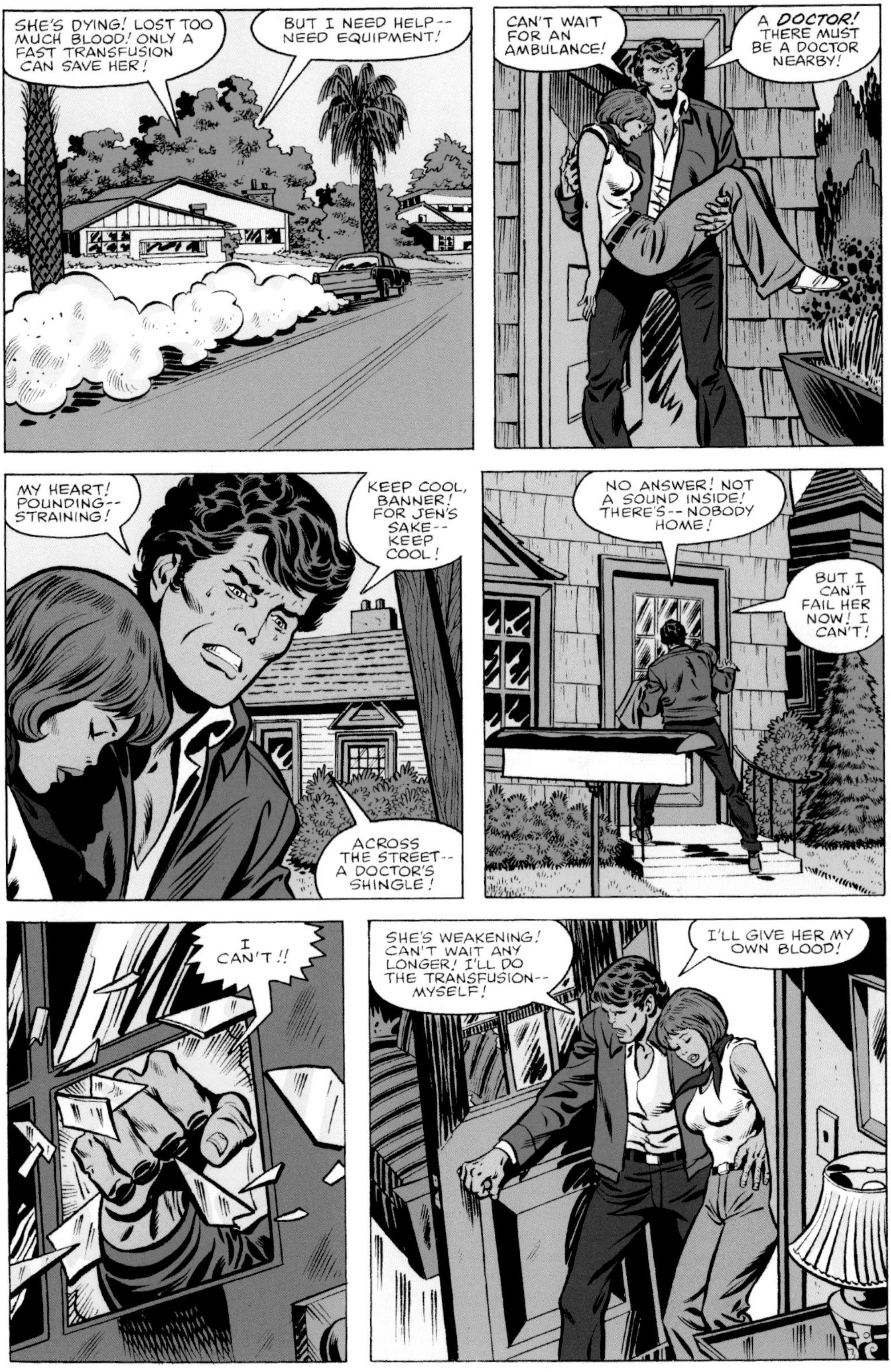
SHE'S DYING! LOST TOO MUCH BLOOD! ONLY A FAST TRANSFUSION CAN SAVE HER!
BUT I NEED HELP-- NEED EQUIPMENT!
CAN'T WAIT FOR AN AMBULANCE!
A DOCTOR! THERE MUST BE A DOCTOR NEARBY!
MY HEART! POUNDING-- STRAINING!
KEEP COOL, BANNER! FOR JEN'S SAKE-- KEEP COOL!
ACROSS THE STREET-- A DOCTOR'S SHINGLE!
NO ANSWER! NOT A SOUND INSIDE! THERE'S-- NOBODY HOME!
BUT I CAN'T FAIL HER NOW! I CAN'T!
I CAN'T!!
SHE'S WEAKENING! CAN'T WAIT ANY LONGER! I'LL DO THE TRANSFUSION-- MYSELF!
I'LL GIVE HER MY OWN BLOOD!

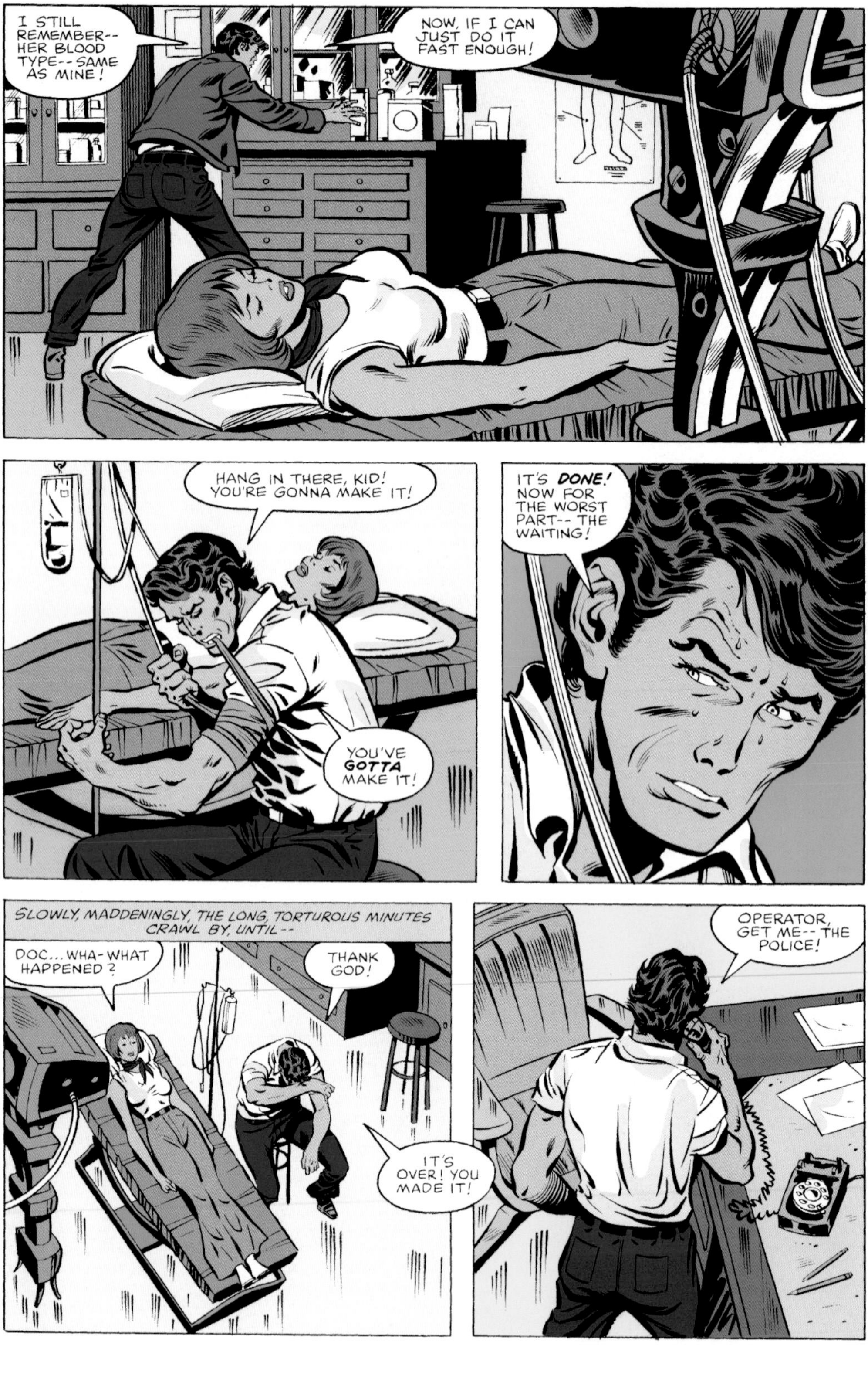

I STILL REMEMBER-- HER BLOOD TYPE-- SAME AS MINE!
NOW, IF I CAN JUST DO IT FAST ENOUGH!
HANG IN THERE, KID! YOU'RE GONNA MAKE IT!
YOU'VE GOTTA MAKE IT!
IT'S DONE! NOW FOR THE WORST PART-- THE WAITING!
SLOWLY, MADDENINGLY, THE LONG, TORTUROUS MINUTES CRAWL BY, UNTIL--
DOC... WHA-WHAT HAPPENED?
THANK GOD!
IT'S OVER! YOU MADE IT!
OPERATOR, GET ME-- THE POLICE!

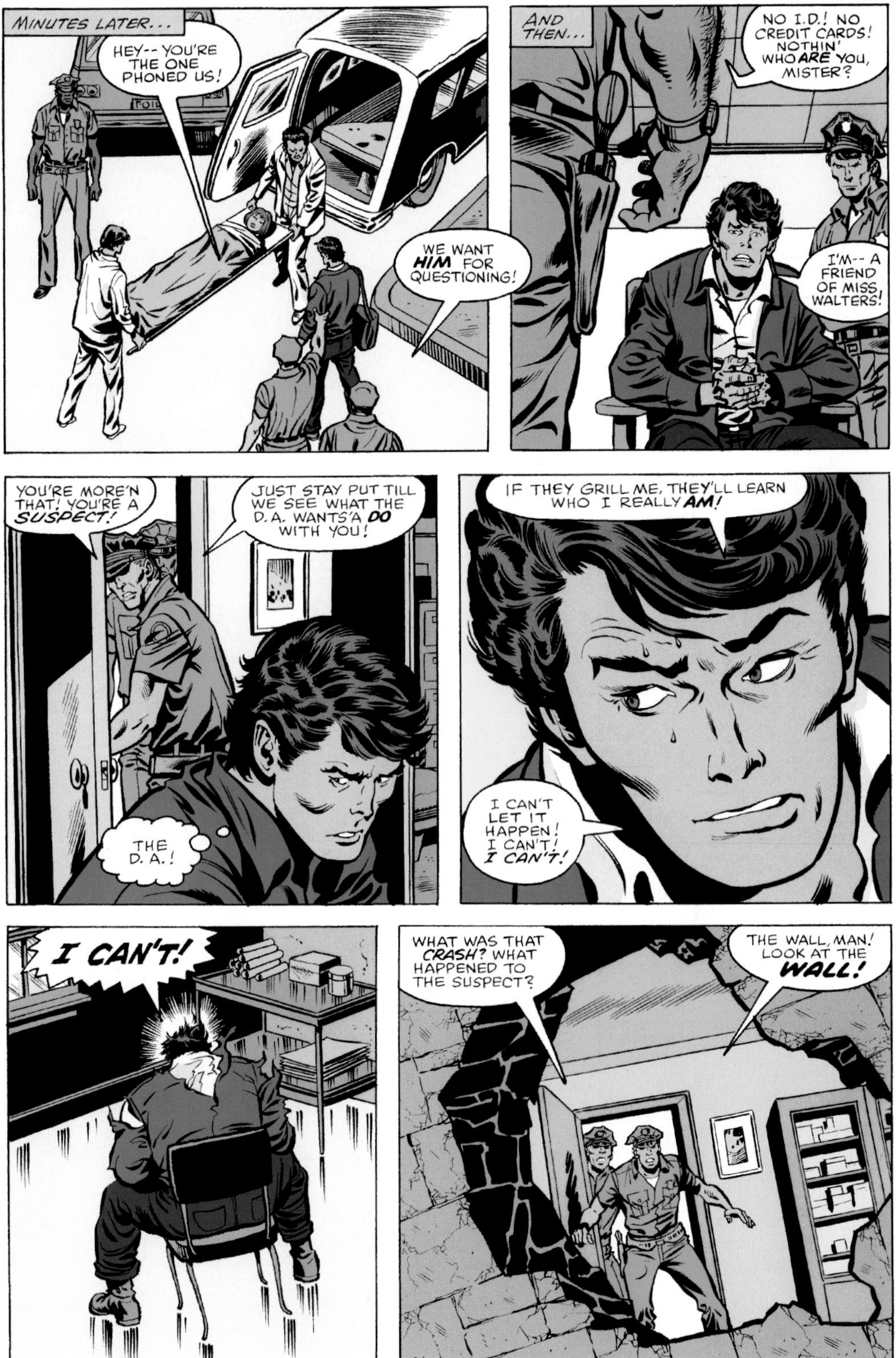
MINUTES LATER...
HEY-- YOU'RE THE ONE PHONED US!
WE WANT HIM FOR QUESTIONING!
AND THEN...
NO I.D.! NO CREDIT CARDS! NOTHIN' WHO ARE YOU, MISTER?
I'M-- A FRIEND OF MISS WALTERS!
YOU'RE MORE'N THAT! YOU'RE A SUSPECT!
JUST STAY PUT TILL WE SEE WHAT THE D.A. WANTS'A DO WITH YOU!
THE D.A.!
IF THEY GRILL ME, THEY'LL LEARN WHO I REALLY AM!
I CAN'T LET IT HAPPEN! I CAN'T! I CAN'T!
I CAN'T!
WHAT WAS THAT CRASH? WHAT HAPPENED TO THE SUSPECT?
THE WALL, MAN! LOOK AT THE WALL!

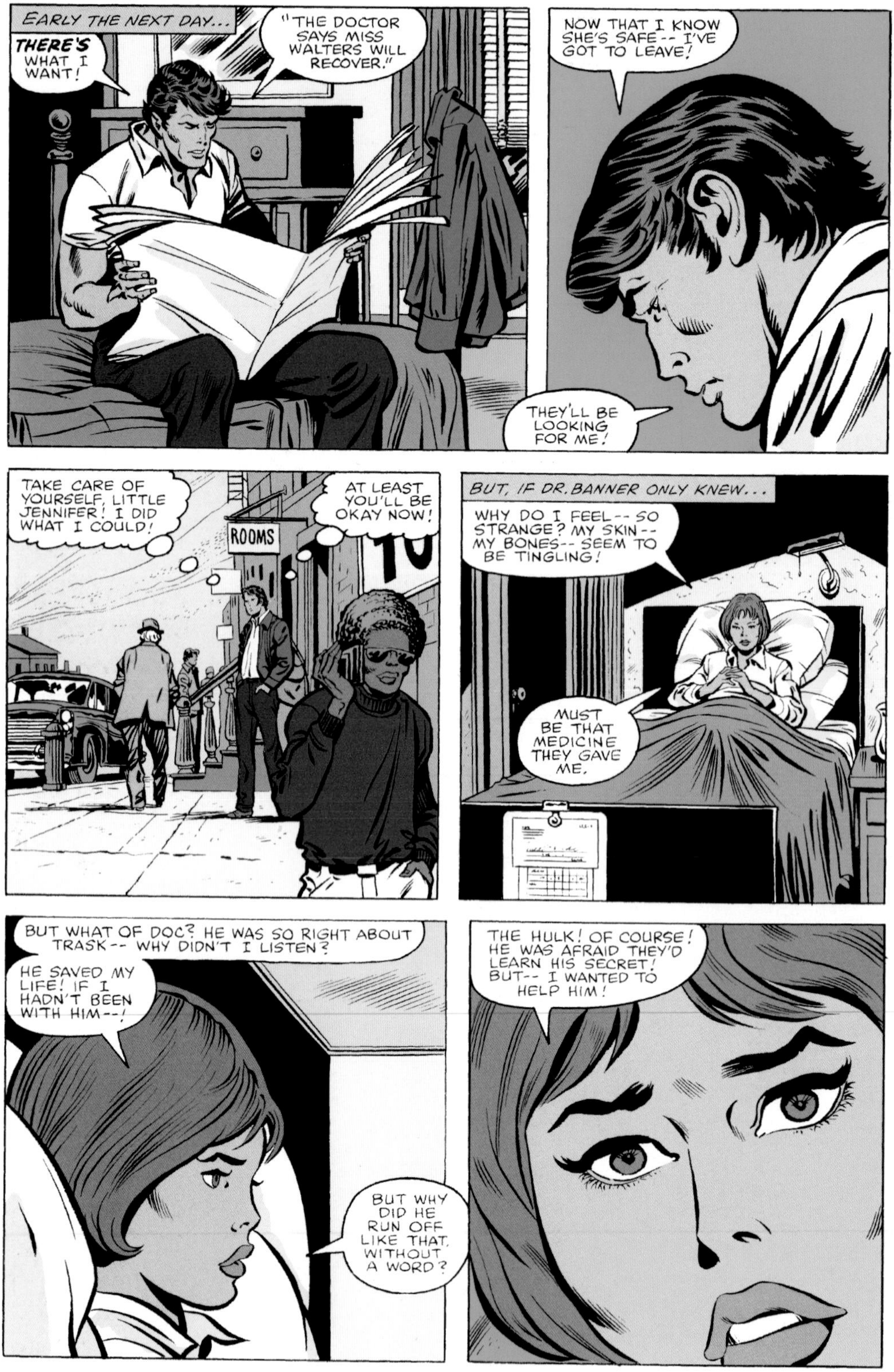
EARLY THE NEXT DAY...
THERE'S WHAT I WANT!
"THE DOCTOR SAYS MISS WALTERS WILL RECOVER."
NOW THAT I KNOW SHE'S SAFE-- I'VE GOT TO LEAVE!
THEY'LL BE LOOKING FOR ME!
TAKE CARE OF YOURSELF, LITTLE JENNIFER! I DID WHAT I COULD!
AT LEAST YOU'LL BE OKAY NOW!
ROOMS
BUT, IF DR. BANNER ONLY KNEW...
WHY DO I FEEL-- SO STRANGE? MY SKIN-- MY BONES-- SEEM TO BE TINGLING!
MUST BE THAT MEDICINE THEY GAVE ME.
BUT WHAT OF DOC? HE WAS SO RIGHT ABOUT TRASK-- WHY DIDN'T I LISTEN?
HE SAVED MY LIFE! IF I HADN'T BEEN WITH HIM--!
BUT WHY DID HE RUN OFF LIKE THAT, WITHOUT A WORD?
THE HULK! OF COURSE! HE WAS AFRAID THEY'D LEARN HIS SECRET! BUT-- I WANTED TO HELP HIM!

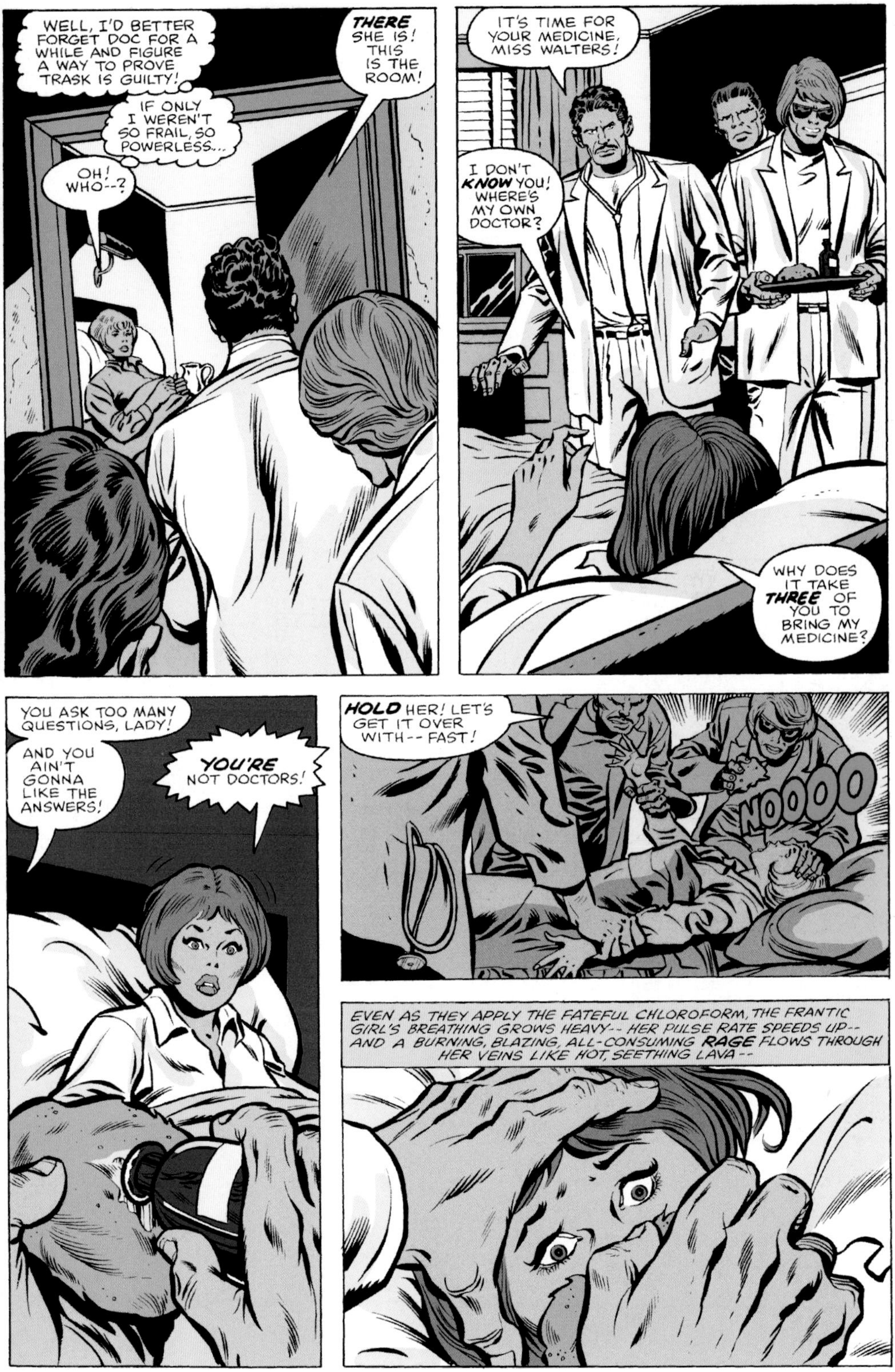
WELL, I'D BETTER FORGET DOC FOR A WHILE AND FIGURE A WAY TO PROVE TRASK IS GUILTY!
IF ONLY I WEREN'T SO FRAIL, SO POWERLESS...
THERE SHE IS! THIS IS THE ROOM!
OH! WHO--?
IT'S TIME FOR YOUR MEDICINE, MISS WALTERS!
I DON'T KNOW YOU! WHERE'S MY OWN DOCTOR?
WHY DOES IT TAKE THREE OF YOU TO BRING MY MEDICINE?
YOU ASK TOO MANY QUESTIONS, LADY!
AND YOU AIN'T GONNA LIKE THE ANSWERS!
YOU'RE NOT DOCTORS!
HOLD HER! LET'S GET IT OVER WITH--FAST!
NOOOO
EVEN AS THEY APPLY THE FATEFUL CHLOROFORM, THE FRANTIC GIRL'S BREATHING GROWS HEAVY-- HER PULSE RATE SPEEDS UP-- AND A BURNING, BLAZING, ALL-CONSUMING RAGE FLOWS THROUGH HER VEINS LIKE HOT, SEETHING LAVA--

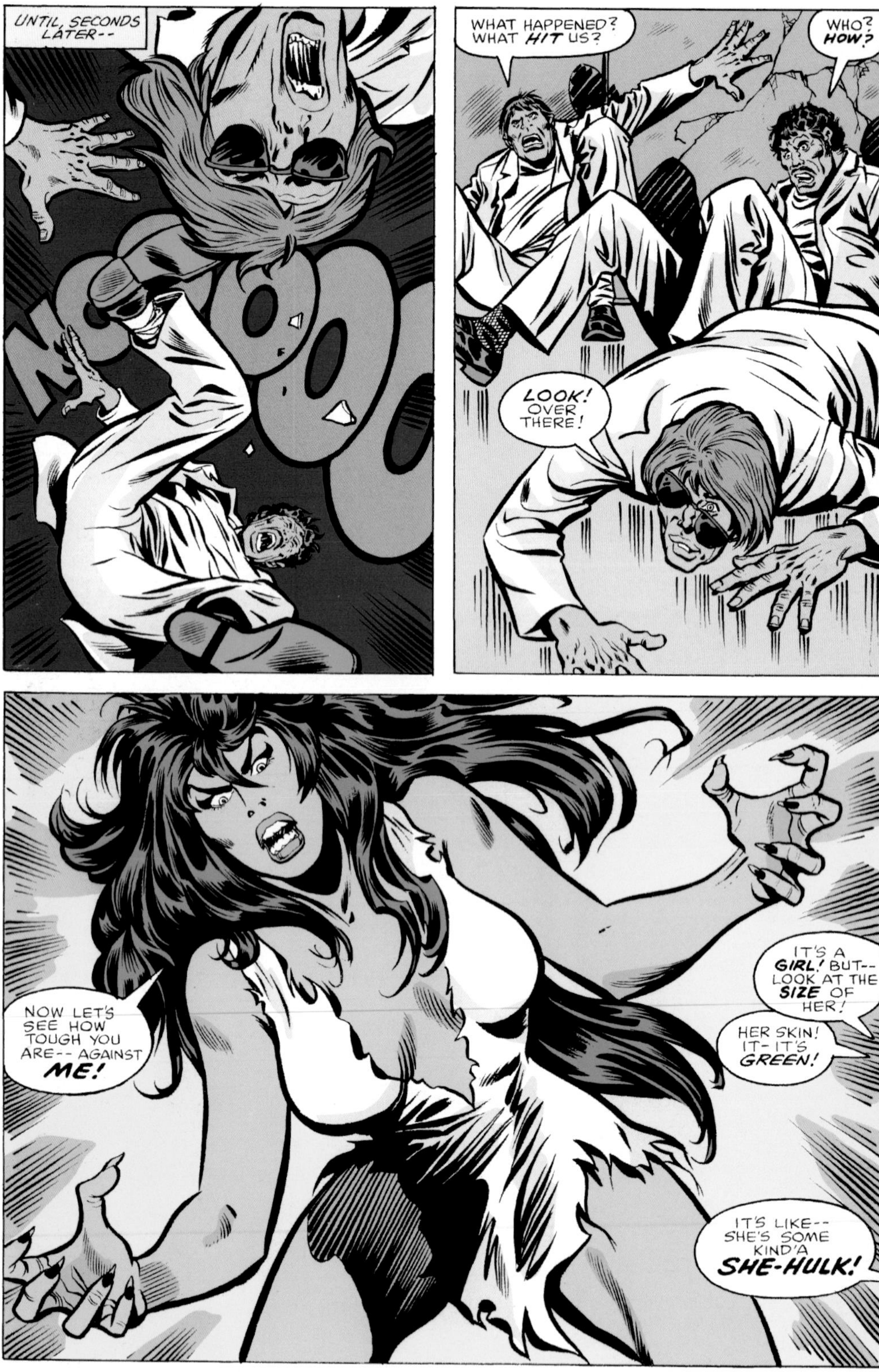
UNTIL, SECONDS LATER--
WHAT HAPPENED? WHAT HIT US?
WHO? HOW?
LOOK! OVER THERE!
NOW LET'S SEE HOW TOUGH YOU ARE-- AGAINST ME!
IT'S A GIRL! BUT-- LOOK AT THE SIZE OF HER!
HER SKIN! IT- IT'S GREEN!
IT'S LIKE-- SHE'S SOME KIND'A SHE-HULK!

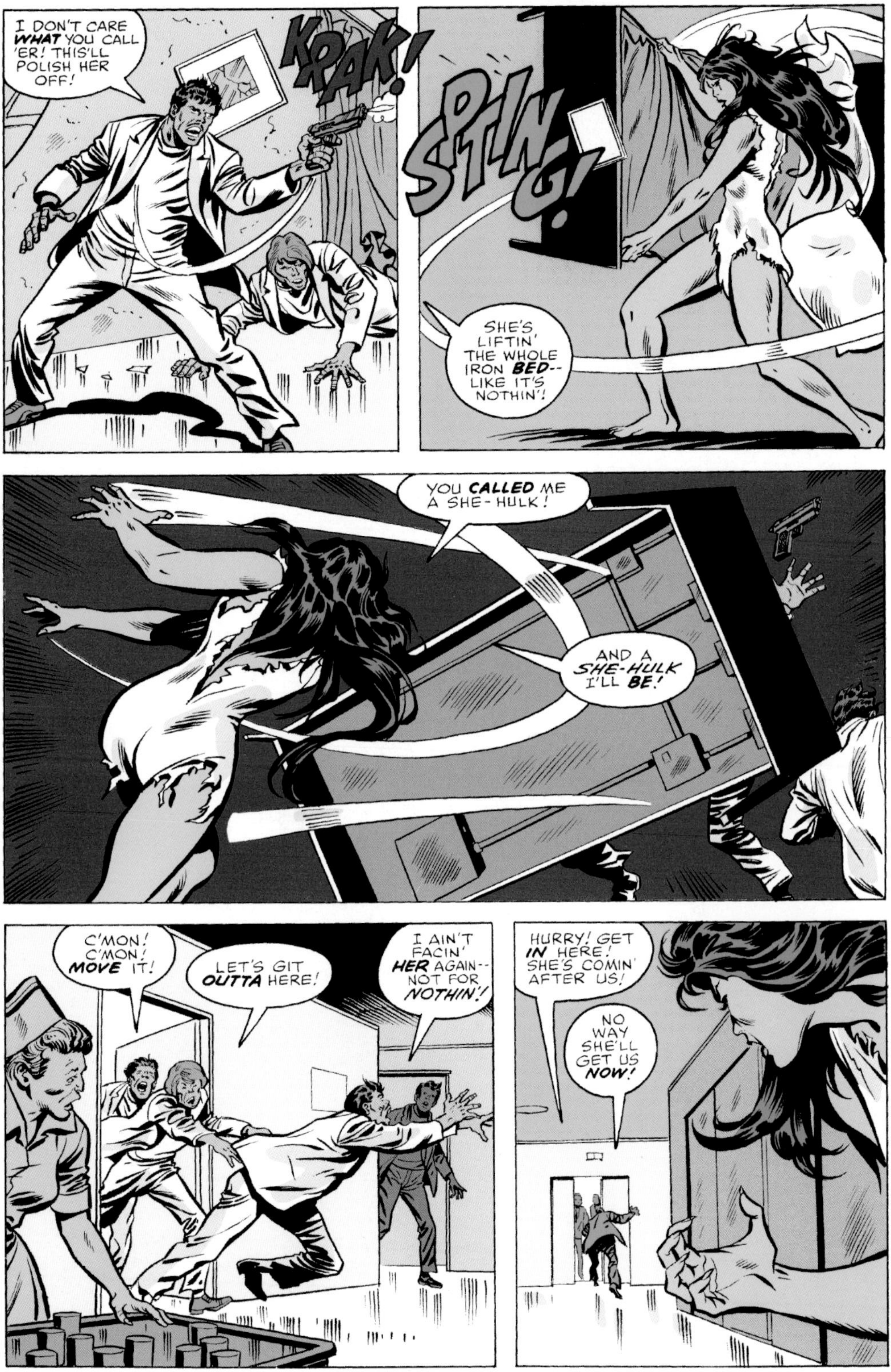
I DON'T CARE WHAT YOU CALL 'ER! THIS'LL POLISH HER OFF!
KRAK!
SPTING!
SHE'S LIFTIN' THE WHOLE IRON BED-- LIKE IT'S NOTHIN'!
YOU CALLED ME A SHE-HULK!
AND A SHE-HULK I'LL BE!
C'MON! C'MON! MOVE IT!
LET'S GIT OUTTA HERE!
I AIN'T FACIN' HER AGAIN-- NOT FOR NOTHIN'!
HURRY! GET IN HERE! SHE'S COMIN' AFTER US!
NO WAY SHE'LL GET US NOW!

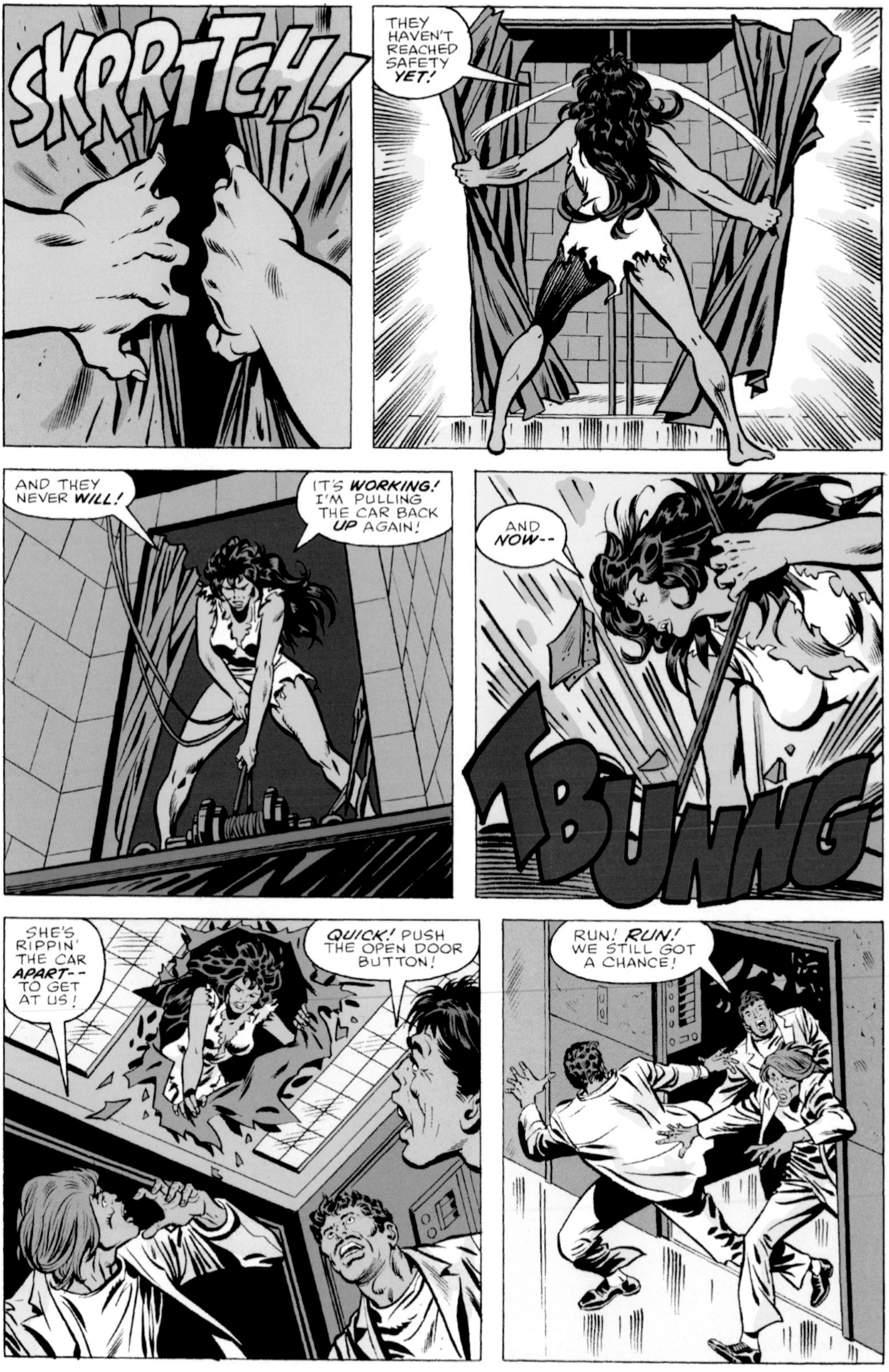
SKRRTCH!
THEY HAVEN'T REACHED SAFETY YET!
AND THEY NEVER WILL!
IT'S WORKING! I'M PULLING THE CAR BACK UP AGAIN!
AND NOW--
TBUNNG
SHE'S RIPPIN' THE CAR APART-- TO GET AT US!
QUICK! PUSH THE OPEN DOOR BUTTON!
RUN! RUN! WE STILL GOT A CHANCE!

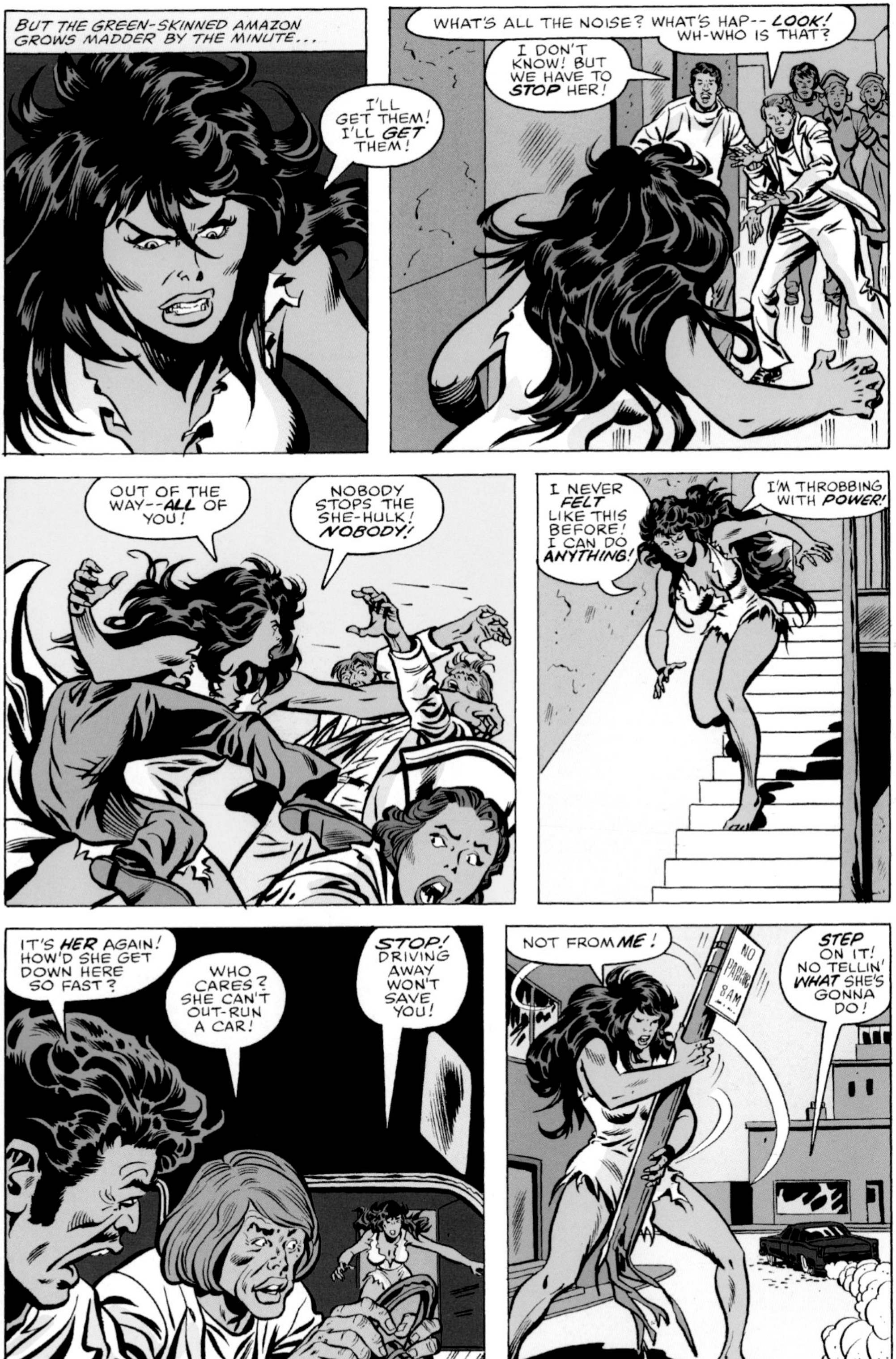
BUT THE GREEN-SKINNED AMAZON GROWS MADDER BY THE MINUTE...
I'LL GET THEM! I'LL GET THEM!
WHAT'S ALL THE NOISE? WHAT'S HAP-- LOOK! WH-WHO IS THAT?
I DON'T KNOW! BUT WE HAVE TO STOP HER!
OUT OF THE WAY--ALL OF YOU!
NOBODY STOPS THE SHE-HULK! NOBODY!
I NEVER FELT LIKE THIS BEFORE! I CAN DO ANYTHING!
I'M THROBBING WITH POWER!
IT'S HER AGAIN! HOW'D SHE GET DOWN HERE SO FAST?
WHO CARES? SHE CAN'T OUT-RUN A CAR!
STOP! DRIVING AWAY WON'T SAVE YOU!
NOT FROM ME!
STEP ON IT! NO TELLIN' WHAT SHE'S GONNA DO!

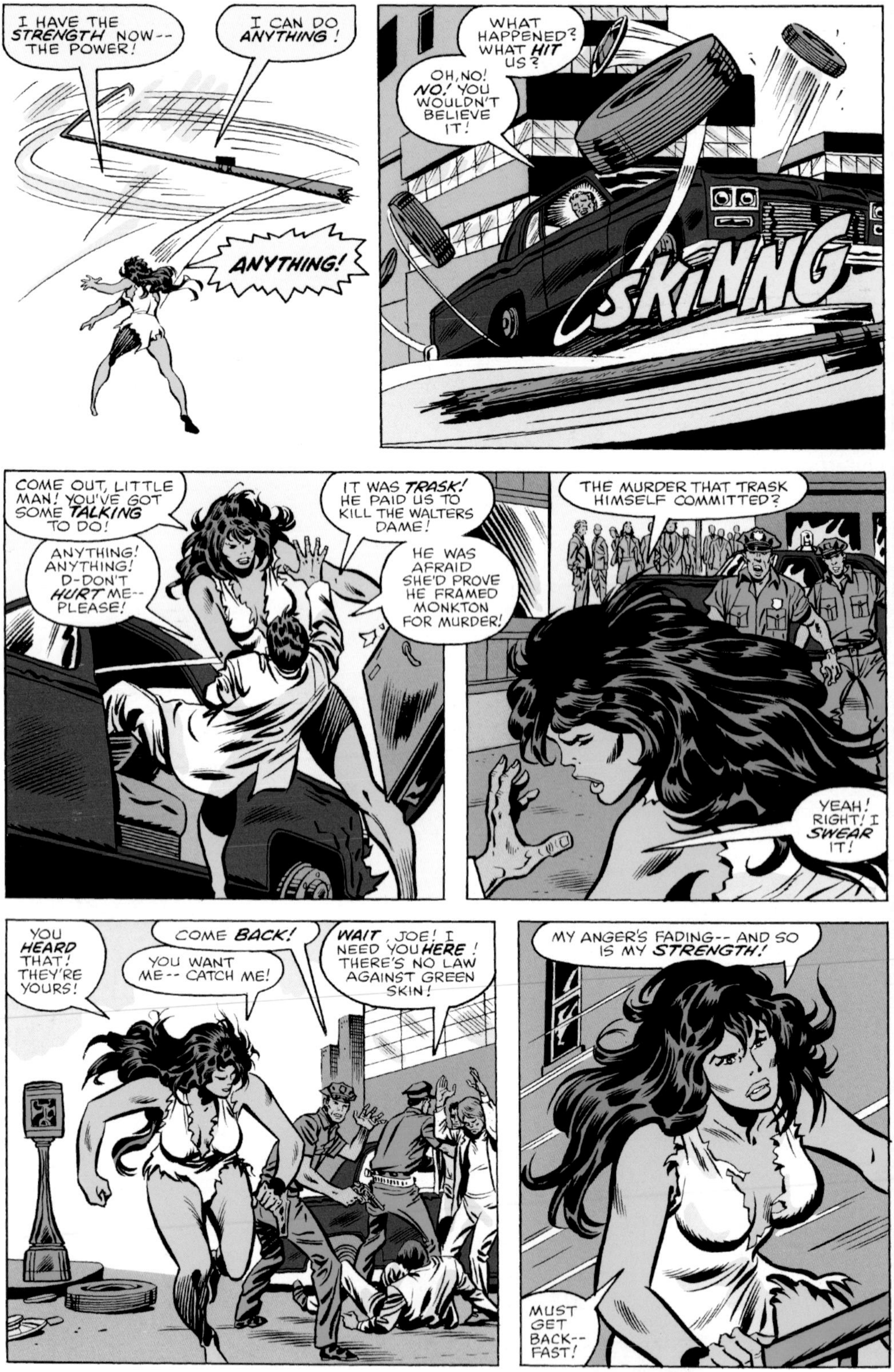
I HAVE THE STRENGTH NOW-- THE POWER!
I CAN DO ANYTHING!
ANYTHING!
WHAT HAPPENED? WHAT HIT US?
OH, NO! NO! YOU WOULDN'T BELIEVE IT!
SKINNG
COME OUT, LITTLE MAN! YOU'VE GOT SOME TALKING TO DO!
ANYTHING! ANYTHING! D-DON'T HURT ME-- PLEASE!
IT WAS TRASK! HE PAID US TO KILL THE WALTERS DAME!
HE WAS AFRAID SHE'D PROVE HE FRAMED MONKTON FOR MURDER!
THE MURDER THAT TRASK HIMSELF COMMITTED?
YEAH! RIGHT! I SWEAR IT!
YOU HEARD THAT! THEY'RE YOURS!
COME BACK!
YOU WANT ME-- CATCH ME!
WAIT, JOE! I NEED YOU HERE! THERE'S NO LAW AGAINST GREEN SKIN!
MY ANGER'S FADING-- AND SO IS MY STRENGTH!
MUST GET BACK-- FAST!

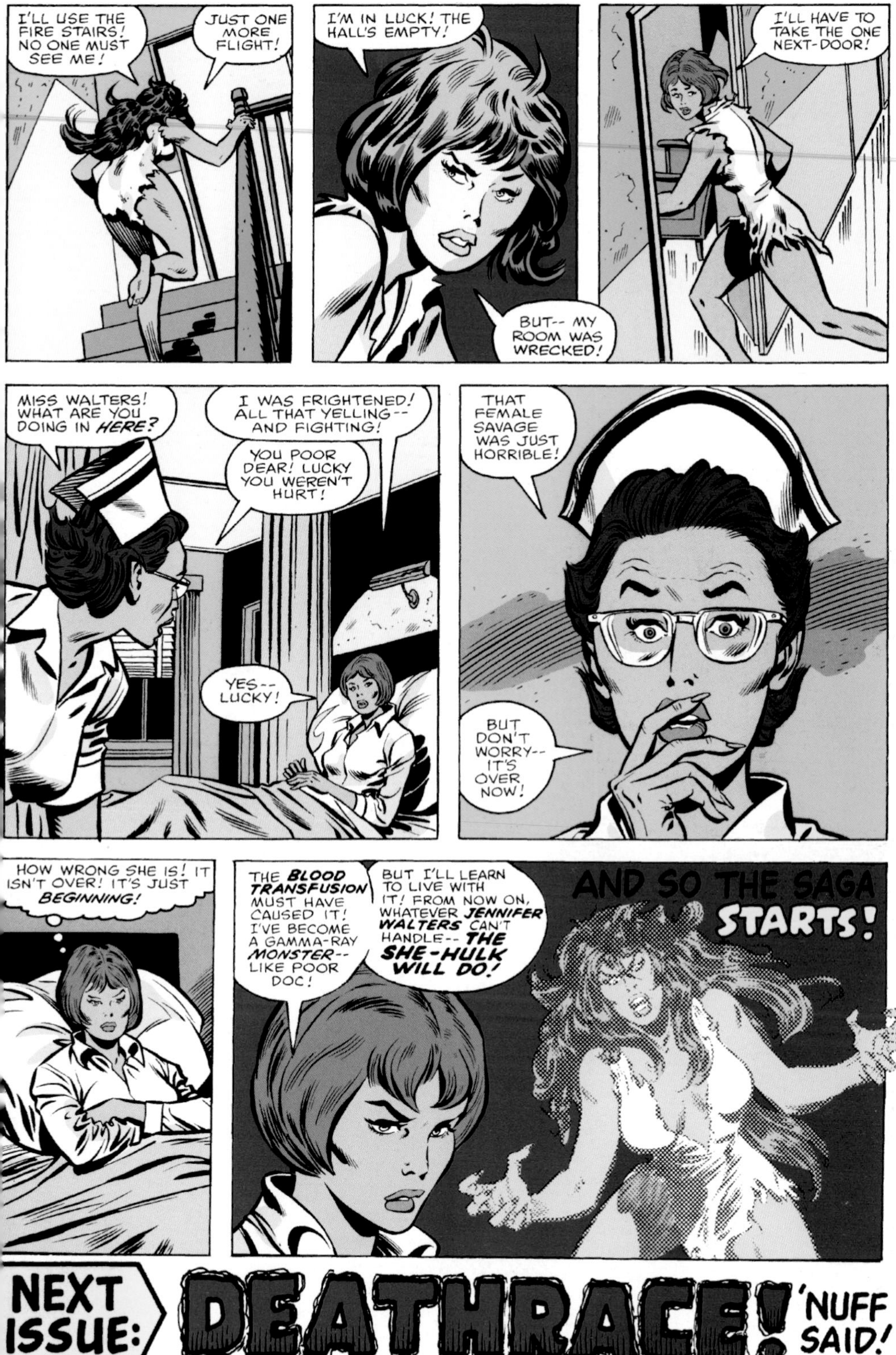
I'LL USE THE FIRE STAIRS! NO ONE MUST SEE ME!
JUST ONE MORE FLIGHT!
I'M IN LUCK! THE HALL'S EMPTY!
BUT-- MY ROOM WAS WRECKED!
I'LL HAVE TO TAKE THE ONE NEXT-DOOR!
MISS WALTERS! WHAT ARE YOU DOING IN HERE?
I WAS FRIGHTENED! ALL THAT YELLING-- AND FIGHTING!
YOU POOR DEAR! LUCKY YOU WEREN'T HURT!
YES-- LUCKY!
THAT FEMALE SAVAGE WAS JUST HORRIBLE!
BUT DON'T WORRY-- IT'S OVER NOW!
HOW WRONG SHE IS! IT ISN'T OVER! IT'S JUST BEGINNING!
THE BLOOD TRANSFUSION MUST HAVE CAUSED IT! I'VE BECOME A GAMMA-RAY MONSTER-- LIKE POOR DOC!
BUT I'LL LEARN TO LIVE WITH IT! FROM NOW ON, WHATEVER JENNIFER WALTERS CAN'T HANDLE-- THE SHE-HULK WILL DO!
AND SO THE SAGA STARTS!
NEXT ISSUE:
DEATHRACE!
'NUFF SAID!

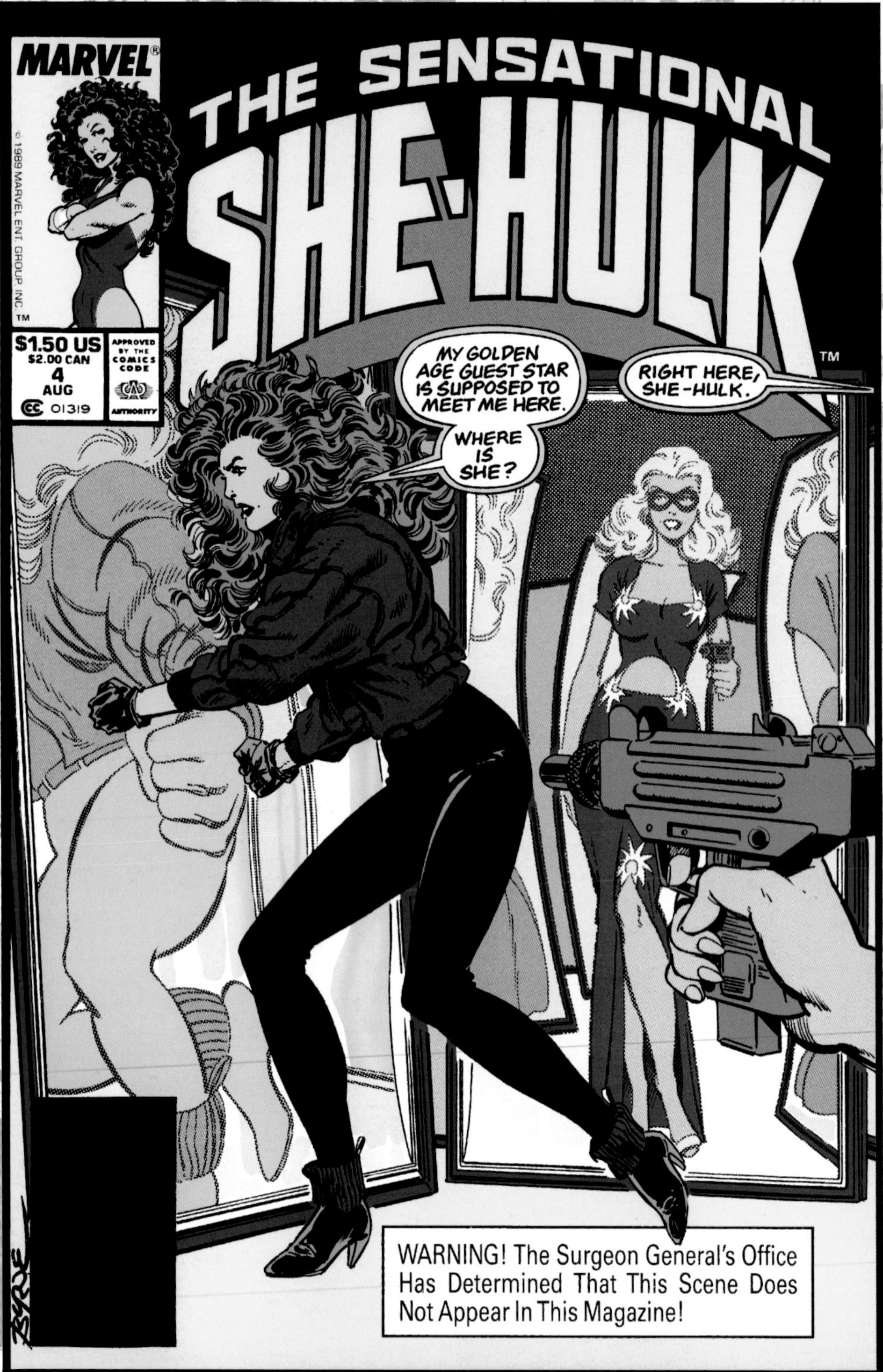
MARVEL®
THE SENSATIONAL
SHE-HULK
© 1989 MARVEL ENT. GROUP, INC.
TM
$1.50 US
$2.00 CAN
4
AUG
01319
APPROVED BY THE COMICS CODE AUTHORITY
TM
MY GOLDEN AGE GUEST STAR IS SUPPOSED TO MEET ME HERE.
WHERE IS SHE?
RIGHT HERE, SHE-HULK.
WARNING! The Surgeon General's Office Has Determined That This Scene Does Not Appear In This Magazine!

SENSATIONAL SHE-HULK #4

JENNIFER WALTERS TAKES ON ONE OF THE BIGGEST CHALLENGES THAT FACE ALL OF US! THE DREADED JOB INTERVIEW!

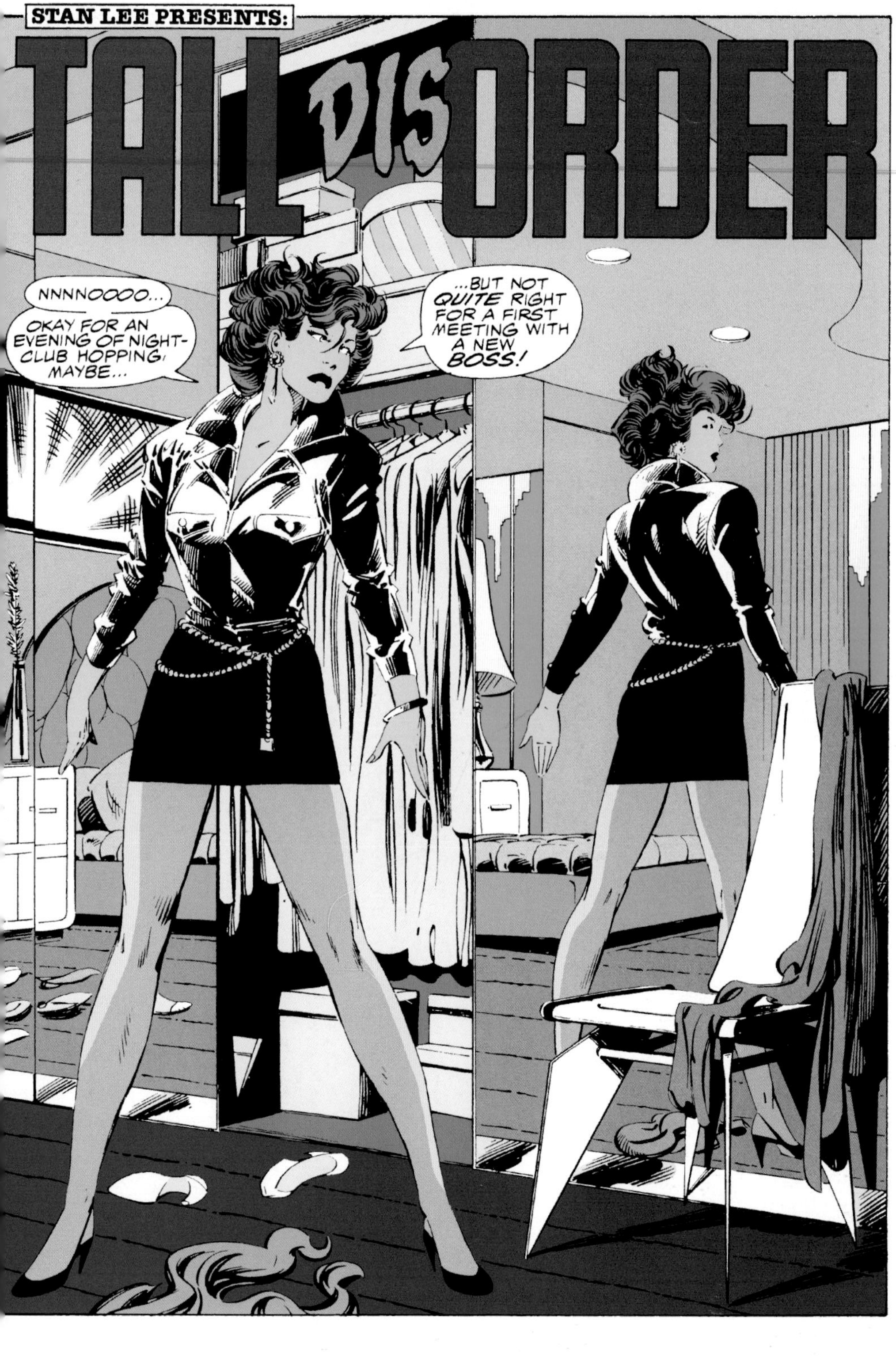
STAN LEE PRESENTS:
TALL DIS ORDER
NNNNOOOO...
OKAY FOR AN EVENING OF NIGHT-CLUB HOPPING, MAYBE...
...BUT NOT QUITE RIGHT FOR A FIRST MEETING WITH A NEW BOSS!

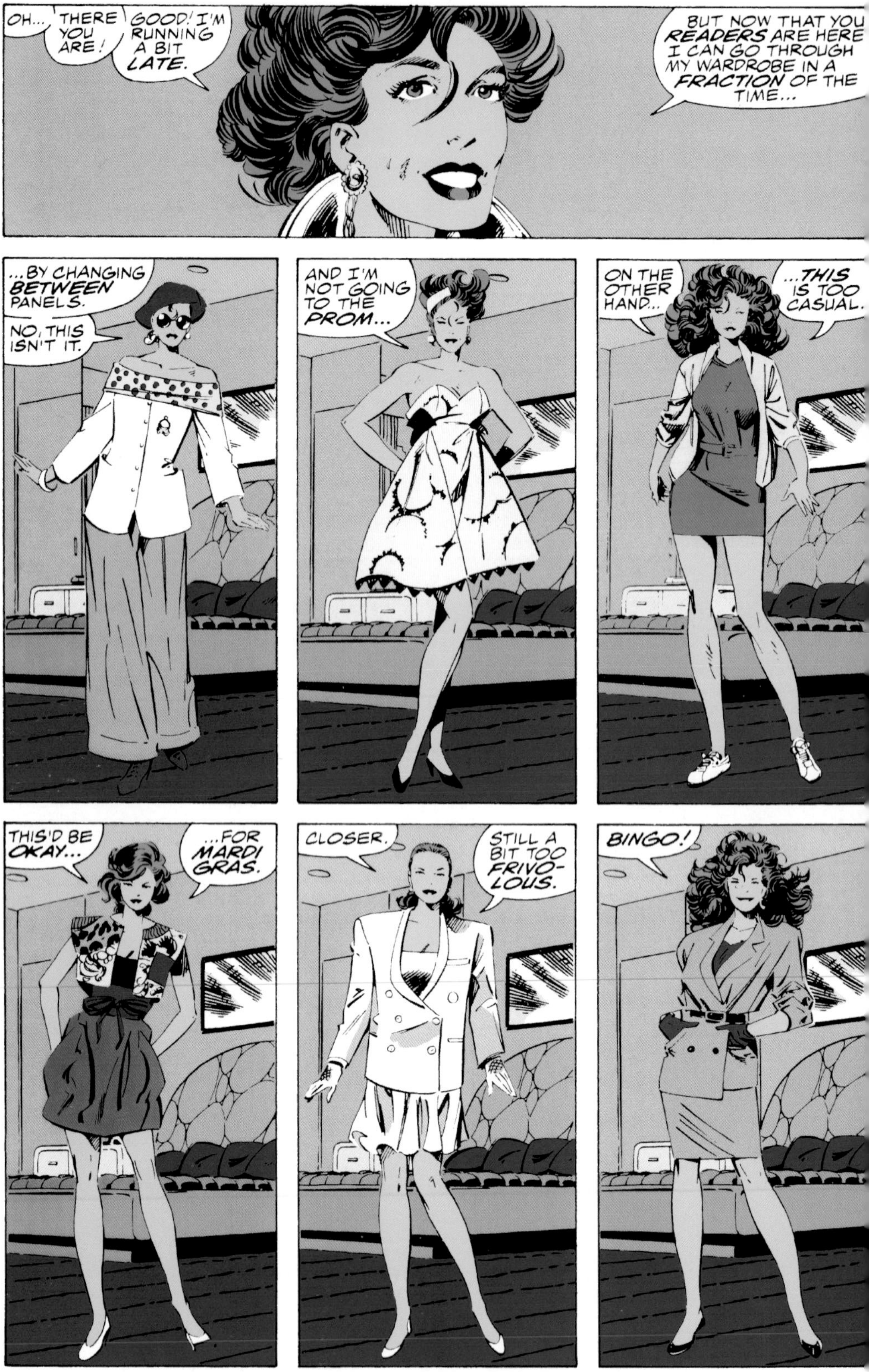

OH...
THERE YOU ARE!
GOOD! I'M RUNNING A BIT LATE.
BUT NOW THAT YOU READERS ARE HERE I CAN GO THROUGH MY WARDROBE IN A FRACTION OF THE TIME...
...BY CHANGING BETWEEN PANELS.
NO, THIS ISN'T IT.
AND I'M NOT GOING TO THE PROM...
ON THE OTHER HAND...
...THIS IS TOO CASUAL.
THIS'D BE OKAY...
...FOR MARDI GRAS.
CLOSER.
STILL A BIT TOO FRIVO-LOUS.
BINGO!

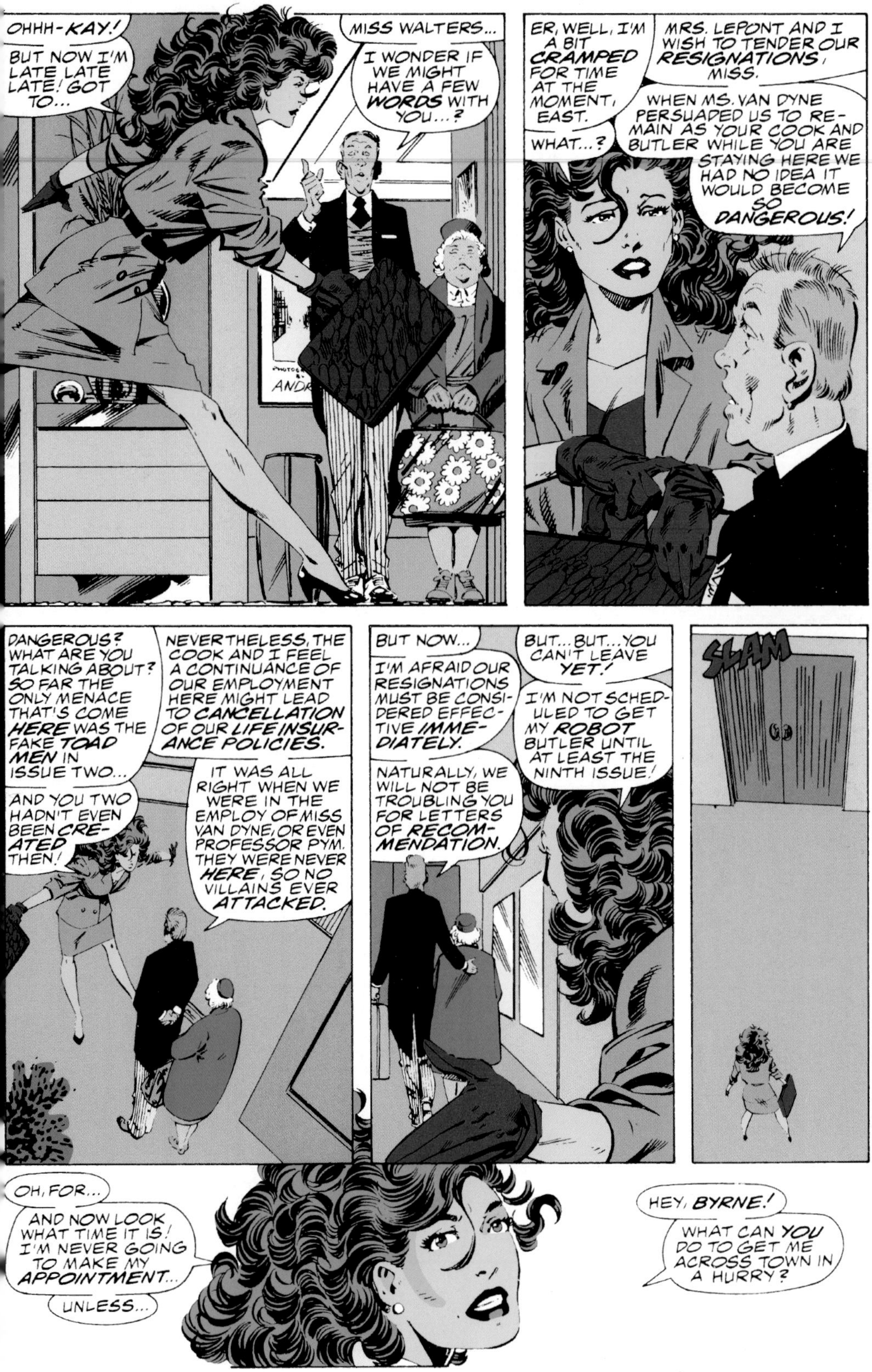

OHHH-KAY!
BUT NOW I'M LATE LATE LATE! GOT TO...
MISS WALTERS...
I WONDER IF WE MIGHT HAVE A FEW WORDS WITH YOU...?
ER, WELL, I'M A BIT CRAMPED FOR TIME AT THE MOMENT, EAST.
WHAT...?
MRS. LEPONT AND I WISH TO TENDER OUR RESIGNATIONS, MISS.
WHEN MS. VAN DYNE PERSUADED US TO RE-MAIN AS YOUR COOK AND BUTLER WHILE YOU ARE STAYING HERE WE HAD NO IDEA IT WOULD BECOME SO DANGEROUS!
DANGEROUS? WHAT ARE YOU TALKING ABOUT? SO FAR THE ONLY MENACE THAT'S COME HERE WAS THE FAKE TOAD MEN IN ISSUE TWO...
AND YOU TWO HADN'T EVEN BEEN CRE-ATED THEN!
NEVERTHELESS, THE COOK AND I FEEL A CONTINUANCE OF OUR EMPLOYMENT HERE MIGHT LEAD TO CANCELLATION OF OUR LIFE INSUR-ANCE POLICIES.
IT WAS ALL RIGHT WHEN WE WERE IN THE EMPLOY OF MISS VAN DYNE, OR EVEN PROFESSOR PYM. THEY WERE NEVER HERE, SO NO VILLAINS EVER ATTACKED.
BUT NOW...
I'M AFRAID OUR RESIGNATIONS MUST BE CONSI-DERED EFFEC-TIVE IMME-DIATELY.
NATURALLY, WE WILL NOT BE TROUBLING YOU FOR LETTERS OF RECOM-MENDATION.
BUT...BUT...YOU CAN'T LEAVE YET!
I'M NOT SCHED-ULED TO GET MY ROBOT BUTLER UNTIL AT LEAST THE NINTH ISSUE!
SLAM
OH, FOR...
AND NOW LOOK WHAT TIME IT IS! I'M NEVER GOING TO MAKE MY APPOINTMENT...
UNLESS...
HEY, BYRNE!
WHAT CAN YOU DO TO GET ME ACROSS TOWN IN A HURRY?

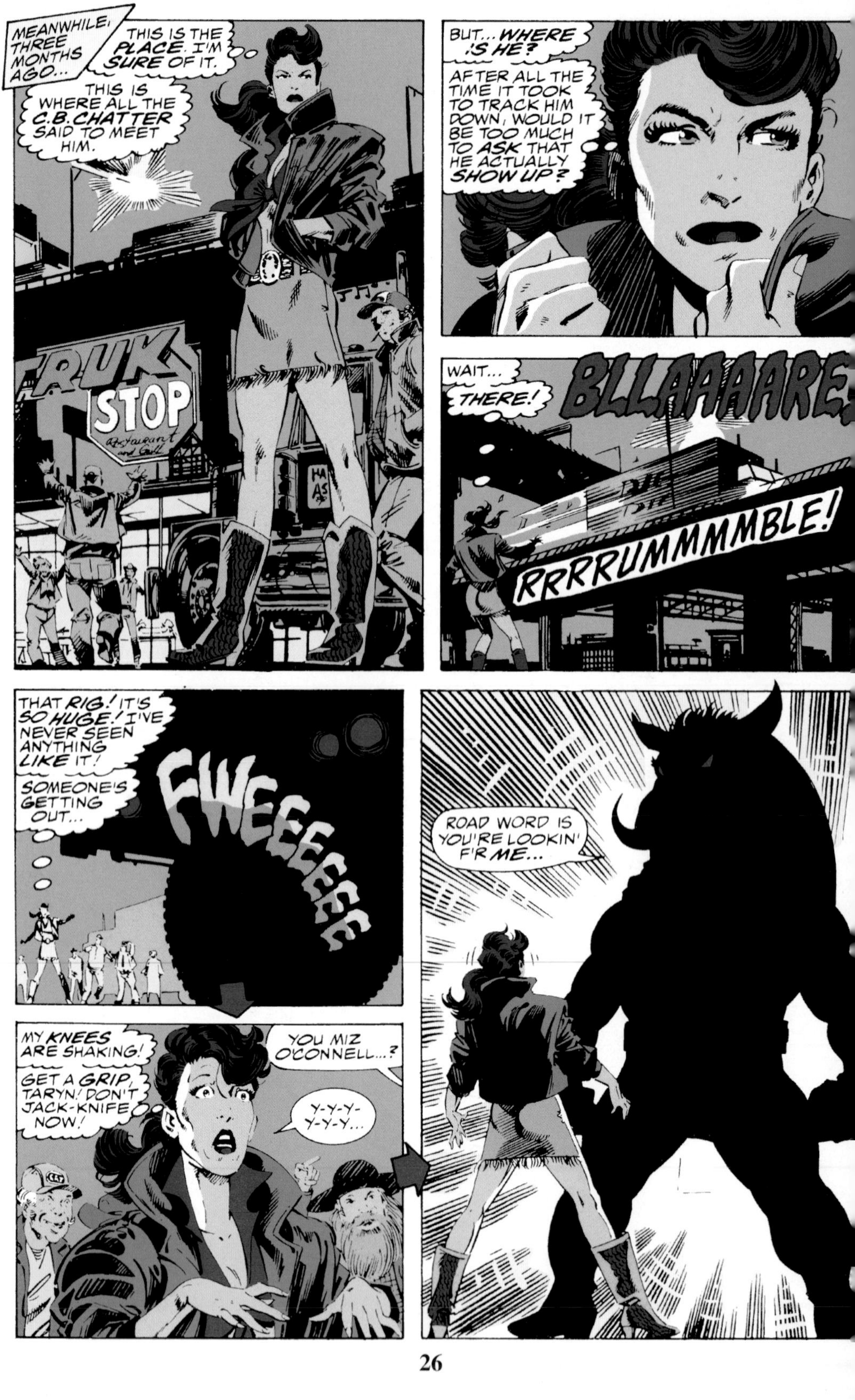
MEANWHILE, THREE MONTHS AGO...
THIS IS THE PLACE. I'M SURE OF IT.
THIS IS WHERE ALL THE C.B. CHATTER SAID TO MEET HIM.
TRUK STOP
Restaurant and Grill
BUT... WHERE IS HE?
AFTER ALL THE TIME IT TOOK TO TRACK HIM DOWN, WOULD IT BE TOO MUCH TO ASK THAT HE ACTUALLY SHOW UP?
WAIT...
THERE!
BLLAAAARE
RRRRUMMMMMBLE!
THAT RIG! IT'S SO HUGE! I'VE NEVER SEEN ANYTHING LIKE IT!
SOMEONE'S GETTING OUT...
FWEEEEEEE
ROAD WORD IS YOU'RE LOOKIN' F'R ME...
MY KNEES ARE SHAKING!
GET A GRIP, TARYN! DON'T JACK-KNIFE NOW!
YOU MIZ O'CONNELL...?
Y-Y-Y-Y-Y-Y...

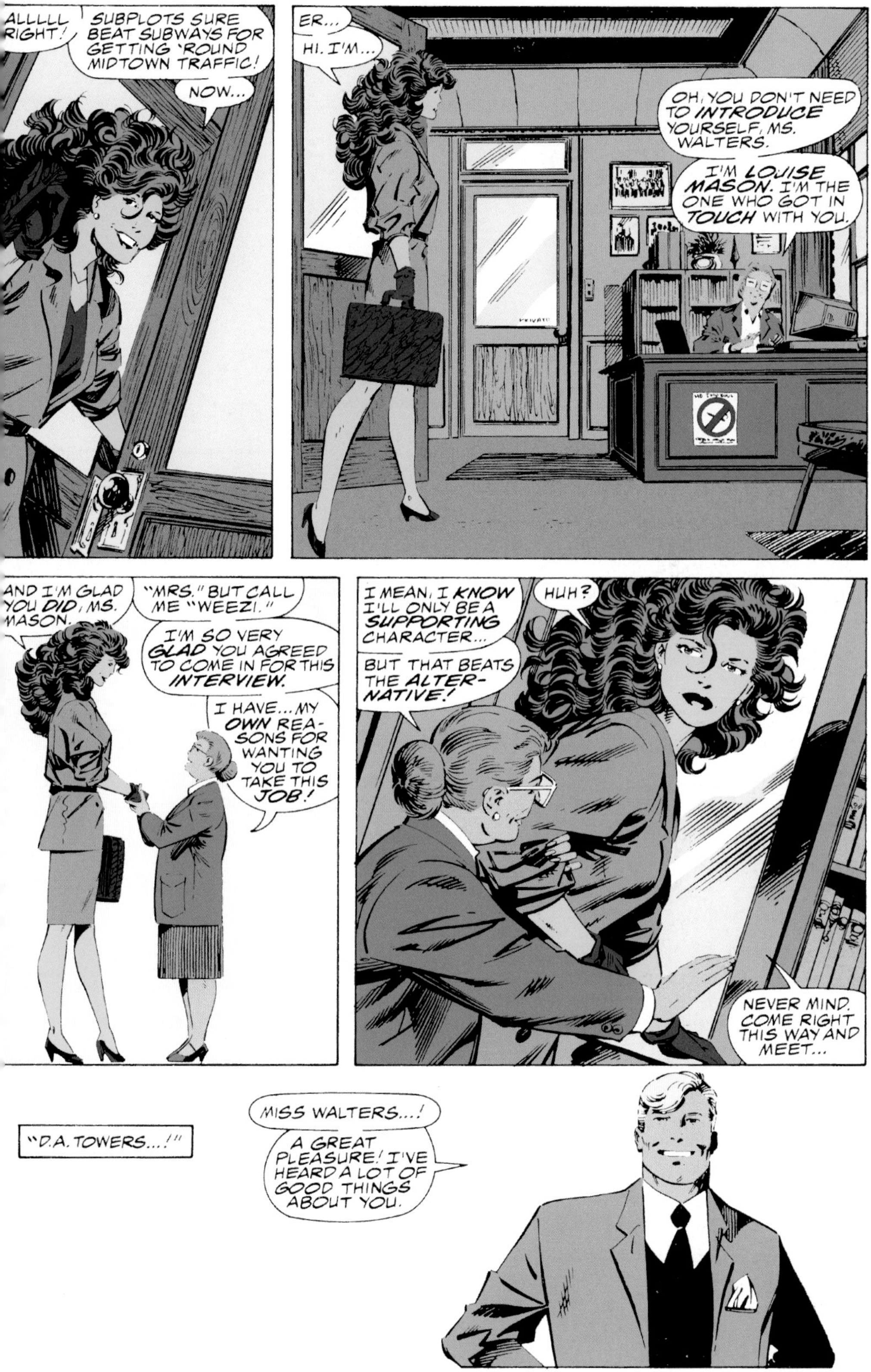
ALLLLL RIGHT!
SUBPLOTS SURE BEAT SUBWAYS FOR GETTING 'ROUND MIDTOWN TRAFFIC!
NOW...
ER...
HI. I'M...
OH, YOU DON'T NEED TO INTRODUCE YOURSELF, MS. WALTERS.
I'M LOUISE MASON. I'M THE ONE WHO GOT IN TOUCH WITH YOU.
AND I'M GLAD YOU DID, MS. MASON.
"MRS." BUT CALL ME "WEEZI."
I'M SO VERY GLAD YOU AGREED TO COME IN FOR THIS INTERVIEW.
I HAVE... MY OWN REASONS FOR WANTING YOU TO TAKE THIS JOB!
I MEAN, I KNOW I'LL ONLY BE A SUPPORTING CHARACTER...
BUT THAT BEATS THE ALTERNATIVE!
HUH?
NEVER MIND. COME RIGHT THIS WAY AND MEET...
"D.A. TOWERS...!"
MISS WALTERS...!
A GREAT PLEASURE! I'VE HEARD A LOT OF GOOD THINGS ABOUT YOU.

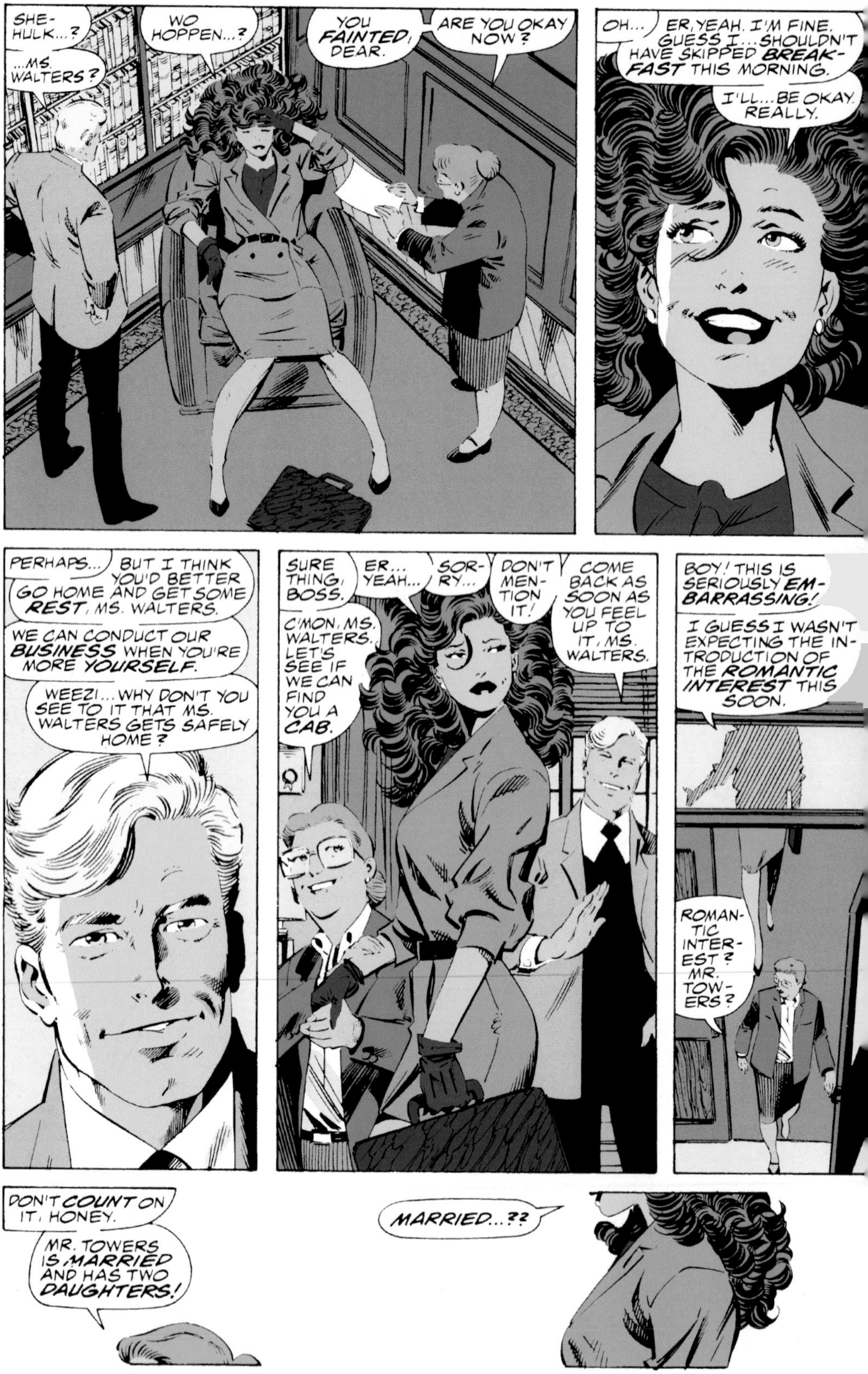
SHE-HULK...?
...MS. WALTERS?
WO HOPPEN...?
YOU FAINTED, DEAR.
ARE YOU OKAY NOW?
OH...
ER, YEAH. I'M FINE. GUESS I...SHOULDN'T HAVE SKIPPED BREAKFAST THIS MORNING.
I'LL...BE OKAY. REALLY.
PERHAPS...
BUT I THINK YOU'D BETTER GO HOME AND GET SOME REST, MS. WALTERS.
WE CAN CONDUCT OUR BUSINESS WHEN YOU'RE MORE YOURSELF.
WEEZI...WHY DON'T YOU SEE TO IT THAT MS. WALTERS GETS SAFELY HOME?
SURE THING, BOSS.
C'MON, MS. WALTERS. LET'S SEE IF WE CAN FIND YOU A CAB.
ER...YEAH...
SORRY...
DON'T MENTION IT!
COME BACK AS SOON AS YOU FEEL UP TO IT, MS. WALTERS.
BOY! THIS IS SERIOUSLY EMBARRASSING!
I GUESS I WASN'T EXPECTING THE INTRODUCTION OF THE ROMANTIC INTEREST THIS SOON.
ROMANTIC INTEREST? MR. TOWERS?
DON'T COUNT ON IT, HONEY.
MR. TOWERS IS MARRIED AND HAS TWO DAUGHTERS!
MARRIED...??

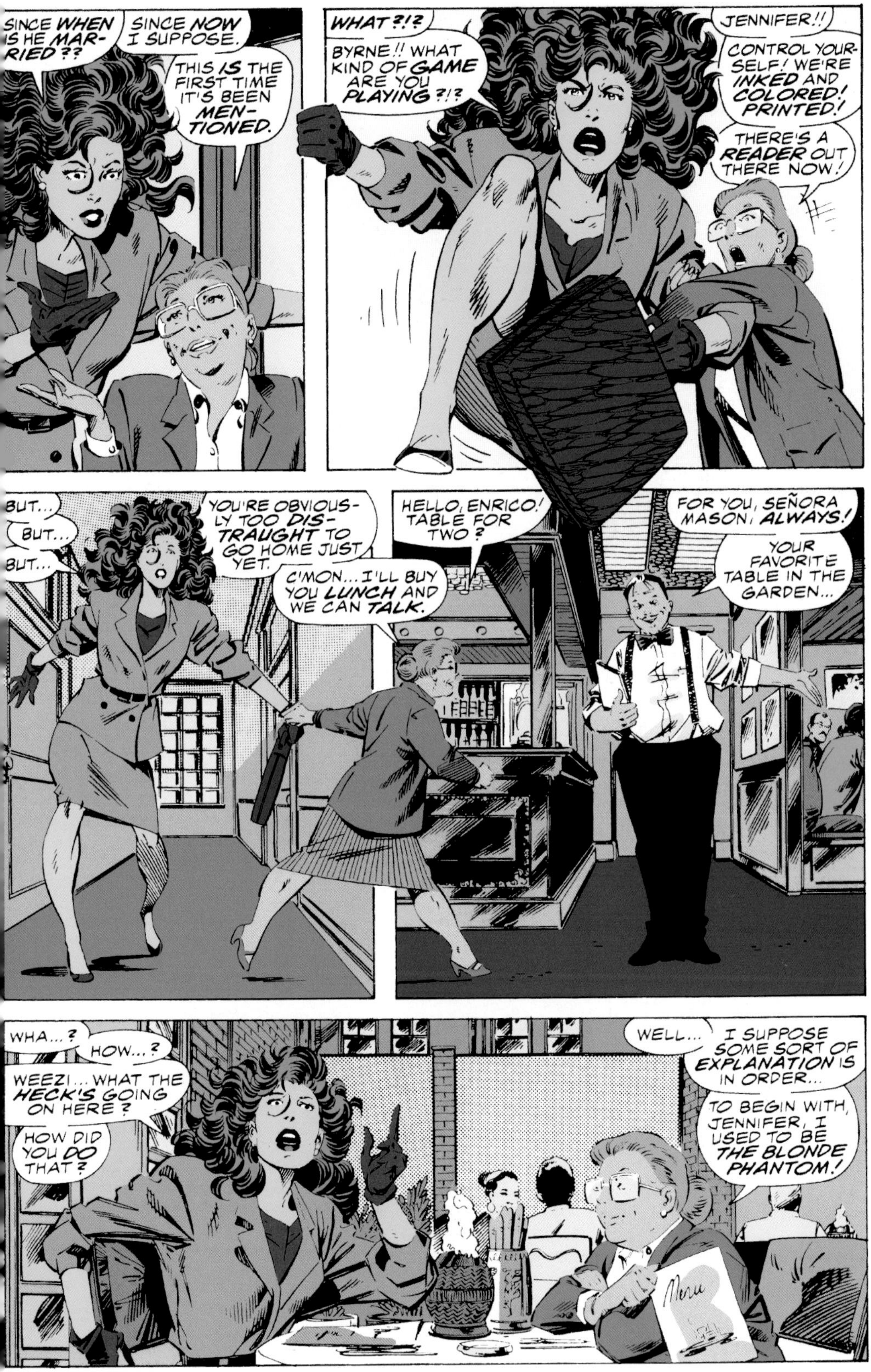
SINCE WHEN IS HE MAR-RIED??
SINCE NOW I SUPPOSE.
THIS IS THE FIRST TIME IT'S BEEN MEN-TIONED.
WHAT?!?
BYRNE!! WHAT KIND OF GAME ARE YOU PLAYING?!?
JENNIFER!!
CONTROL YOUR-SELF! WE'RE INKED AND COLORED! PRINTED!
THERE'S A READER OUT THERE NOW!
BUT...
BUT...
BUT...
YOU'RE OBVIOUS-LY TOO DIS-TRAUGHT TO GO HOME JUST YET.
C'MON... I'LL BUY YOU LUNCH AND WE CAN TALK.
HELLO, ENRICO! TABLE FOR TWO?
FOR YOU, SEÑORA MASON, ALWAYS!
YOUR FAVORITE TABLE IN THE GARDEN...
WHA...?
HOW...?
WEEZI... WHAT THE HECK'S GOING ON HERE?
HOW DID YOU DO THAT?
WELL...
I SUPPOSE SOME SORT OF EXPLANATION IS IN ORDER...
TO BEGIN WITH, JENNIFER, I USED TO BE THE BLONDE PHANTOM!
Menu

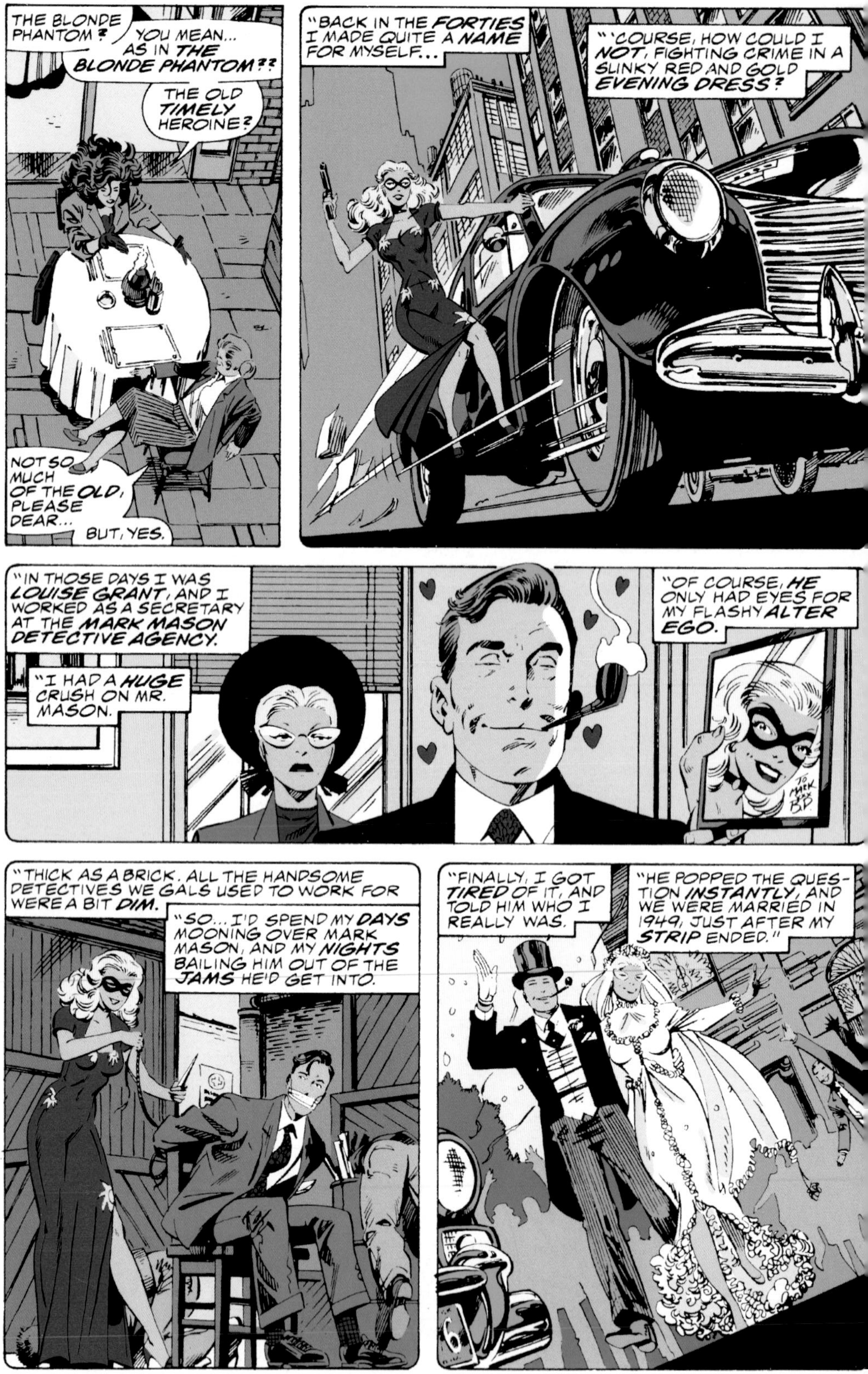
THE BLONDE PHANTOM?
YOU MEAN... AS IN THE BLONDE PHANTOM??
THE OLD TIMELY HEROINE?
NOT SO MUCH OF THE OLD, PLEASE DEAR... BUT, YES.
"BACK IN THE FORTIES I MADE QUITE A NAME FOR MYSELF...
"'COURSE, HOW COULD I NOT, FIGHTING CRIME IN A SLINKY RED AND GOLD EVENING DRESS?
"IN THOSE DAYS I WAS LOUISE GRANT, AND I WORKED AS A SECRETARY AT THE MARK MASON DETECTIVE AGENCY.
"I HAD A HUGE CRUSH ON MR. MASON.
"OF COURSE, HE ONLY HAD EYES FOR MY FLASHY ALTER EGO.
"THICK AS A BRICK. ALL THE HANDSOME DETECTIVES WE GALS USED TO WORK FOR WERE A BIT DIM.
"SO... I'D SPEND MY DAYS MOONING OVER MARK MASON, AND MY NIGHTS BAILING HIM OUT OF THE JAMS HE'D GET INTO.
"FINALLY, I GOT TIRED OF IT, AND TOLD HIM WHO I REALLY WAS.
"HE POPPED THE QUESTION INSTANTLY, AND WE WERE MARRIED IN 1949, JUST AFTER MY STRIP ENDED."

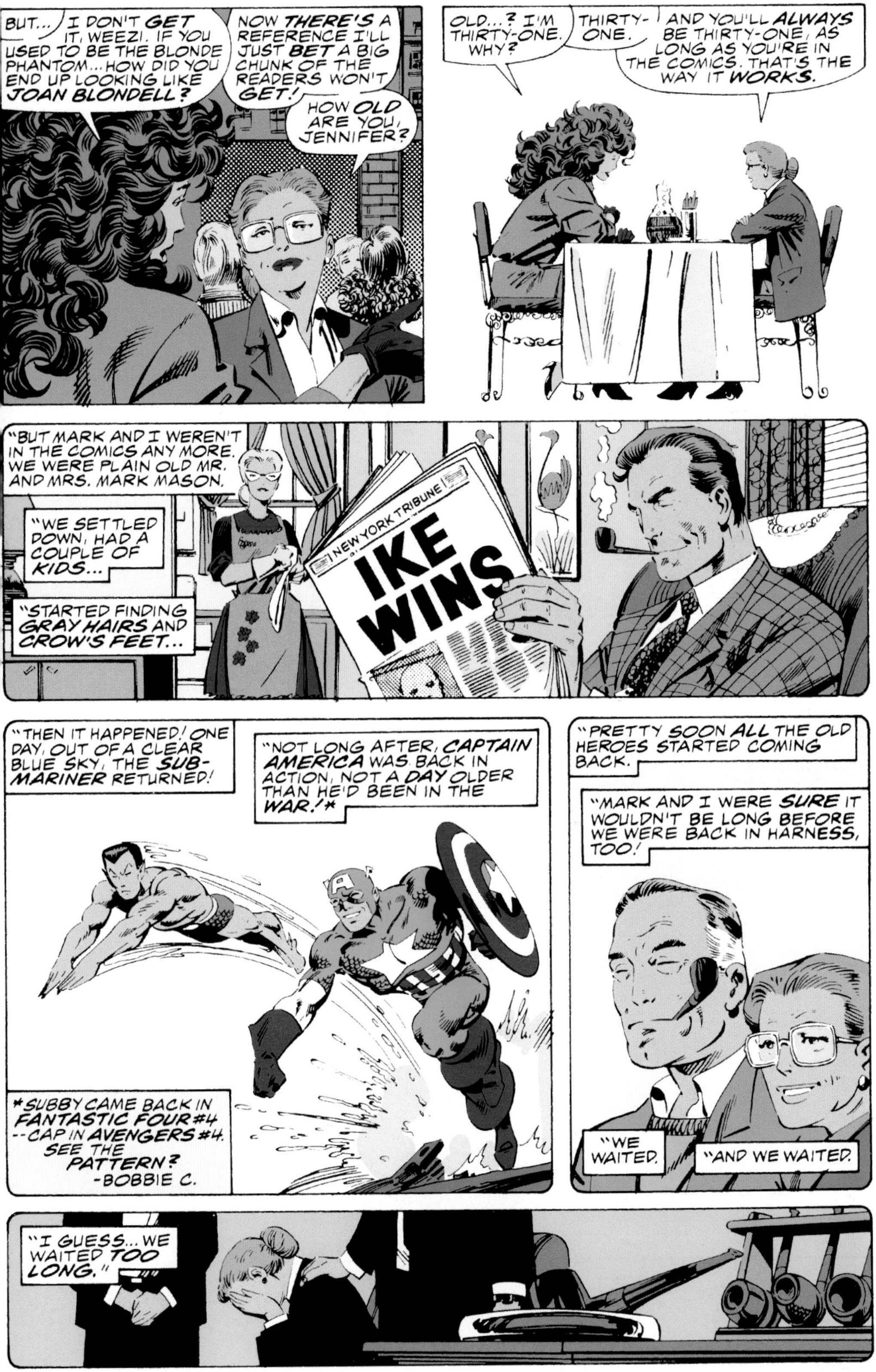

BUT...I DON'T GET IT, WEEZI. IF YOU USED TO BE THE BLONDE PHANTOM...HOW DID YOU END UP LOOKING LIKE JOAN BLONDELL?
NOW THERE'S A REFERENCE I'LL JUST BET A BIG CHUNK OF THE READERS WON'T GET!
HOW OLD ARE YOU, JENNIFER?
OLD...? I'M THIRTY-ONE. WHY?
THIRTY-ONE.
AND YOU'LL ALWAYS BE THIRTY-ONE, AS LONG AS YOU'RE IN THE COMICS. THAT'S THE WAY IT WORKS.
"BUT MARK AND I WEREN'T IN THE COMICS ANY MORE. WE WERE PLAIN OLD MR. AND MRS. MARK MASON.
"WE SETTLED DOWN, HAD A COUPLE OF KIDS...
"STARTED FINDING GRAY HAIRS AND CROW'S FEET...
NEW YORK TRIBUNE
IKE WINS
"THEN IT HAPPENED! ONE DAY, OUT OF A CLEAR BLUE SKY, THE SUB-MARINER RETURNED!
"NOT LONG AFTER, CAPTAIN AMERICA WAS BACK IN ACTION, NOT A DAY OLDER THAN HE'D BEEN IN THE WAR!*
*SUBBY CAME BACK IN FANTASTIC FOUR #4 --CAP IN AVENGERS #4. SEE THE PATTERN? -BOBBIE C.
"PRETTY SOON ALL THE OLD HEROES STARTED COMING BACK.
"MARK AND I WERE SURE IT WOULDN'T BE LONG BEFORE WE WERE BACK IN HARNESS, TOO!
"WE WAITED.
"AND WE WAITED.
"I GUESS...WE WAITED TOO LONG."

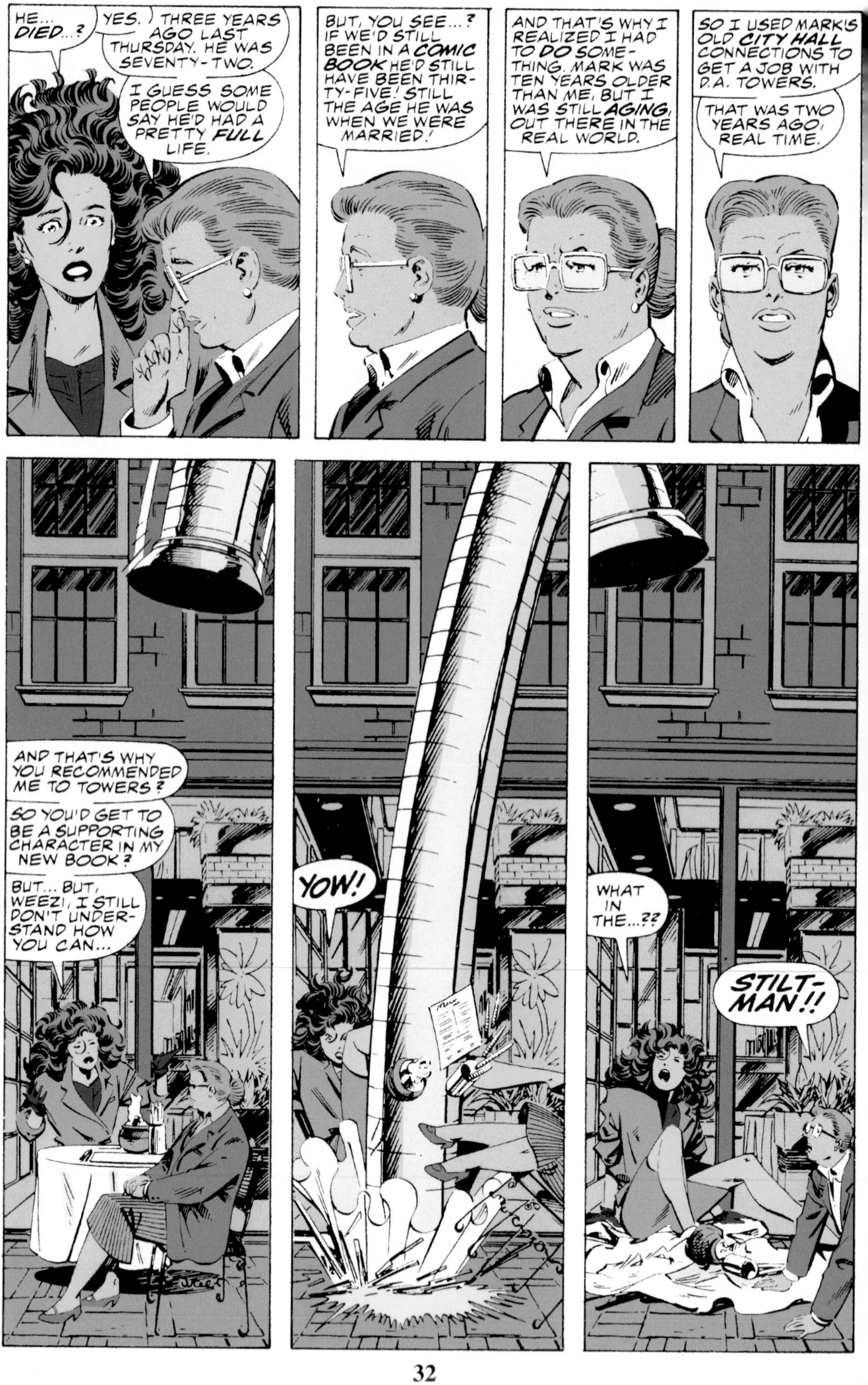

HE... DIED...?
YES. THREE YEARS AGO LAST THURSDAY. HE WAS SEVENTY-TWO.
I GUESS SOME PEOPLE WOULD SAY HE'D HAD A PRETTY FULL LIFE.
BUT, YOU SEE...? IF WE'D STILL BEEN IN A COMIC BOOK HE'D STILL HAVE BEEN THIRTY-FIVE! STILL THE AGE HE WAS WHEN WE WERE MARRIED!
AND THAT'S WHY I REALIZED I HAD TO DO SOMETHING. MARK WAS TEN YEARS OLDER THAN ME, BUT I WAS STILL AGING, OUT THERE IN THE REAL WORLD.
SO I USED MARK'S OLD CITY HALL CONNECTIONS TO GET A JOB WITH D.A. TOWERS.
THAT WAS TWO YEARS AGO, REAL TIME.
AND THAT'S WHY YOU RECOMMENDED ME TO TOWERS?
SO YOU'D GET TO BE A SUPPORTING CHARACTER IN MY NEW BOOK?
BUT... BUT, WEEZI, I STILL DON'T UNDERSTAND HOW YOU CAN...
YOW!
WHAT IN THE...??
STILT-MAN!!

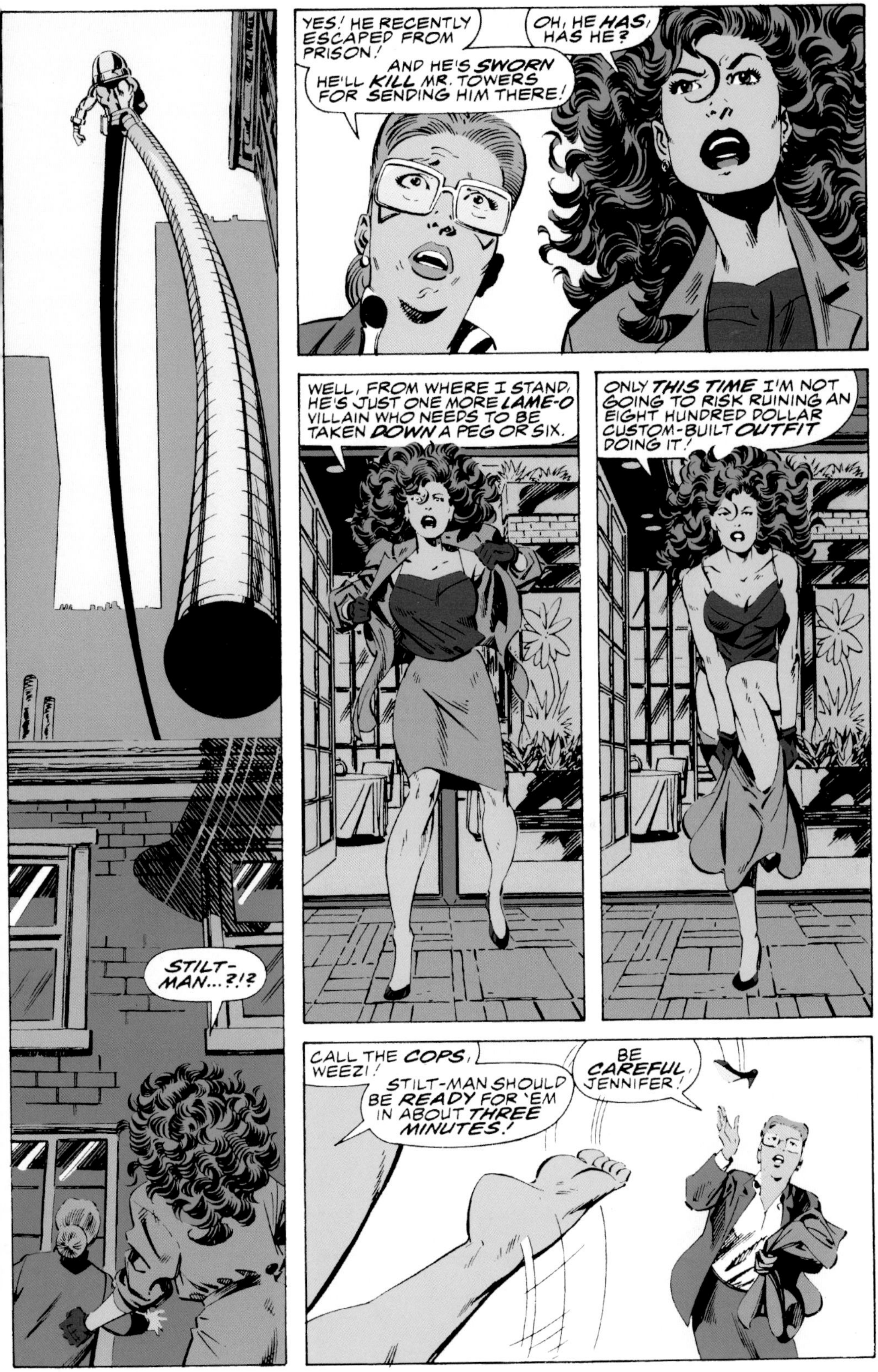
YES! HE RECENTLY ESCAPED FROM PRISON!
AND HE'S SWORN HE'LL KILL MR. TOWERS FOR SENDING HIM THERE!
OH, HE HAS, HAS HE?
STILT-MAN...?!?
WELL, FROM WHERE I STAND, HE'S JUST ONE MORE LAME-O VILLAIN WHO NEEDS TO BE TAKEN DOWN A PEG OR SIX.
ONLY THIS TIME I'M NOT GOING TO RISK RUINING AN EIGHT HUNDRED DOLLAR CUSTOM-BUILT OUTFIT DOING IT!
CALL THE COPS, WEEZI!
STILT-MAN SHOULD BE READY FOR 'EM IN ABOUT THREE MINUTES!
BE CAREFUL, JENNIFER!

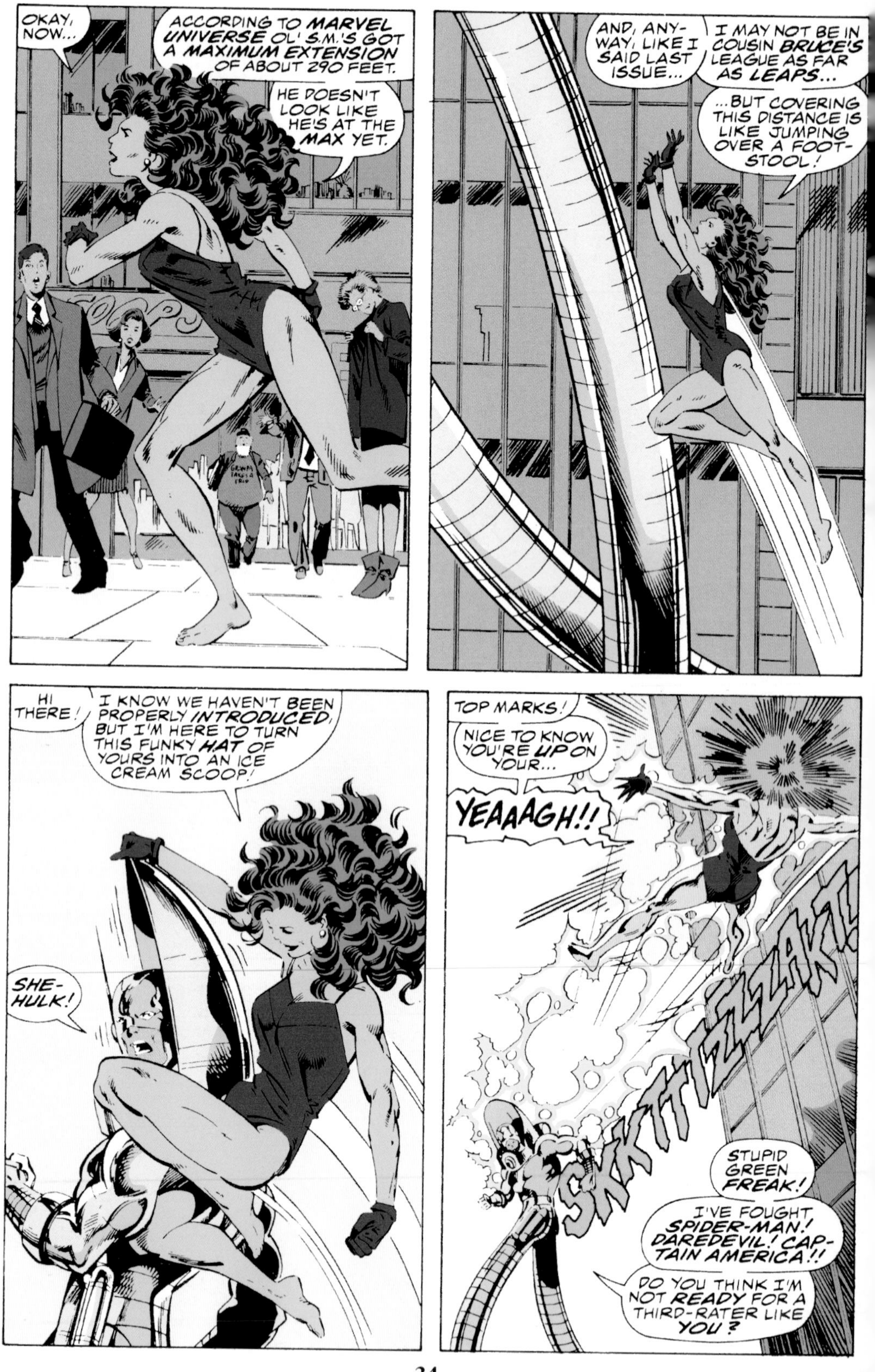
OKAY, NOW...
ACCORDING TO MARVEL UNIVERSE OL' S.M.'S GOT A MAXIMUM EXTENSION OF ABOUT 290 FEET.
HE DOESN'T LOOK LIKE HE'S AT THE MAX YET.
AND, ANY-WAY, LIKE I SAID LAST ISSUE...
I MAY NOT BE IN COUSIN BRUCE'S LEAGUE AS FAR AS LEAPS...
...BUT COVERING THIS DISTANCE IS LIKE JUMPING OVER A FOOT-STOOL!
HI THERE!
I KNOW WE HAVEN'T BEEN PROPERLY INTRODUCED, BUT I'M HERE TO TURN THIS FUNKY HAT OF YOURS INTO AN ICE CREAM SCOOP!
SHE-HULK!
TOP MARKS!
NICE TO KNOW YOU'RE UP ON YOUR...
YEAAAGH!!
SKKTTTZZZAKT!
STUPID GREEN FREAK!
I'VE FOUGHT SPIDER-MAN! DAREDEVIL! CAPTAIN AMERICA!!
DO YOU THINK I'M NOT READY FOR A THIRD-RATER LIKE YOU?

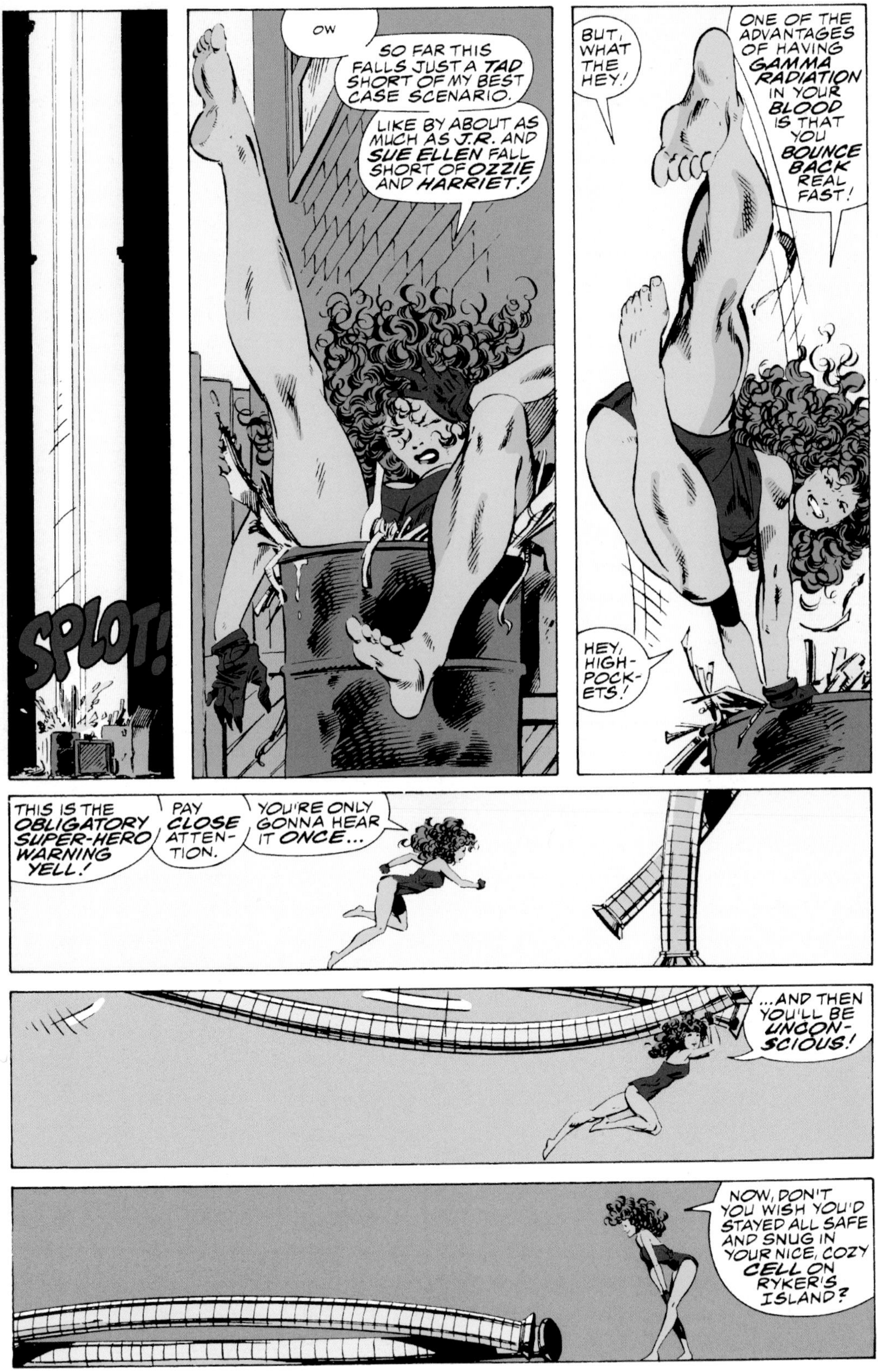
SPLOT!
OW
SO FAR THIS FALLS JUST A TAD SHORT OF MY BEST CASE SCENARIO.
LIKE BY ABOUT AS MUCH AS J.R. AND SUE ELLEN FALL SHORT OF OZZIE AND HARRIET!
BUT, WHAT THE HEY!
ONE OF THE ADVANTAGES OF HAVING GAMMA RADIATION IN YOUR BLOOD IS THAT YOU BOUNCE BACK REAL FAST!
HEY, HIGH-POCK-ETS!
THIS IS THE OBLIGATORY SUPER-HERO WARNING YELL!
PAY CLOSE ATTEN-TION.
YOU'RE ONLY GONNA HEAR IT ONCE...
...AND THEN YOU'LL BE UNCON-SCIOUS!
NOW, DON'T YOU WISH YOU'D STAYED ALL SAFE AND SNUG IN YOUR NICE, COZY CELL ON RYKER'S ISLAND?

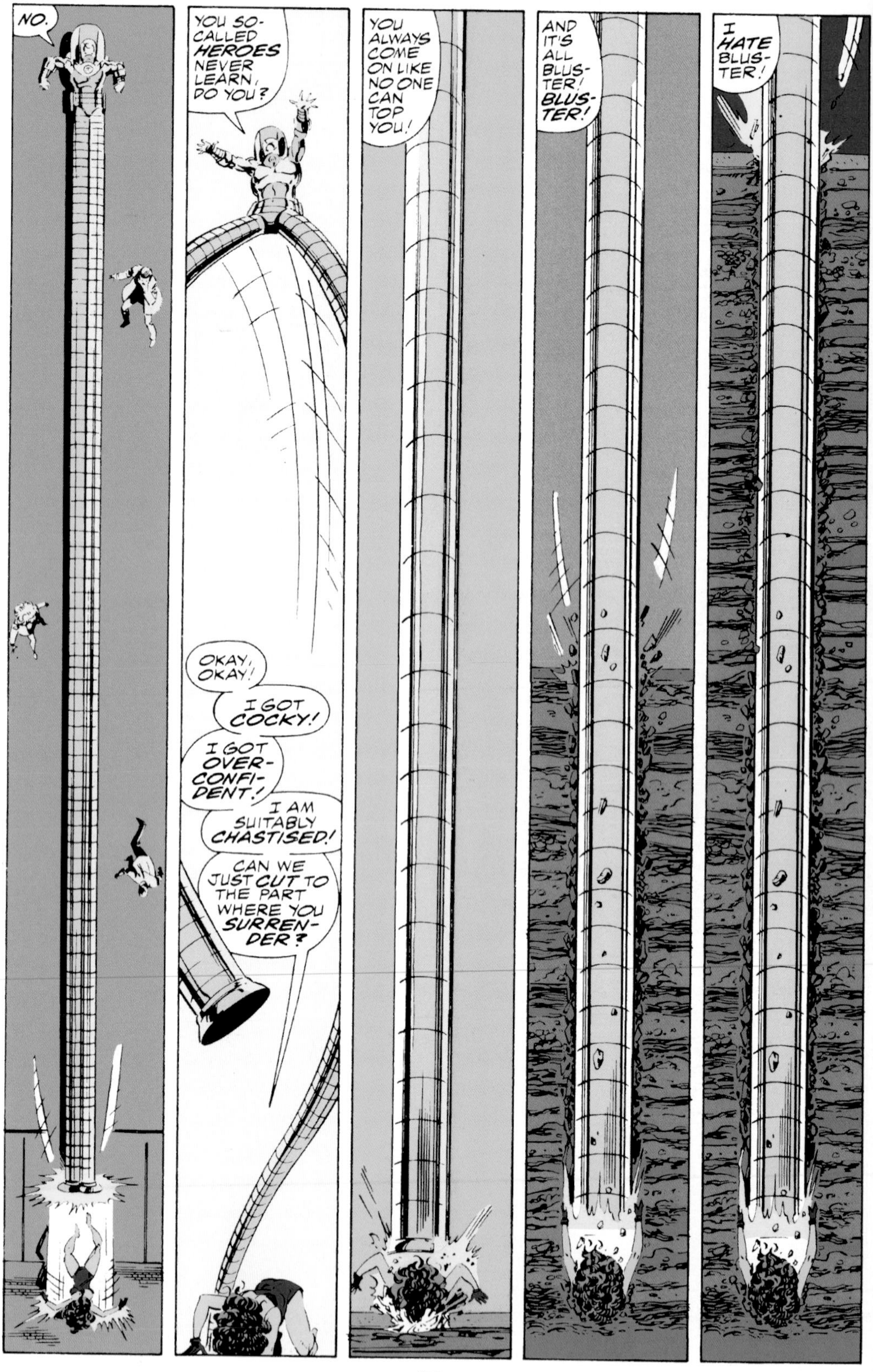
NO.
YOU SO-CALLED HEROES NEVER LEARN, DO YOU?
OKAY, OKAY!
I GOT COCKY!
I GOT OVER-CONFI-DENT!
I AM SUITABLY CHASTISED!
CAN WE JUST CUT TO THE PART WHERE YOU SURREN-DER?
YOU ALWAYS COME ON LIKE NO ONE CAN TOP YOU!
AND IT'S ALL BLUS-TER! BLUS-TER!
I HATE BLUS-TER!

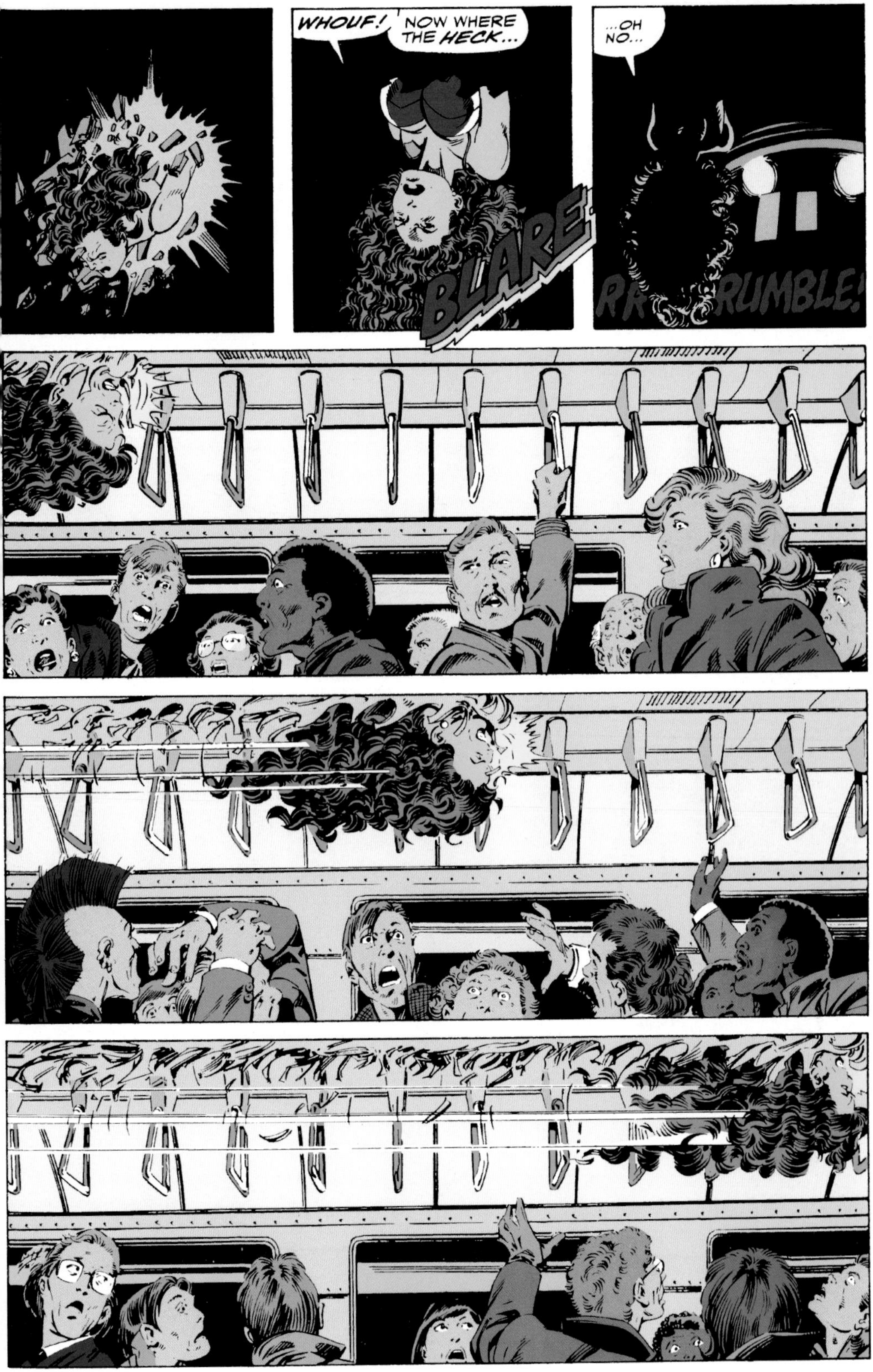
WHOUF!
NOW WHERE THE HECK...
BLARE
...OH NO...
RR
RUMBLE!

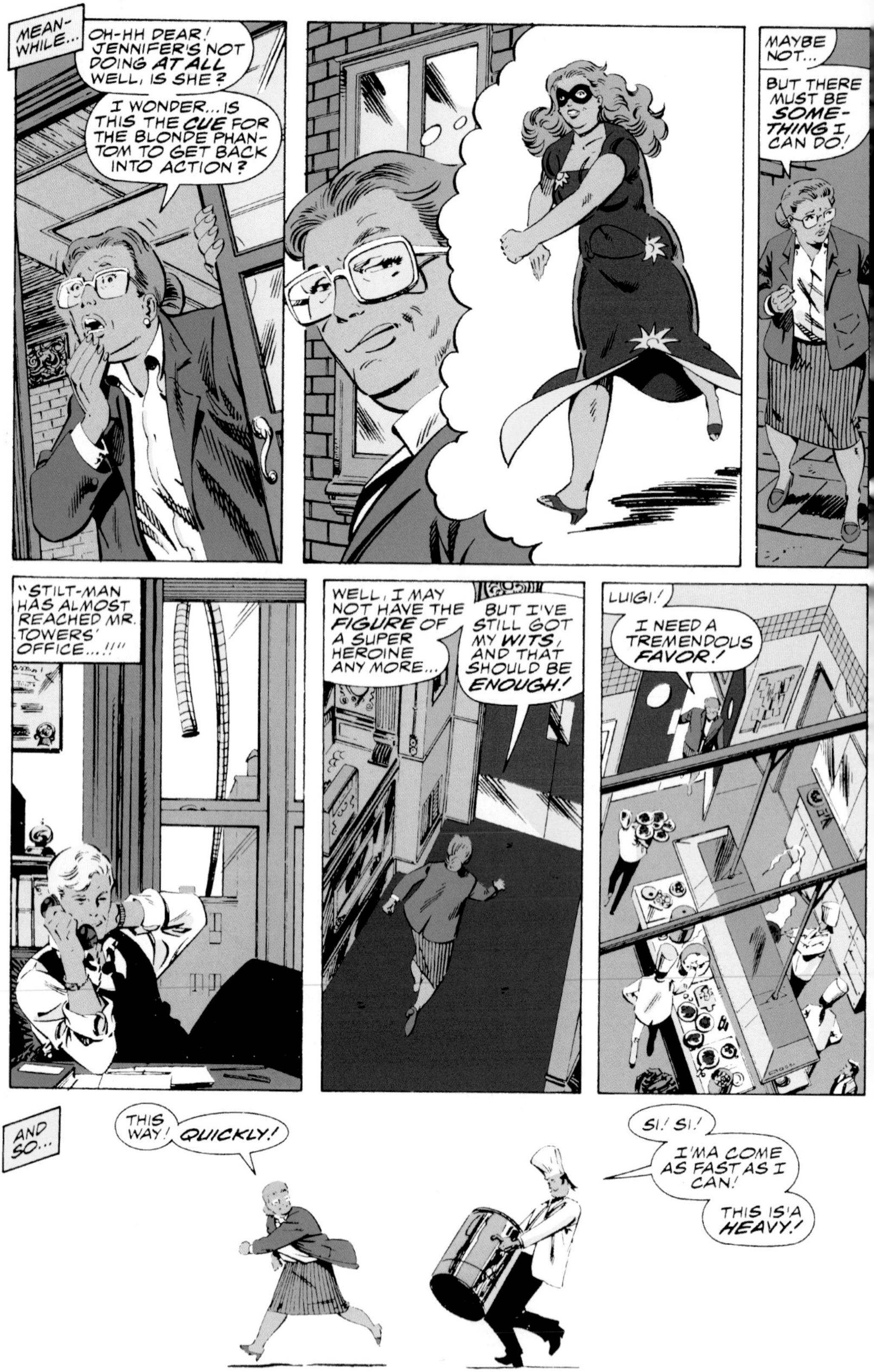
MEAN-WHILE...
OH-HH DEAR! JENNIFER'S NOT DOING AT ALL WELL, IS SHE?
I WONDER... IS THIS THE CUE FOR THE BLONDE PHANTOM TO GET BACK INTO ACTION?
MAYBE NOT...
BUT THERE MUST BE SOME-THING I CAN DO!
"STILT-MAN HAS ALMOST REACHED MR. TOWERS' OFFICE...!!"
WELL, I MAY NOT HAVE THE FIGURE OF A SUPER HEROINE ANY MORE...
BUT I'VE STILL GOT MY WITS, AND THAT SHOULD BE ENOUGH!
LUIGI!
I NEED A TREMENDOUS FAVOR!
AND SO...
THIS WAY! QUICKLY!
SI! SI!
I'MA COME AS FAST AS I CAN!
THIS IS'A HEAVY!

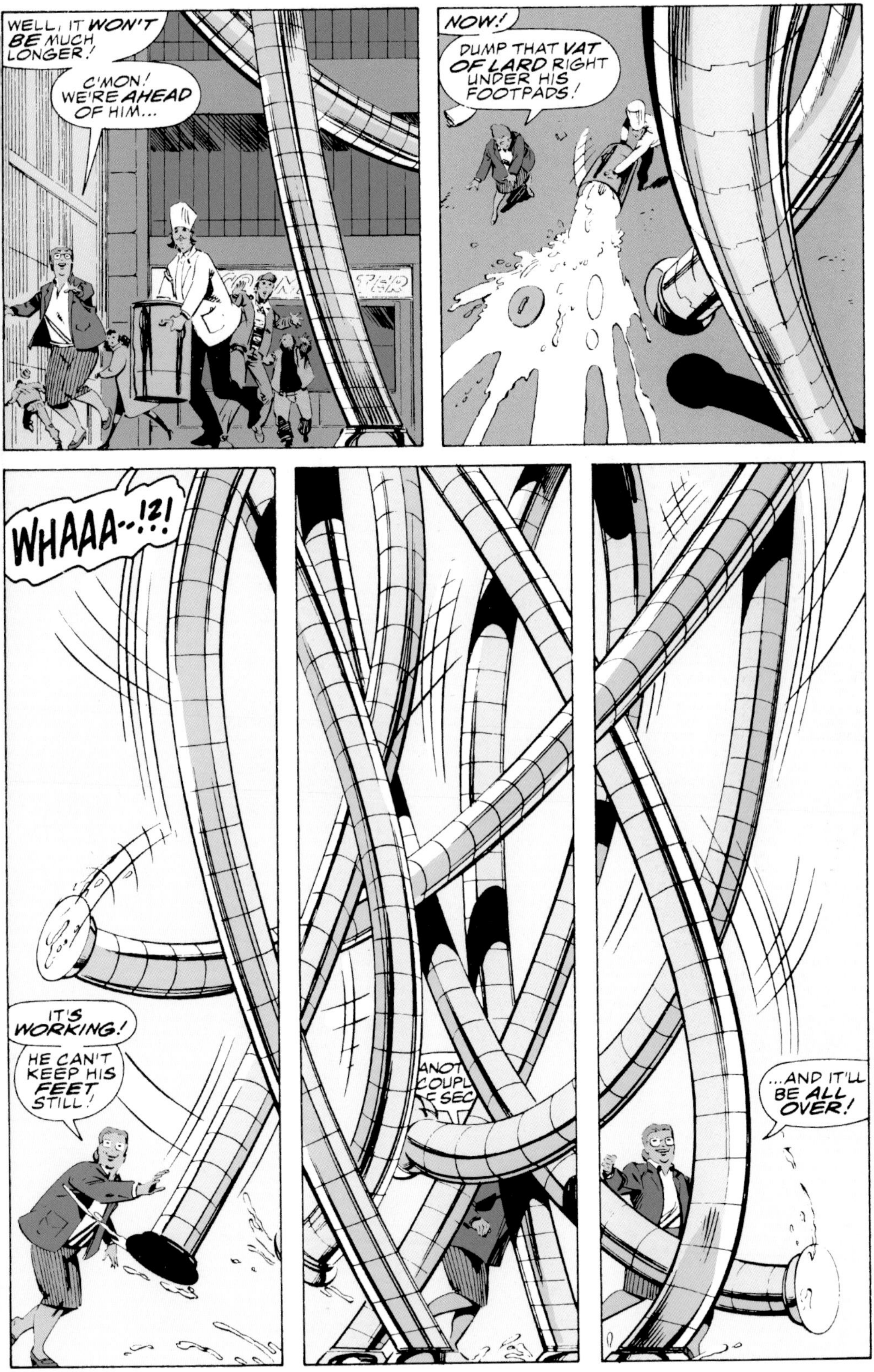
WELL, IT WON'T BE MUCH LONGER!
C'MON! WE'RE AHEAD OF HIM...
NOW!
DUMP THAT VAT OF LARD RIGHT UNDER HIS FOOTPADS!
WHAAA--!?!
IT'S WORKING!
HE CAN'T KEEP HIS FEET STILL!
ANOT COUPL E SEC
...AND IT'LL BE ALL OVER!

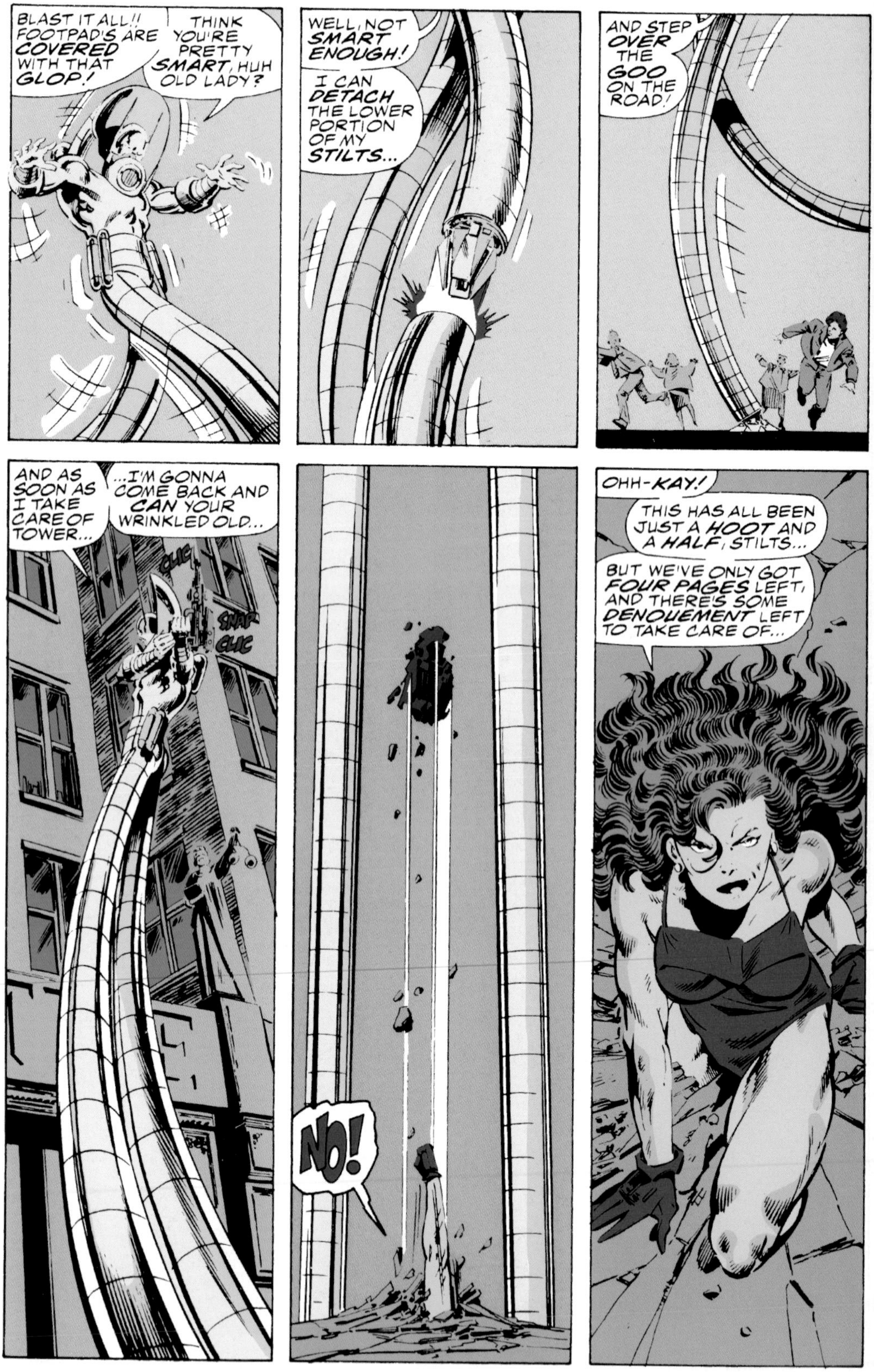
BLAST IT ALL!! FOOTPAD'S ARE COVERED WITH THAT GLOP!
THINK YOU'RE PRETTY SMART, HUH OLD LADY?
WELL, NOT SMART ENOUGH!
I CAN DETACH THE LOWER PORTION OF MY STILTS...
AND STEP OVER THE GOO ON THE ROAD!
AND AS SOON AS I TAKE CARE OF TOWER...
...I'M GONNA COME BACK AND CAN YOUR WRINKLED OLD...
CLIC
SNAP
CLIC
NO!
OHH-KAY!
THIS HAS ALL BEEN JUST A HOOT AND A HALF, STILTS...
BUT WE'VE ONLY GOT FOUR PAGES LEFT, AND THERE'S SOME DENOUEMENT LEFT TO TAKE CARE OF...

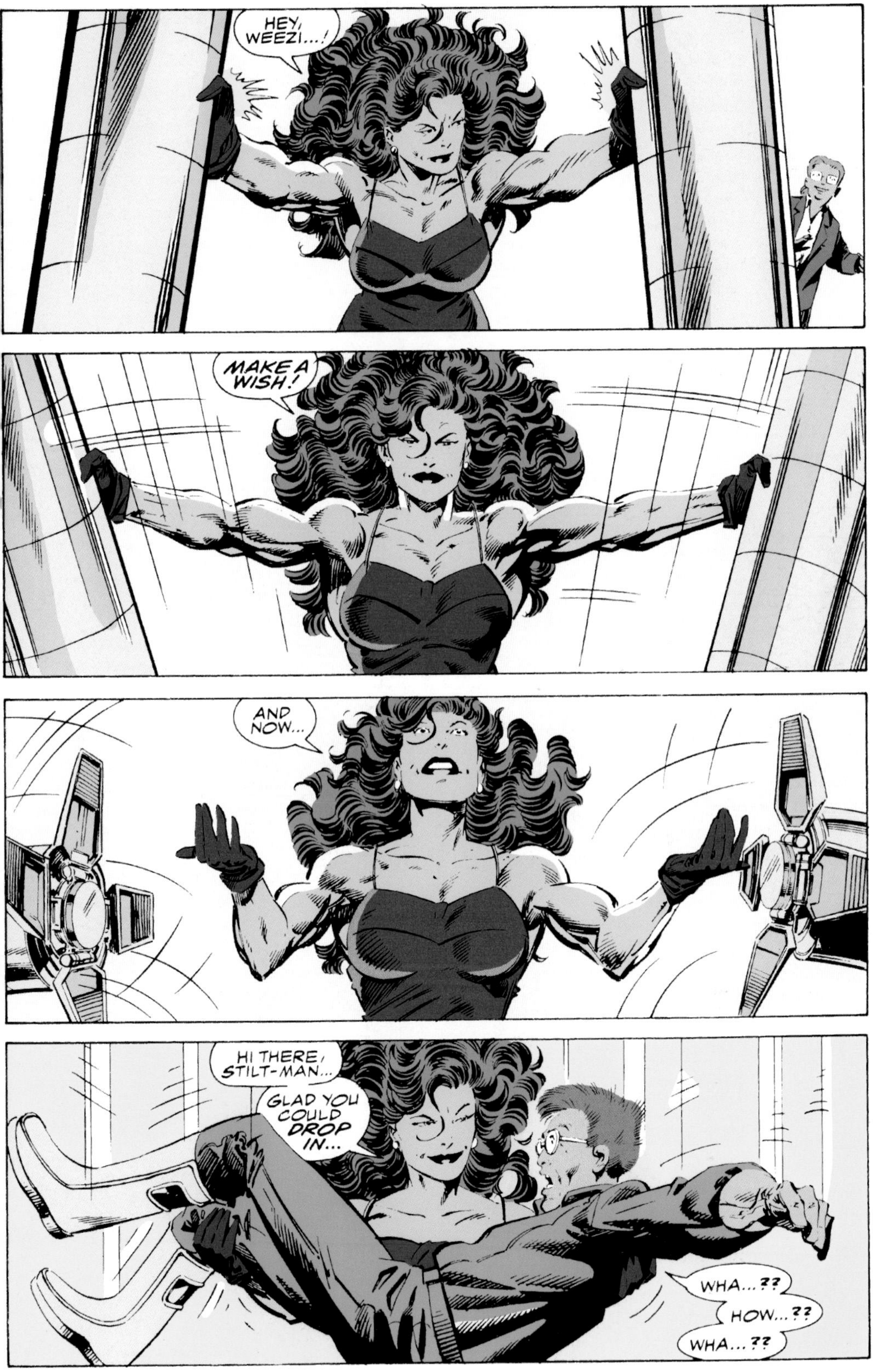
HEY, WEEZI...!
MAKE A WISH!
AND NOW...
HI THERE, STILT-MAN...
GLAD YOU COULD DROP IN...
WHA...??
HOW...??
WHA...??

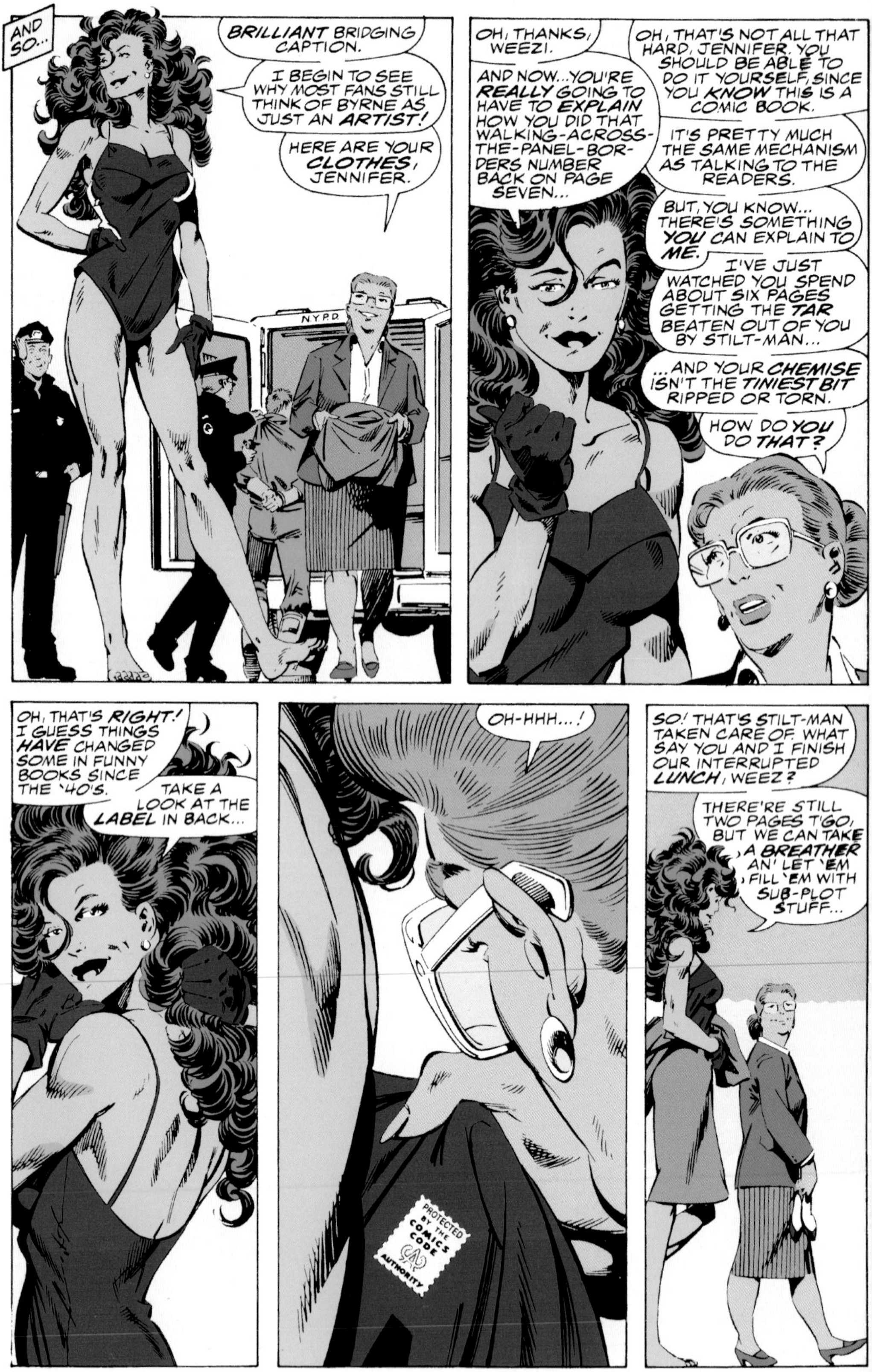
AND SO...
BRILLIANT BRIDGING CAPTION.
I BEGIN TO SEE WHY MOST FANS STILL THINK OF BYRNE AS JUST AN ARTIST!
HERE ARE YOUR CLOTHES, JENNIFER.
N.Y.P.D.
OH, THANKS, WEEZI.
AND NOW... YOU'RE REALLY GOING TO HAVE TO EXPLAIN HOW YOU DID THAT WALKING-ACROSS-THE-PANEL-BORDERS NUMBER BACK ON PAGE SEVEN...
OH, THAT'S NOT ALL THAT HARD, JENNIFER. YOU SHOULD BE ABLE TO DO IT YOURSELF, SINCE YOU KNOW THIS IS A COMIC BOOK.
IT'S PRETTY MUCH THE SAME MECHANISM AS TALKING TO THE READERS.
BUT, YOU KNOW... THERE'S SOMETHING YOU CAN EXPLAIN TO ME.
I'VE JUST WATCHED YOU SPEND ABOUT SIX PAGES GETTING THE TAR BEATEN OUT OF YOU BY STILT-MAN...
...AND YOUR CHEMISE ISN'T THE TINIEST BIT RIPPED OR TORN.
HOW DO YOU DO THAT?
OH, THAT'S RIGHT! I GUESS THINGS HAVE CHANGED SOME IN FUNNY BOOKS SINCE THE '40'S.
TAKE A LOOK AT THE LABEL IN BACK...
OH-HHH...!
PROTECTED BY THE COMICS CODE AUTHORITY
SO! THAT'S STILT-MAN TAKEN CARE OF. WHAT SAY YOU AND I FINISH OUR INTERRUPTED LUNCH, WEEZ?
THERE'RE STILL TWO PAGES T'GO, BUT WE CAN TAKE A BREATHER AN' LET 'EM FILL 'EM WITH SUB-PLOT STUFF...

AND SO... ~~I MEAN~~ ... ELSEWHERE...

THERE WE GO.

579

I MUST SAY, THIS IS THE *FIRST TIME* I'VE EVER HAD ANYONE REQUEST A *NINETY-NINE YEAR LEASE!* YOU MUST BE PLANNING ON BEING WITH US *QUITE A WHILE!*

AND, SINCE YOUR CREDIT REFERENCES ARE *IMPECCABLE...*

YOU'RE QUITE SURE YOU DON'T WANT TO SEE THE APARTMENT? YOU WERE SO VERY *SPECIFIC* ABOUT THE UNIT YOU WANTED, BUYING OUT THE PREVIOUS TENANTS AND ALL...

NO? WELL, I'LL BE LOOKING FOR YOU TO MOVE IN NEXT WEEK, SHALL I?

I'LL JUST PUT YOUR NICE, NEW *NAME PLATE* IN PLACE HERE.

YOU'RE JOINING QUITE AN *ILLUSTRIOUS* LIST, AS YOU CAN SEE...

20 A	JENNIFER WALTERS ATTORNEY AT LAW	20 B	JOHN BYRNE WRITER/PENCILER
19 A	MR. POWERS ADVENTURER	19 B	BOB WIACEK INKER
	TOM DEFALCO EDITOR-IN-C	18 B	GLYNIS OLIVER COLORIST
17 A	RICK		17 B	JIM NOVAK LETTERER
	ERTZ GEON	16 B	BOBBIE CHASE EDITOR

WELL, SINCE THERE DOESN'T SEEM TO BE ANYTHING ELSE TO TAKE *CARE* OF, I'LL JUST SAY *GOOD-BYE* FOR NOW, MR. POWERS.

WOW!

WHAT A *HUNK!*

EXCUSE ME, ARE YOU THE MANAGER?

I HAVE THAT *PRIVILEGE.* HOW MAY I *HELP* YOU?

I HAVE AN IMPORTANT *MESSAGE* FOR THE SHE-HULK. IS SHE AT HOME?

43

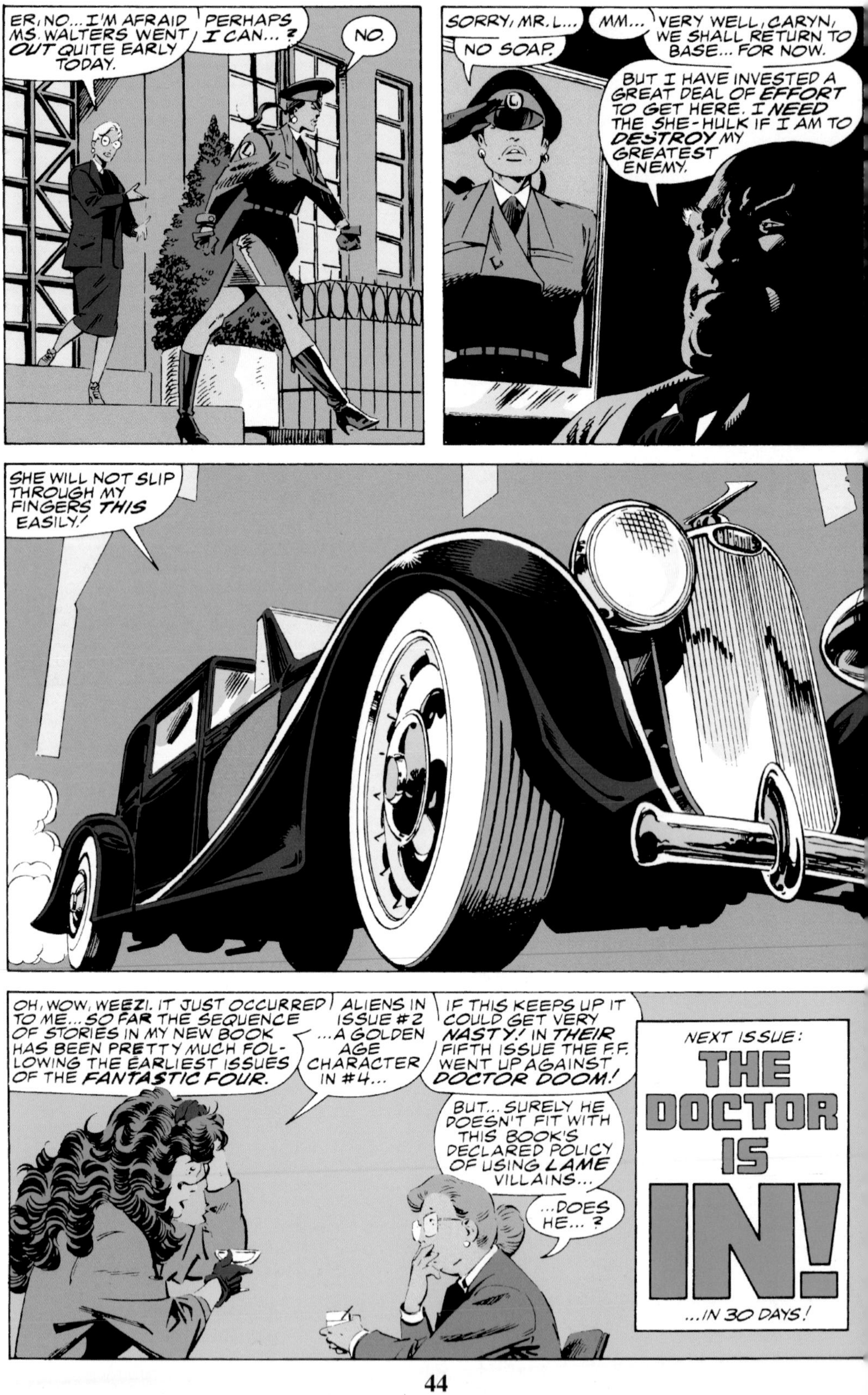

ER, NO... I'M AFRAID MS. WALTERS WENT OUT QUITE EARLY TODAY.
PERHAPS I CAN... ?
NO.
SORRY, MR. L... NO SOAP.
MM... VERY WELL, CARYN, WE SHALL RETURN TO BASE... FOR NOW.
BUT I HAVE INVESTED A GREAT DEAL OF EFFORT TO GET HERE. I NEED THE SHE-HULK IF I AM TO DESTROY MY GREATEST ENEMY.
SHE WILL NOT SLIP THROUGH MY FINGERS THIS EASILY.!
OH, WOW, WEEZI. IT JUST OCCURRED TO ME... SO FAR THE SEQUENCE OF STORIES IN MY NEW BOOK HAS BEEN PRETTY MUCH FOLLOWING THE EARLIEST ISSUES OF THE FANTASTIC FOUR.
ALIENS IN ISSUE #2 ...A GOLDEN AGE CHARACTER IN #4...
IF THIS KEEPS UP IT COULD GET VERY NASTY.! IN THEIR FIFTH ISSUE THE F.F. WENT UP AGAINST DOCTOR DOOM!
BUT... SURELY HE DOESN'T FIT WITH THIS BOOK'S DECLARED POLICY OF USING LAME VILLAINS...
...DOES HE... ?
NEXT ISSUE:
THE DOCTOR IS IN!
...IN 30 DAYS!

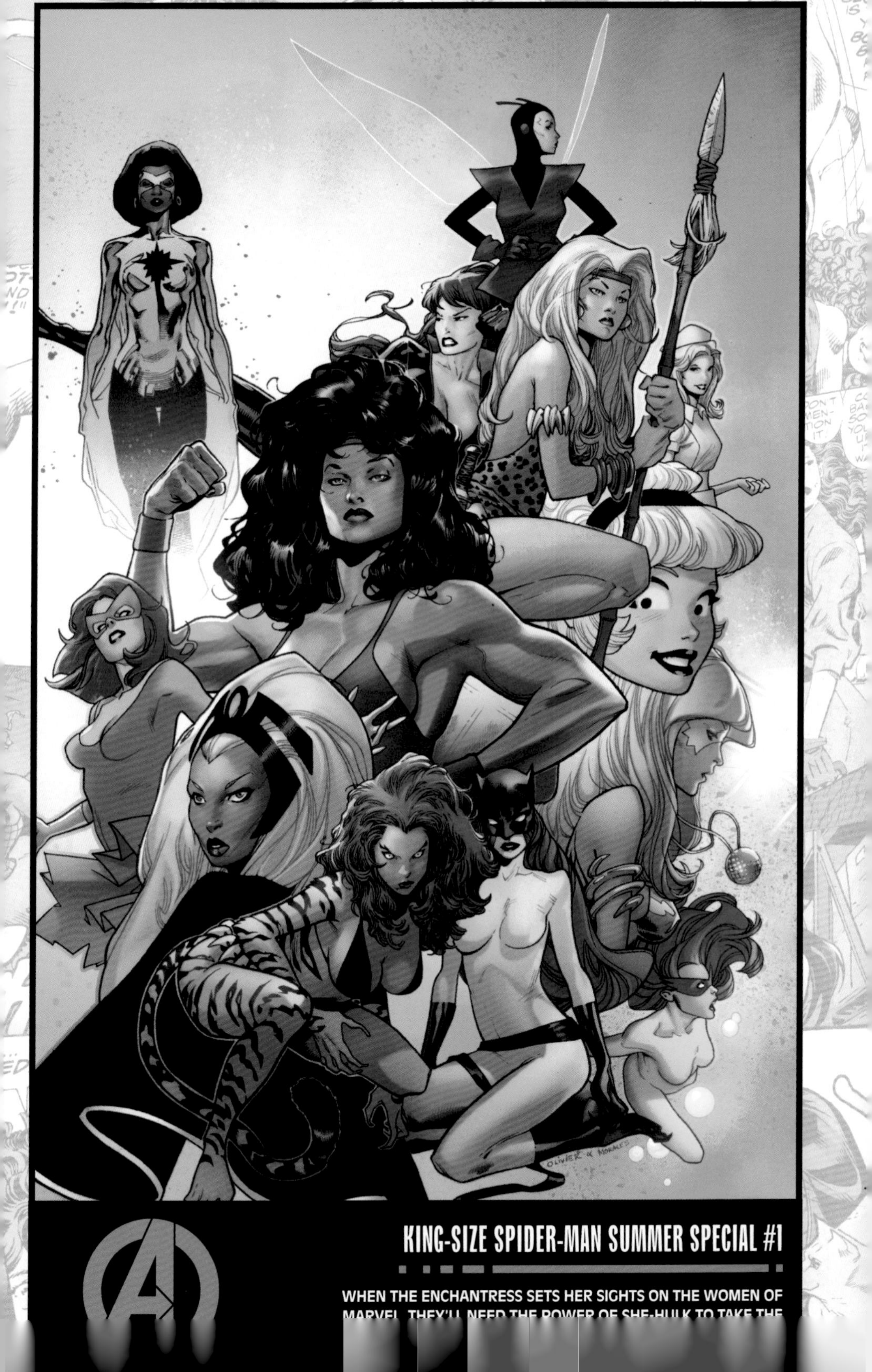
OLIVER & MORALES

KING-SIZE SPIDER-MAN SUMMER SPECIAL #1

WHEN THE ENCHANTRESS SETS HER SIGHTS ON THE WOMEN OF MARVEL, THEY'LL NEED THE POWER OF SHE-HULK TO TAKE THE

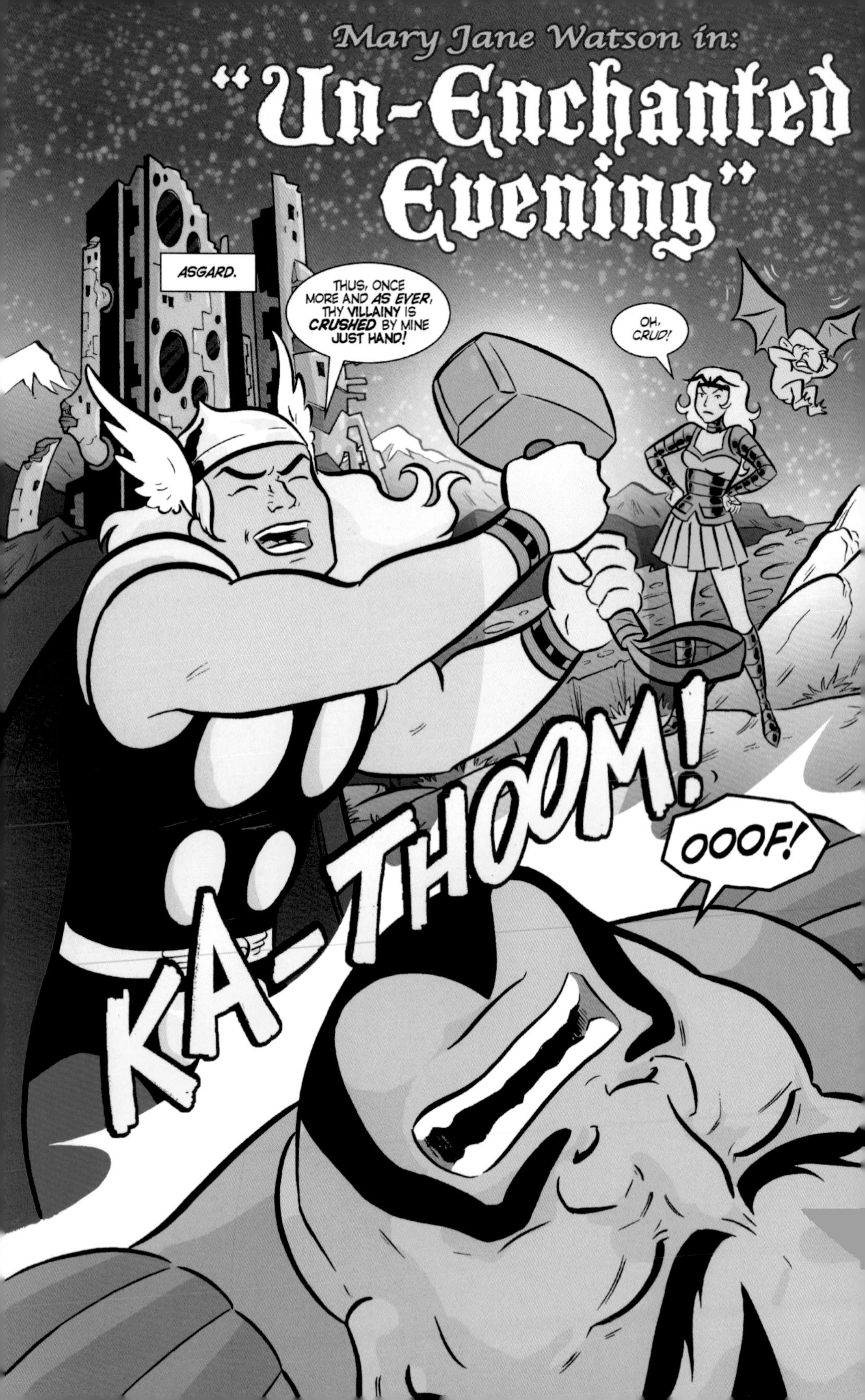
Mary Jane Watson in:
"Un-Enchanted Evening"
ASGARD.
THUS, ONCE MORE AND AS EVER, THY VILLAINY IS CRUSHED BY MINE JUST HAND!
OH, CRUD!
KA-THOOOM!
OOOF!

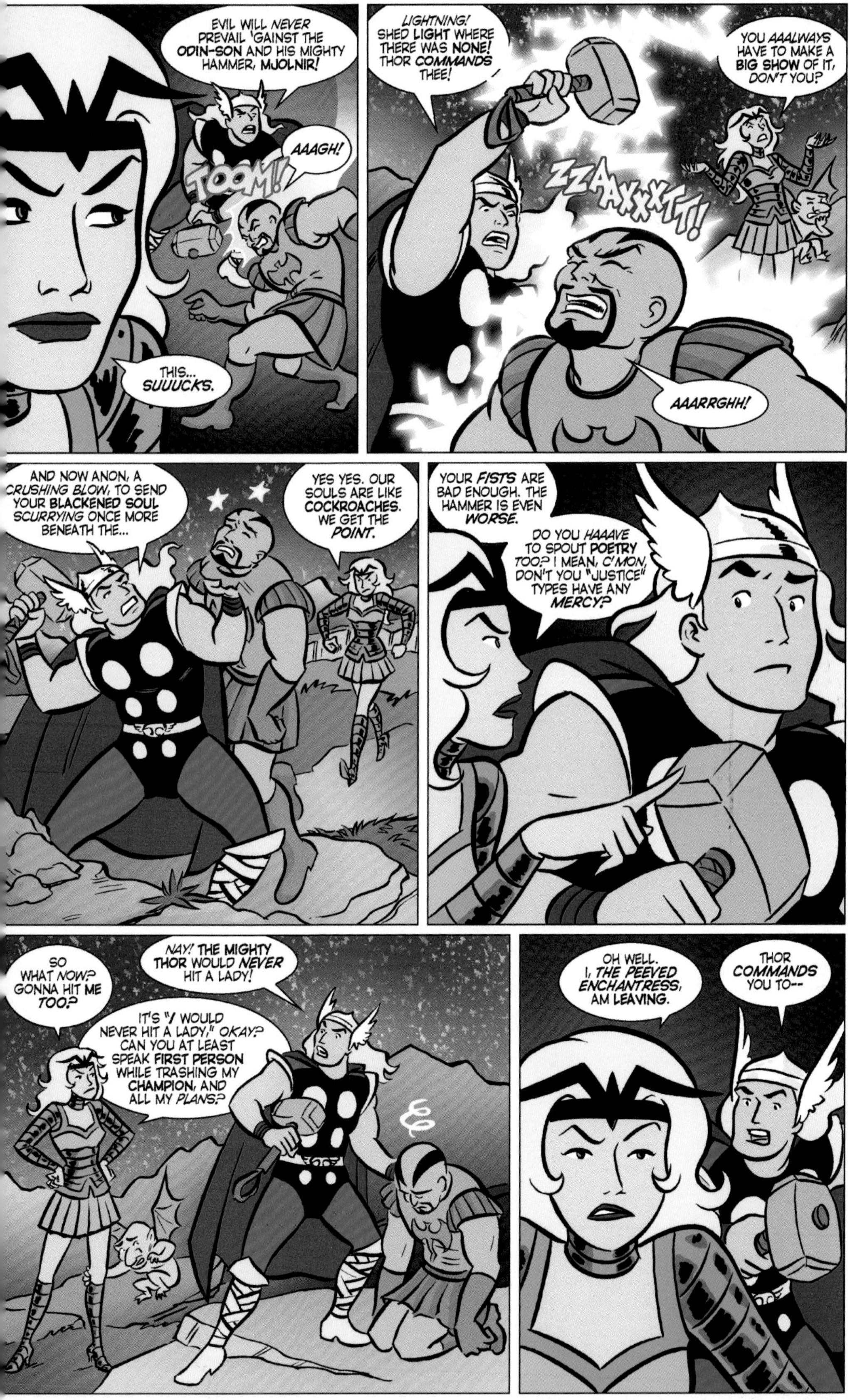
EVIL WILL NEVER PREVAIL 'GAINST THE ODIN-SON AND HIS MIGHTY HAMMER, MJOLNIR!
TOOM!
AAAGH!
THIS... SUUUCKS.
LIGHTNING! SHED LIGHT WHERE THERE WAS NONE! THOR COMMANDS THEE!
YOU AAALWAYS HAVE TO MAKE A BIG SHOW OF IT, DON'T YOU?
ZZAAXXXTT!
AAARRGHH!
AND NOW ANON, A CRUSHING BLOW, TO SEND YOUR BLACKENED SOUL SCURRYING ONCE MORE BENEATH THE...
YES YES. OUR SOULS ARE LIKE COCKROACHES. WE GET THE POINT.
YOUR FISTS ARE BAD ENOUGH. THE HAMMER IS EVEN WORSE.
DO YOU HAAAVE TO SPOUT POETRY TOO? I MEAN, C'MON, DON'T YOU "JUSTICE" TYPES HAVE ANY MERCY?
SO WHAT NOW? GONNA HIT ME TOO?
NAY! THE MIGHTY THOR WOULD NEVER HIT A LADY!
IT'S "I WOULD NEVER HIT A LADY," OKAY? CAN YOU AT LEAST SPEAK FIRST PERSON WHILE TRASHING MY CHAMPION, AND ALL MY PLANS?
OH WELL. I, THE PEEVED ENCHANTRESS, AM LEAVING.
THOR COMMANDS YOU TO--

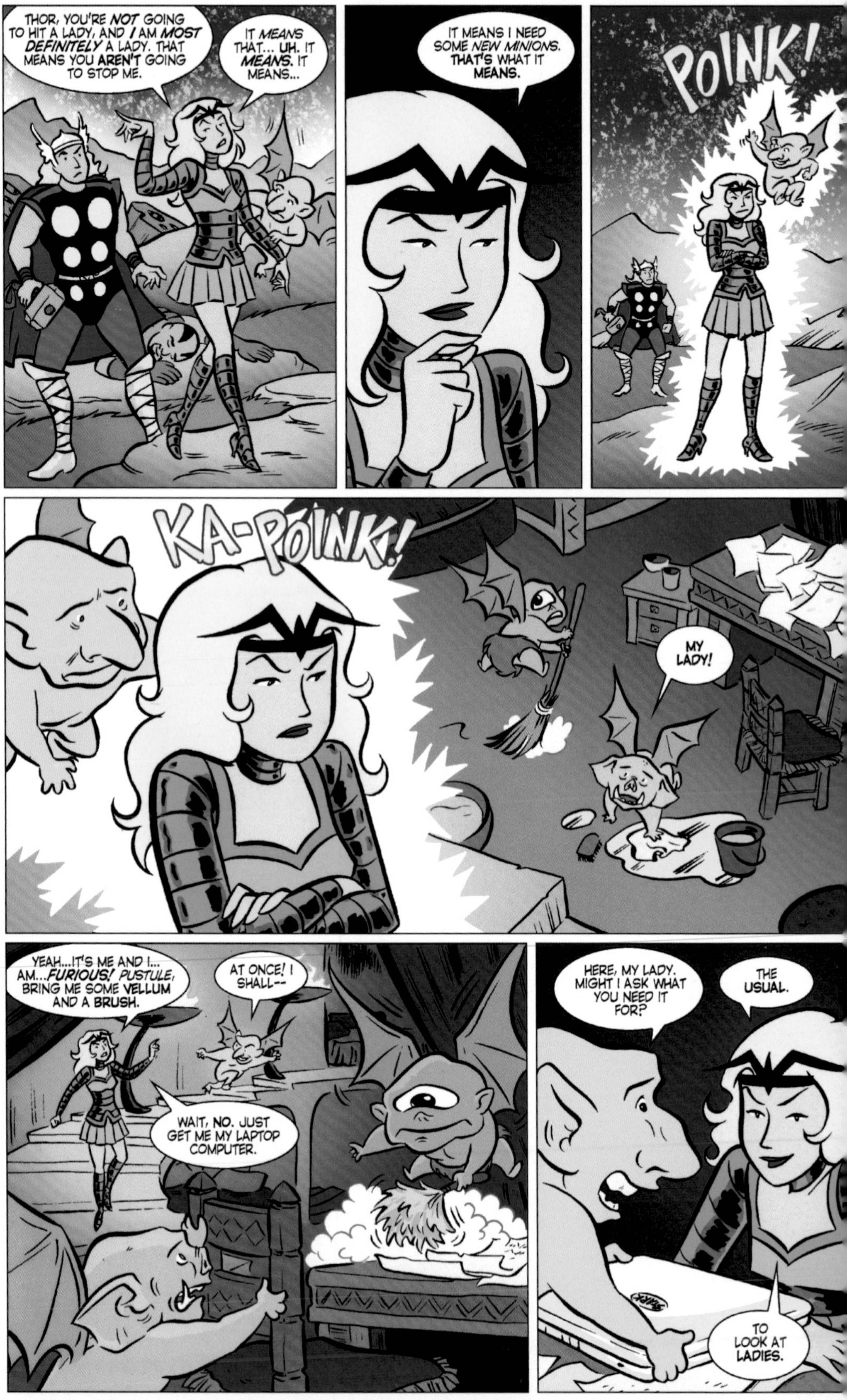
THOR, YOU'RE **NOT** GOING TO HIT A LADY, AND **I** AM ***MOST DEFINITELY*** A LADY. THAT MEANS YOU **AREN'T** GOING TO STOP ME.
IT *MEANS* THAT... **UH.** IT ***MEANS.*** IT MEANS...
IT MEANS I NEED SOME *NEW MINIONS.* **THAT'S** WHAT IT **MEANS.**
POINK!
KA-POINK!
MY LADY!
YEAH...IT'S ME AND I... AM...***FURIOUS!*** *PUSTULE,* BRING ME SOME **VELLUM** AND A **BRUSH.**
AT ONCE! I SHALL--
WAIT, **NO.** JUST GET ME MY LAPTOP COMPUTER.
HERE, MY LADY. MIGHT I ASK WHAT YOU NEED IT FOR?
THE **USUAL.**
TO LOOK AT **LADIES.**

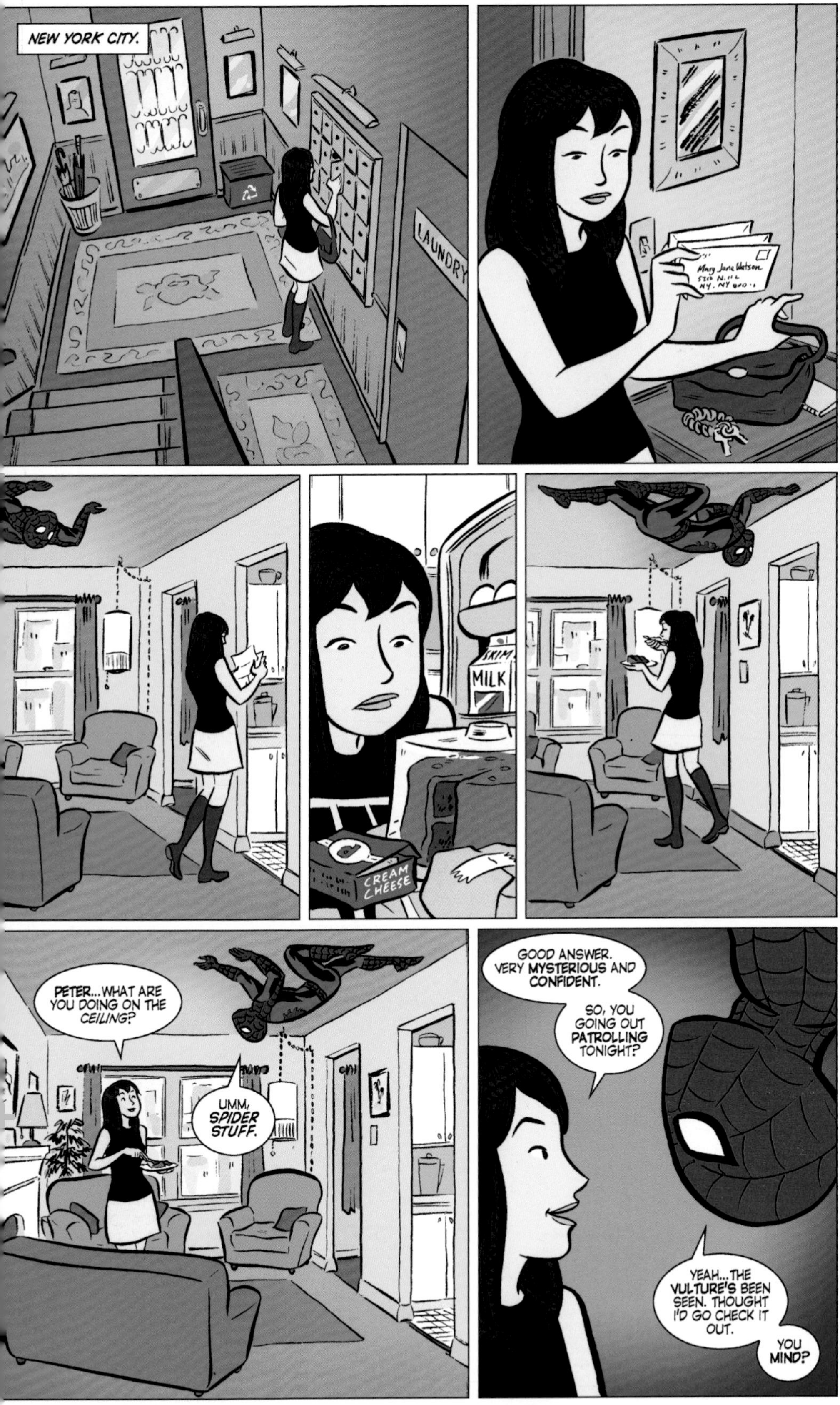
NEW YORK CITY.
LAUNDRY
Mary Jane Watson
SKIM MILK
CREAM CHEESE
PETER...WHAT ARE YOU DOING ON THE *CEILING*?
UMM, *SPIDER STUFF.*
GOOD ANSWER. VERY **MYSTERIOUS** AND **CONFIDENT**.
SO, YOU GOING OUT **PATROLLING** TONIGHT?
YEAH...THE **VULTURE'S** BEEN SEEN. THOUGHT I'D GO CHECK IT OUT.
YOU **MIND?**

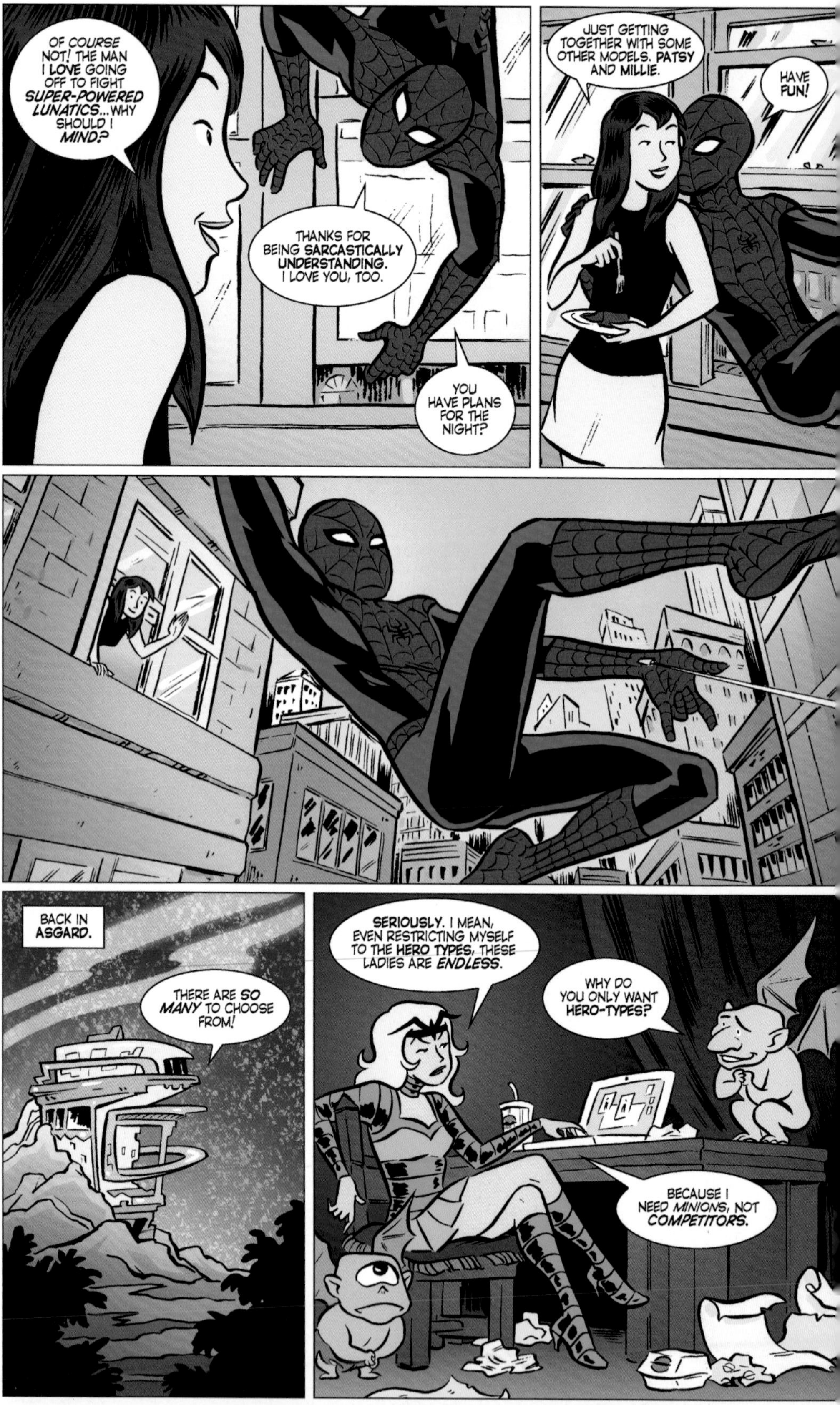
OF COURSE NOT! THE MAN I LOVE GOING OFF TO FIGHT SUPER-POWERED LUNATICS... WHY SHOULD I MIND?
THANKS FOR BEING SARCASTICALLY UNDERSTANDING. I LOVE YOU, TOO.
YOU HAVE PLANS FOR THE NIGHT?
JUST GETTING TOGETHER WITH SOME OTHER MODELS. PATSY AND MILLIE.
HAVE FUN!
BACK IN ASGARD.
THERE ARE SO MANY TO CHOOSE FROM!
SERIOUSLY. I MEAN, EVEN RESTRICTING MYSELF TO THE HERO TYPES, THESE LADIES ARE ENDLESS.
WHY DO YOU ONLY WANT HERO-TYPES?
BECAUSE I NEED MINIONS, NOT COMPETITORS.

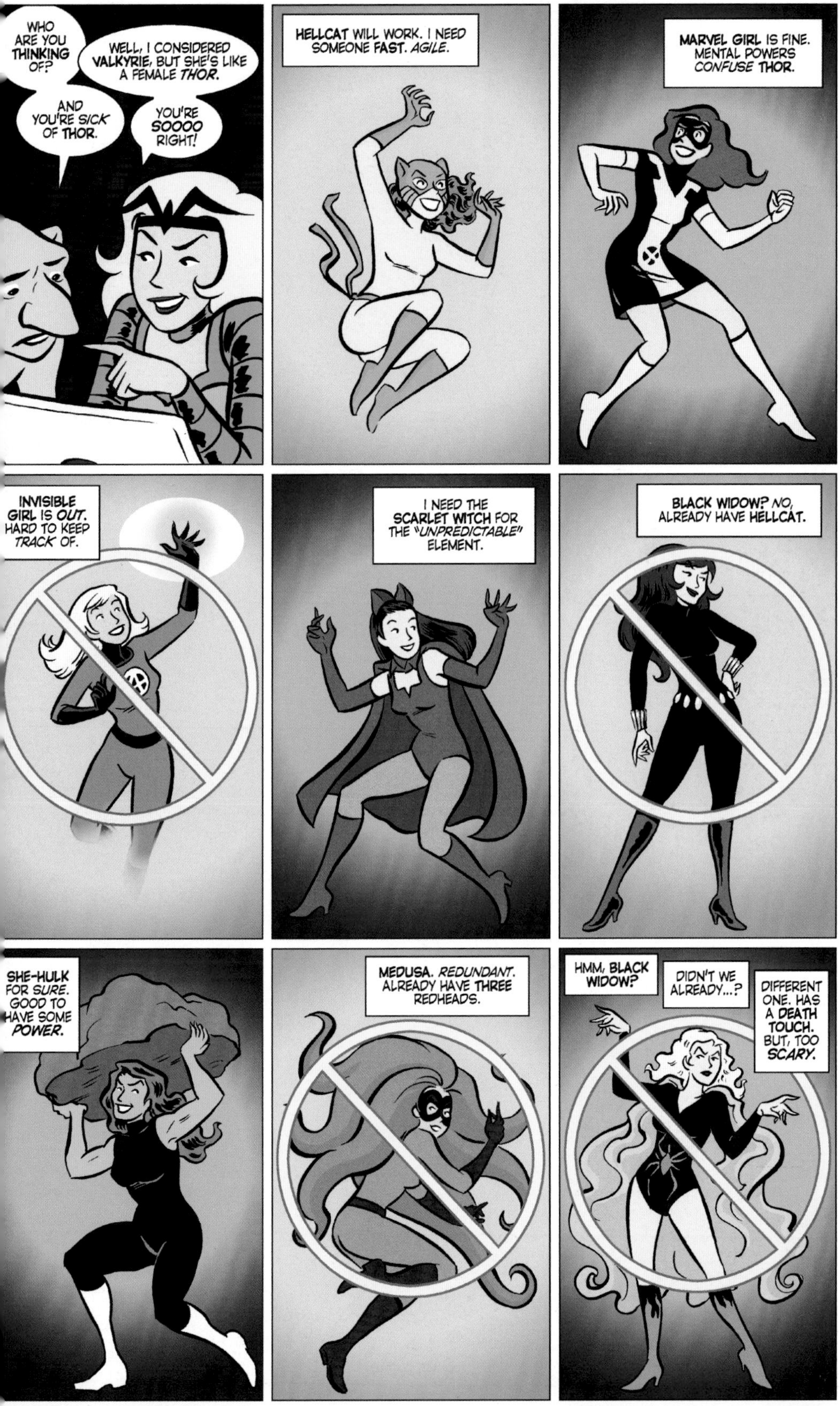
WHO ARE YOU THINKING OF?
WELL, I CONSIDERED VALKYRIE, BUT SHE'S LIKE A FEMALE THOR.
AND YOU'RE SICK OF THOR.
YOU'RE SOOOO RIGHT!
HELLCAT WILL WORK. I NEED SOMEONE FAST. AGILE.
MARVEL GIRL IS FINE. MENTAL POWERS CONFUSE THOR.
INVISIBLE GIRL IS OUT. HARD TO KEEP TRACK OF.
I NEED THE SCARLET WITCH FOR THE "UNPREDICTABLE" ELEMENT.
BLACK WIDOW? NO, ALREADY HAVE HELLCAT.
SHE-HULK FOR SURE. GOOD TO HAVE SOME POWER.
MEDUSA. REDUNDANT. ALREADY HAVE THREE REDHEADS.
HMM, BLACK WIDOW?
DIDN'T WE ALREADY...?
DIFFERENT ONE. HAS A DEATH TOUCH. BUT, TOO SCARY.

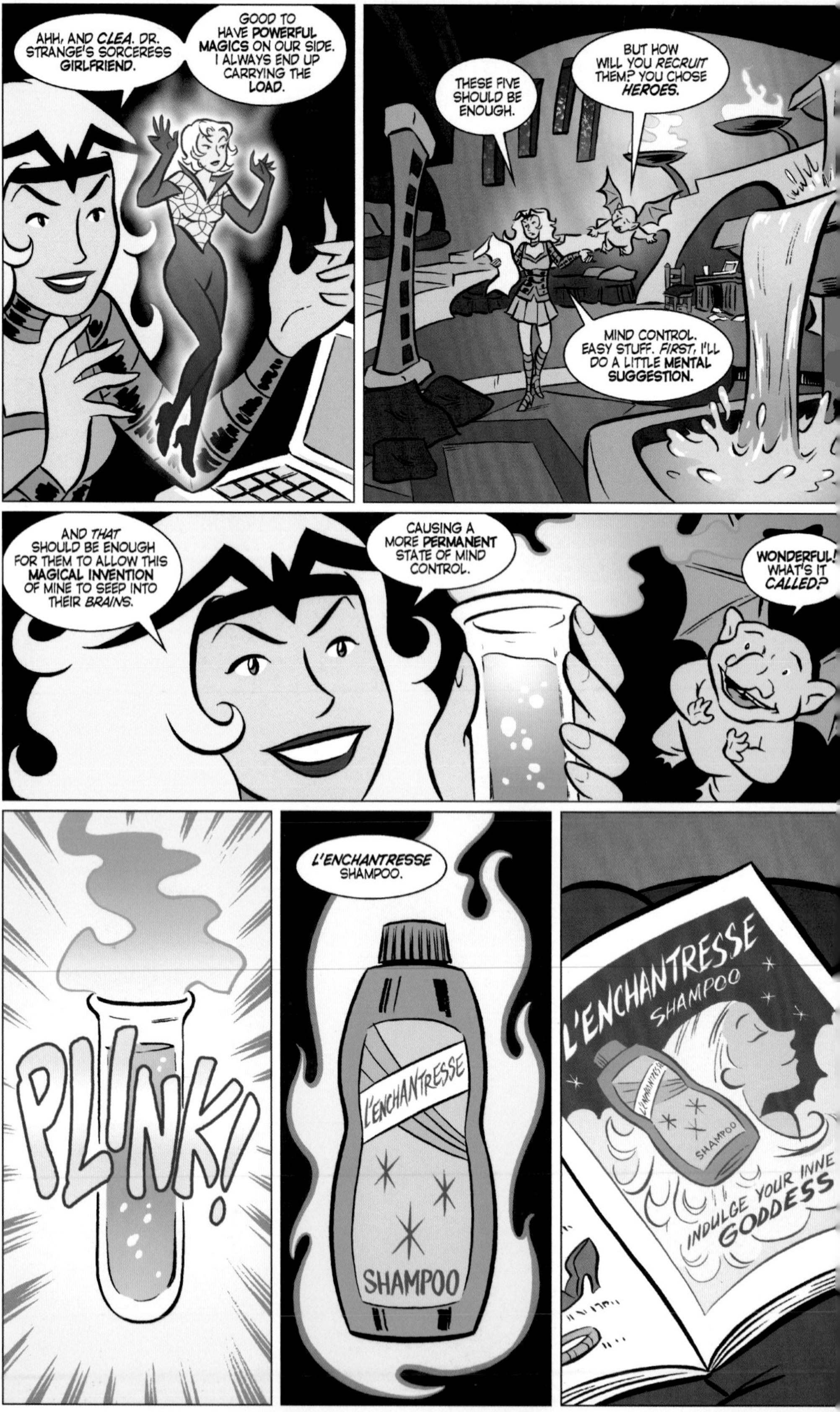
AHH, AND CLEA. DR. STRANGE'S SORCERESS GIRLFRIEND.
GOOD TO HAVE POWERFUL MAGICS ON OUR SIDE. I ALWAYS END UP CARRYING THE LOAD.
THESE FIVE SHOULD BE ENOUGH.
BUT HOW WILL YOU RECRUIT THEM? YOU CHOSE HEROES.
MIND CONTROL. EASY STUFF. FIRST, I'LL DO A LITTLE MENTAL SUGGESTION.
AND THAT SHOULD BE ENOUGH FOR THEM TO ALLOW THIS MAGICAL INVENTION OF MINE TO SEEP INTO THEIR BRAINS.
CAUSING A MORE PERMANENT STATE OF MIND CONTROL.
WONDERFUL! WHAT'S IT CALLED?
PLINK!
L'ENCHANTRESSE SHAMPOO.
L'ENCHANTRESSE
SHAMPOO
L'ENCHANTRESSE
SHAMPOO
INDULGE YOUR INNE
GODDESS

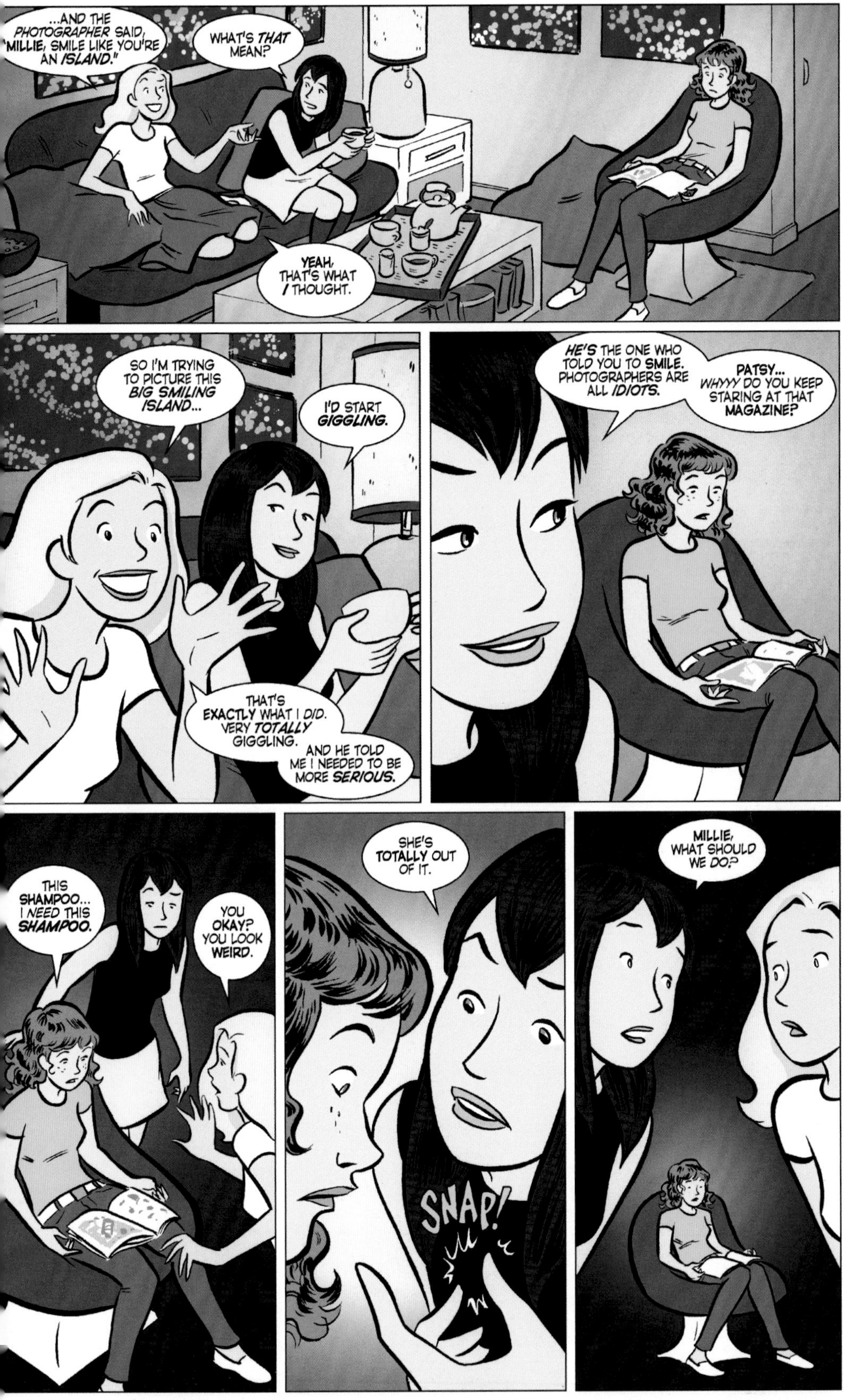

...AND THE PHOTOGRAPHER SAID, "MILLIE, SMILE LIKE YOU'RE AN ISLAND."
WHAT'S THAT MEAN?
YEAH, THAT'S WHAT I THOUGHT.
SO I'M TRYING TO PICTURE THIS BIG SMILING ISLAND...
I'D START GIGGLING.
THAT'S EXACTLY WHAT I DID. VERY TOTALLY GIGGLING.
AND HE TOLD ME I NEEDED TO BE MORE SERIOUS.
HE'S THE ONE WHO TOLD YOU TO SMILE. PHOTOGRAPHERS ARE ALL IDIOTS.
PATSY... WHYYY DO YOU KEEP STARING AT THAT MAGAZINE?
THIS SHAMPOO... I NEED THIS SHAMPOO.
YOU OKAY? YOU LOOK WEIRD.
SHE'S TOTALLY OUT OF IT.
SNAP!
MILLIE, WHAT SHOULD WE DO?

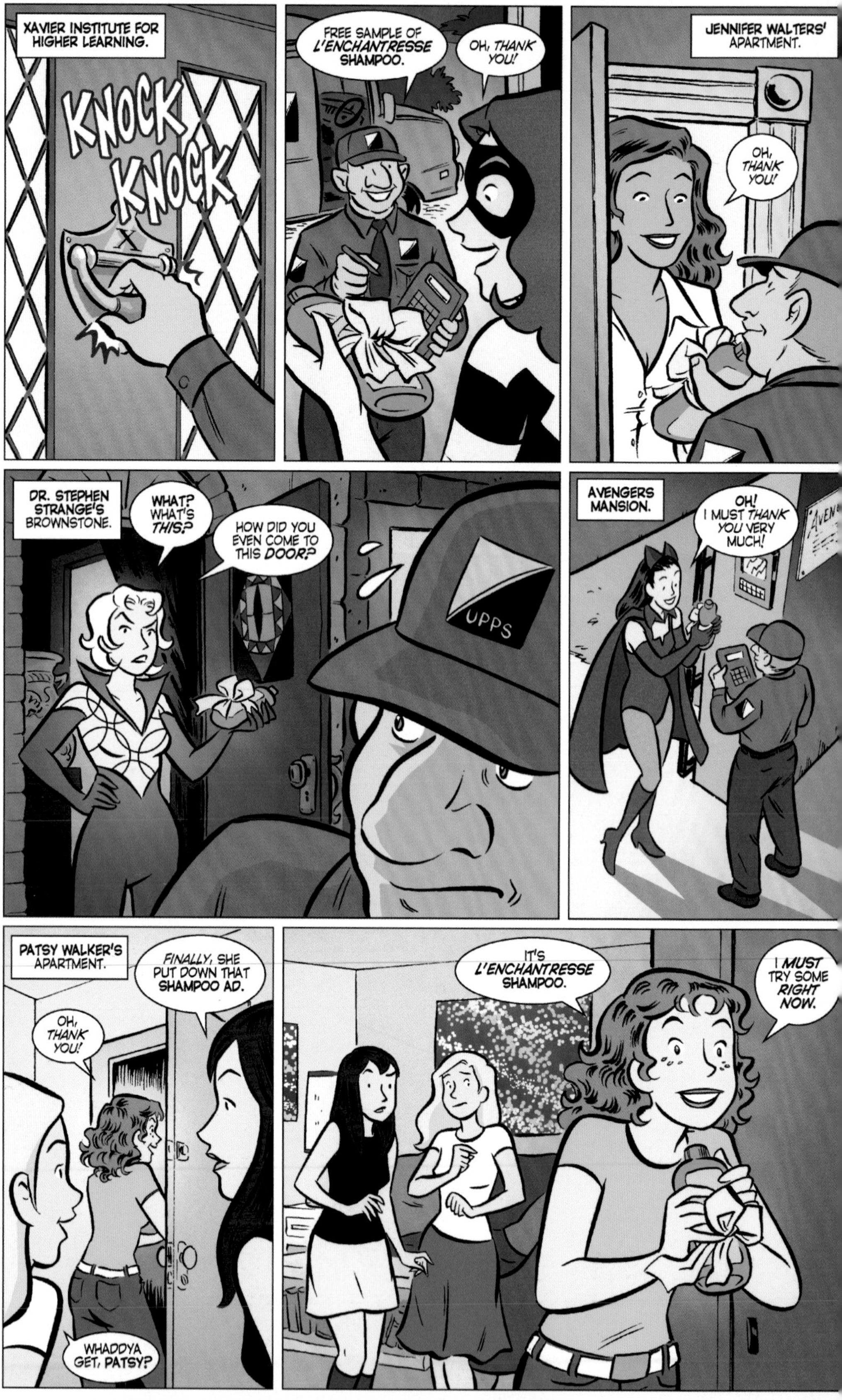
XAVIER INSTITUTE FOR HIGHER LEARNING.
KNOCK KNOCK
X
FREE SAMPLE OF L'ENCHANTRESSE SHAMPOO.
OH, THANK YOU!
JENNIFER WALTERS' APARTMENT.
OH, THANK YOU!
DR. STEPHEN STRANGE'S BROWNSTONE.
WHAT? WHAT'S THIS?
HOW DID YOU EVEN COME TO THIS DOOR?
UPPS
AVENGERS MANSION.
OH! I MUST THANK YOU VERY MUCH!
PATSY WALKER'S APARTMENT.
FINALLY, SHE PUT DOWN THAT SHAMPOO AD.
OH, THANK YOU!
WHADDYA GET, PATSY?
IT'S L'ENCHANTRESSE SHAMPOO.
I MUST TRY SOME RIGHT NOW.

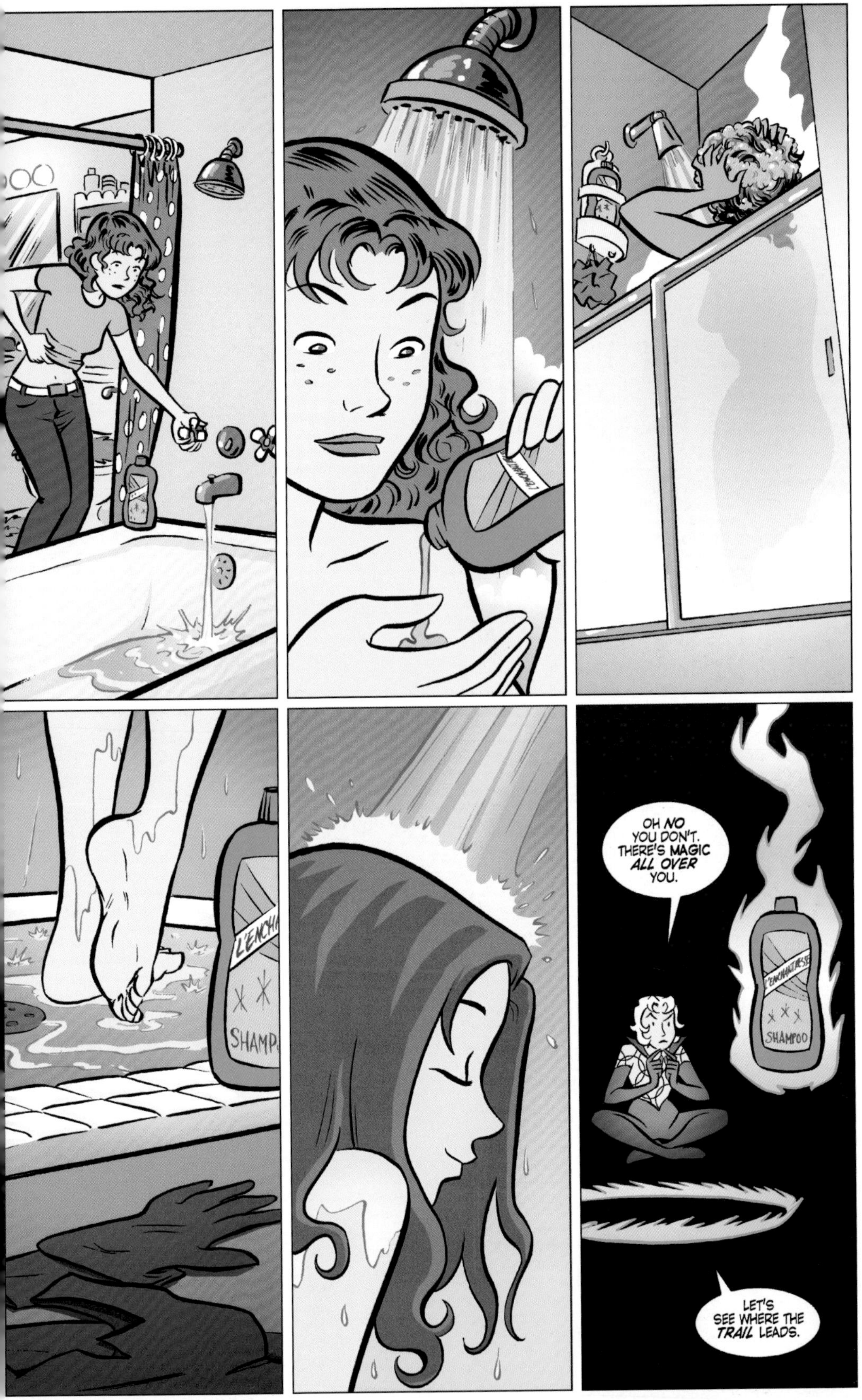
L'ENCHA
SHAMP
OH NO YOU DON'T. THERE'S MAGIC ALL OVER YOU.
SHAMPOO
LET'S SEE WHERE THE TRAIL LEADS.

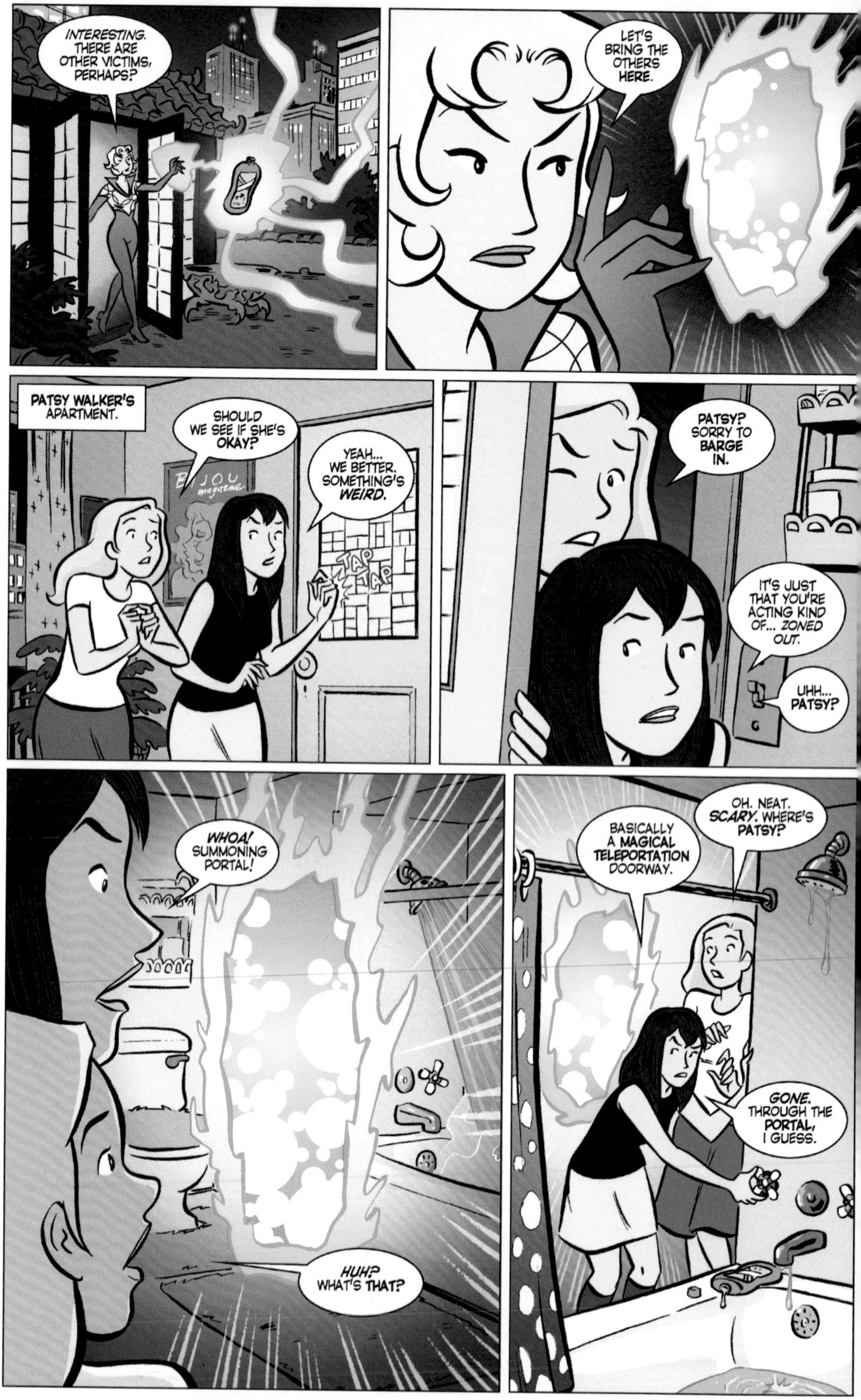
INTERESTING. THERE ARE OTHER VICTIMS, PERHAPS?
LET'S BRING THE OTHERS HERE.
PATSY WALKER'S APARTMENT.
SHOULD WE SEE IF SHE'S OKAY?
YEAH... WE BETTER. SOMETHING'S WEIRD.
TAP TAP
PATSY? SORRY TO BARGE IN.
IT'S JUST THAT YOU'RE ACTING KIND OF... ZONED OUT.
UHH... PATSY?
WHOA! SUMMONING PORTAL!
HUH? WHAT'S THAT?
BASICALLY A MAGICAL TELEPORTATION DOORWAY.
OH. NEAT. SCARY. WHERE'S PATSY?
GONE. THROUGH THE PORTAL, I GUESS.

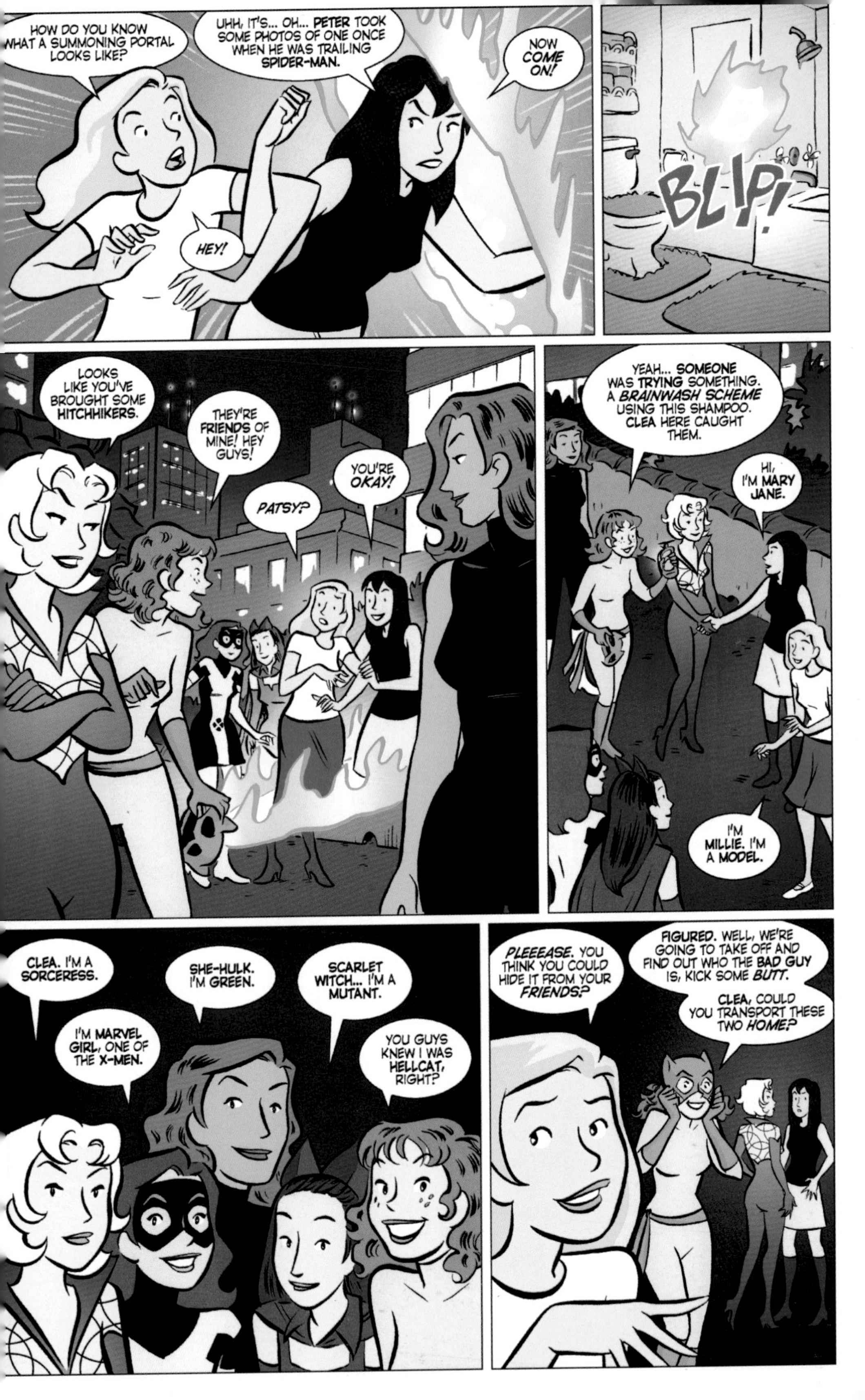
HOW DO YOU KNOW WHAT A SUMMONING PORTAL LOOKS LIKE?
UHH, IT'S... OH... PETER TOOK SOME PHOTOS OF ONE ONCE WHEN HE WAS TRAILING SPIDER-MAN.
NOW COME ON!
HEY!
BLIP!
LOOKS LIKE YOU'VE BROUGHT SOME HITCHHIKERS.
THEY'RE FRIENDS OF MINE! HEY GUYS!
PATSY?
YOU'RE OKAY!
YEAH... SOMEONE WAS TRYING SOMETHING. A BRAINWASH SCHEME USING THIS SHAMPOO. CLEA HERE CAUGHT THEM.
HI, I'M MARY JANE.
I'M MILLIE. I'M A MODEL.
CLEA. I'M A SORCERESS.
I'M MARVEL GIRL, ONE OF THE X-MEN.
SHE-HULK. I'M GREEN.
SCARLET WITCH... I'M A MUTANT.
YOU GUYS KNEW I WAS HELLCAT, RIGHT?
PLEEEASE. YOU THINK YOU COULD HIDE IT FROM YOUR FRIENDS?
FIGURED. WELL, WE'RE GOING TO TAKE OFF AND FIND OUT WHO THE BAD GUY IS, KICK SOME BUTT.
CLEA, COULD YOU TRANSPORT THESE TWO HOME?

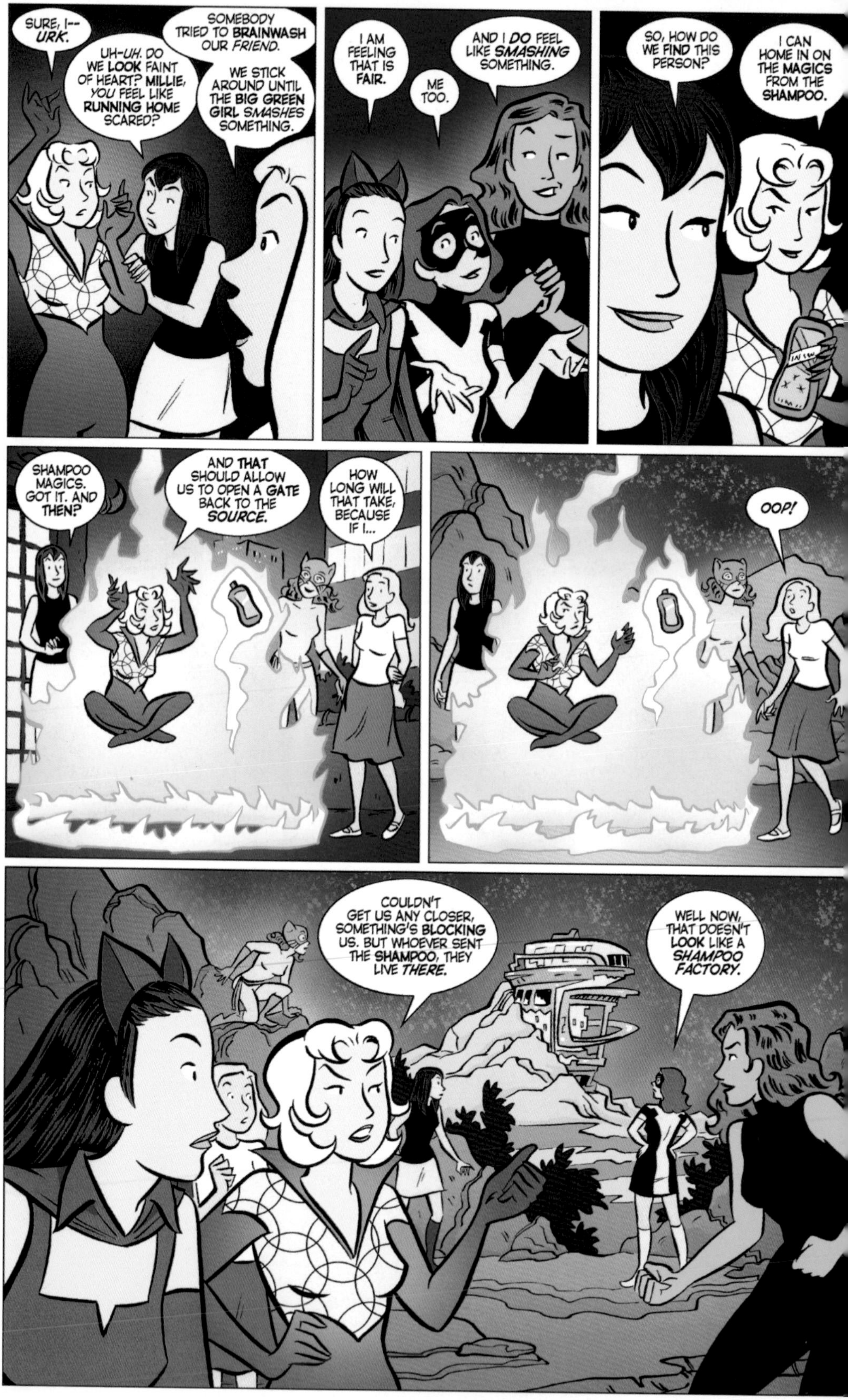
SURE, I-- URK.
UH-UH. DO WE LOOK FAINT OF HEART? MILLIE, YOU FEEL LIKE RUNNING HOME SCARED?
SOMEBODY TRIED TO BRAINWASH OUR FRIEND.
WE STICK AROUND UNTIL THE BIG GREEN GIRL SMASHES SOMETHING.
I AM FEELING THAT IS FAIR.
ME TOO.
AND I DO FEEL LIKE SMASHING SOMETHING.
SO, HOW DO WE FIND THIS PERSON?
I CAN HOME IN ON THE MAGICS FROM THE SHAMPOO.
SHAMPOO MAGICS. GOT IT. AND THEN?
AND THAT SHOULD ALLOW US TO OPEN A GATE BACK TO THE SOURCE.
HOW LONG WILL THAT TAKE, BECAUSE IF I...
OOP!
COULDN'T GET US ANY CLOSER, SOMETHING'S BLOCKING US. BUT WHOEVER SENT THE SHAMPOO, THEY LIVE THERE.
WELL NOW, THAT DOESN'T LOOK LIKE A SHAMPOO FACTORY.

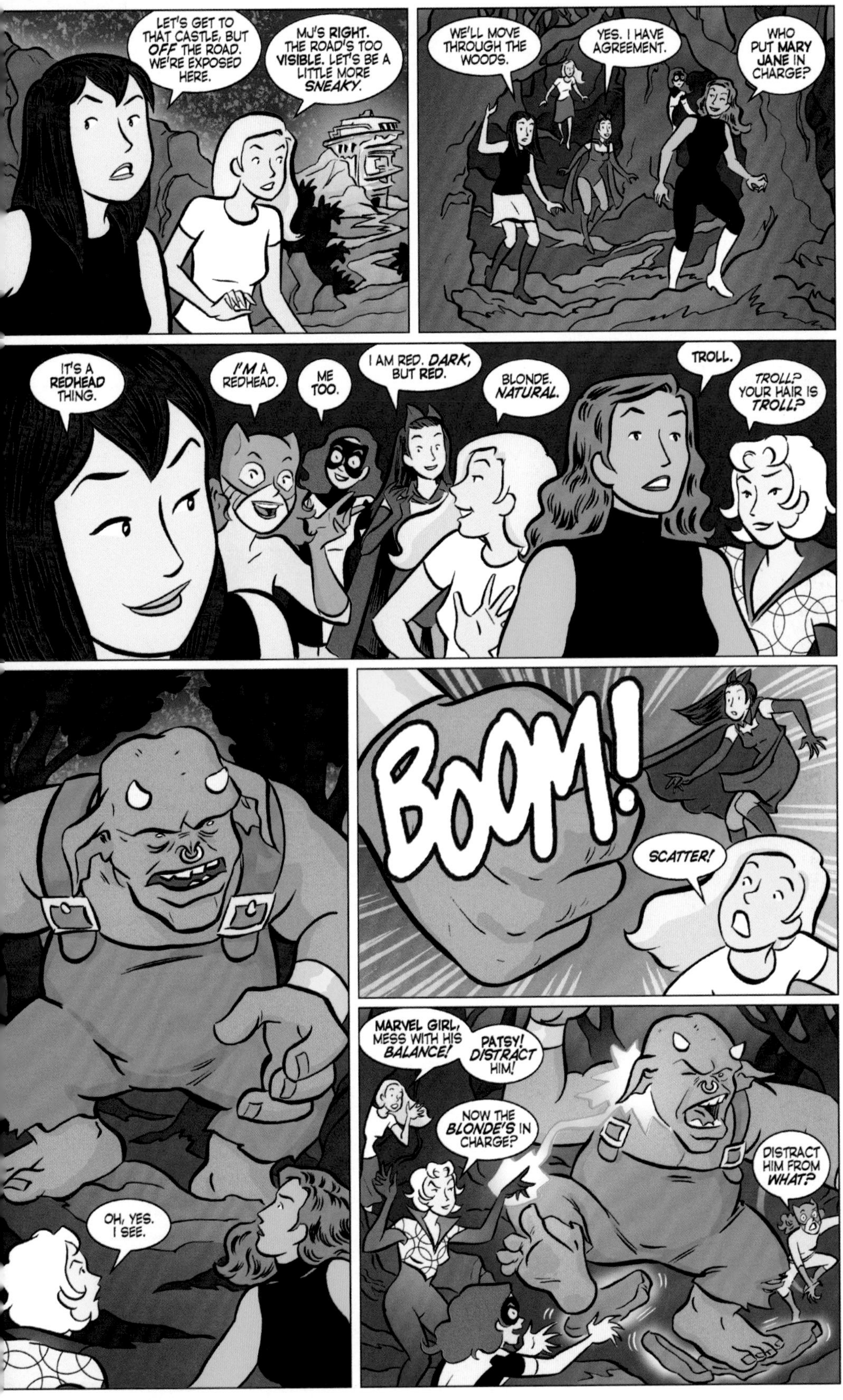
LET'S GET TO THAT CASTLE, BUT OFF THE ROAD. WE'RE EXPOSED HERE.
MJ'S RIGHT. THE ROAD'S TOO VISIBLE. LET'S BE A LITTLE MORE SNEAKY.
WE'LL MOVE THROUGH THE WOODS.
YES. I HAVE AGREEMENT.
WHO PUT MARY JANE IN CHARGE?
IT'S A REDHEAD THING.
I'M A REDHEAD.
ME TOO.
I AM RED. DARK, BUT RED.
BLONDE. NATURAL.
TROLL.
TROLL? YOUR HAIR IS TROLL?
OH, YES. I SEE.
BOOM!
SCATTER!
MARVEL GIRL, MESS WITH HIS BALANCE!
PATSY! DISTRACT HIM!
NOW THE BLONDE'S IN CHARGE?
DISTRACT HIM FROM WHAT?

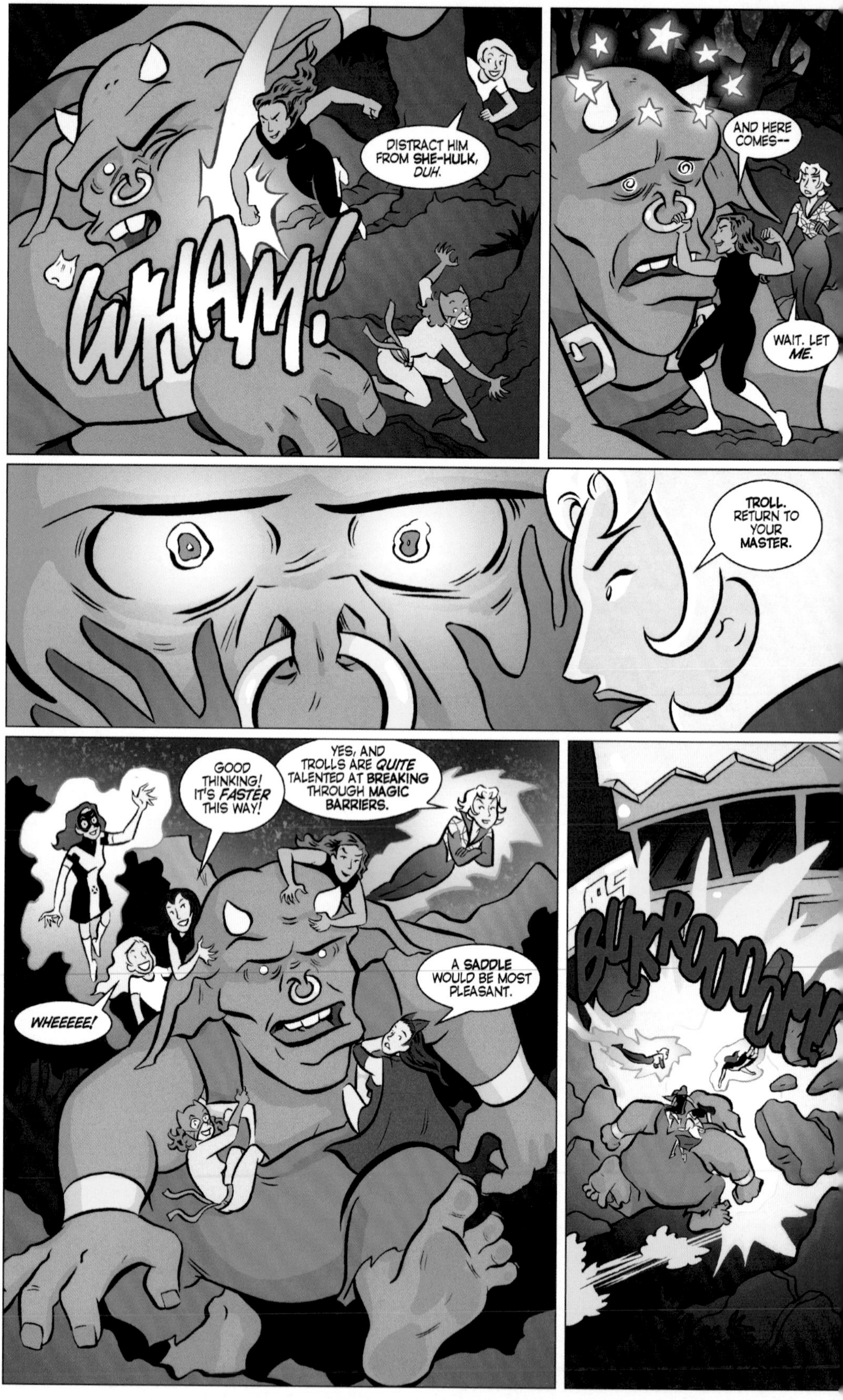
DISTRACT HIM FROM SHE-HULK, DUH.
WHAM!
AND HERE COMES--
WAIT. LET ME.
TROLL. RETURN TO YOUR MASTER.
GOOD THINKING! IT'S FASTER THIS WAY!
YES, AND TROLLS ARE QUITE TALENTED AT BREAKING THROUGH MAGIC BARRIERS.
WHEEEEE!
A SADDLE WOULD BE MOST PLEASANT.
BUKROOOOOM!

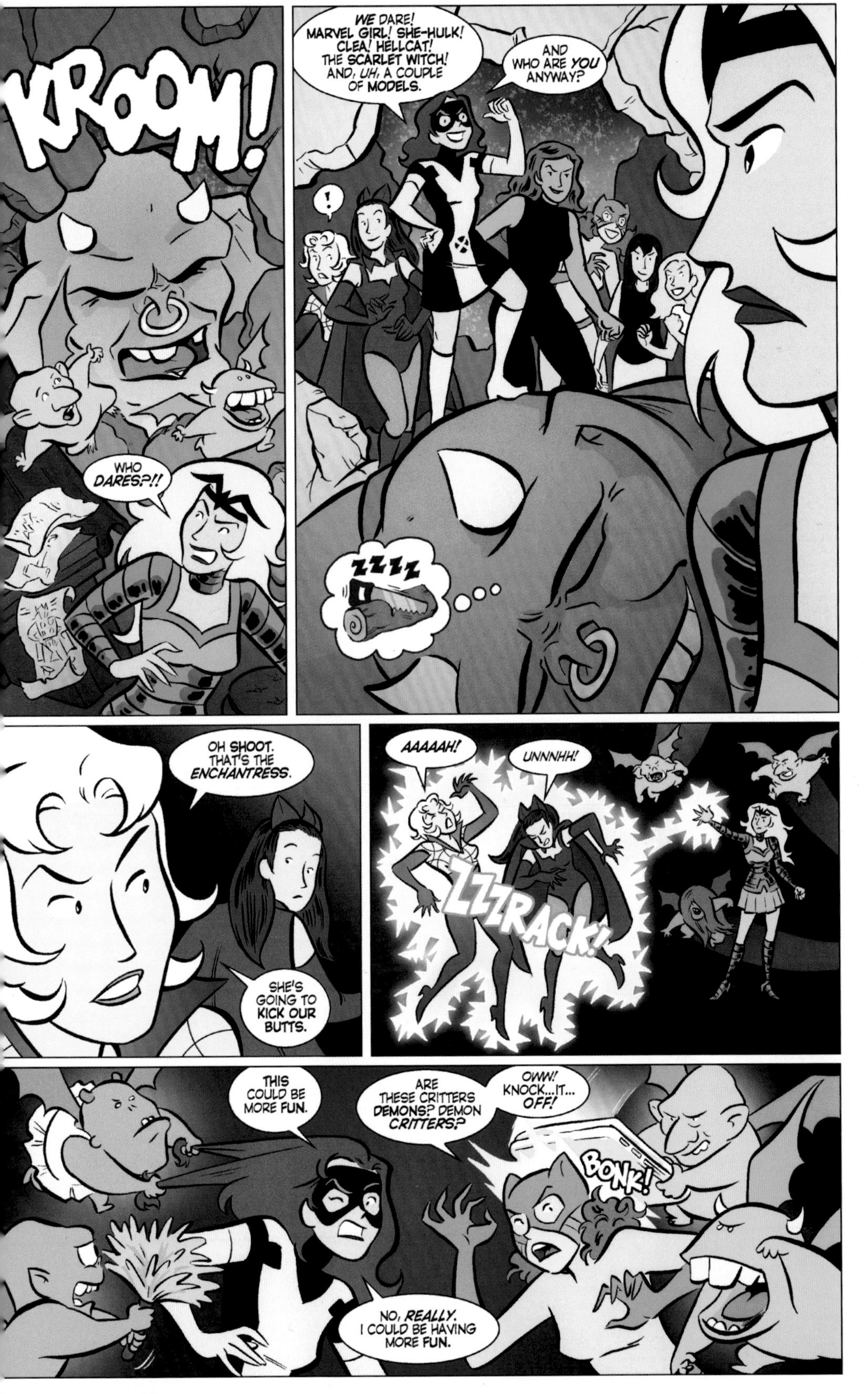

KROOM!
WHO DARES?!!
WE DARE! MARVEL GIRL! SHE-HULK! CLEA! HELLCAT! THE SCARLET WITCH! AND, UH, A COUPLE OF MODELS.
AND WHO ARE YOU ANYWAY?
!
ZZZZ
OH SHOOT. THAT'S THE ENCHANTRESS.
SHE'S GOING TO KICK OUR BUTTS.
AAAAAH!
UNNNHH!
ZZZRACK!
THIS COULD BE MORE FUN.
ARE THESE CRITTERS DEMONS? DEMON CRITTERS?
OWW! KNOCK...IT... OFF!
BONK!
NO, REALLY. I COULD BE HAVING MORE FUN.

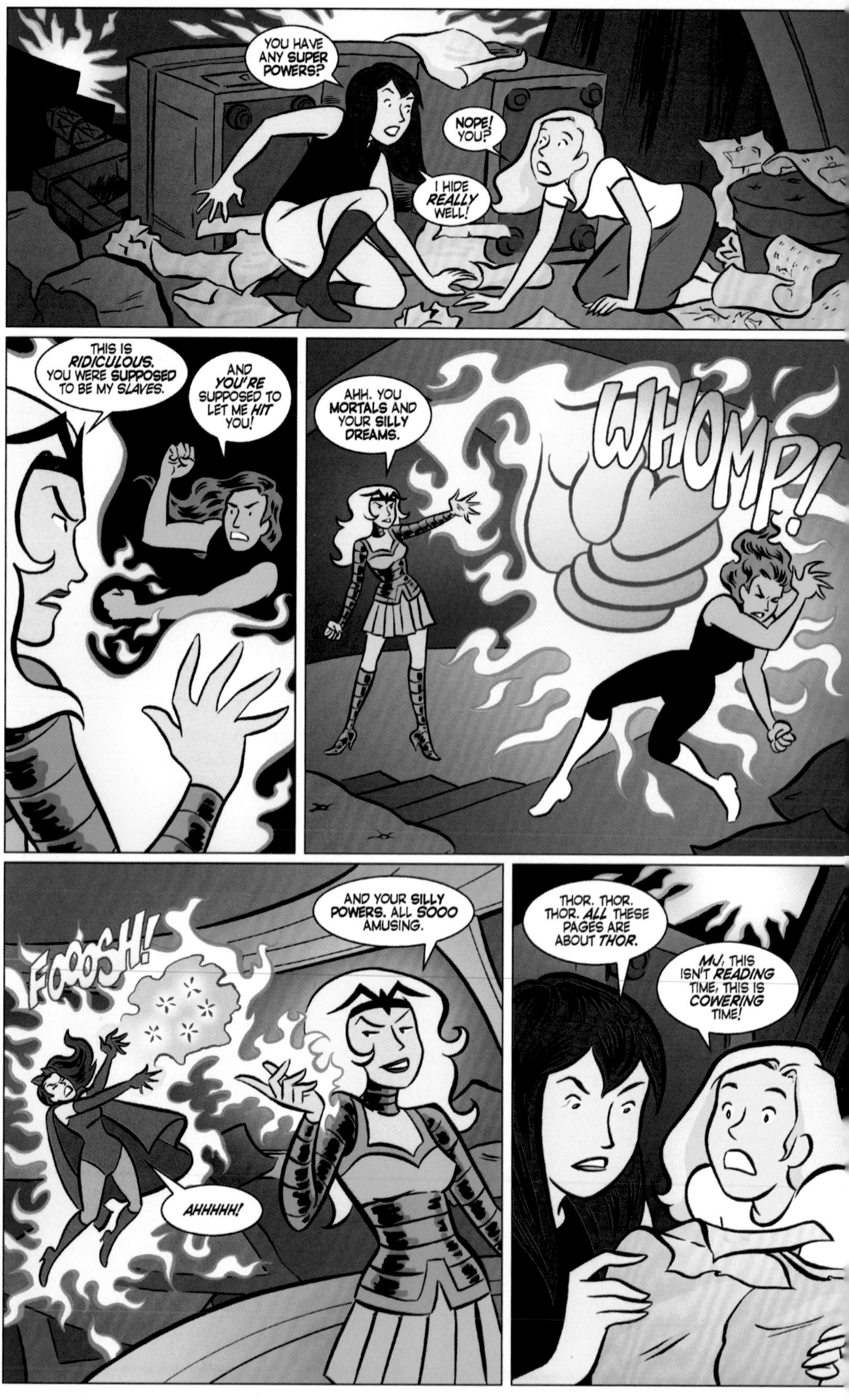

YOU HAVE ANY SUPER POWERS?
NOPE! YOU?
I HIDE REALLY WELL!
THIS IS RIDICULOUS. YOU WERE SUPPOSED TO BE MY SLAVES.
AND YOU'RE SUPPOSED TO LET ME HIT YOU!
AHH. YOU MORTALS AND YOUR SILLY DREAMS.
WHOMP!
AND YOUR SILLY POWERS. ALL SOOO AMUSING.
FOOOSH!
AHHHHH!
THOR. THOR. THOR. ALL THESE PAGES ARE ABOUT THOR.
MJ, THIS ISN'T READING TIME, THIS IS COWERING TIME!

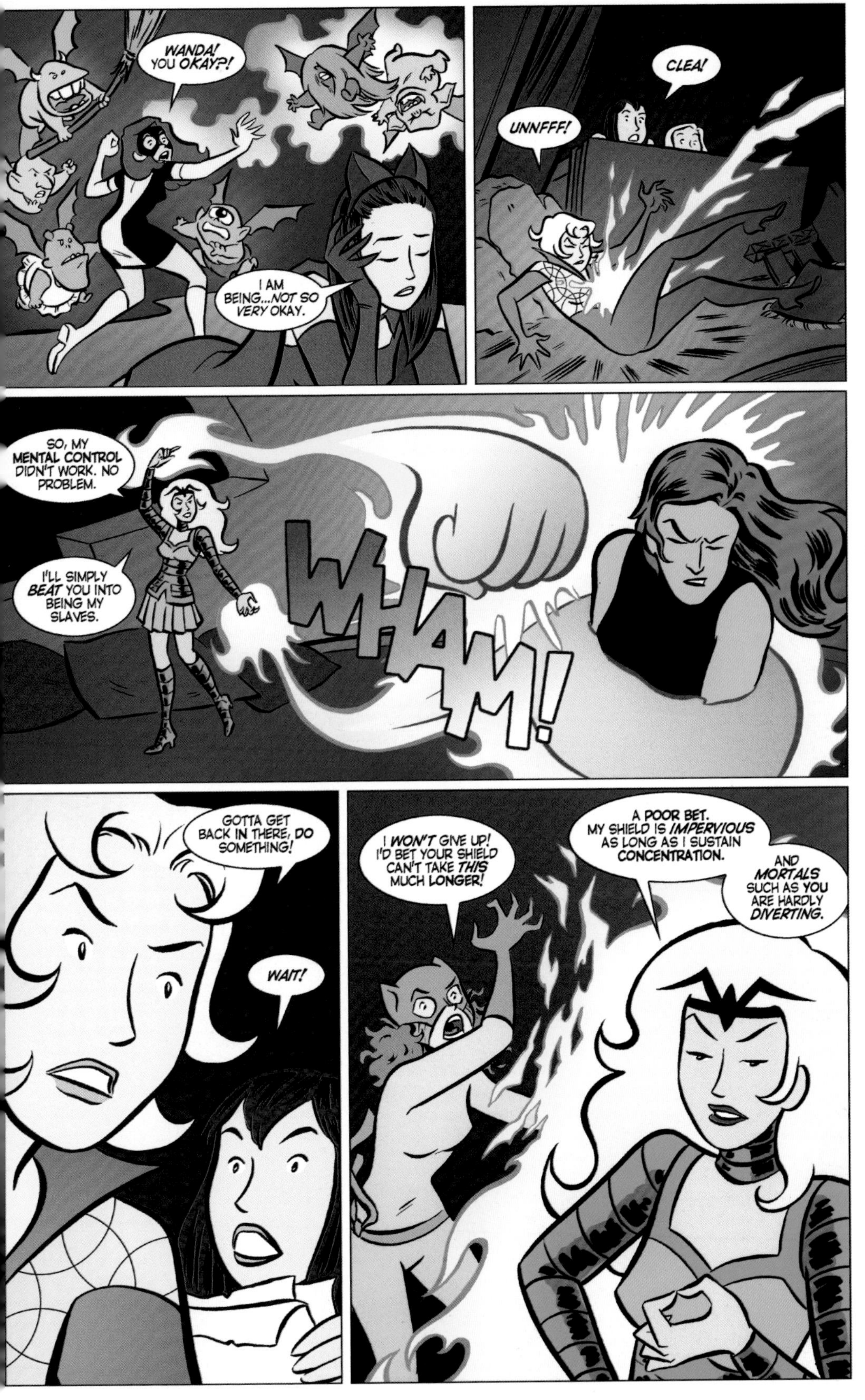
WANDA! YOU OKAY?!
I AM BEING...NOT SO VERY OKAY.
CLEA!
UNNFFF!
SO, MY MENTAL CONTROL DIDN'T WORK. NO PROBLEM.
I'LL SIMPLY BEAT YOU INTO BEING MY SLAVES.
WHAM!
GOTTA GET BACK IN THERE, DO SOMETHING!
WAIT!
I WON'T GIVE UP! I'D BET YOUR SHIELD CAN'T TAKE THIS MUCH LONGER!
A POOR BET. MY SHIELD IS IMPERVIOUS AS LONG AS I SUSTAIN CONCENTRATION.
AND MORTALS SUCH AS YOU ARE HARDLY DIVERTING.

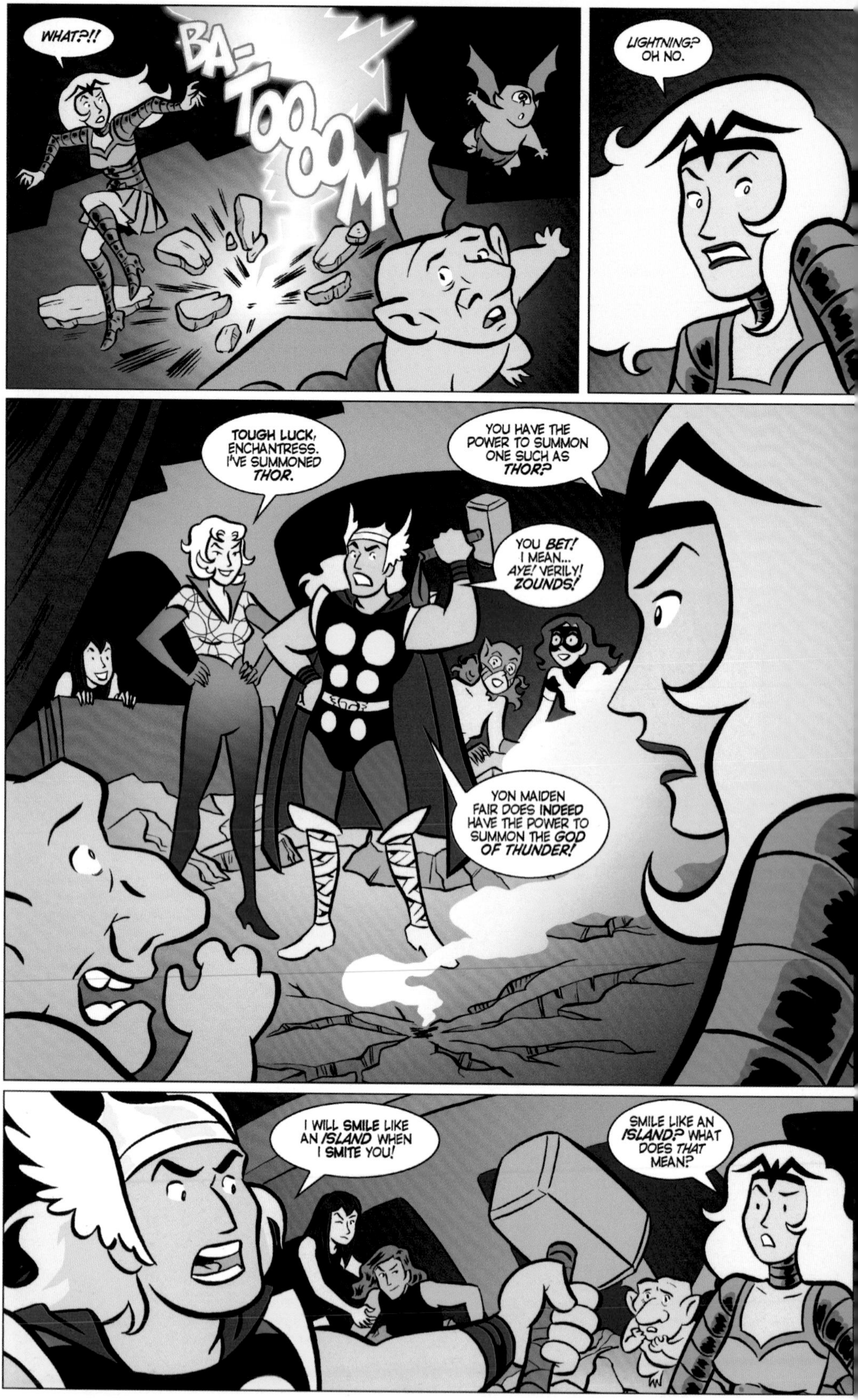
WHAT?!!
BA-TOOOOOM!
LIGHTNING? OH NO.
TOUGH LUCK, ENCHANTRESS. I'VE SUMMONED THOR.
YOU HAVE THE POWER TO SUMMON ONE SUCH AS THOR?
YOU BET! I MEAN... AYE! VERILY! ZOUNDS!
YON MAIDEN FAIR DOES INDEED HAVE THE POWER TO SUMMON THE GOD OF THUNDER!
I WILL SMILE LIKE AN ISLAND WHEN I SMITE YOU!
SMILE LIKE AN ISLAND? WHAT DOES THAT MEAN?

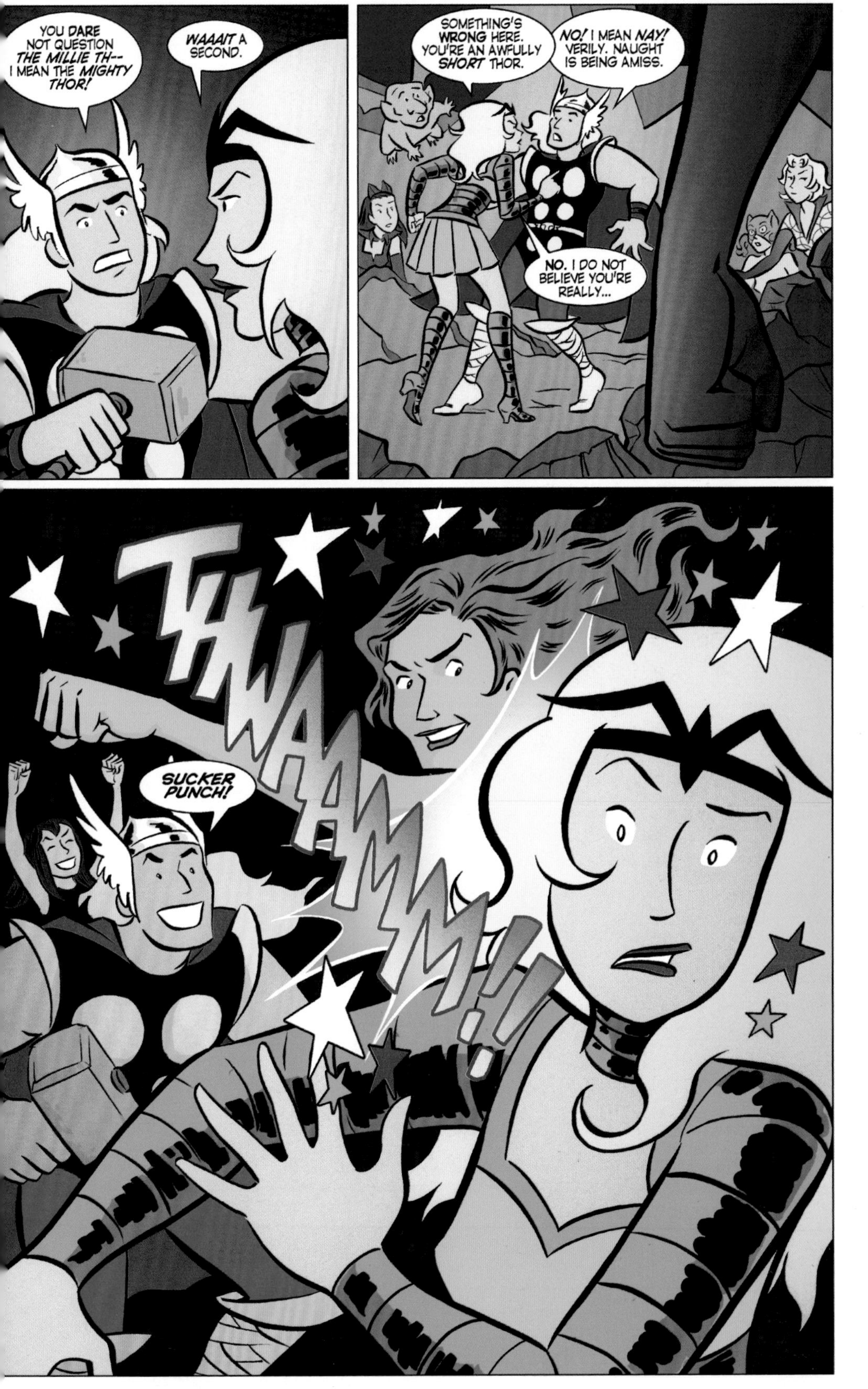

YOU DARE NOT QUESTION THE MILLIE TH-- I MEAN THE MIGHTY THOR!
WAAAIT A SECOND.
SOMETHING'S WRONG HERE. YOU'RE AN AWFULLY SHORT THOR.
NO! I MEAN NAY! VERILY. NAUGHT IS BEING AMISS.
NO. I DO NOT BELIEVE YOU'RE REALLY...
THWAAMMM!!!
SUCKER PUNCH!

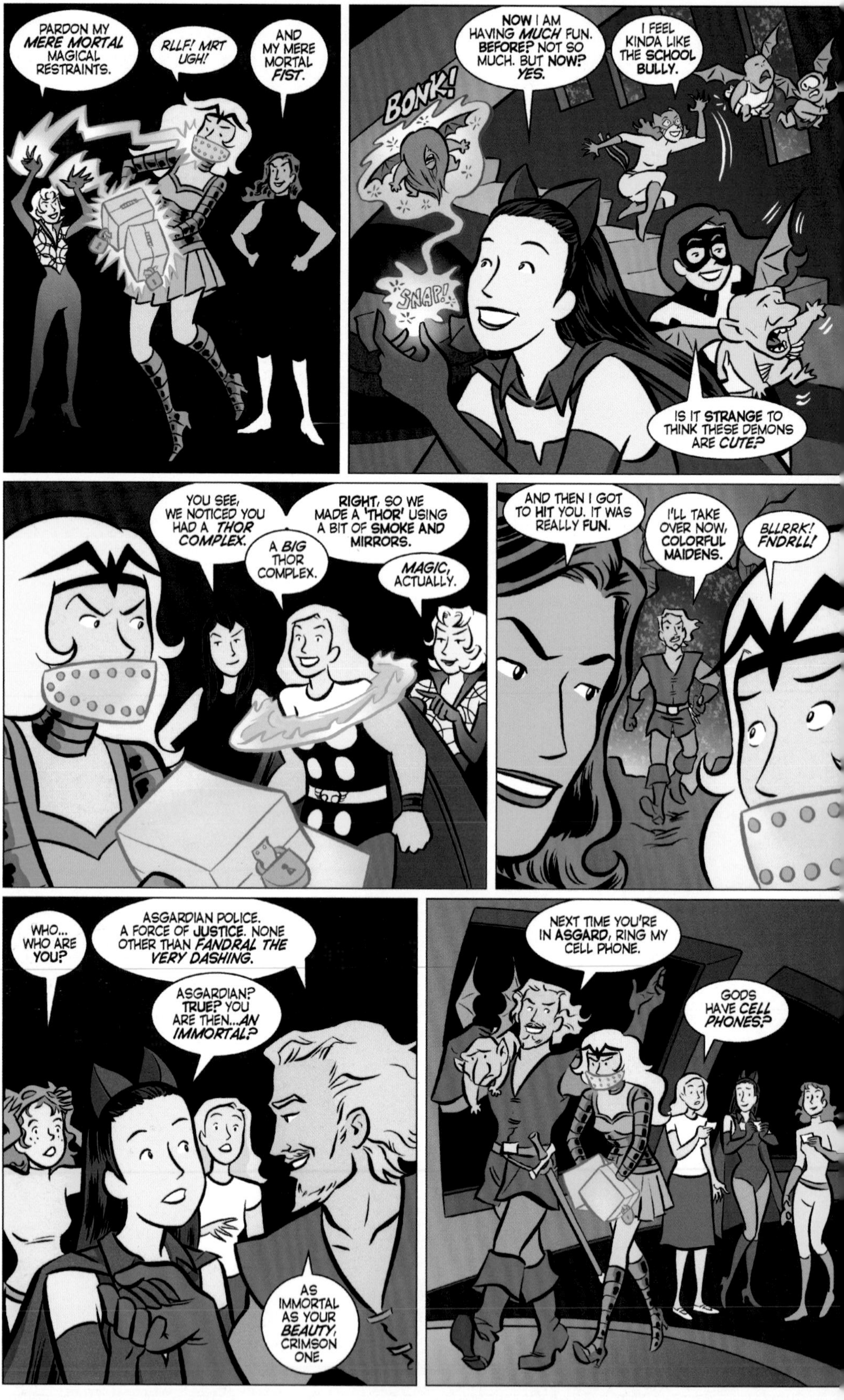

PARDON MY MERE MORTAL MAGICAL RESTRAINTS.
RLLF! MRT UGH!
AND MY MERE MORTAL FIST.
BONK!
SNAP!
NOW I AM HAVING MUCH FUN. BEFORE? NOT SO MUCH. BUT NOW? YES.
I FEEL KINDA LIKE THE SCHOOL BULLY.
IS IT STRANGE TO THINK THESE DEMONS ARE CUTE?
YOU SEE, WE NOTICED YOU HAD A THOR COMPLEX.
RIGHT, SO WE MADE A 'THOR' USING A BIT OF SMOKE AND MIRRORS.
A BIG THOR COMPLEX.
MAGIC, ACTUALLY.
AND THEN I GOT TO HIT YOU. IT WAS REALLY FUN.
I'LL TAKE OVER NOW, COLORFUL MAIDENS.
BLLRRK! FNDRLL!
WHO... WHO ARE YOU?
ASGARDIAN POLICE. A FORCE OF JUSTICE. NONE OTHER THAN FANDRAL THE VERY DASHING.
ASGARDIAN? TRUE? YOU ARE THEN...AN IMMORTAL?
AS IMMORTAL AS YOUR BEAUTY, CRIMSON ONE.
NEXT TIME YOU'RE IN ASGARD, RING MY CELL PHONE.
GODS HAVE CELL PHONES?

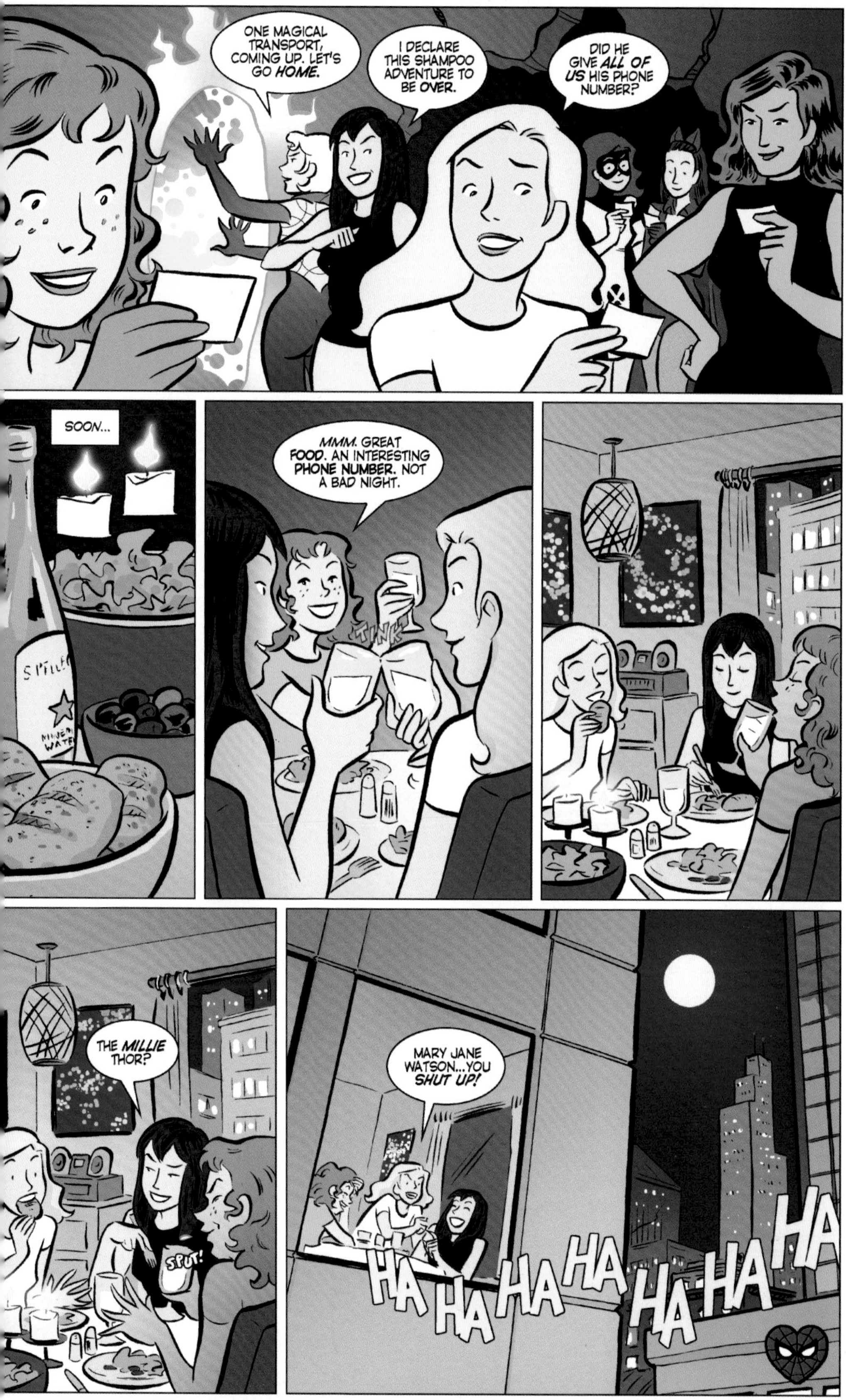
ONE MAGICAL TRANSPORT, COMING UP. LET'S GO HOME.
I DECLARE THIS SHAMPOO ADVENTURE TO BE OVER.
DID HE GIVE ALL OF US HIS PHONE NUMBER?
SOON...
MMM. GREAT FOOD. AN INTERESTING PHONE NUMBER. NOT A BAD NIGHT.
TINK
THE MILLIE THOR?
SPUT!
MARY JANE WATSON...YOU SHUT UP!
HA HA HA HA HA HA HA HA HA

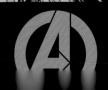

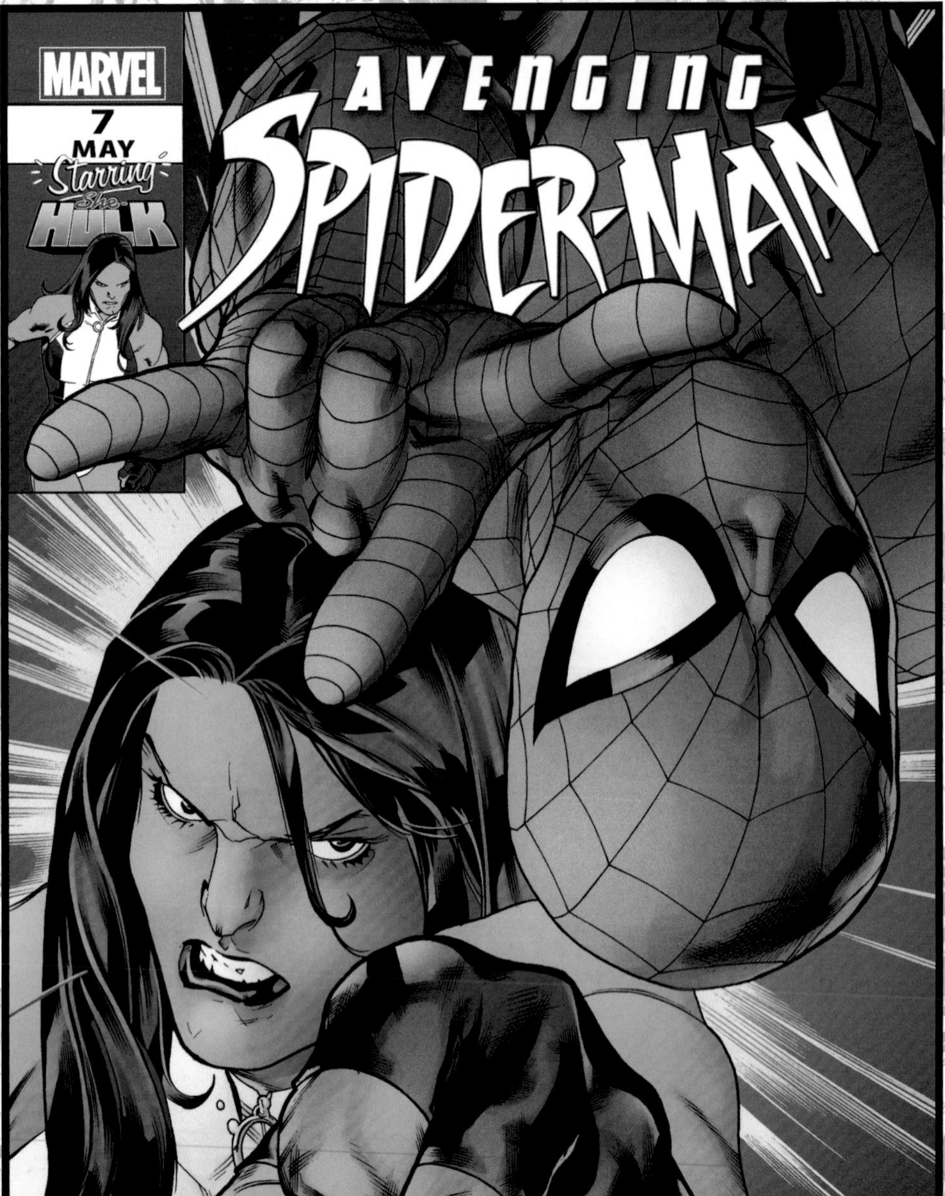
MARVEL
7
MAY
Starring She-Hulk
AVENGING SPIDER-MAN

AVENGING SPIDER-MAN #7

IT'S A STORY OF CONSTANT THWIPPING AND QUIPPING AS SHE-HULK AND SPIDER-MAN SPEND A NIGHT ON THE TOWN!

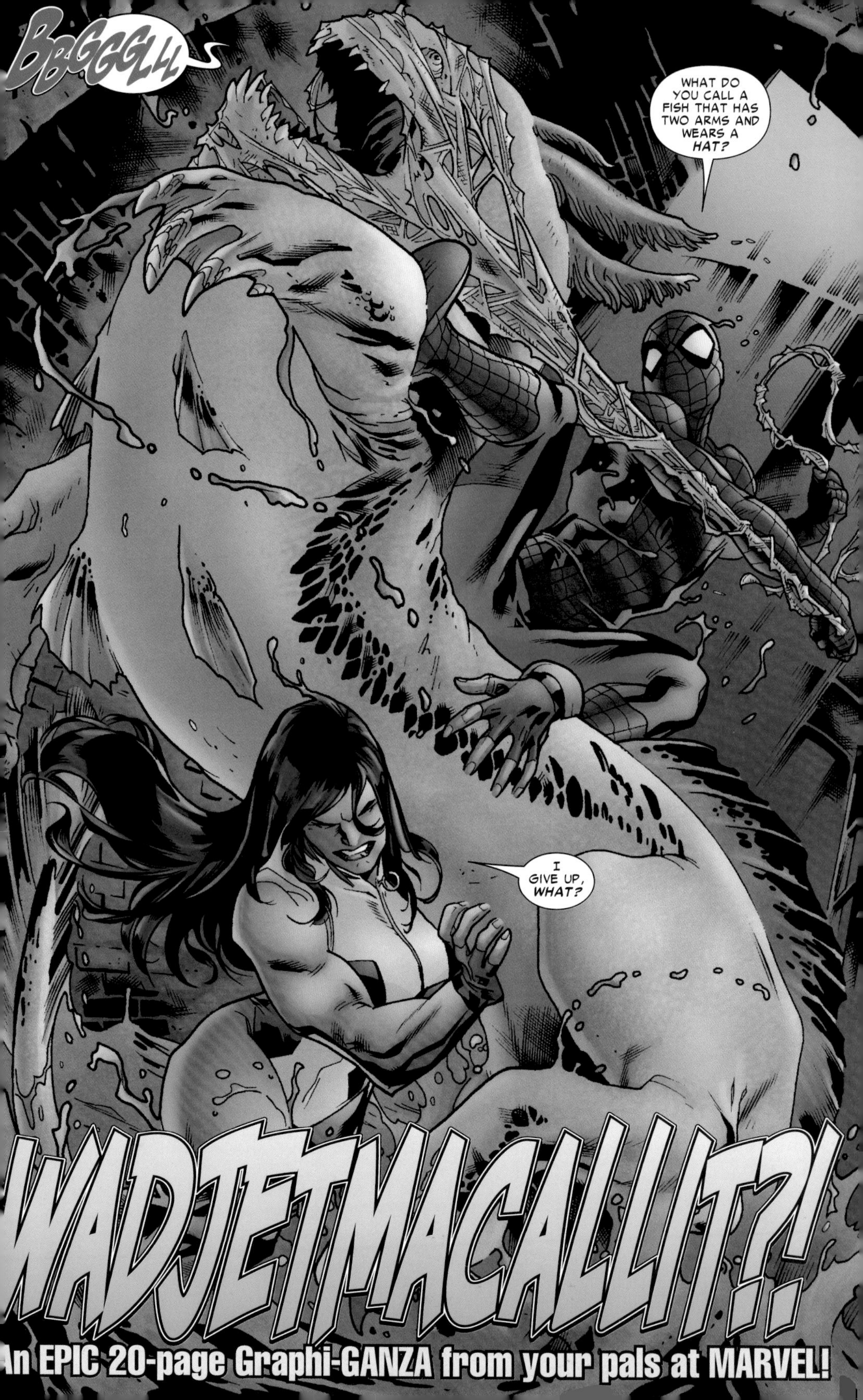
BBGGGLLL
WHAT DO YOU CALL A FISH THAT HAS TWO ARMS AND WEARS A HAT?
I GIVE UP, WHAT?
WADJETMACALLIT?!
An EPIC 20-page Graphi-GANZA from your pals at MARVEL!

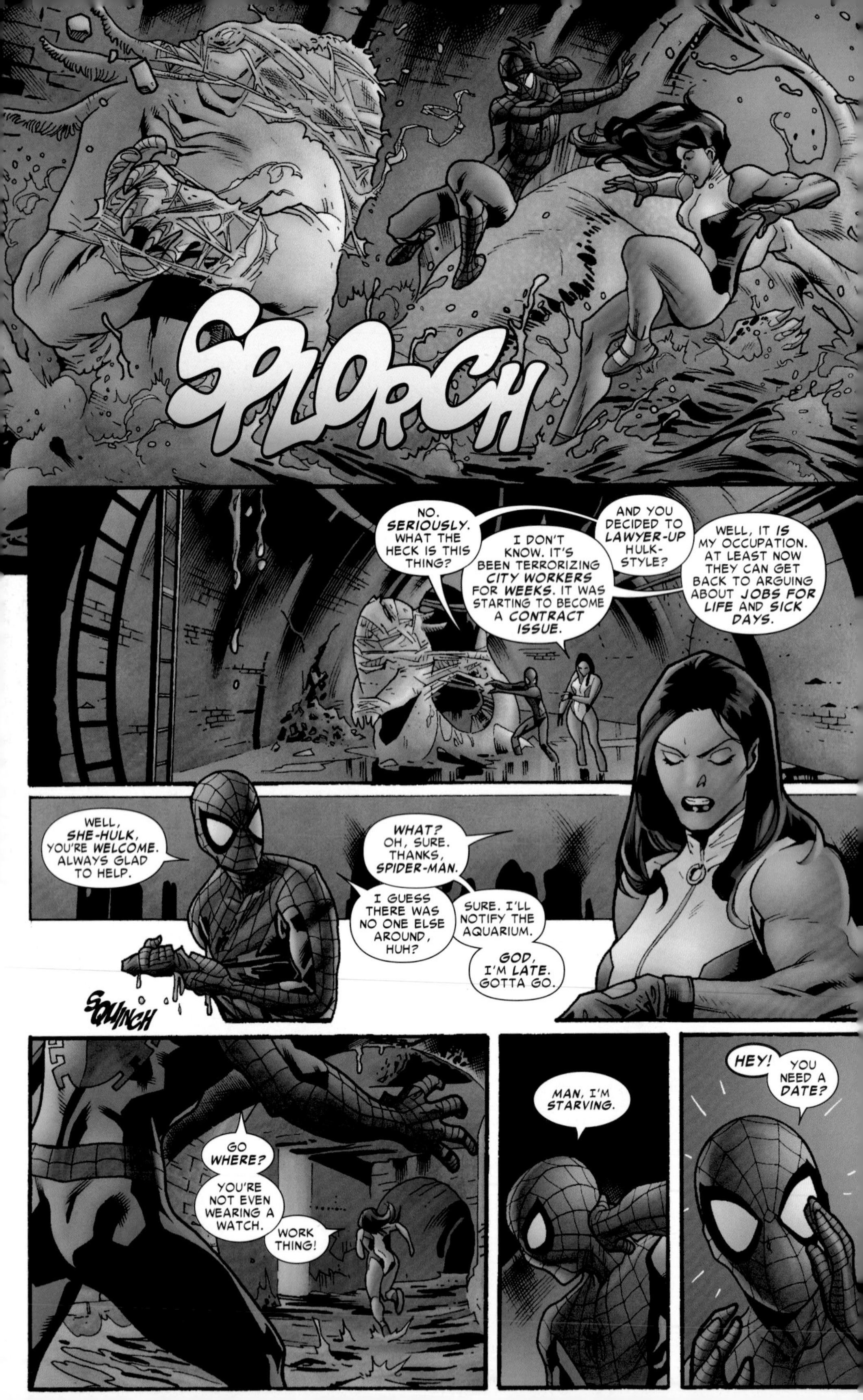
SPLORCH
NO. SERIOUSLY. WHAT THE HECK IS THIS THING?
I DON'T KNOW. IT'S BEEN TERRORIZING CITY WORKERS FOR WEEKS. IT WAS STARTING TO BECOME A CONTRACT ISSUE.
AND YOU DECIDED TO LAWYER-UP HULK-STYLE?
WELL, IT IS MY OCCUPATION. AT LEAST NOW THEY CAN GET BACK TO ARGUING ABOUT JOBS FOR LIFE AND SICK DAYS.
WELL, SHE-HULK, YOU'RE WELCOME. ALWAYS GLAD TO HELP.
WHAT? OH, SURE. THANKS, SPIDER-MAN.
I GUESS THERE WAS NO ONE ELSE AROUND, HUH?
SURE. I'LL NOTIFY THE AQUARIUM.
GOD, I'M LATE. GOTTA GO.
SQUINCH
GO WHERE?
YOU'RE NOT EVEN WEARING A WATCH.
WORK THING!
MAN, I'M STARVING.
HEY!
YOU NEED A DATE?

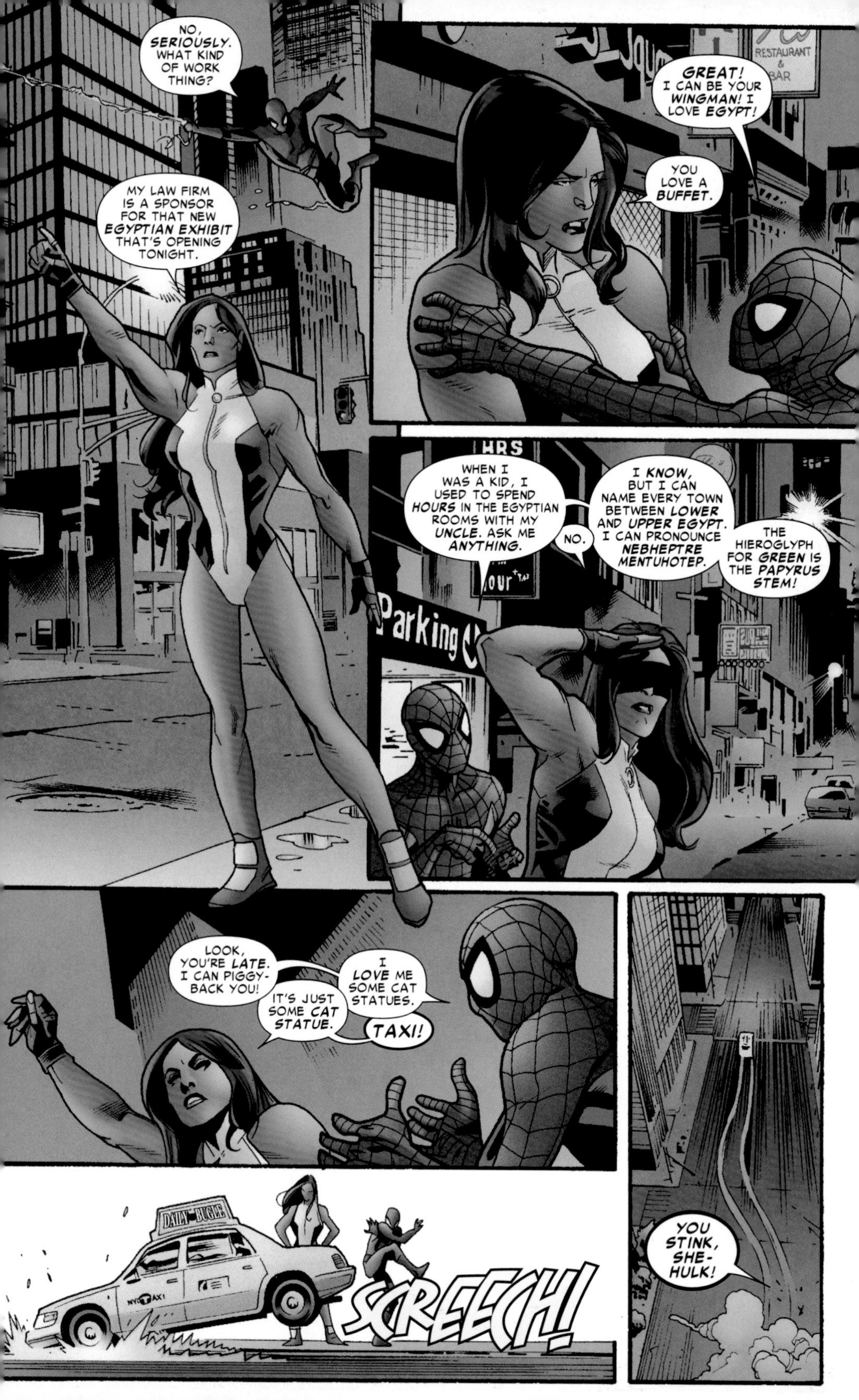
NO, SERIOUSLY. WHAT KIND OF WORK THING?
MY LAW FIRM IS A SPONSOR FOR THAT NEW EGYPTIAN EXHIBIT THAT'S OPENING TONIGHT.
RESTAURANT & BAR
GREAT! I CAN BE YOUR WINGMAN! I LOVE EGYPT!
YOU LOVE A BUFFET.
HRS
WHEN I WAS A KID, I USED TO SPEND HOURS IN THE EGYPTIAN ROOMS WITH MY UNCLE. ASK ME ANYTHING.
NO.
I KNOW, BUT I CAN NAME EVERY TOWN BETWEEN LOWER AND UPPER EGYPT. I CAN PRONOUNCE NEBHEPTRE MENTUHOTEP.
THE HIEROGLYPH FOR GREEN IS THE PAPYRUS STEM!
Parking
LOOK, YOU'RE LATE. I CAN PIGGY-BACK YOU!
IT'S JUST SOME CAT STATUE.
I LOVE ME SOME CAT STATUES.
TAXI!
DAILY BUGLE
NYC TAXI
SCREECH!
YOU STINK, SHE-HULK!

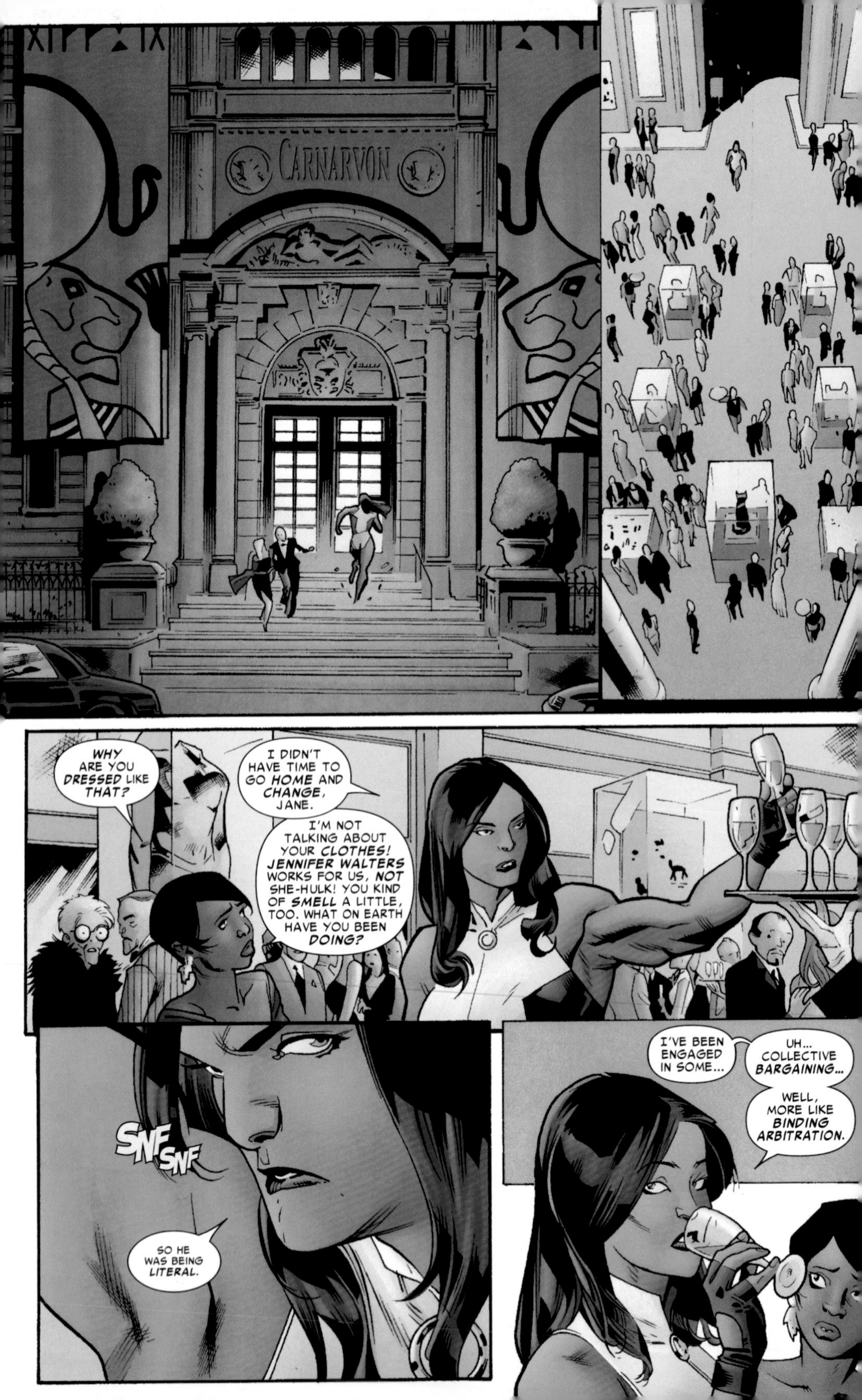

CARNARVON
WHY ARE YOU DRESSED LIKE THAT?
I DIDN'T HAVE TIME TO GO HOME AND CHANGE, JANE.
I'M NOT TALKING ABOUT YOUR CLOTHES! JENNIFER WALTERS WORKS FOR US, NOT SHE-HULK! YOU KIND OF SMELL A LITTLE, TOO. WHAT ON EARTH HAVE YOU BEEN DOING?
SNF SNF
SO HE WAS BEING LITERAL.
I'VE BEEN ENGAGED IN SOME...
UH... COLLECTIVE BARGAINING...
WELL, MORE LIKE BINDING ARBITRATION.

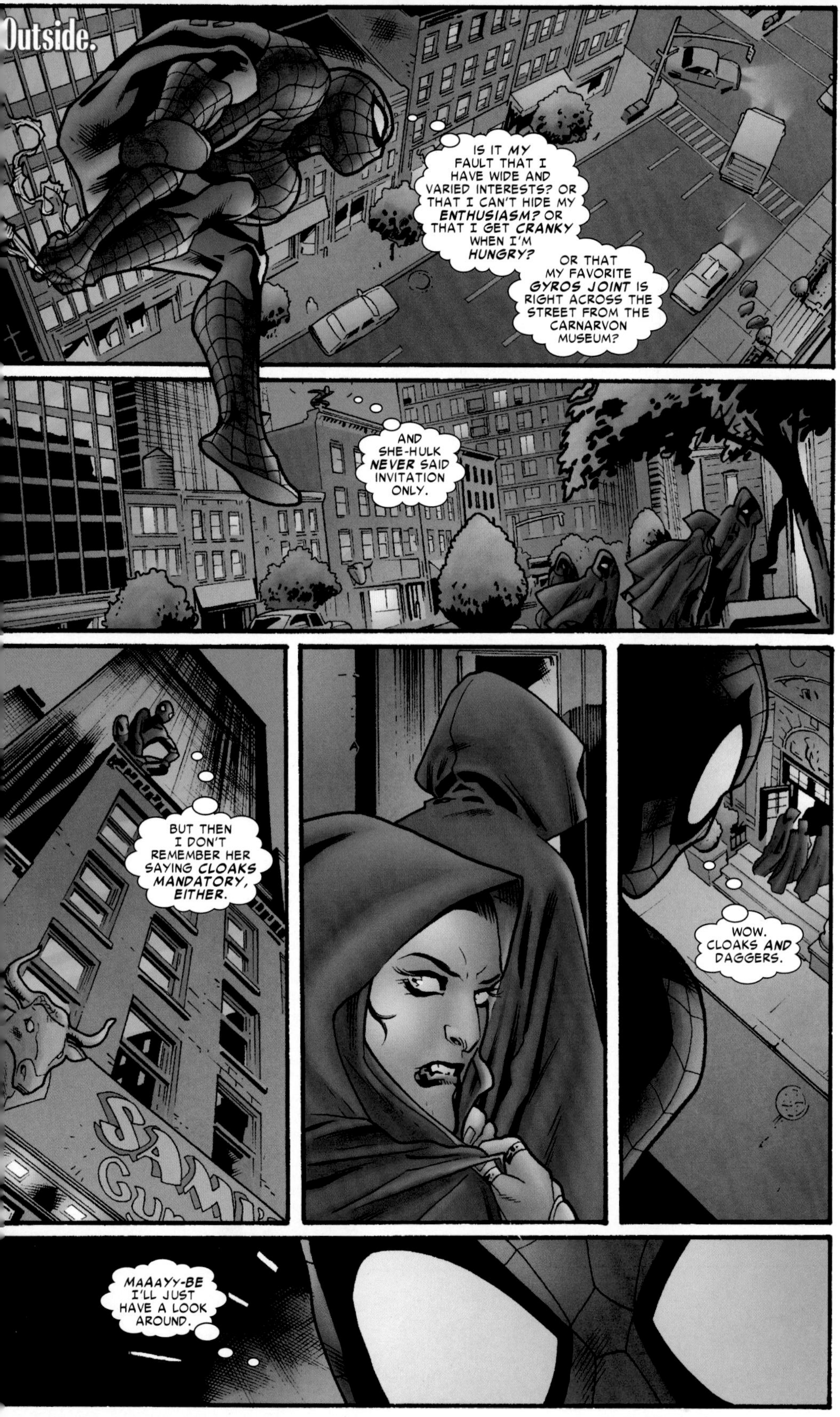
Outside.
IS IT MY FAULT THAT I HAVE WIDE AND VARIED INTERESTS? OR THAT I CAN'T HIDE MY ENTHUSIASM? OR THAT I GET CRANKY WHEN I'M HUNGRY?
OR THAT MY FAVORITE GYROS JOINT IS RIGHT ACROSS THE STREET FROM THE CARNARVON MUSEUM?
AND SHE-HULK NEVER SAID INVITATION ONLY.
BUT THEN I DON'T REMEMBER HER SAYING CLOAKS MANDATORY, EITHER.
WOW. CLOAKS AND DAGGERS.
MAAAYY-BE I'LL JUST HAVE A LOOK AROUND.

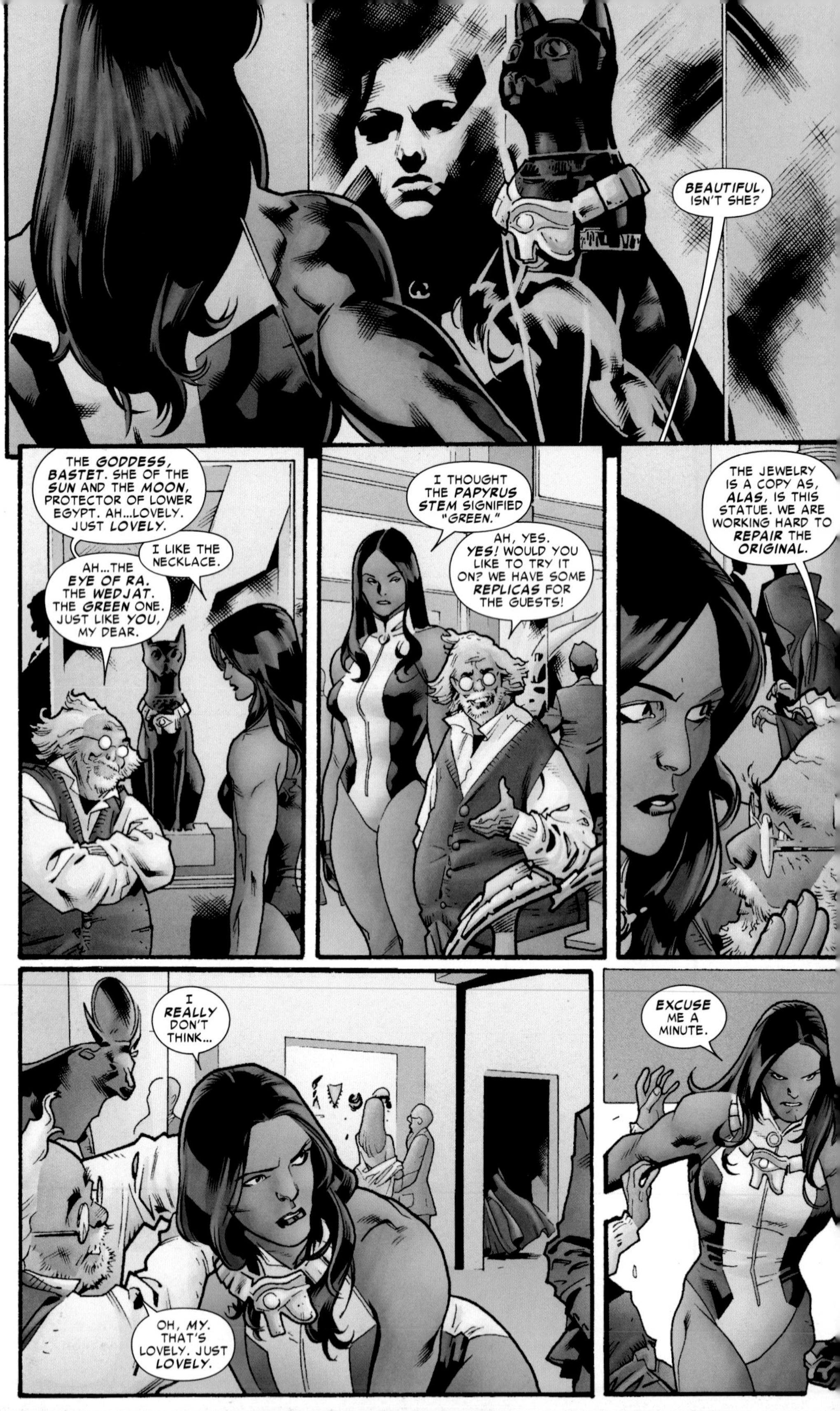
BEAUTIFUL, ISN'T SHE?
THE GODDESS, BASTET. SHE OF THE SUN AND THE MOON, PROTECTOR OF LOWER EGYPT. AH...LOVELY. JUST LOVELY.
I LIKE THE NECKLACE.
AH...THE EYE OF RA. THE WEDJAT. THE GREEN ONE. JUST LIKE YOU, MY DEAR.
I THOUGHT THE PAPYRUS STEM SIGNIFIED "GREEN."
AH, YES. YES! WOULD YOU LIKE TO TRY IT ON? WE HAVE SOME REPLICAS FOR THE GUESTS!
THE JEWELRY IS A COPY AS, ALAS, IS THIS STATUE. WE ARE WORKING HARD TO REPAIR THE ORIGINAL.
I REALLY DON'T THINK...
OH, MY. THAT'S LOVELY. JUST LOVELY.
EXCUSE ME A MINUTE.

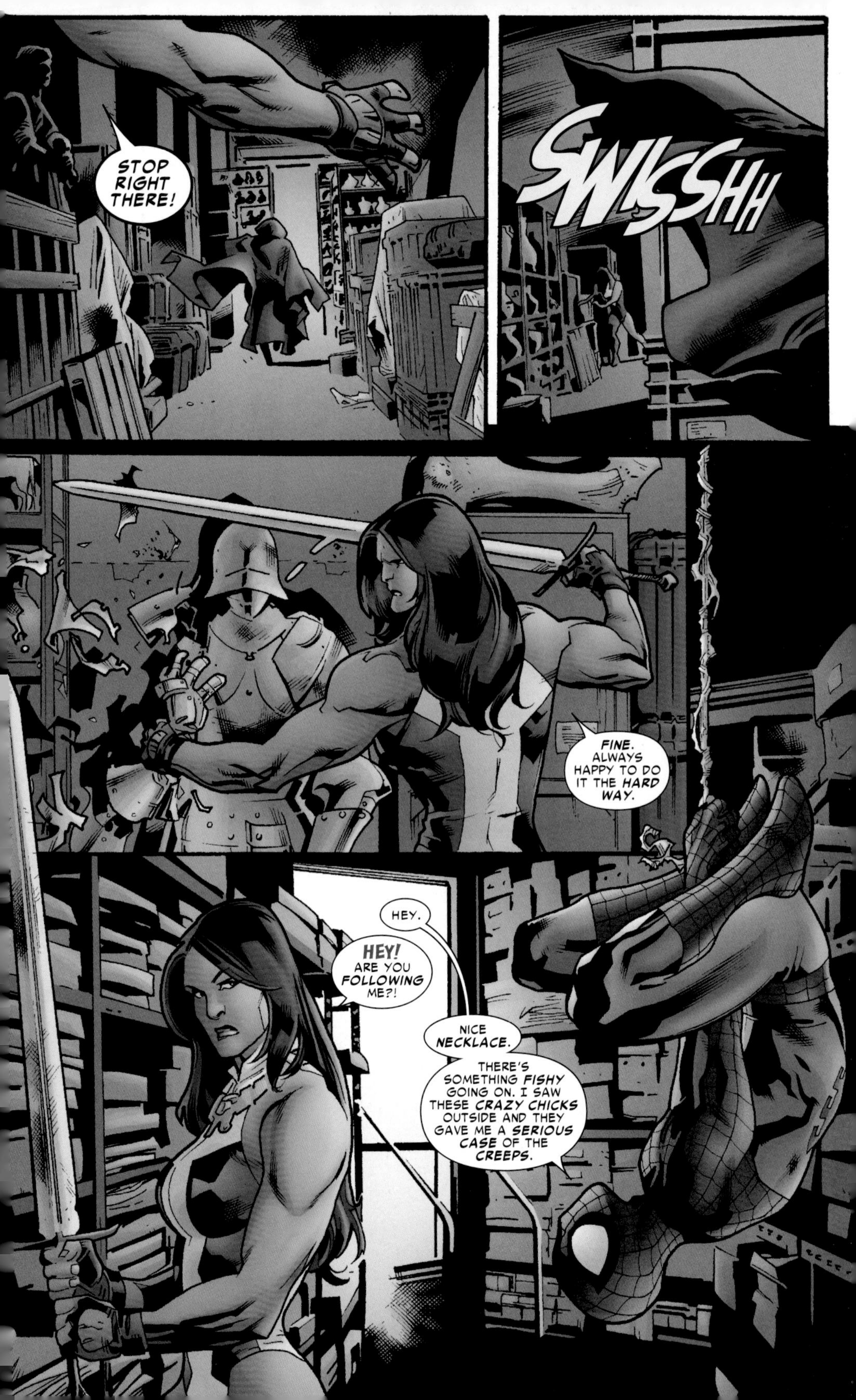
STOP RIGHT THERE!
SWISSHH
FINE. ALWAYS HAPPY TO DO IT THE HARD WAY.
HEY.
HEY! ARE YOU FOLLOWING ME?!
NICE NECKLACE.
THERE'S SOMETHING FISHY GOING ON. I SAW THESE CRAZY CHICKS OUTSIDE AND THEY GAVE ME A SERIOUS CASE OF THE CREEPS.

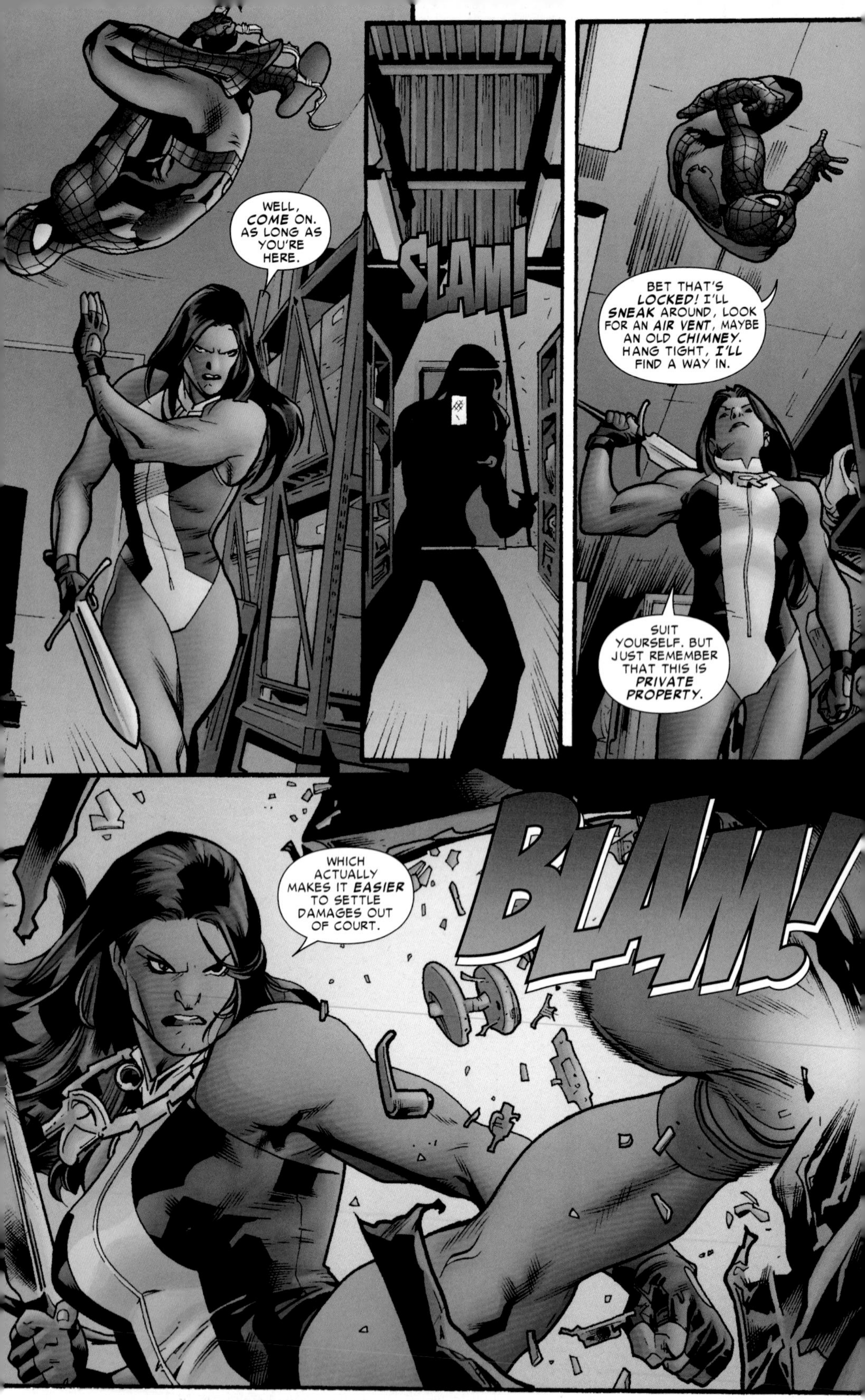
WELL, COME ON. AS LONG AS YOU'RE HERE.
SLAM!
BET THAT'S LOCKED! I'LL SNEAK AROUND, LOOK FOR AN AIR VENT, MAYBE AN OLD CHIMNEY. HANG TIGHT, I'LL FIND A WAY IN.
SUIT YOURSELF. BUT JUST REMEMBER THAT THIS IS PRIVATE PROPERTY.
WHICH ACTUALLY MAKES IT EASIER TO SETTLE DAMAGES OUT OF COURT.
BLAM!

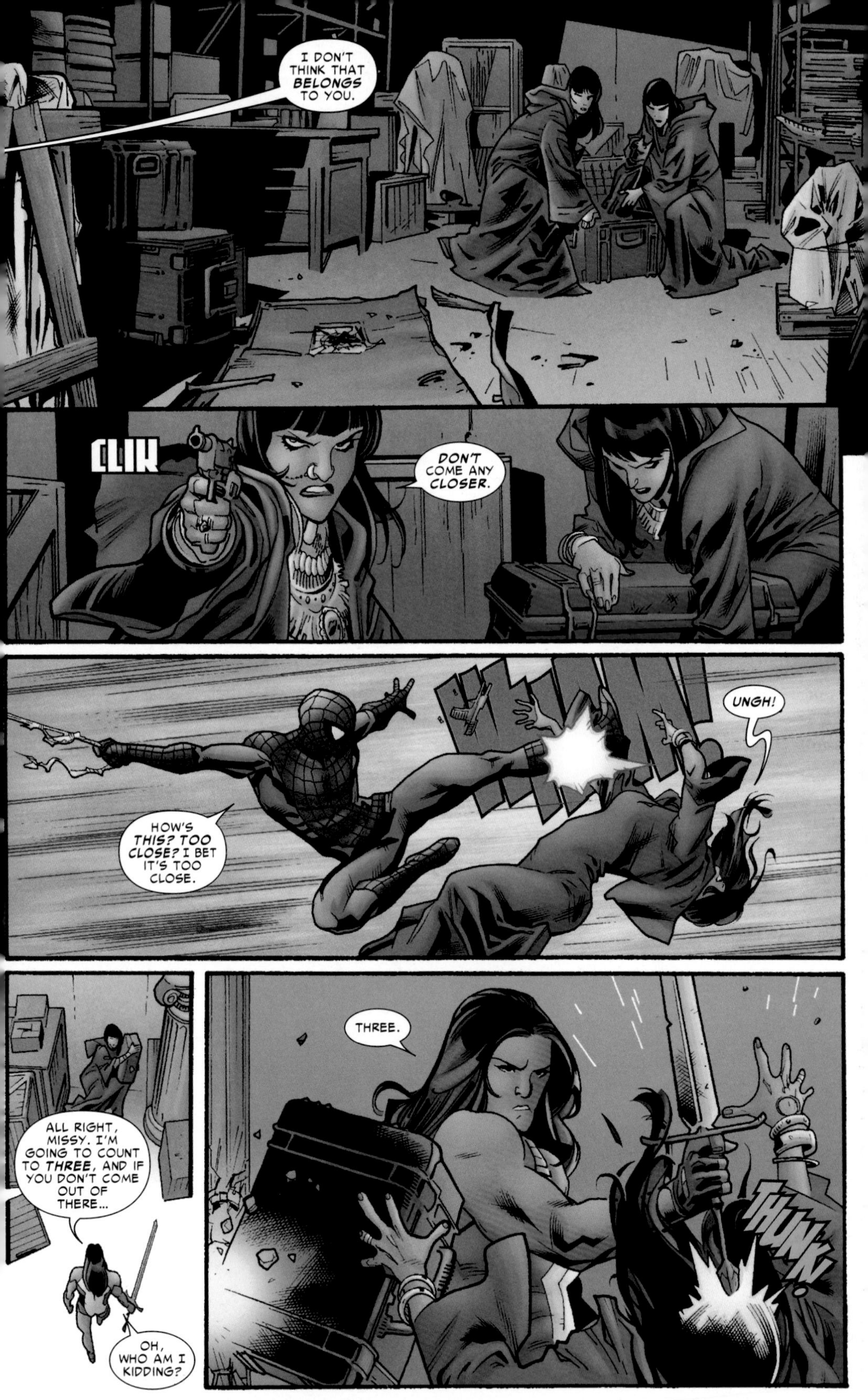
I DON'T THINK THAT BELONGS TO YOU.
CLIK
DON'T COME ANY CLOSER.
UNGH!
HOW'S THIS? TOO CLOSE? I BET IT'S TOO CLOSE.
ALL RIGHT, MISSY. I'M GOING TO COUNT TO THREE, AND IF YOU DON'T COME OUT OF THERE...
OH, WHO AM I KIDDING?
THREE.
THUNK!

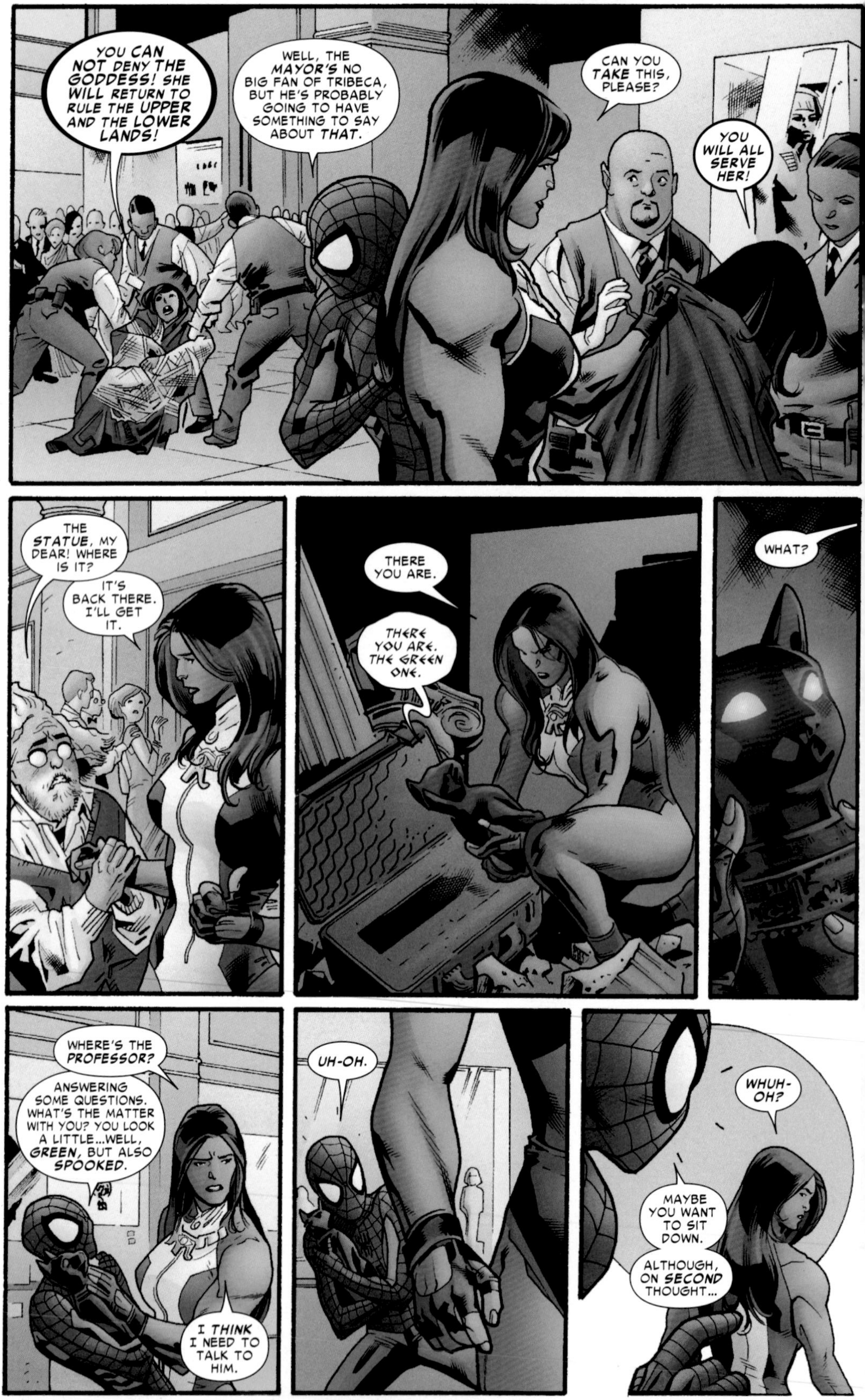
YOU CAN NOT DENY THE GODDESS! SHE WILL RETURN TO RULE THE UPPER AND THE LOWER LANDS!
WELL, THE MAYOR'S NO BIG FAN OF TRIBECA, BUT HE'S PROBABLY GOING TO HAVE SOMETHING TO SAY ABOUT THAT.
CAN YOU TAKE THIS, PLEASE?
YOU WILL ALL SERVE HER!
THE STATUE, MY DEAR! WHERE IS IT?
IT'S BACK THERE. I'LL GET IT.
THERE YOU ARE.
THERE YOU ARE. THE GREEN ONE.
WHAT?
WHERE'S THE PROFESSOR?
ANSWERING SOME QUESTIONS. WHAT'S THE MATTER WITH YOU? YOU LOOK A LITTLE...WELL, GREEN, BUT ALSO SPOOKED.
I THINK I NEED TO TALK TO HIM.
UH-OH.
WHUH-OH?
MAYBE YOU WANT TO SIT DOWN.
ALTHOUGH, ON SECOND THOUGHT...

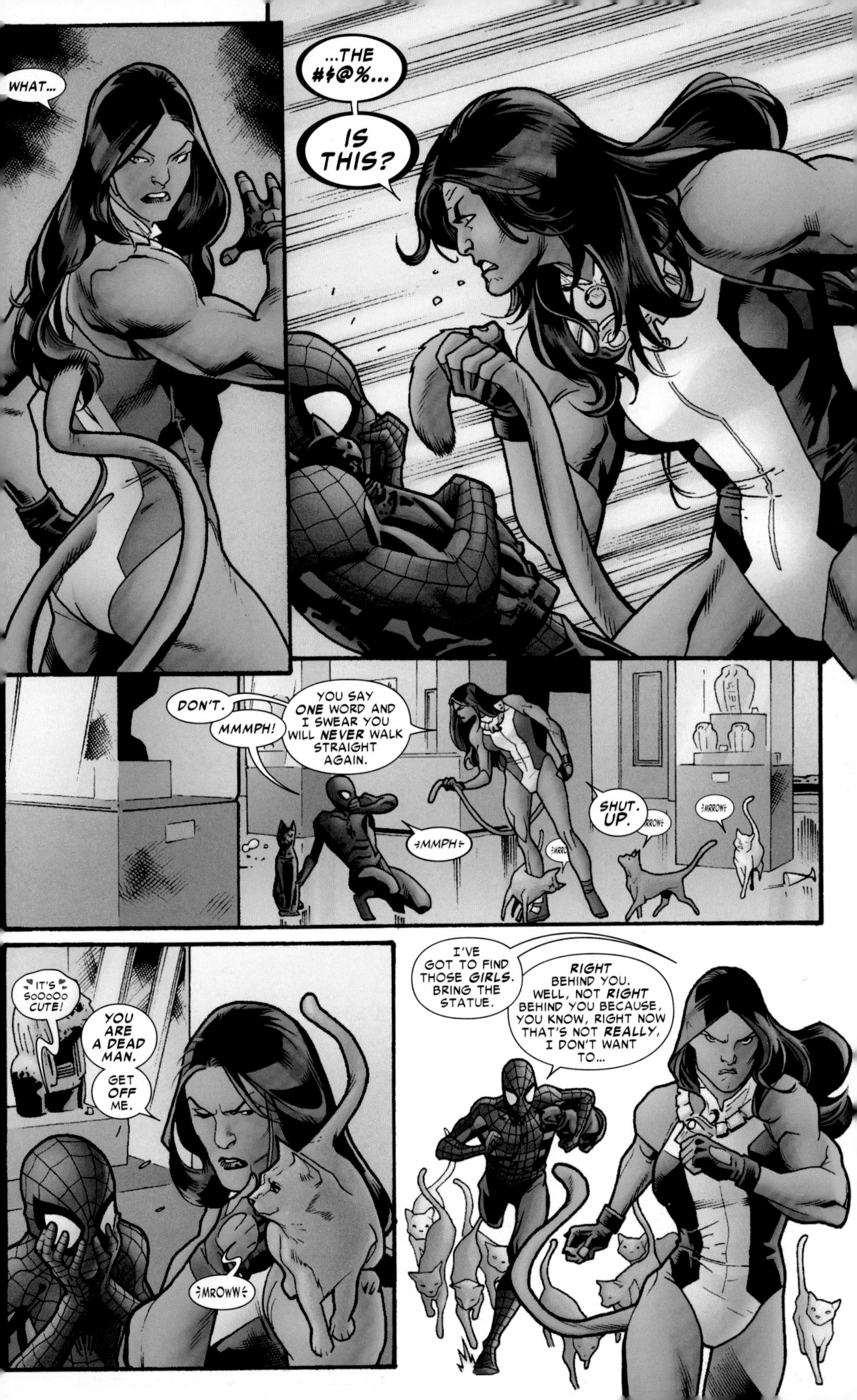
WHAT...
...THE
#$@%...
IS THIS?
DON'T.
MMMPH!
YOU SAY ONE WORD AND I SWEAR YOU WILL NEVER WALK STRAIGHT AGAIN.
MMPH
SHUT. UP.
MRRO
MRROW
MRROW
IT'S SOOOOO CUTE!
YOU ARE A DEAD MAN.
GET OFF ME.
MROWW
I'VE GOT TO FIND THOSE GIRLS. BRING THE STATUE.
RIGHT BEHIND YOU. WELL, NOT RIGHT BEHIND YOU BECAUSE, YOU KNOW, RIGHT NOW THAT'S NOT REALLY, I DON'T WANT TO...

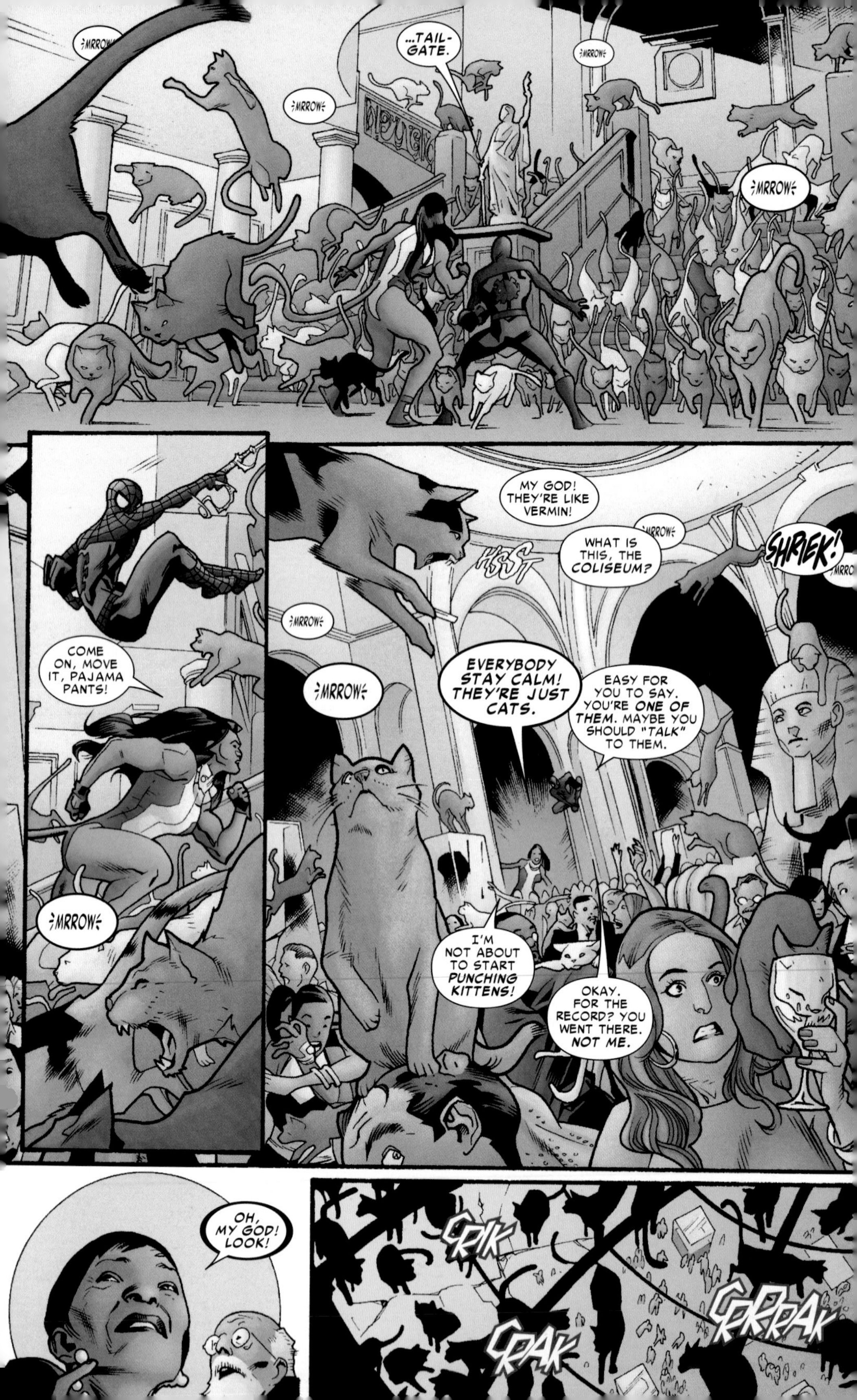
MRROW
...TAIL-GATE.
MRROW
MRROW
MRROW
COME ON, MOVE IT, PAJAMA PANTS!
MRROW
MY GOD! THEY'RE LIKE VERMIN!
MRROW
WHAT IS THIS, THE COLISEUM?
HSST
SHRIEK!
MRROW
MRROW
EVERYBODY STAY CALM! THEY'RE JUST CATS.
EASY FOR YOU TO SAY. YOU'RE ONE OF THEM. MAYBE YOU SHOULD "TALK" TO THEM.
I'M NOT ABOUT TO START PUNCHING KITTENS!
OKAY. FOR THE RECORD? YOU WENT THERE. NOT ME.
OH, MY GOD! LOOK!
CRIK
CRAK
CRRRRAK

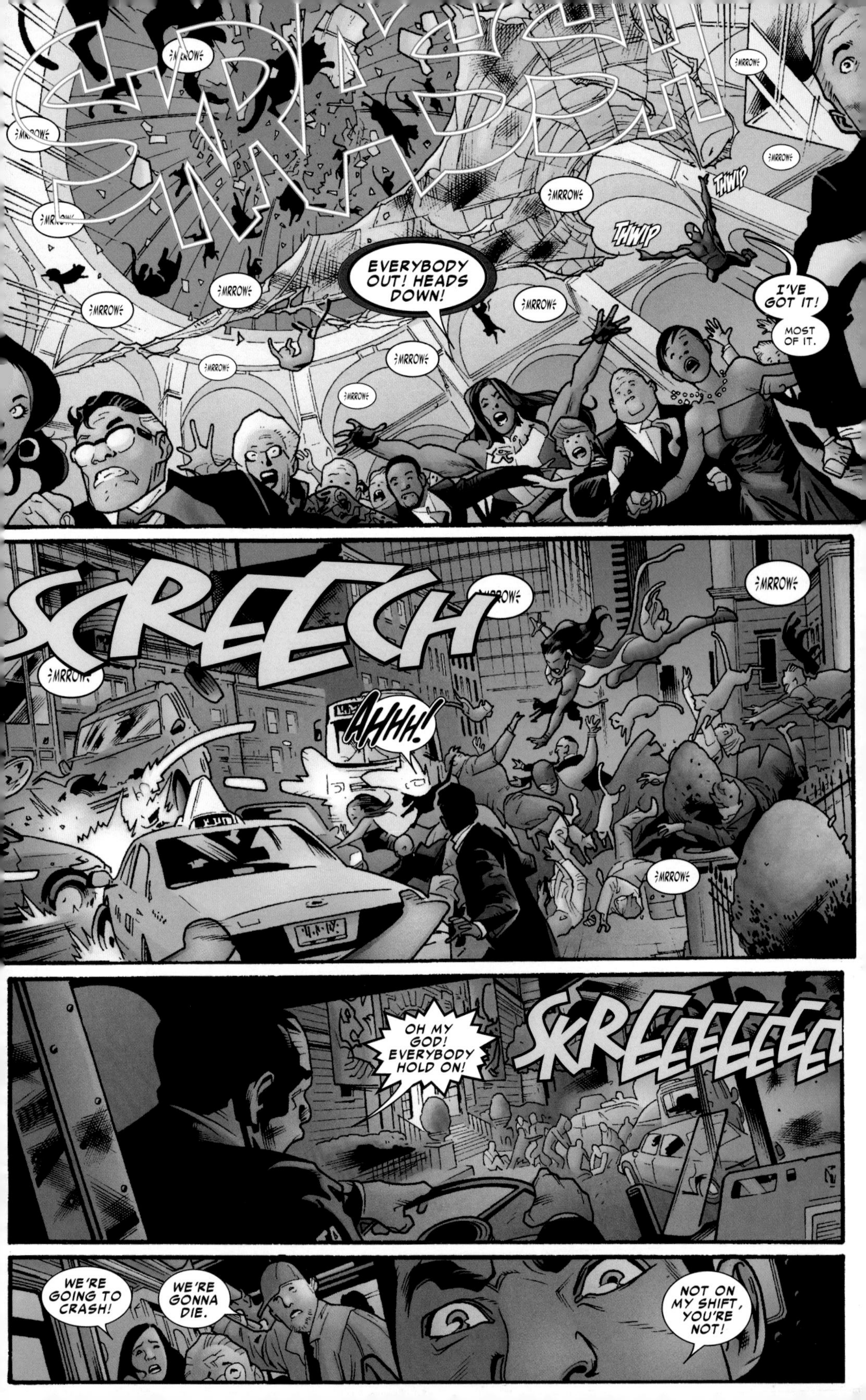
CRASH
SMASH
MRROW
MRROW
MRROW
MRROW
MRROW
MRROW
MRROW
MRROW
MRROW
MRROW
THWIP
THWIP
EVERYBODY OUT! HEADS DOWN!
I'VE GOT IT!
MOST OF IT.
SCREECH
MRROW
MRROW
MRROW
AHHH!
MRROW
OH MY GOD! EVERYBODY HOLD ON!
SKREEEEEEE
WE'RE GOING TO CRASH!
WE'RE GONNA DIE.
NOT ON MY SHIFT, YOU'RE NOT!

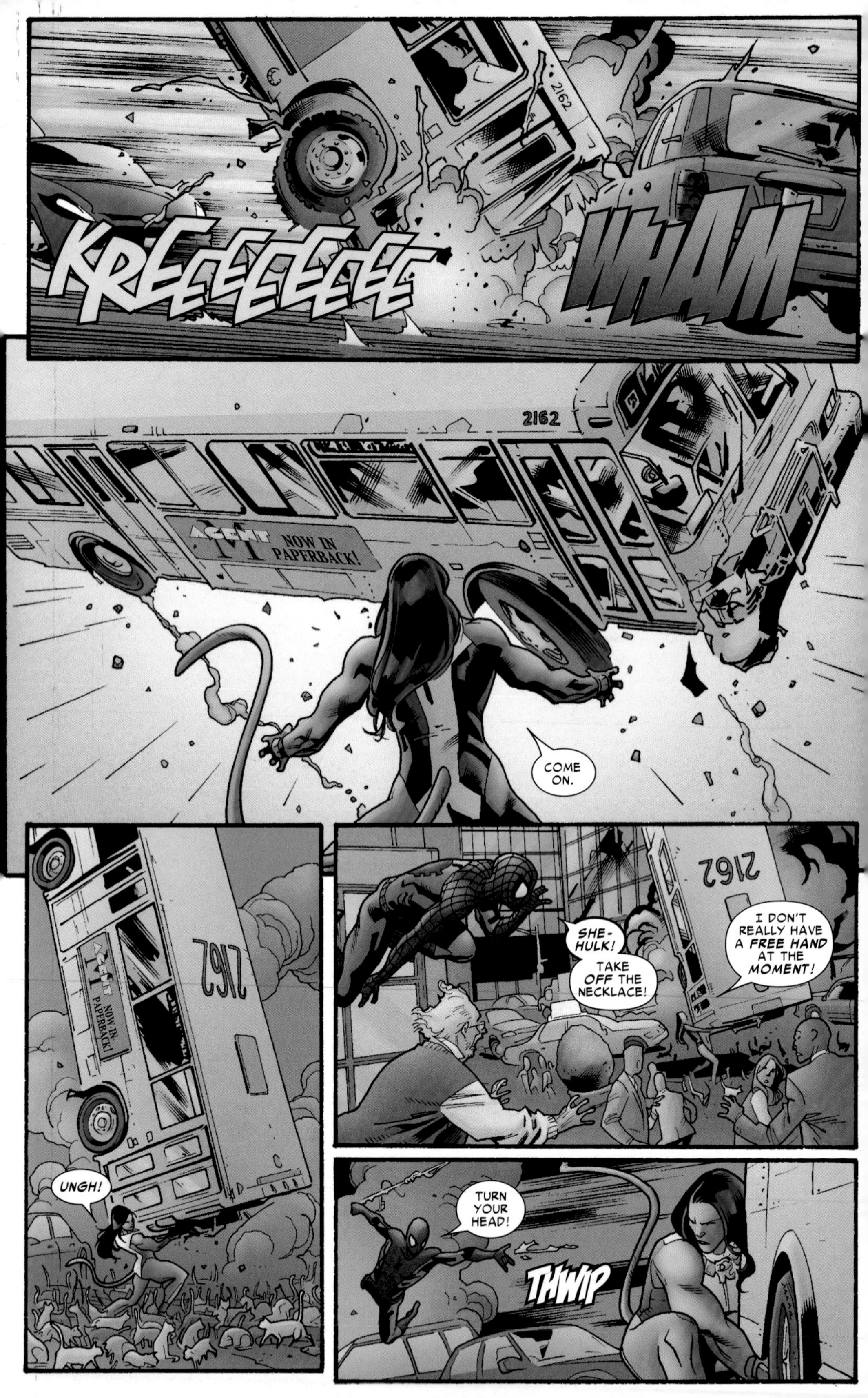
KREEEEEEEEEE
WHAM
2162
AGENT M NOW IN PAPERBACK!
COME ON.
2162
AGENT M NOW IN PAPERBACK!
UNGH!
2162
SHE-HULK! TAKE OFF THE NECKLACE!
I DON'T REALLY HAVE A FREE HAND AT THE MOMENT!
TURN YOUR HEAD!
THWIP

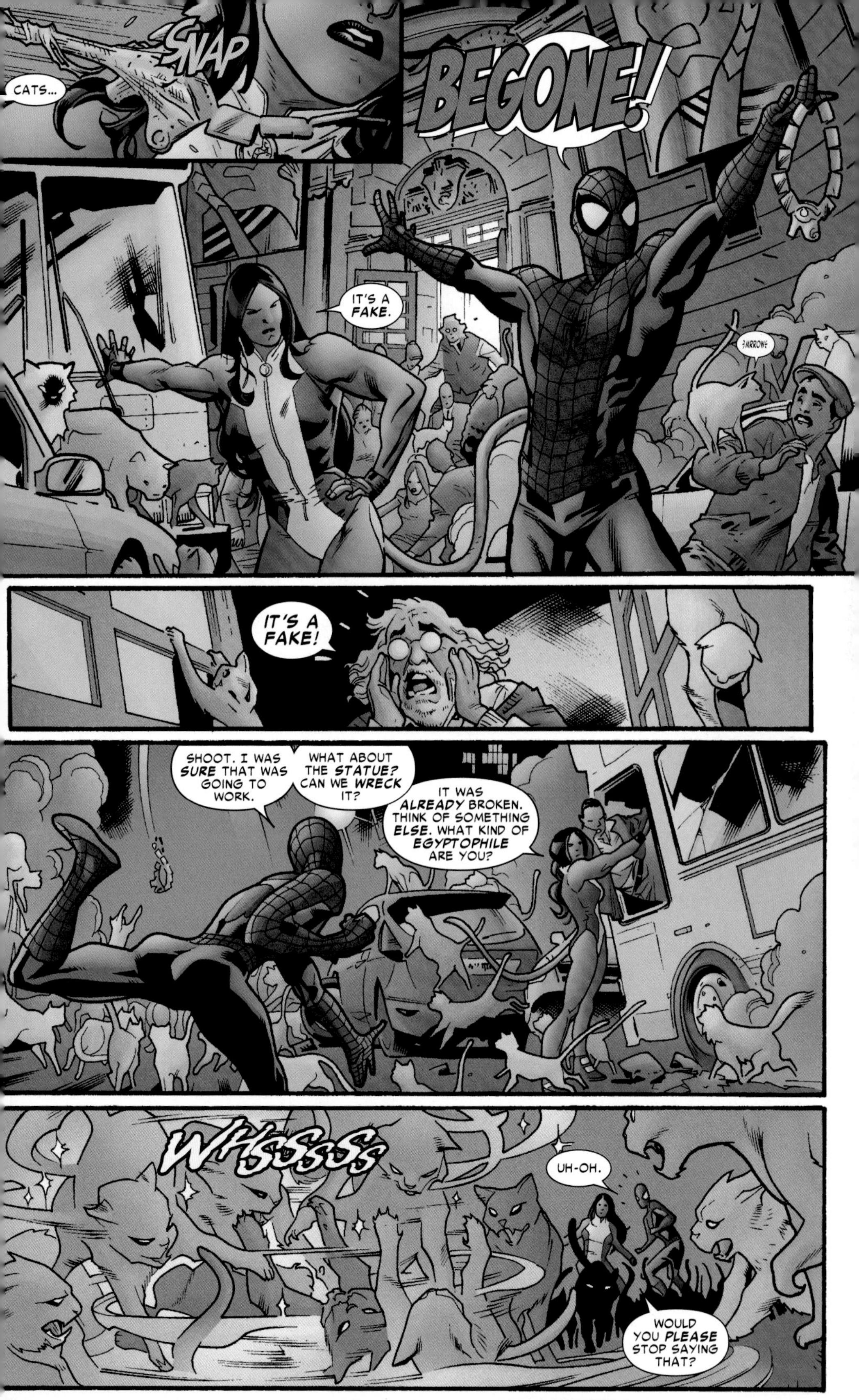
SNAP
CATS...
BEGONE!
IT'S A FAKE.
MIRROW
IT'S A FAKE!
SHOOT. I WAS SURE THAT WAS GOING TO WORK.
WHAT ABOUT THE STATUE? CAN WE WRECK IT?
IT WAS ALREADY BROKEN. THINK OF SOMETHING ELSE. WHAT KIND OF EGYPTOPHILE ARE YOU?
WHSSSSS
UH-OH.
WOULD YOU PLEASE STOP SAYING THAT?

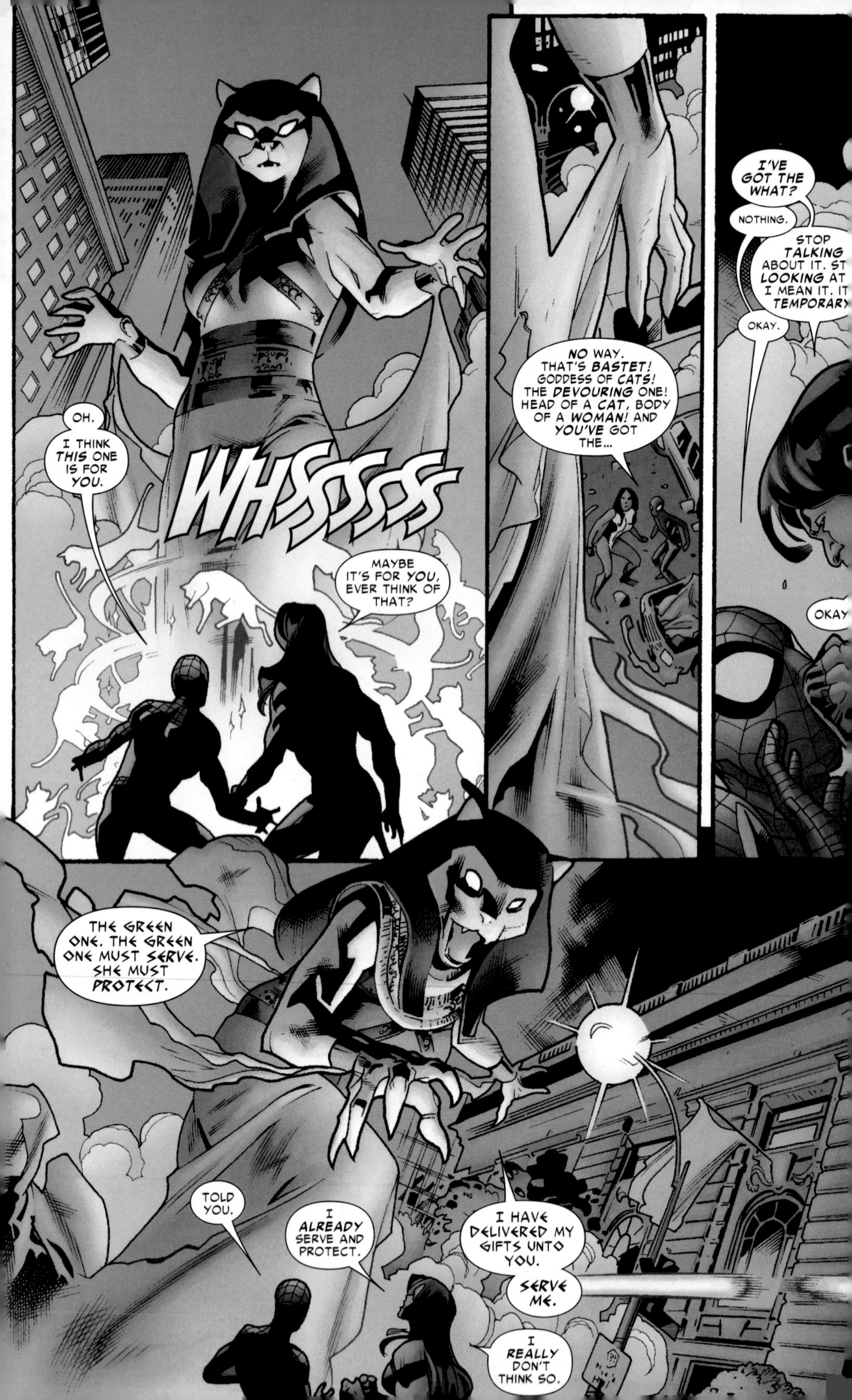
OH.
I THINK THIS ONE IS FOR YOU.
WHSSSSS
MAYBE IT'S FOR YOU, EVER THINK OF THAT?
NO WAY. THAT'S BASTET! GODDESS OF CATS! THE DEVOURING ONE! HEAD OF A CAT, BODY OF A WOMAN! AND YOU'VE GOT THE...
I'VE GOT THE WHAT?
NOTHING.
STOP TALKING ABOUT IT.
I MEAN IT.
OKAY.
OKAY
THE GREEN ONE. THE GREEN ONE MUST SERVE. SHE MUST PROTECT.
TOLD YOU.
I ALREADY SERVE AND PROTECT.
I HAVE DELIVERED MY GIFTS UNTO YOU.
SERVE ME.
I REALLY DON'T THINK SO.

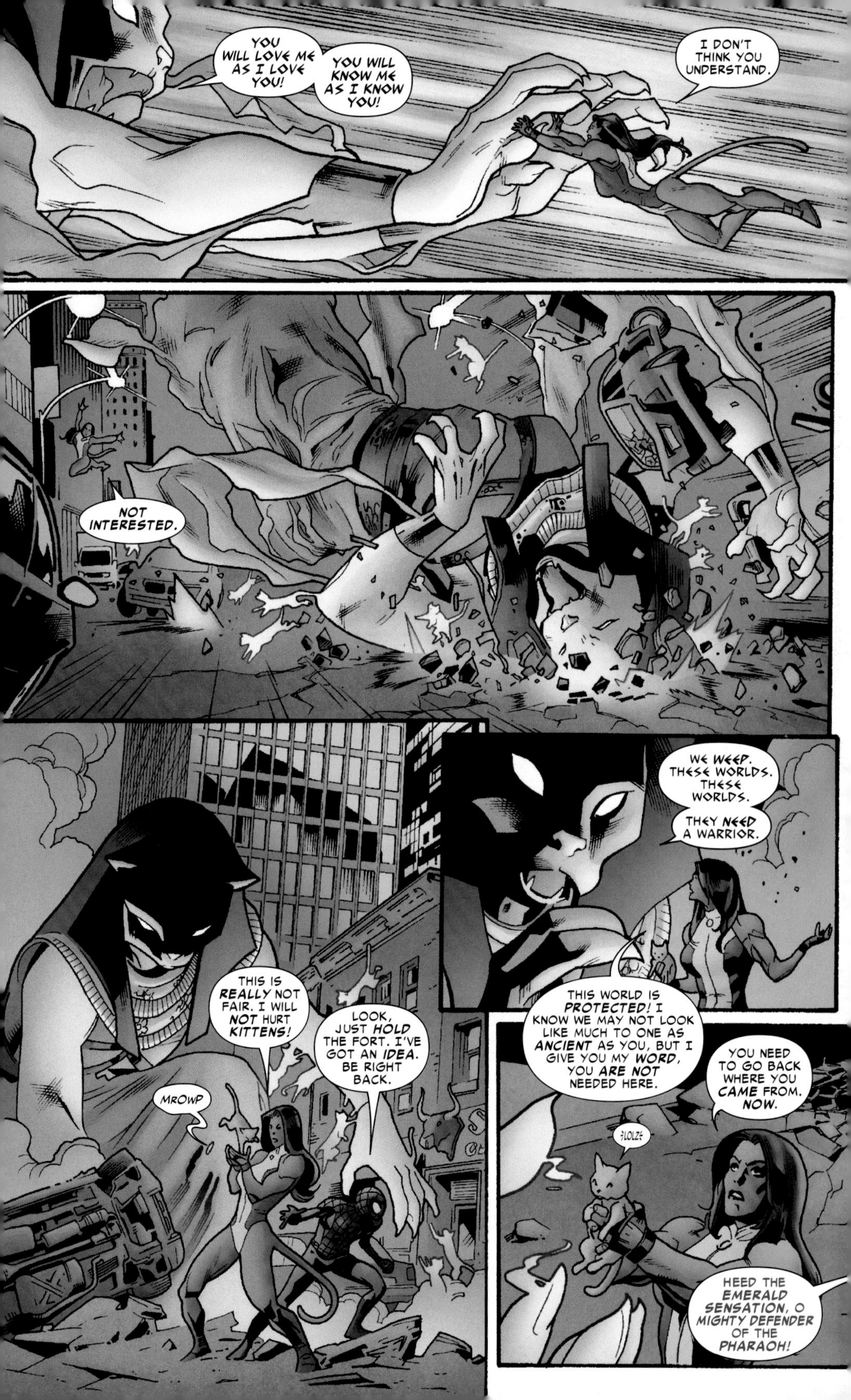
YOU WILL LOVE ME AS I LOVE YOU!
YOU WILL KNOW ME AS I KNOW YOU!
I DON'T THINK YOU UNDERSTAND.
NOT INTERESTED.
THIS IS REALLY NOT FAIR. I WILL NOT HURT KITTENS!
MROWP
LOOK, JUST HOLD THE FORT. I'VE GOT AN IDEA. BE RIGHT BACK.
WE WEEP. THESE WORLDS. THESE WORLDS.
THEY NEED A WARRIOR.
THIS WORLD IS PROTECTED! I KNOW WE MAY NOT LOOK LIKE MUCH TO ONE AS ANCIENT AS YOU, BUT I GIVE YOU MY WORD, YOU ARE NOT NEEDED HERE.
YOU NEED TO GO BACK WHERE YOU CAME FROM. NOW.
LOLZ
HEED THE EMERALD SENSATION, O MIGHTY DEFENDER OF THE PHARAOH!

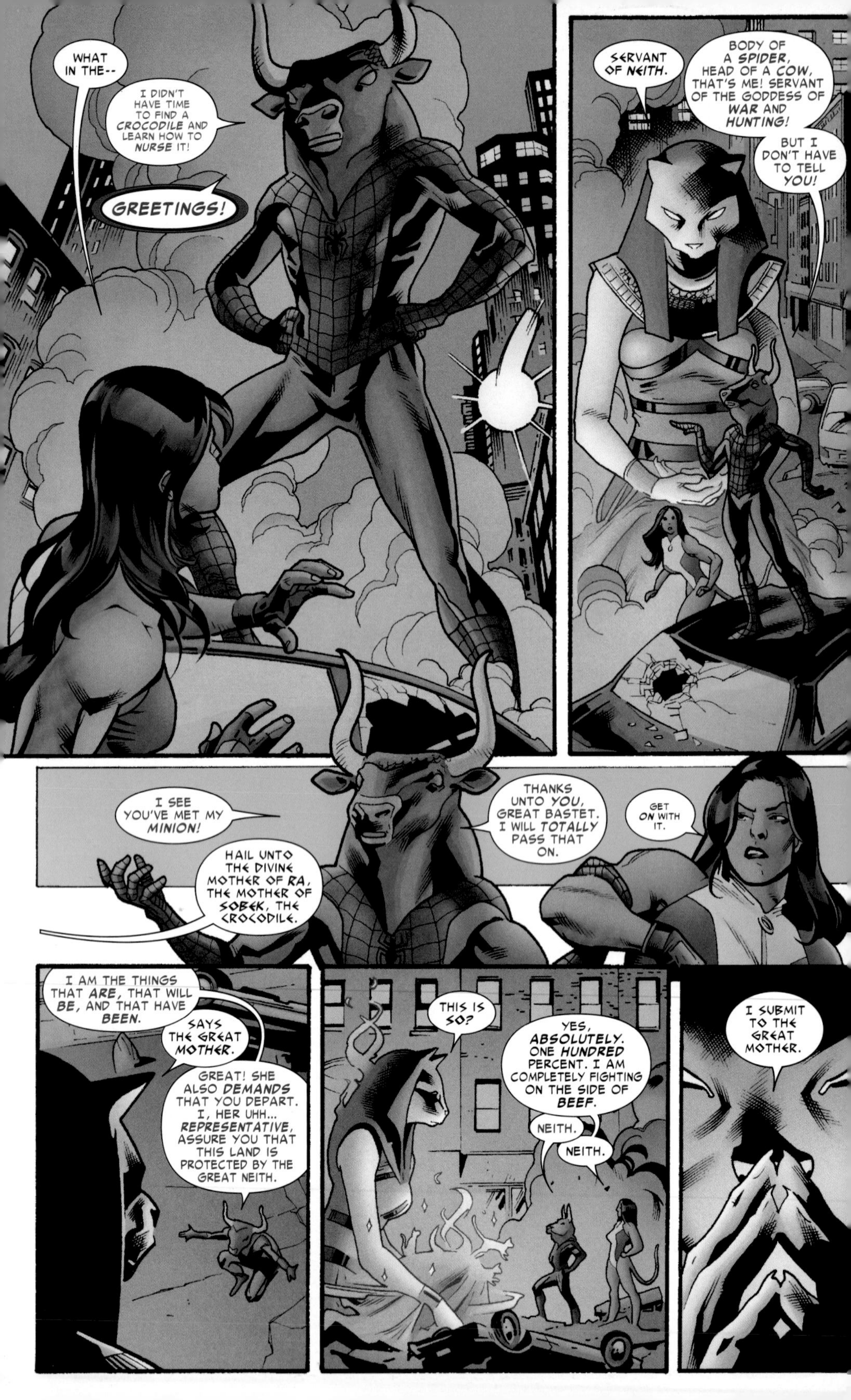
WHAT IN THE--
I DIDN'T HAVE TIME TO FIND A CROCODILE AND LEARN HOW TO NURSE IT!
GREETINGS!
SERVANT OF NEITH.
BODY OF A SPIDER, HEAD OF A COW, THAT'S ME! SERVANT OF THE GODDESS OF WAR AND HUNTING!
BUT I DON'T HAVE TO TELL YOU!
I SEE YOU'VE MET MY MINION!
HAIL UNTO THE DIVINE MOTHER OF RA, THE MOTHER OF SOBEK, THE CROCODILE.
THANKS UNTO YOU, GREAT BASTET. I WILL TOTALLY PASS THAT ON.
GET ON WITH IT.
I AM THE THINGS THAT ARE, THAT WILL BE, AND THAT HAVE BEEN.
SAYS THE GREAT MOTHER.
GREAT! SHE ALSO DEMANDS THAT YOU DEPART. I, HER UHH... REPRESENTATIVE, ASSURE YOU THAT THIS LAND IS PROTECTED BY THE GREAT NEITH.
THIS IS SO?
YES, ABSOLUTELY. ONE HUNDRED PERCENT. I AM COMPLETELY FIGHTING ON THE SIDE OF BEEF.
NEITH.
NEITH.
I SUBMIT TO THE GREAT MOTHER.

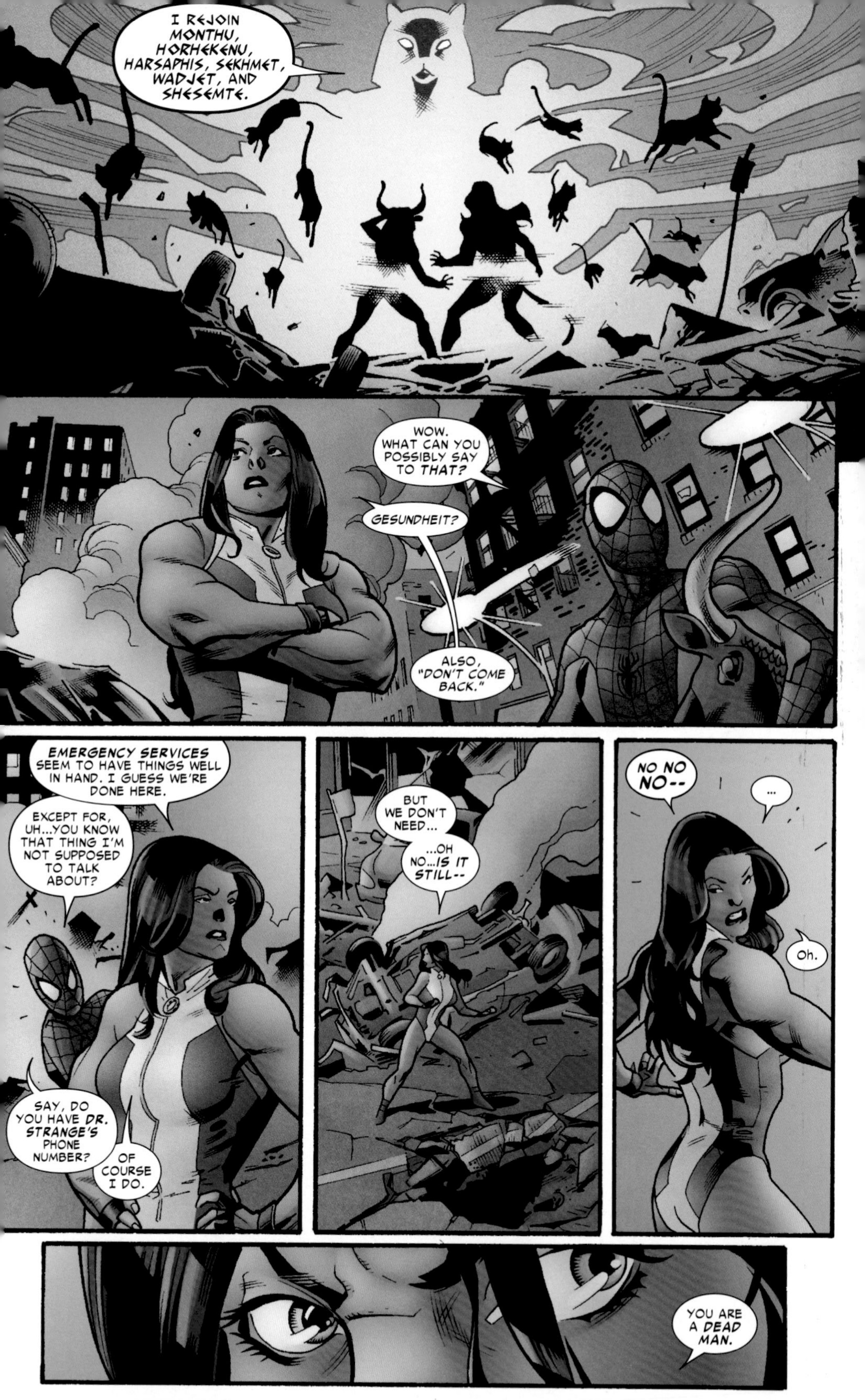
I REJOIN MONTHU, HORHEKENU, HARSAPHIS, SEKHMET, WADJET, AND SHESEMTE.
WOW. WHAT CAN YOU POSSIBLY SAY TO THAT?
GESUNDHEIT?
ALSO, "DON'T COME BACK."
EMERGENCY SERVICES SEEM TO HAVE THINGS WELL IN HAND. I GUESS WE'RE DONE HERE.
EXCEPT FOR, UH...YOU KNOW THAT THING I'M NOT SUPPOSED TO TALK ABOUT?
SAY, DO YOU HAVE DR. STRANGE'S PHONE NUMBER?
OF COURSE I DO.
BUT WE DON'T NEED...
...OH NO...IS IT STILL--
NO NO NO--
...
Oh.
YOU ARE A DEAD MAN.

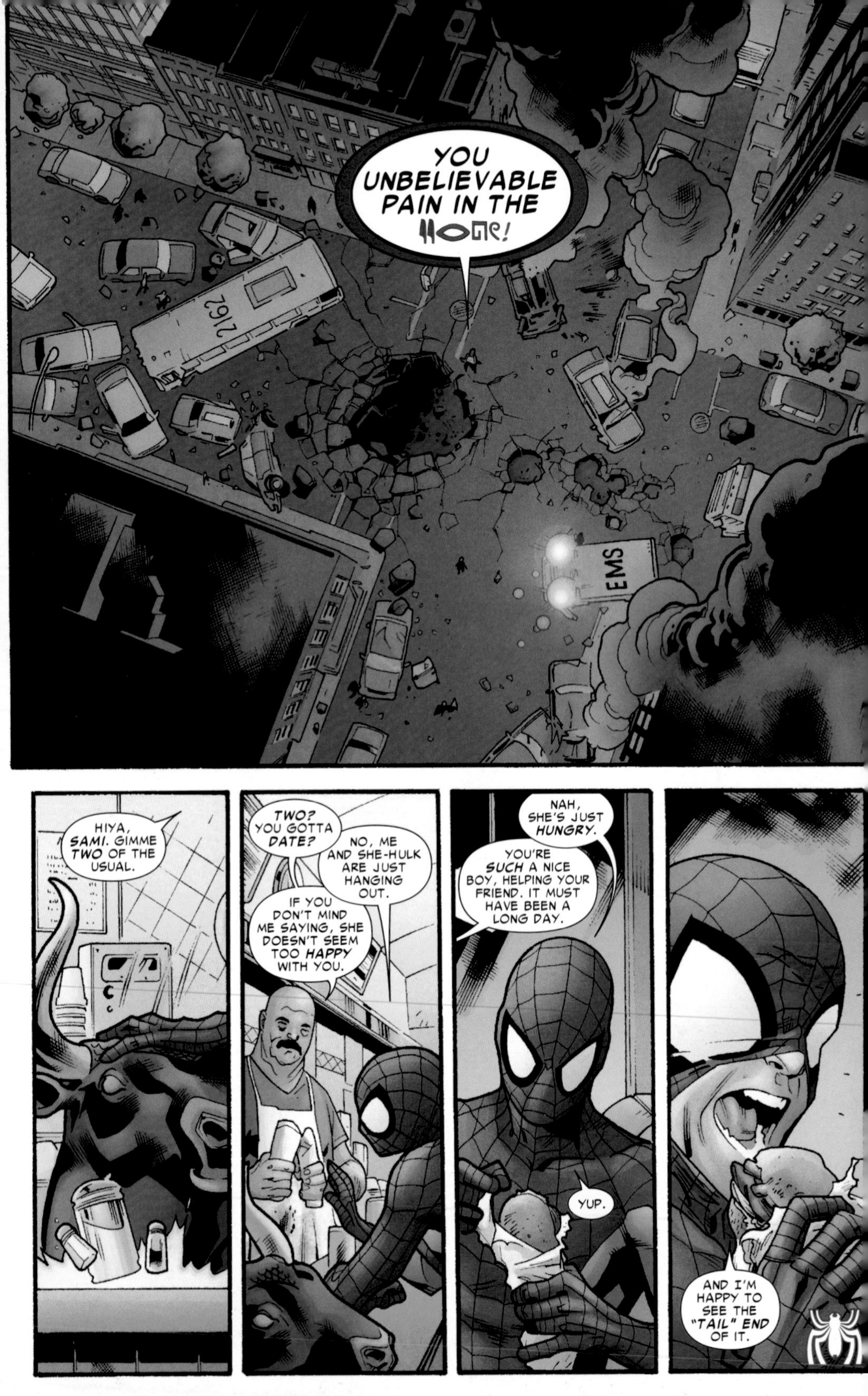
YOU UNBELIEVABLE PAIN IN THE
HIYA, SAMI. GIMME TWO OF THE USUAL.
TWO? YOU GOTTA DATE?
NO, ME AND SHE-HULK ARE JUST HANGING OUT.
IF YOU DON'T MIND ME SAYING, SHE DOESN'T SEEM TOO HAPPY WITH YOU.
NAH, SHE'S JUST HUNGRY.
YOU'RE SUCH A NICE BOY, HELPING YOUR FRIEND. IT MUST HAVE BEEN A LONG DAY.
YUP.
AND I'M HAPPY TO SEE THE "TAIL" END OF IT.

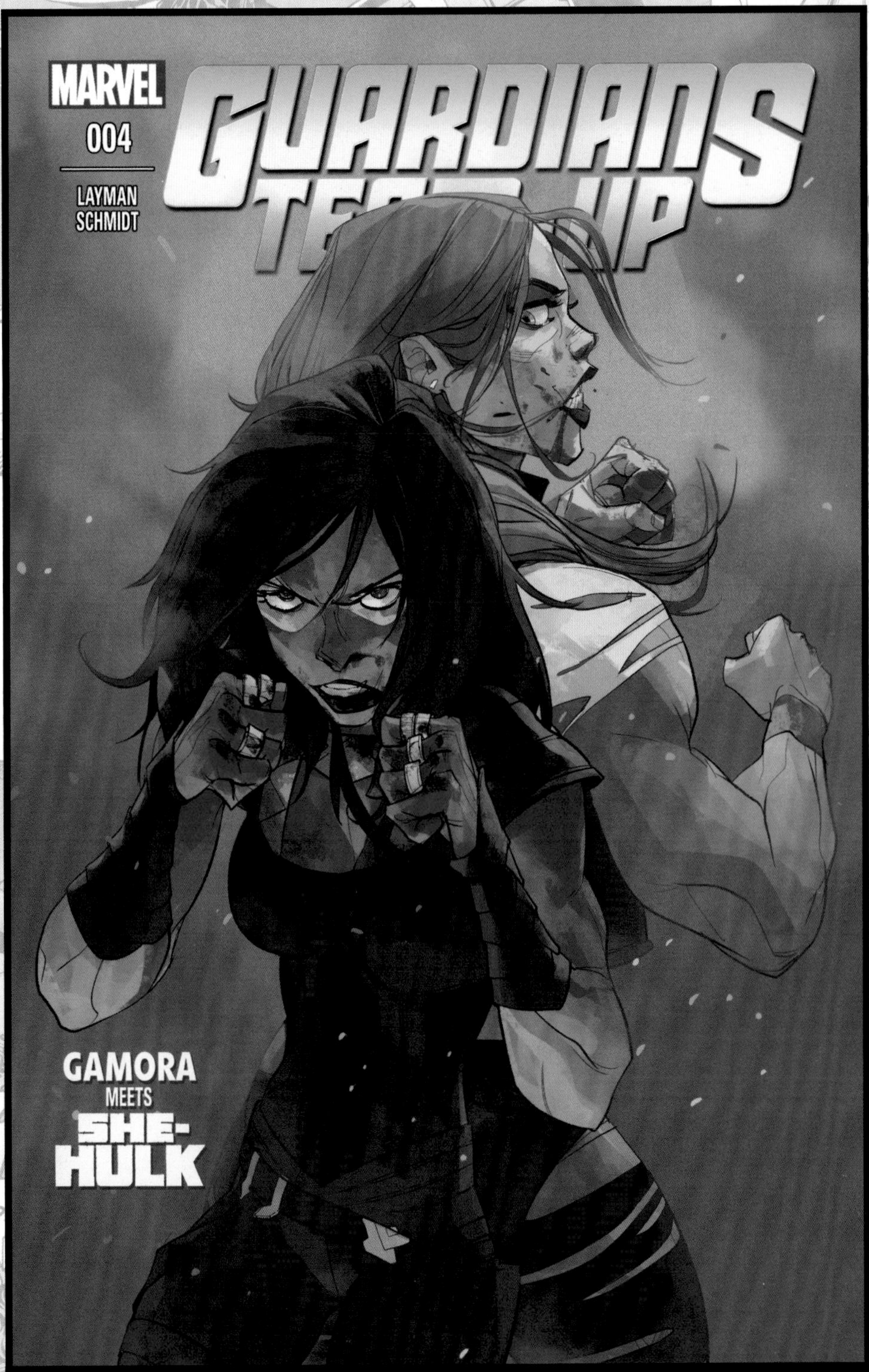
MARVEL
004
LAYMAN
SCHMIDT
GUARDIANS
GAMORA
MEETS
SHE-HULK

GUARDIANS TEAM-UP #4

IT'S NOT EASY BEING GREEN — IN FACT, IT'S TOUGH. BUT A BAND OF INTERGALACTIC BOUNTY HUNTERS ARE ABOUT TO FIND OUT THAT SO ARE SHE-HULK AND GAMORA!

PROLOGUE:

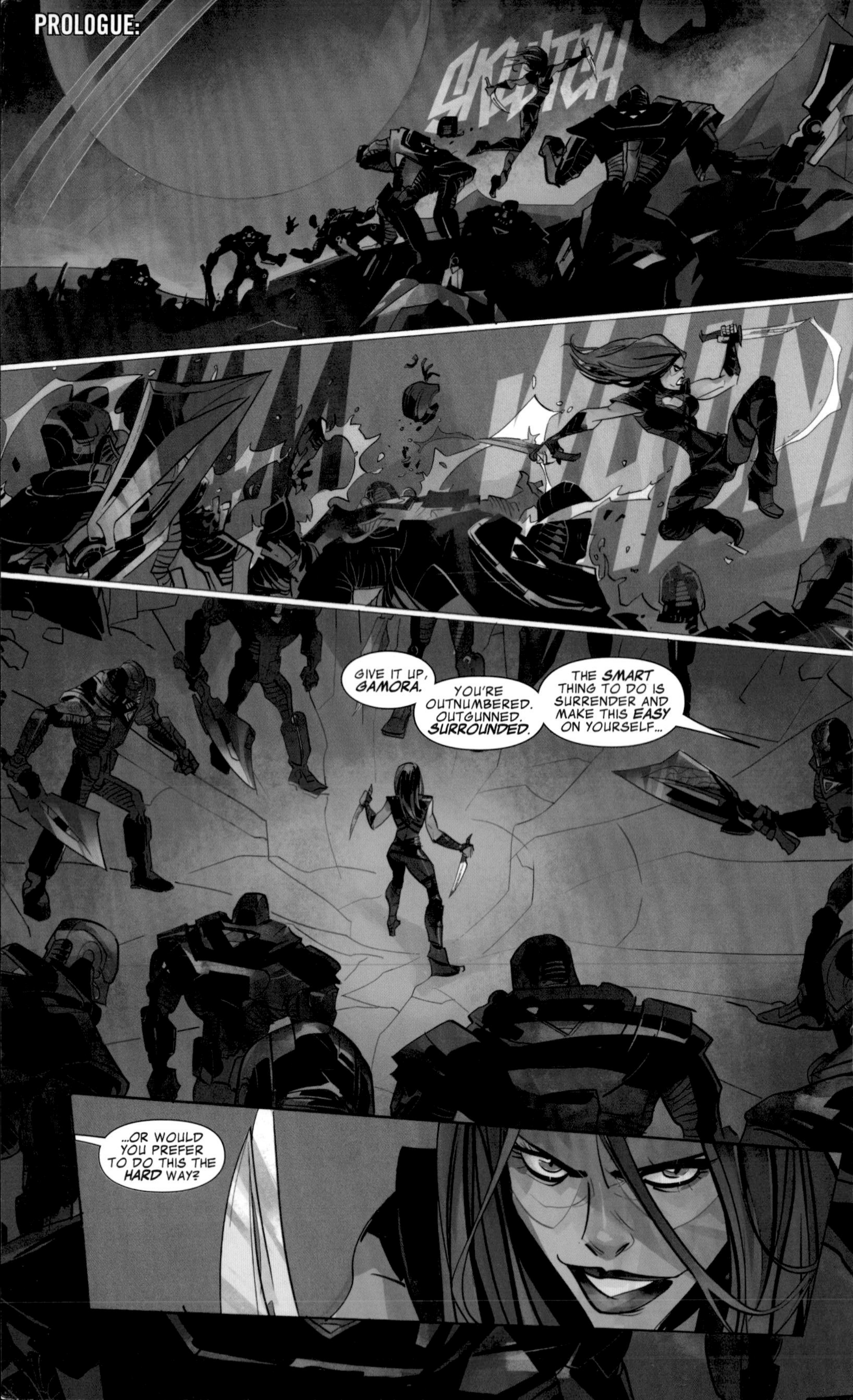
GIVE IT UP, GAMORA.
YOU'RE OUTNUMBERED. OUTGUNNED. SURROUNDED.
THE SMART THING TO DO IS SURRENDER AND MAKE THIS EASY ON YOURSELF...
...OR WOULD YOU PREFER TO DO THIS THE HARD WAY?

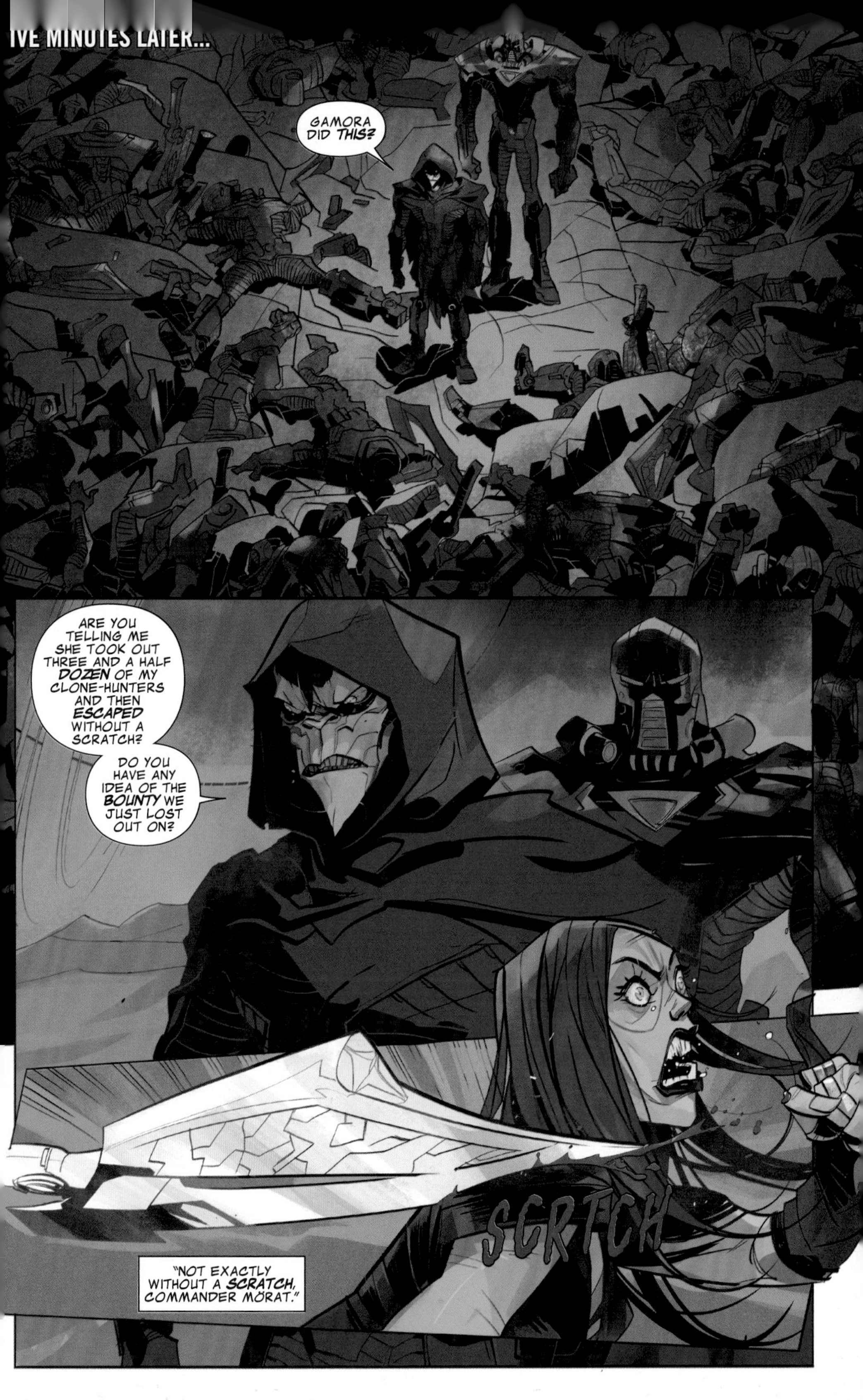
IVE MINUTES LATER...
GAMORA DID THIS?
ARE YOU TELLING ME SHE TOOK OUT THREE AND A HALF DOZEN OF MY CLONE-HUNTERS AND THEN ESCAPED WITHOUT A SCRATCH?
DO YOU HAVE ANY IDEA OF THE BOUNTY WE JUST LOST OUT ON?
SCRTCH
"NOT EXACTLY WITHOUT A SCRATCH, COMMANDER MORAT."

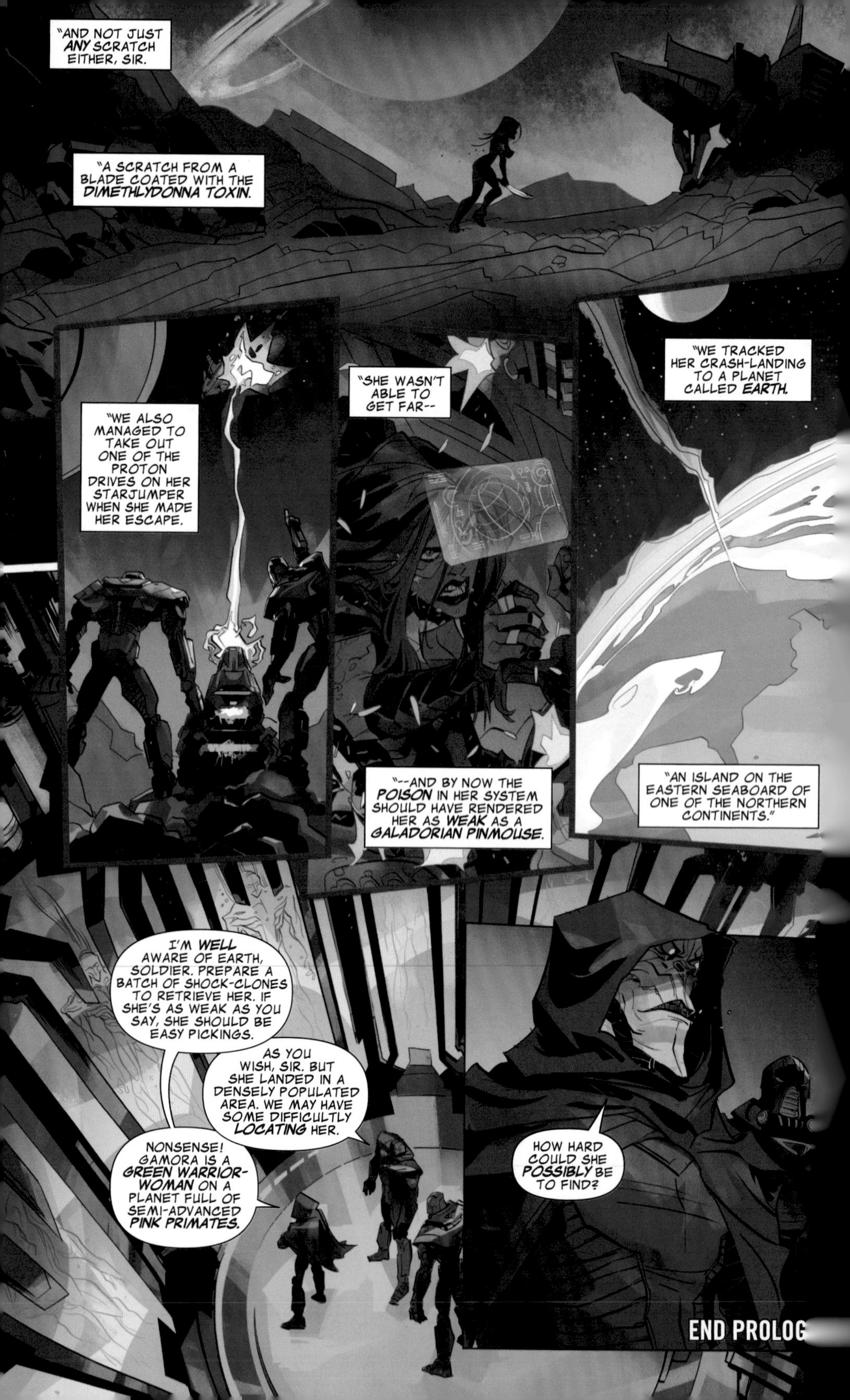
"AND NOT JUST ANY SCRATCH EITHER, SIR.
"A SCRATCH FROM A BLADE COATED WITH THE DIMETHLYDONNA TOXIN.
"WE ALSO MANAGED TO TAKE OUT ONE OF THE PROTON DRIVES ON HER STARJUMPER WHEN SHE MADE HER ESCAPE.
"SHE WASN'T ABLE TO GET FAR--
"--AND BY NOW THE POISON IN HER SYSTEM SHOULD HAVE RENDERED HER AS WEAK AS A GALADORIAN PINMOUSE.
"WE TRACKED HER CRASH-LANDING TO A PLANET CALLED EARTH.
"AN ISLAND ON THE EASTERN SEABOARD OF ONE OF THE NORTHERN CONTINENTS."
I'M WELL AWARE OF EARTH, SOLDIER. PREPARE A BATCH OF SHOCK-CLONES TO RETRIEVE HER. IF SHE'S AS WEAK AS YOU SAY, SHE SHOULD BE EASY PICKINGS.
AS YOU WISH, SIR. BUT SHE LANDED IN A DENSELY POPULATED AREA. WE MAY HAVE SOME DIFFICULTLY LOCATING HER.
NONSENSE! GAMORA IS A GREEN WARRIOR-WOMAN ON A PLANET FULL OF SEMI-ADVANCED PINK PRIMATES.
HOW HARD COULD SHE POSSIBLY BE TO FIND?
END PROLOG

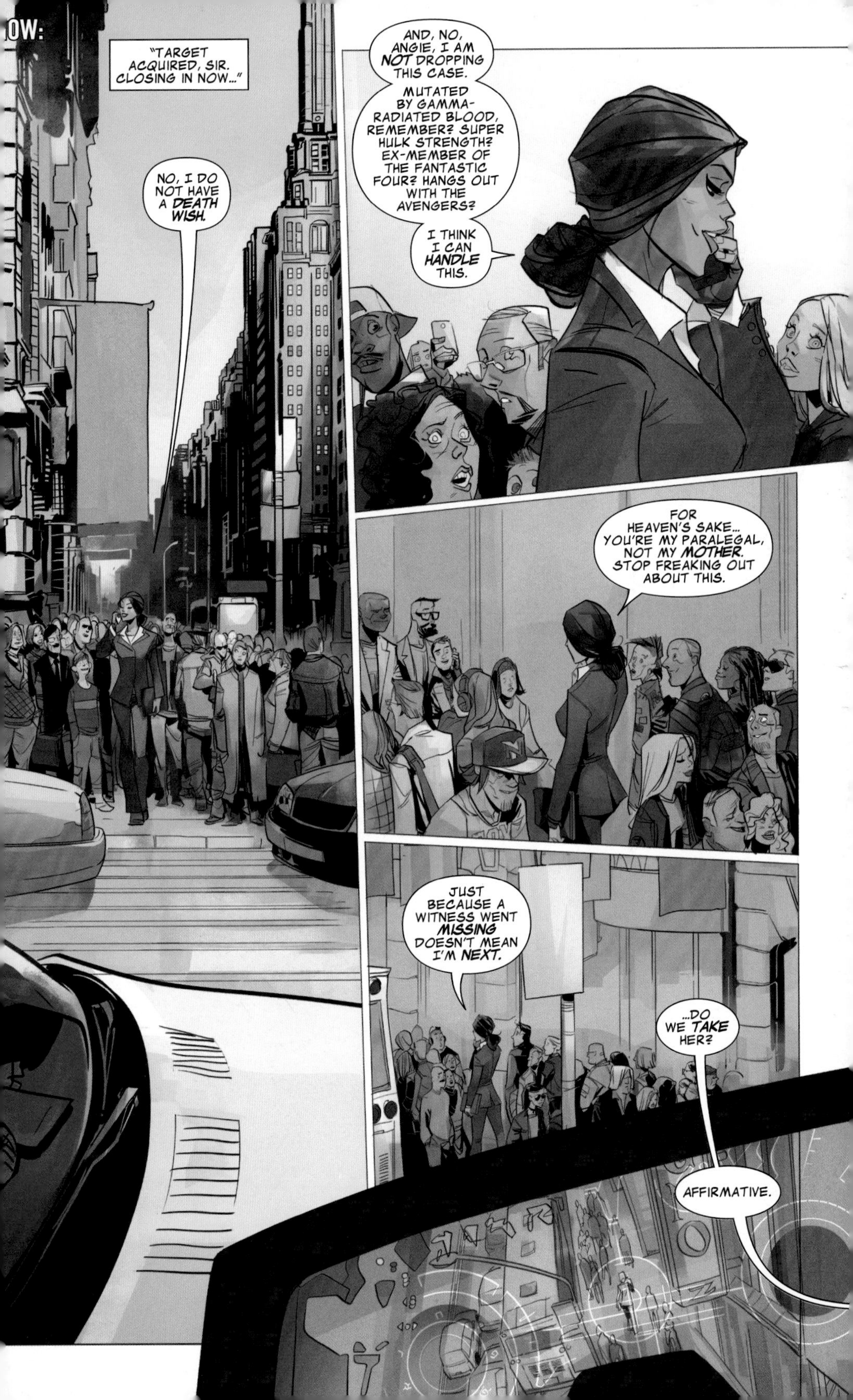
OW:
"TARGET ACQUIRED, SIR. CLOSING IN NOW..."
NO, I DO NOT HAVE A DEATH WISH.
AND, NO, ANGIE, I AM NOT DROPPING THIS CASE.
MUTATED BY GAMMA-RADIATED BLOOD, REMEMBER? SUPER HULK STRENGTH? EX-MEMBER OF THE FANTASTIC FOUR? HANGS OUT WITH THE AVENGERS?
I THINK I CAN HANDLE THIS.
FOR HEAVEN'S SAKE... YOU'RE MY PARALEGAL, NOT MY MOTHER. STOP FREAKING OUT ABOUT THIS.
JUST BECAUSE A WITNESS WENT MISSING DOESN'T MEAN I'M NEXT.
...DO WE TAKE HER?
AFFIRMATIVE.

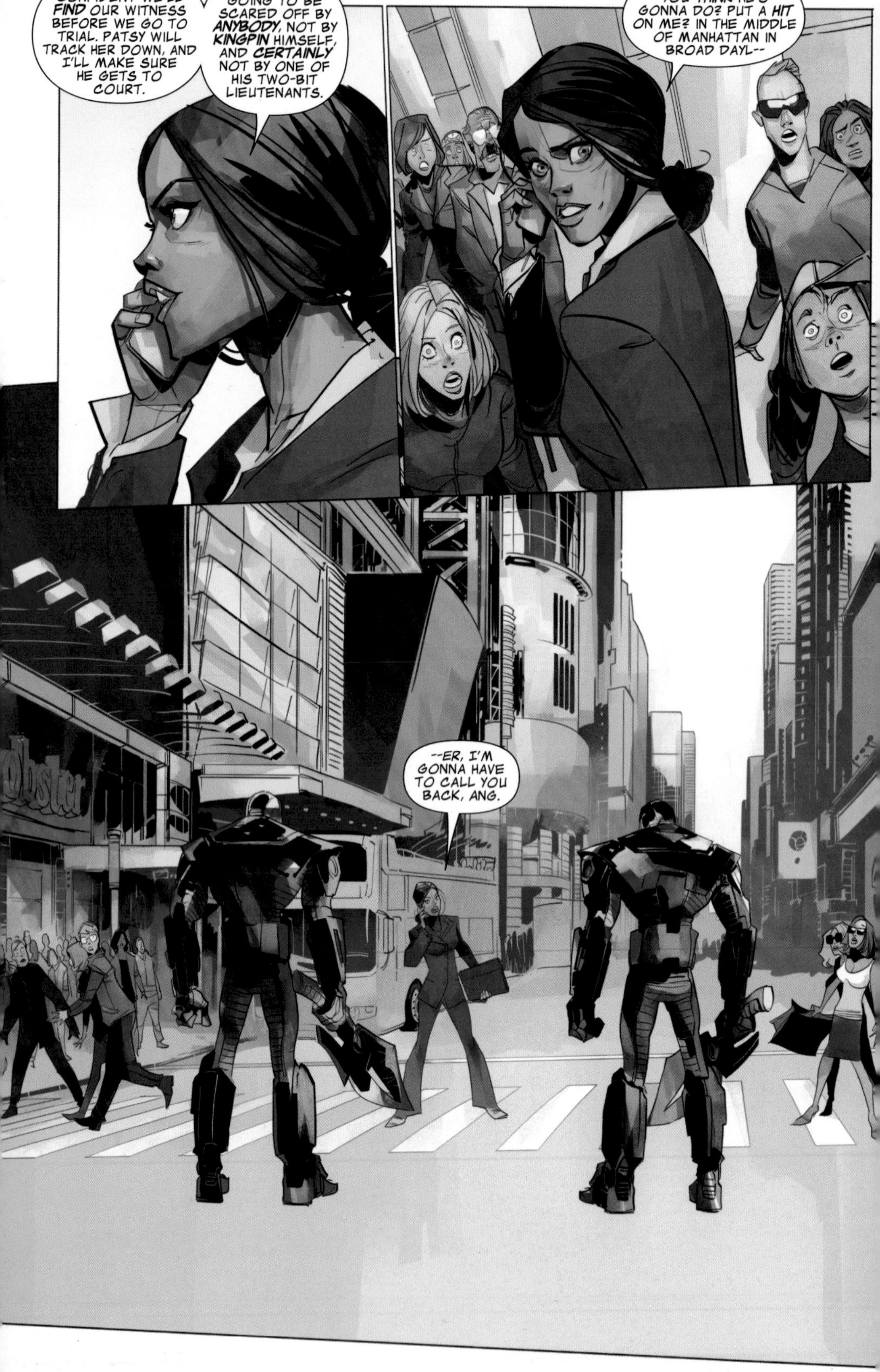
NO, I'M CONFIDENT WE'LL FIND OUR WITNESS BEFORE WE GO TO TRIAL. PATSY WILL TRACK HER DOWN, AND I'LL MAKE SURE HE GETS TO COURT.
I'M NOT GOING TO BE SCARED OFF BY ANYBODY, NOT BY KINGPIN HIMSELF, AND CERTAINLY NOT BY ONE OF HIS TWO-BIT LIEUTENANTS.
WHAT DO YOU THINK HE'S GONNA DO? PUT A HIT ON ME? IN THE MIDDLE OF MANHATTAN IN BROAD DAYL--
--ER, I'M GONNA HAVE TO CALL YOU BACK, ANG.

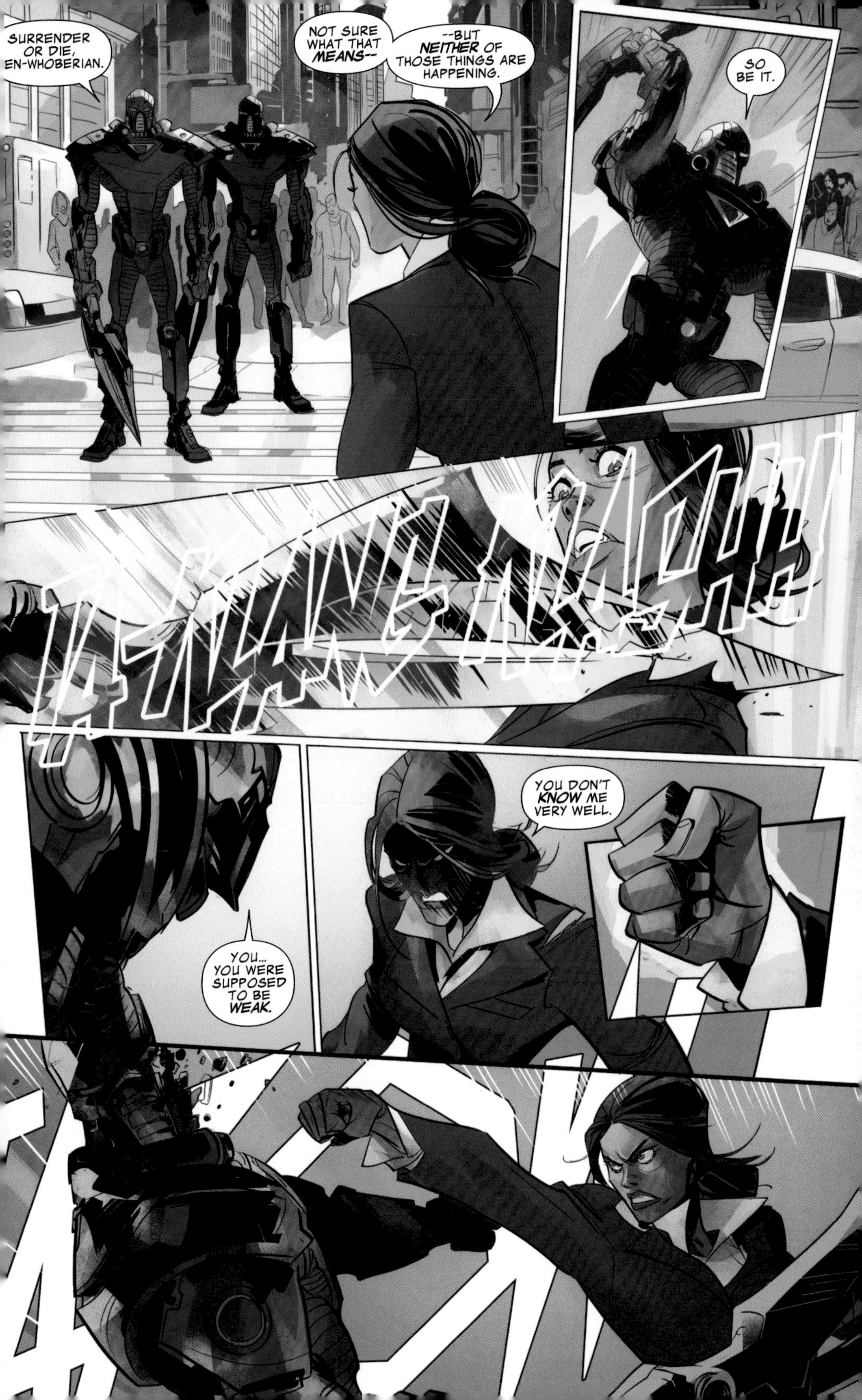
SURRENDER OR DIE, EN-WHOBERIAN.
NOT SURE WHAT THAT MEANS--
--BUT NEITHER OF THOSE THINGS ARE HAPPENING.
SO BE IT.
YOU DON'T KNOW ME VERY WELL.
YOU... YOU WERE SUPPOSED TO BE WEAK.

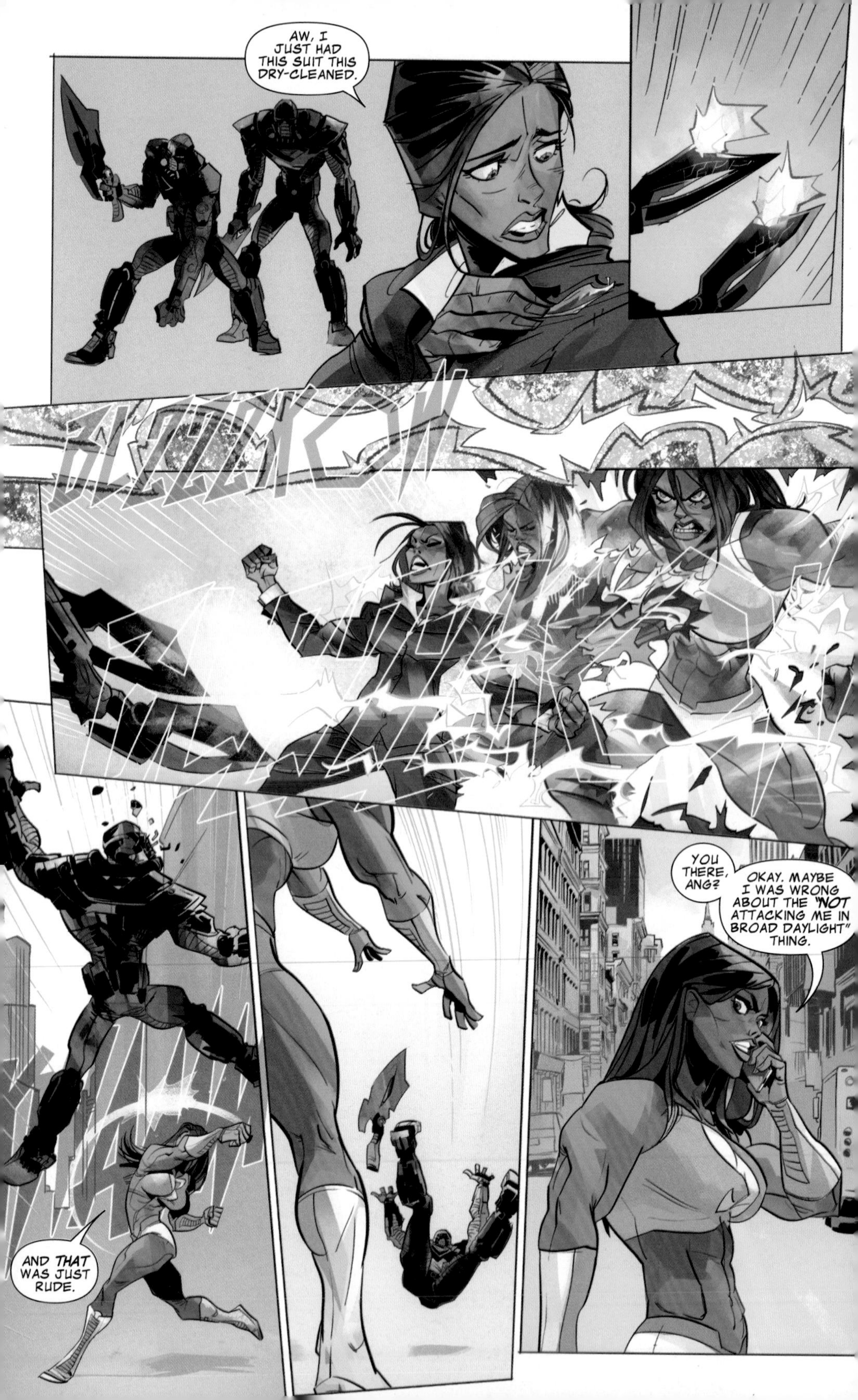
AW, I JUST HAD THIS SUIT THIS DRY-CLEANED.
AND THAT WAS JUST RUDE.
YOU THERE, ANG?
OKAY. MAYBE I WAS WRONG ABOUT THE "NOT ATTACKING ME IN BROAD DAYLIGHT" THING.

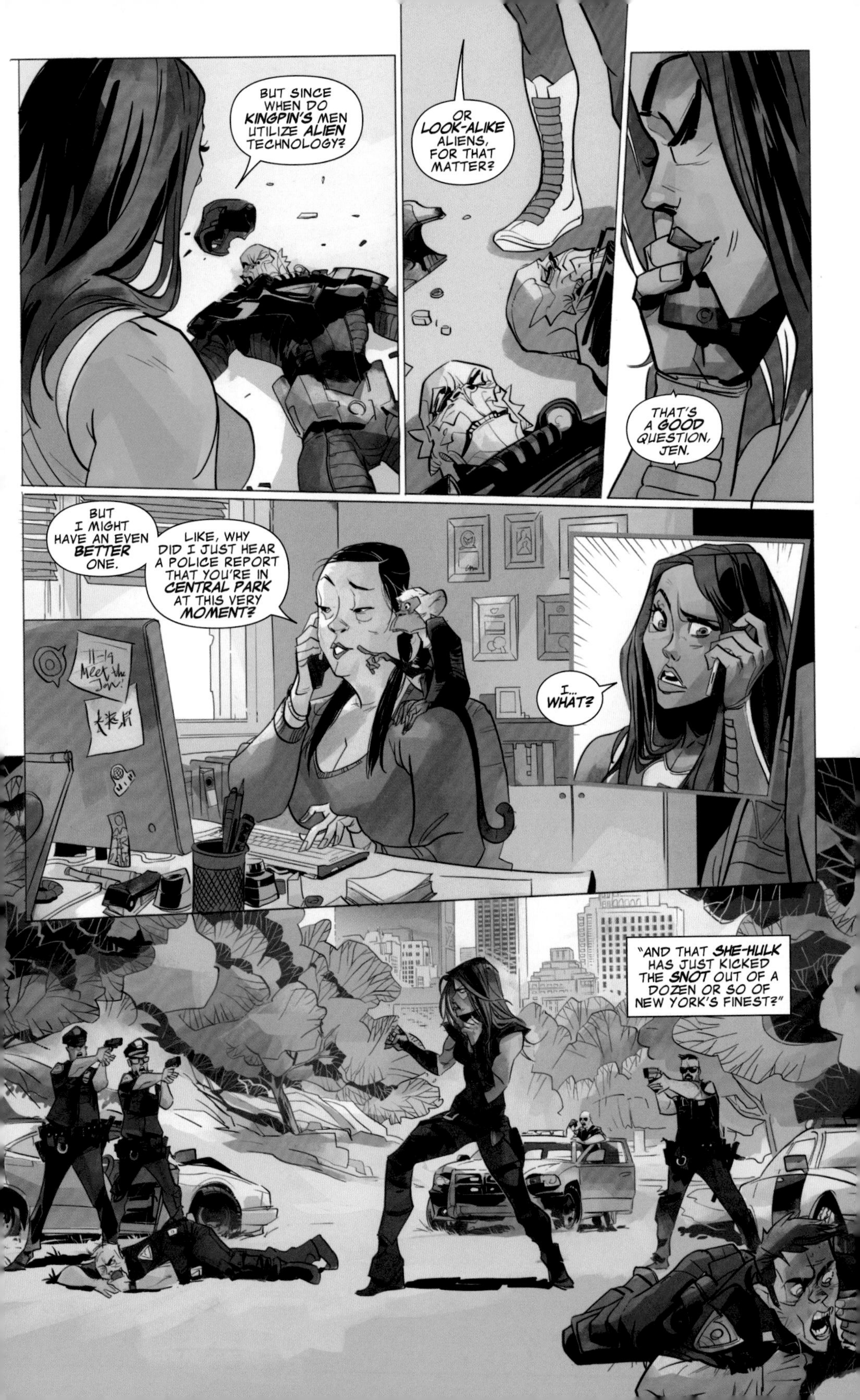
BUT SINCE WHEN DO KINGPIN'S MEN UTILIZE ALIEN TECHNOLOGY?
OR LOOK-ALIKE ALIENS, FOR THAT MATTER?
THAT'S A GOOD QUESTION, JEN.
BUT I MIGHT HAVE AN EVEN BETTER ONE.
LIKE, WHY DID I JUST HEAR A POLICE REPORT THAT YOU'RE IN CENTRAL PARK AT THIS VERY MOMENT?
I... WHAT?
"AND THAT SHE-HULK HAS JUST KICKED THE SNOT OUT OF A DOZEN OR SO OF NEW YORK'S FINEST?"

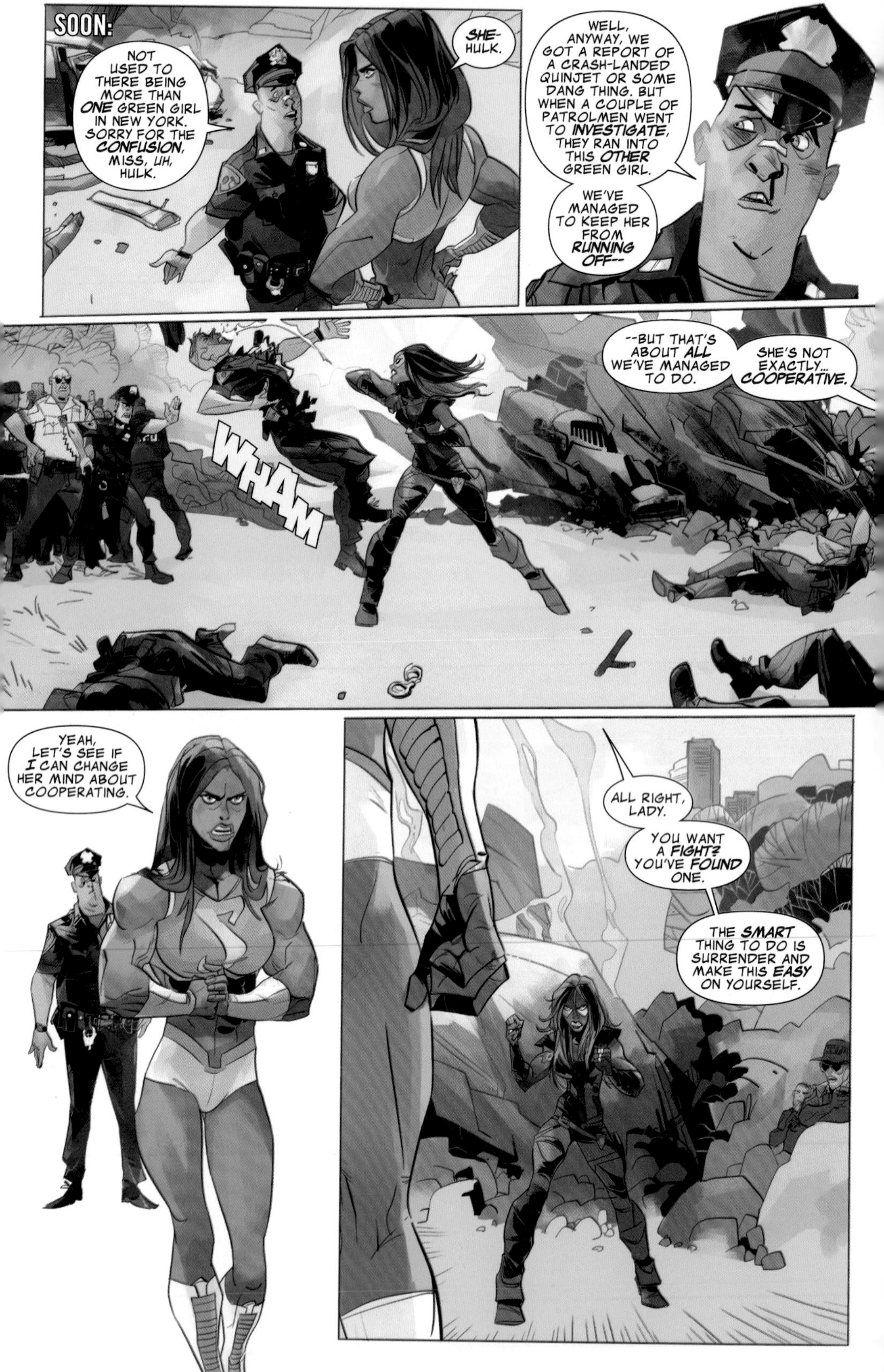
SOON:
NOT USED TO THERE BEING MORE THAN ONE GREEN GIRL IN NEW YORK. SORRY FOR THE CONFUSION, MISS, UH, HULK.
SHE-HULK.
WELL, ANYWAY, WE GOT A REPORT OF A CRASH-LANDED QUINJET OR SOME DANG THING. BUT WHEN A COUPLE OF PATROLMEN WENT TO INVESTIGATE, THEY RAN INTO THIS OTHER GREEN GIRL.
WE'VE MANAGED TO KEEP HER FROM RUNNING OFF--
--BUT THAT'S ABOUT ALL WE'VE MANAGED TO DO.
SHE'S NOT EXACTLY... COOPERATIVE.
WHAM
YEAH, LET'S SEE IF I CAN CHANGE HER MIND ABOUT COOPERATING.
ALL RIGHT, LADY.
YOU WANT A FIGHT? YOU'VE FOUND ONE.
THE SMART THING TO DO IS SURRENDER AND MAKE THIS EASY ON YOURSELF.

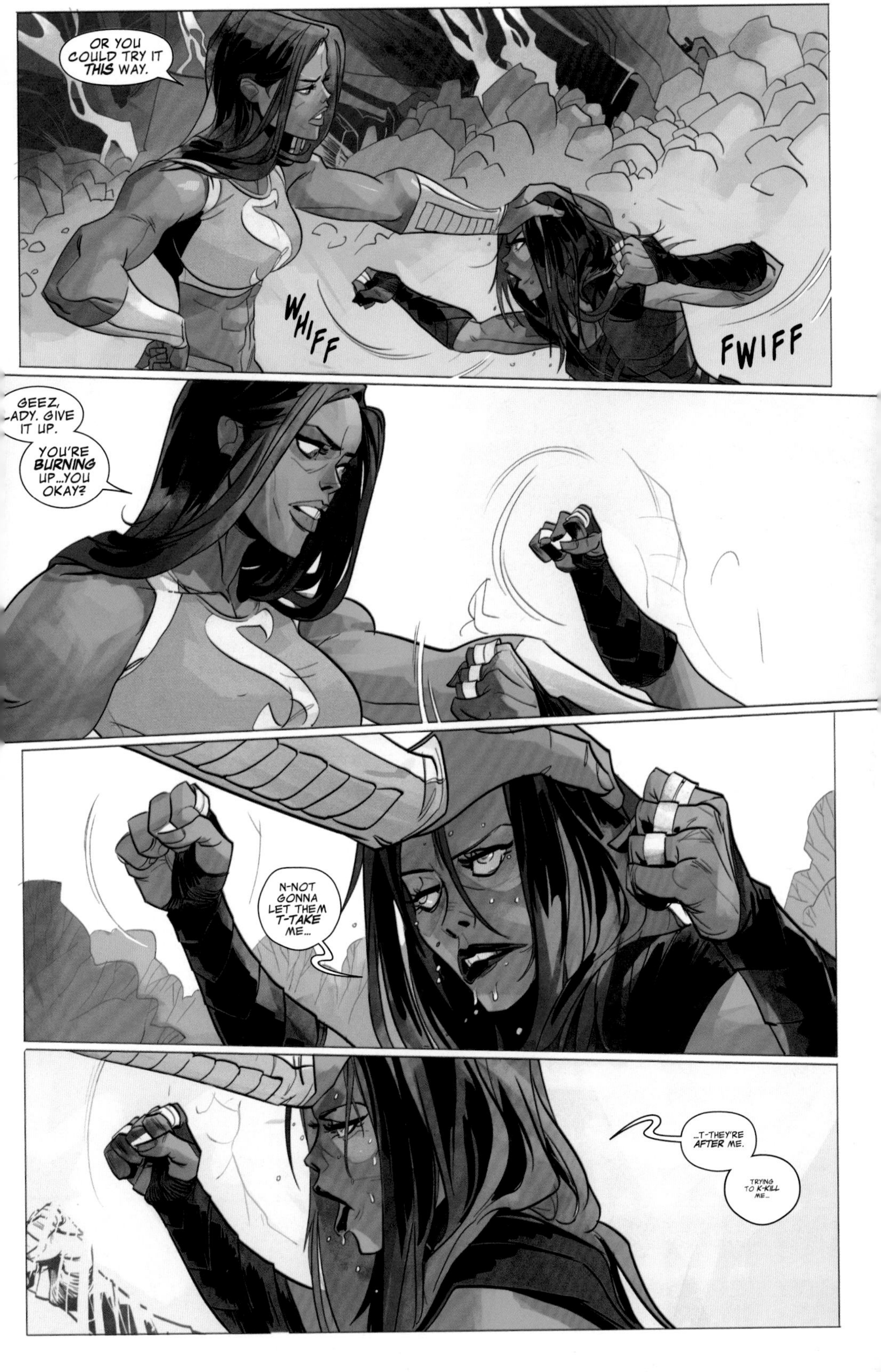
OR YOU COULD TRY IT THIS WAY.
WHIFF
FWIFF
GEEZ, LADY. GIVE IT UP.
YOU'RE BURNING UP...YOU OKAY?
N-NOT GONNA LET THEM T-TAKE ME...
...T-THEY'RE AFTER ME.
TRYING TO K-KILL ME...

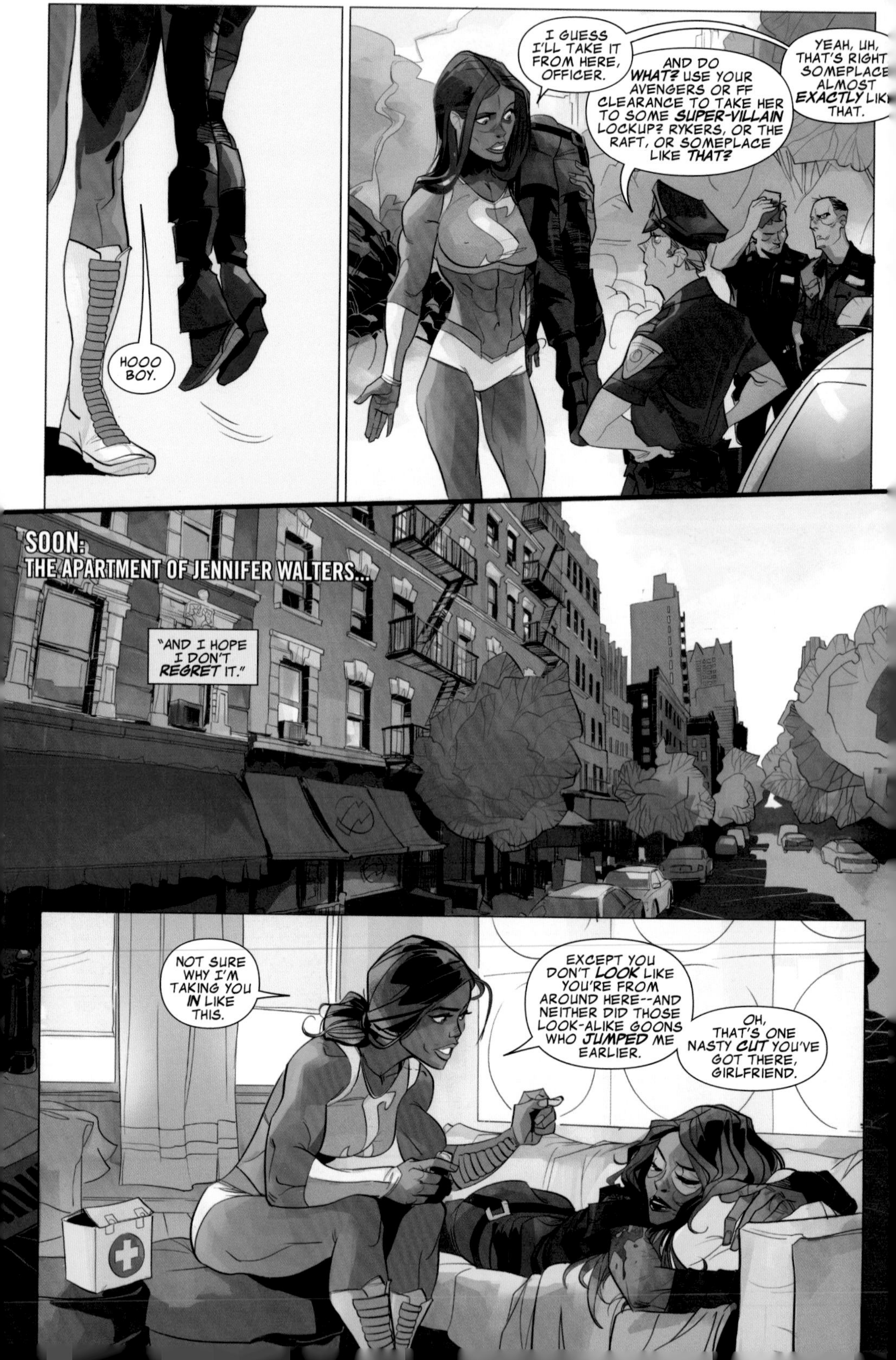
HOOO BOY.
I GUESS I'LL TAKE IT FROM HERE, OFFICER.
AND DO WHAT? USE YOUR AVENGERS OR FF CLEARANCE TO TAKE HER TO SOME SUPER-VILLAIN LOCKUP? RYKERS, OR THE RAFT, OR SOMEPLACE LIKE THAT?
YEAH, UH, THAT'S RIGHT SOMEPLACE ALMOST EXACTLY LIK THAT.
SOON: THE APARTMENT OF JENNIFER WALTERS...
"AND I HOPE I DON'T REGRET IT."
NOT SURE WHY I'M TAKING YOU IN LIKE THIS.
EXCEPT YOU DON'T LOOK LIKE YOU'RE FROM AROUND HERE--AND NEITHER DID THOSE LOOK-ALIKE GOONS WHO JUMPED ME EARLIER.
OH, THAT'S ONE NASTY CUT YOU'VE GOT THERE, GIRLFRIEND.

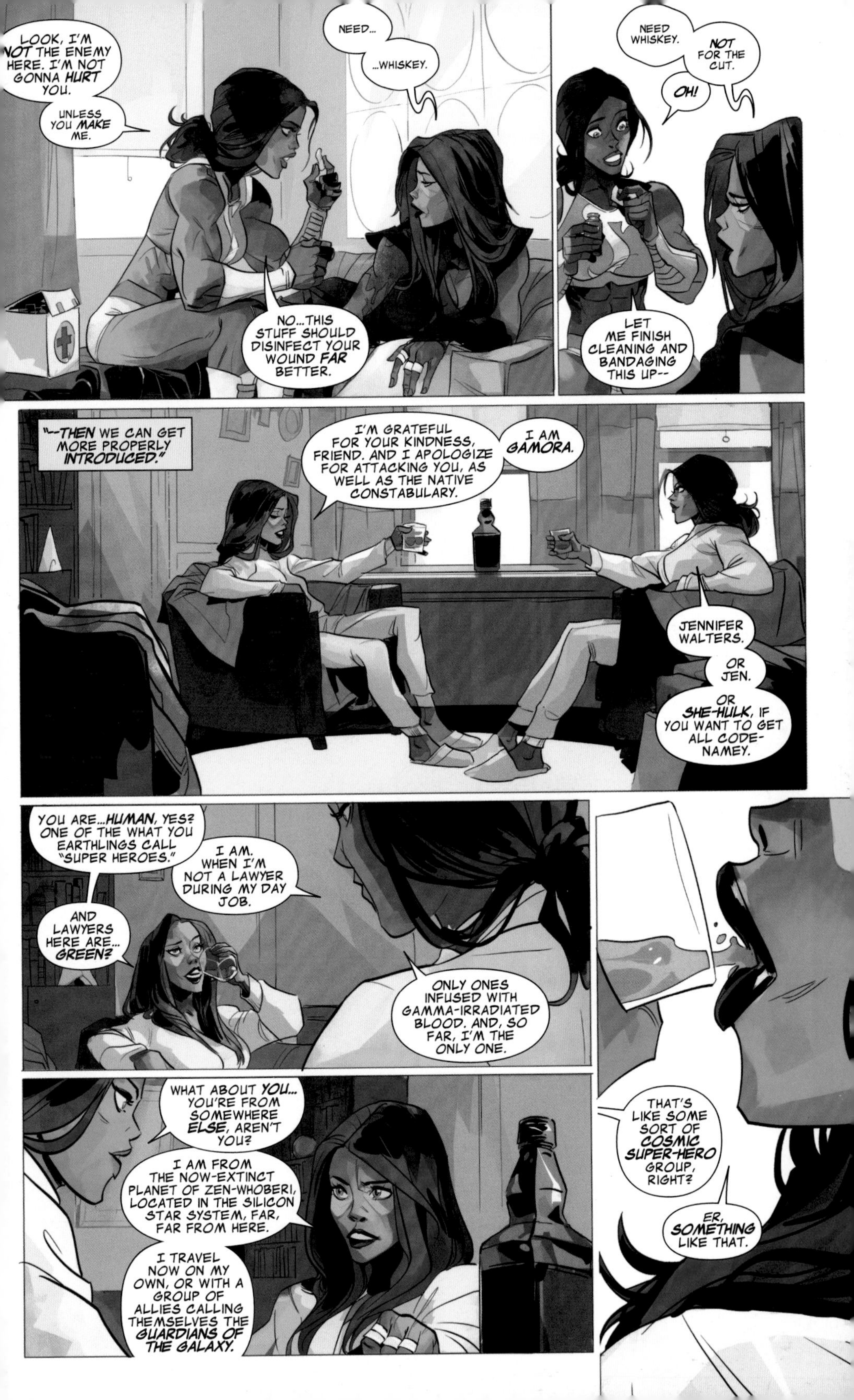
LOOK, I'M NOT THE ENEMY HERE. I'M NOT GONNA HURT YOU.
UNLESS YOU MAKE ME.
NEED...
...WHISKEY.
NO...THIS STUFF SHOULD DISINFECT YOUR WOUND FAR BETTER.
NEED WHISKEY.
NOT FOR THE CUT.
OH!
LET ME FINISH CLEANING AND BANDAGING THIS UP--
"--THEN WE CAN GET MORE PROPERLY INTRODUCED."
I'M GRATEFUL FOR YOUR KINDNESS, FRIEND. AND I APOLOGIZE FOR ATTACKING YOU, AS WELL AS THE NATIVE CONSTABULARY.
I AM GAMORA.
JENNIFER WALTERS.
OR JEN.
OR SHE-HULK, IF YOU WANT TO GET ALL CODE-NAMEY.
YOU ARE...HUMAN, YES? ONE OF THE WHAT YOU EARTHLINGS CALL "SUPER HEROES."
I AM. WHEN I'M NOT A LAWYER DURING MY DAY JOB.
AND LAWYERS HERE ARE... GREEN?
ONLY ONES INFUSED WITH GAMMA-IRRADIATED BLOOD. AND, SO FAR, I'M THE ONLY ONE.
WHAT ABOUT YOU... YOU'RE FROM SOMEWHERE ELSE, AREN'T YOU?
I AM FROM THE NOW-EXTINCT PLANET OF ZEN-WHOBERI, LOCATED IN THE SILICON STAR SYSTEM, FAR, FAR FROM HERE.
I TRAVEL NOW ON MY OWN, OR WITH A GROUP OF ALLIES CALLING THEMSELVES THE GUARDIANS OF THE GALAXY.
THAT'S LIKE SOME SORT OF COSMIC SUPER-HERO GROUP, RIGHT?
ER, SOMETHING LIKE THAT.

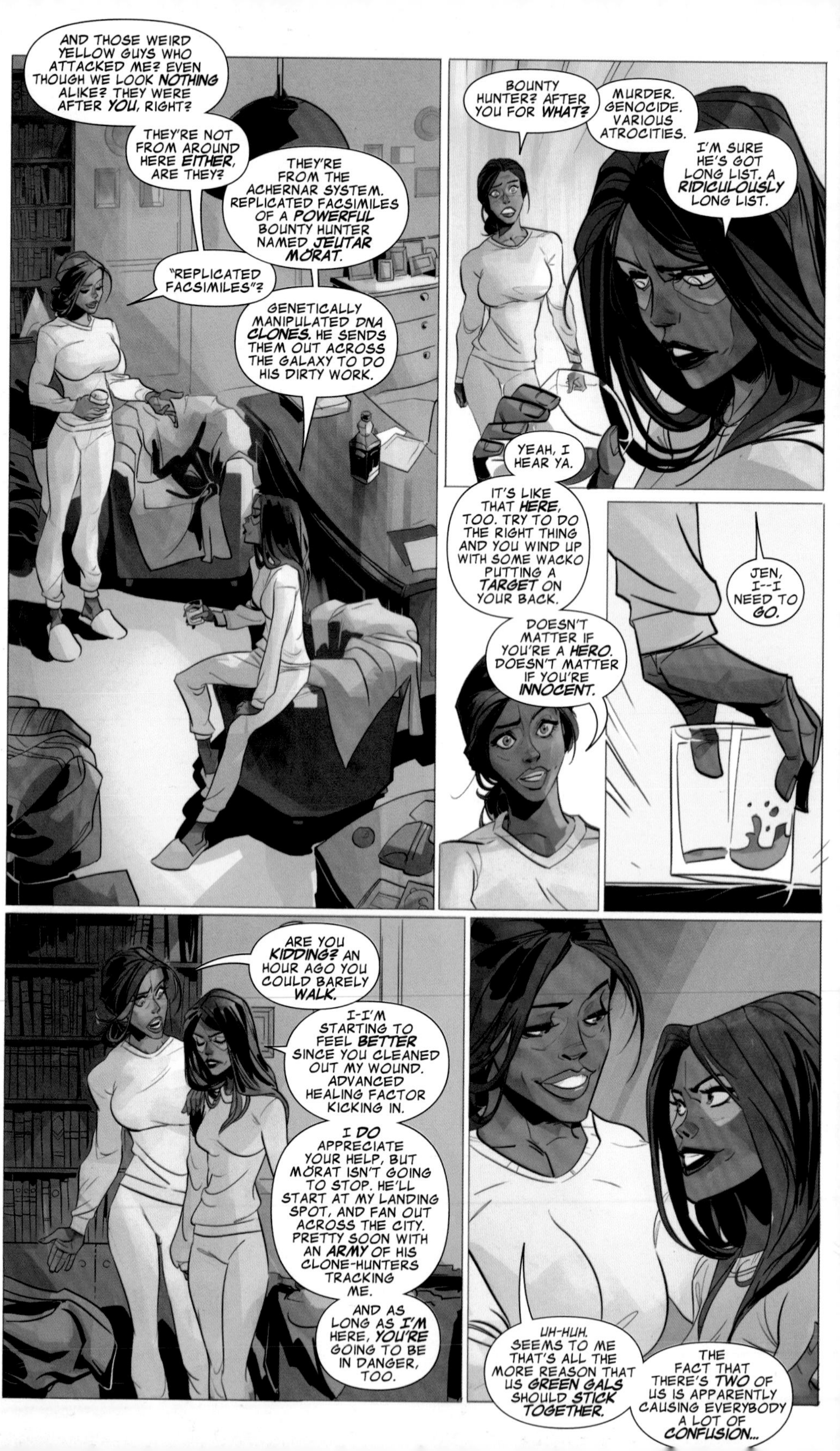
AND THOSE WEIRD YELLOW GUYS WHO ATTACKED ME? EVEN THOUGH WE LOOK NOTHING ALIKE? THEY WERE AFTER YOU, RIGHT?
THEY'RE NOT FROM AROUND HERE EITHER, ARE THEY?
THEY'RE FROM THE ACHERNAR SYSTEM. REPLICATED FACSIMILES OF A POWERFUL BOUNTY HUNTER NAMED JEUTAR MÖRAT.
"REPLICATED FACSIMILES"?
GENETICALLY MANIPULATED DNA CLONES. HE SENDS THEM OUT ACROSS THE GALAXY TO DO HIS DIRTY WORK.
BOUNTY HUNTER? AFTER YOU FOR WHAT?
MURDER. GENOCIDE. VARIOUS ATROCITIES.
I'M SURE HE'S GOT LONG LIST. A RIDICULOUSLY LONG LIST.
YEAH, I HEAR YA.
IT'S LIKE THAT HERE, TOO. TRY TO DO THE RIGHT THING AND YOU WIND UP WITH SOME WACKO PUTTING A TARGET ON YOUR BACK.
DOESN'T MATTER IF YOU'RE A HERO. DOESN'T MATTER IF YOU'RE INNOCENT.
JEN, I--I NEED TO GO.
ARE YOU KIDDING? AN HOUR AGO YOU COULD BARELY WALK.
I-I'M STARTING TO FEEL BETTER SINCE YOU CLEANED OUT MY WOUND. ADVANCED HEALING FACTOR KICKING IN.
I DO APPRECIATE YOUR HELP, BUT MÖRAT ISN'T GOING TO STOP. HE'LL START AT MY LANDING SPOT, AND FAN OUT ACROSS THE CITY. PRETTY SOON WITH AN ARMY OF HIS CLONE-HUNTERS TRACKING ME.
AND AS LONG AS I'M HERE, YOU'RE GOING TO BE IN DANGER, TOO.
UH-HUH. SEEMS TO ME THAT'S ALL THE MORE REASON THAT US GREEN GALS SHOULD STICK TOGETHER.
THE FACT THAT THERE'S TWO OF US IS APPARENTLY CAUSING EVERYBODY A LOT OF CONFUSION...

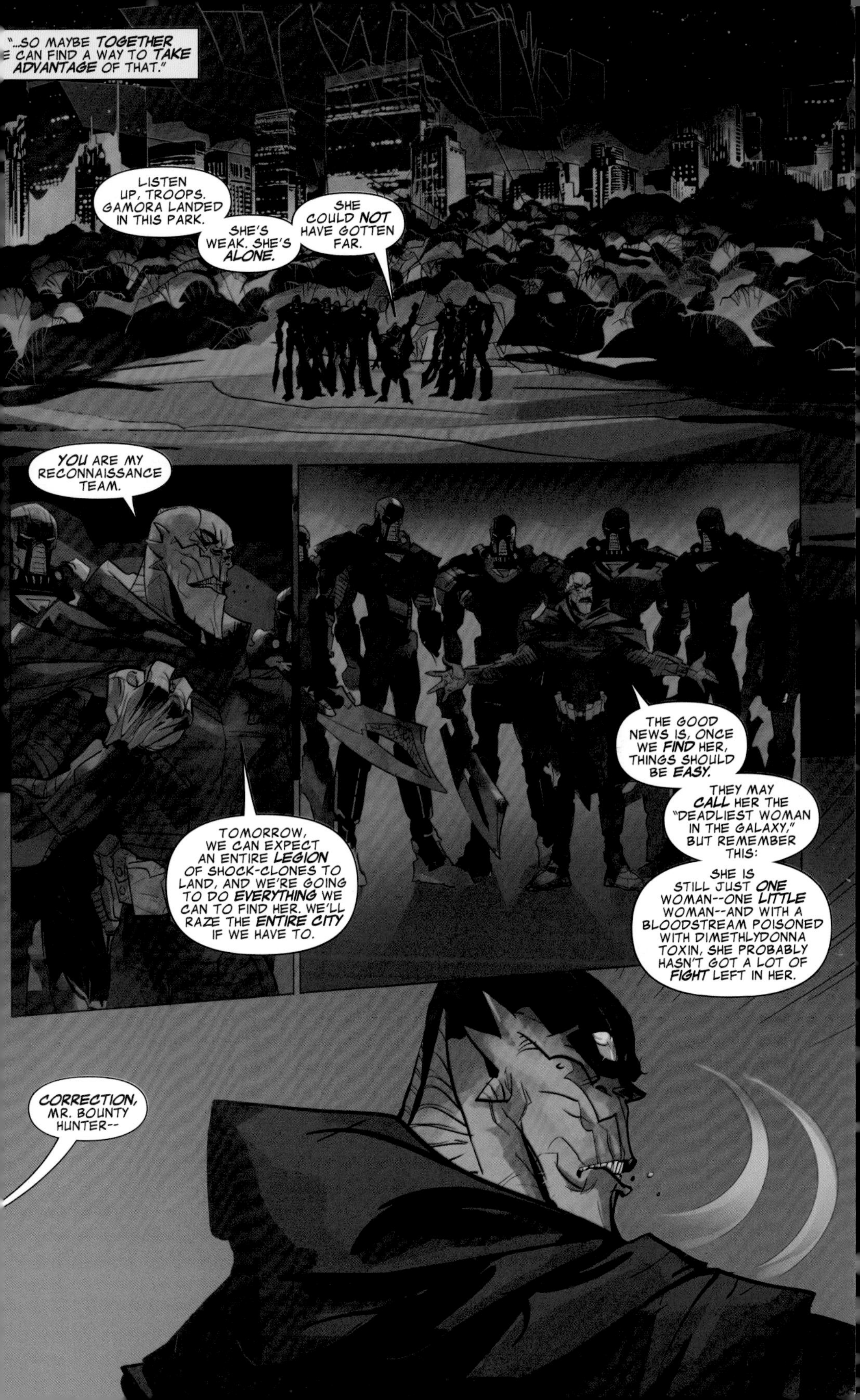
"...SO MAYBE TOGETHER
E CAN FIND A WAY TO TAKE ADVANTAGE OF THAT."
LISTEN UP, TROOPS. GAMORA LANDED IN THIS PARK.
SHE'S WEAK. SHE'S ALONE.
SHE COULD NOT HAVE GOTTEN FAR.
YOU ARE MY RECONNAISSANCE TEAM.
TOMORROW, WE CAN EXPECT AN ENTIRE LEGION OF SHOCK-CLONES TO LAND, AND WE'RE GOING TO DO EVERYTHING WE CAN TO FIND HER. WE'LL RAZE THE ENTIRE CITY IF WE HAVE TO.
THE GOOD NEWS IS, ONCE WE FIND HER, THINGS SHOULD BE EASY.
THEY MAY CALL HER THE "DEADLIEST WOMAN IN THE GALAXY," BUT REMEMBER THIS:
SHE IS STILL JUST ONE WOMAN--ONE LITTLE WOMAN--AND WITH A BLOODSTREAM POISONED WITH DIMETHLYDONNA TOXIN, SHE PROBABLY HASN'T GOT A LOT OF FIGHT LEFT IN HER.
CORRECTION, MR. BOUNTY HUNTER--

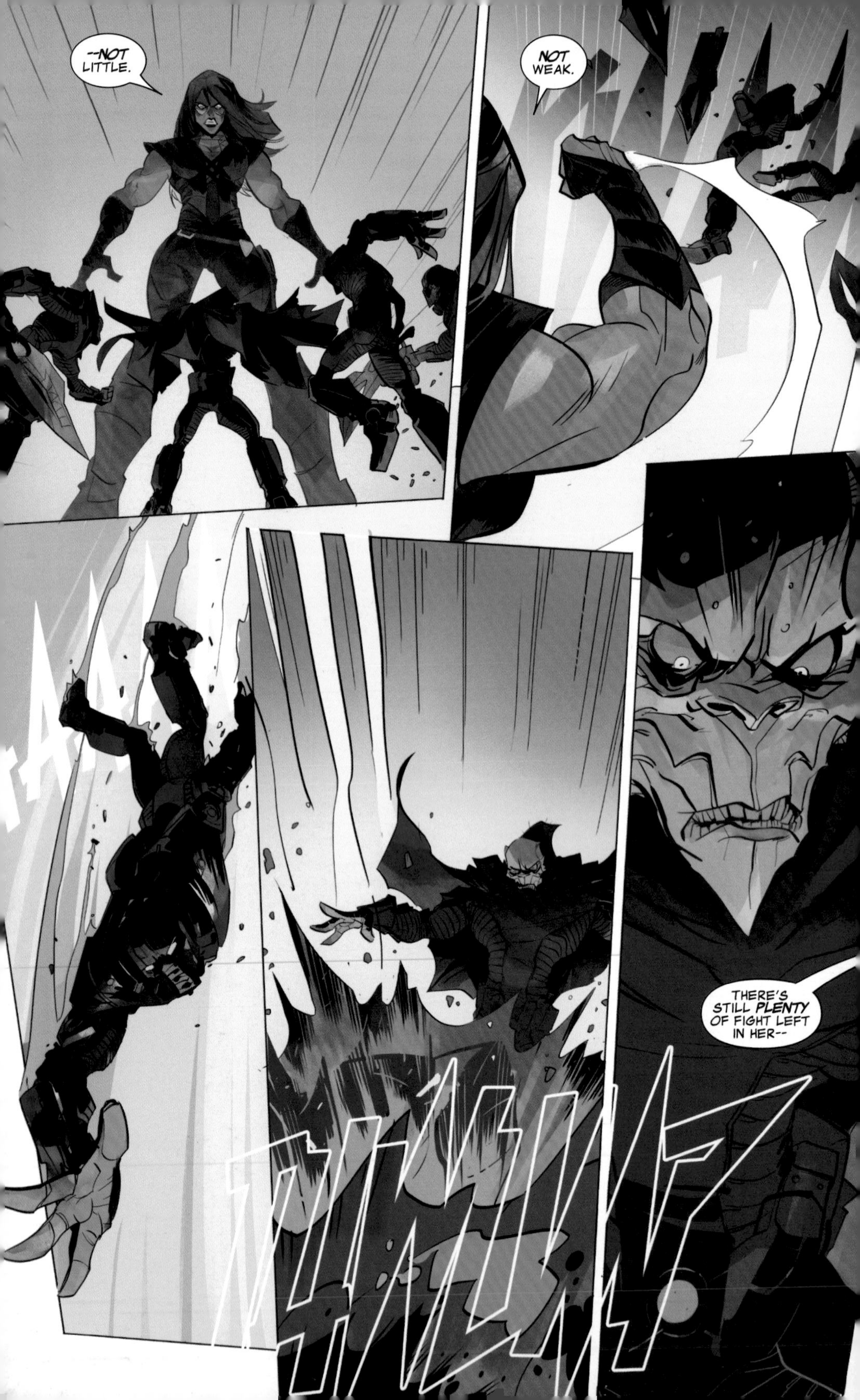
--NOT LITTLE.
NOT WEAK.
THERE'S STILL PLENTY OF FIGHT LEFT IN HER--
THOOM

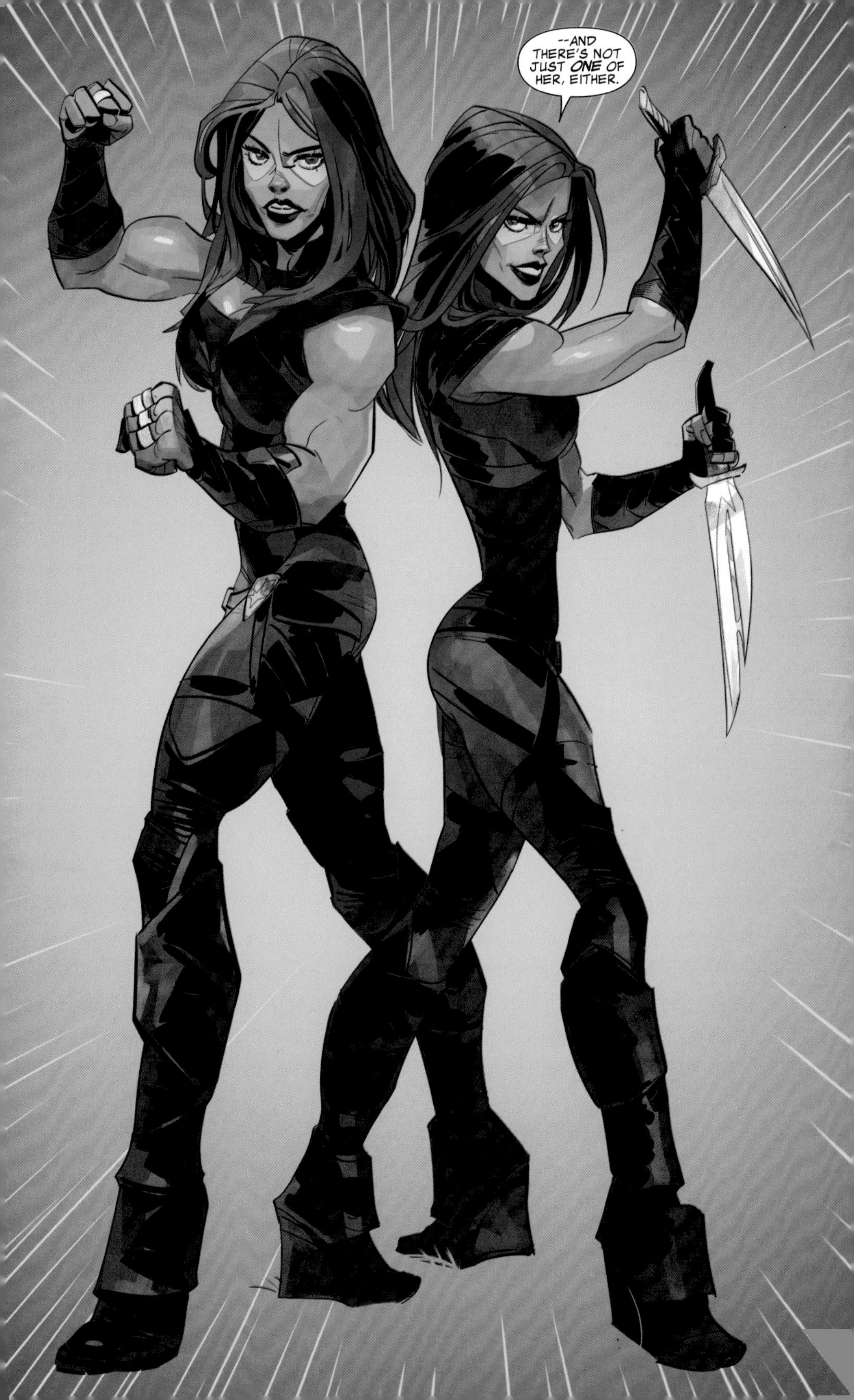
--AND THERE'S NOT JUST ONE OF HER, EITHER.

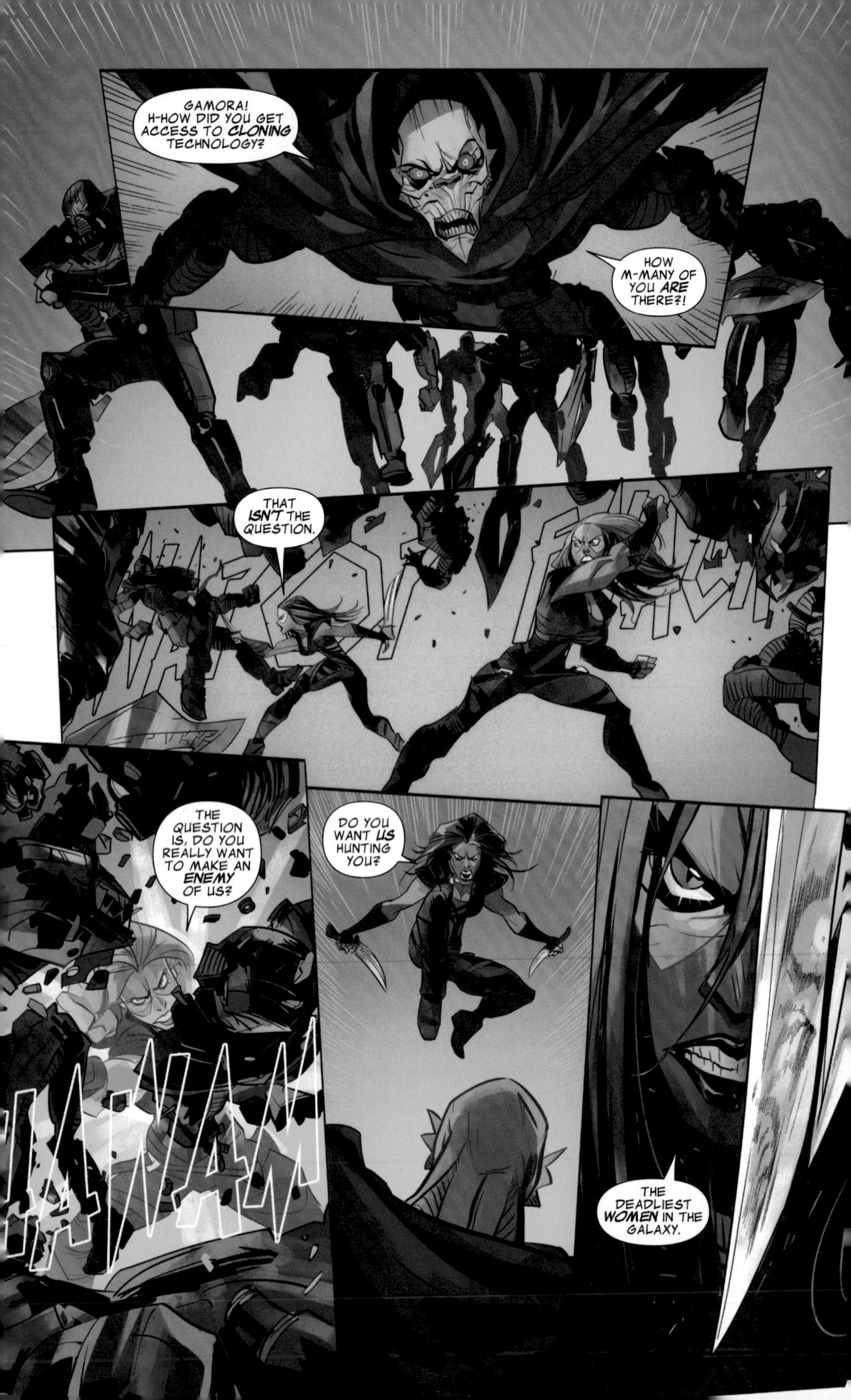
GAMORA! H-HOW DID YOU GET ACCESS TO CLONING TECHNOLOGY?
HOW M-MANY OF YOU ARE THERE?!
THAT ISN'T THE QUESTION.
THE QUESTION IS, DO YOU REALLY WANT TO MAKE AN ENEMY OF US?
DO YOU WANT US HUNTING YOU?
THE DEADLIEST WOMEN IN THE GALAXY.

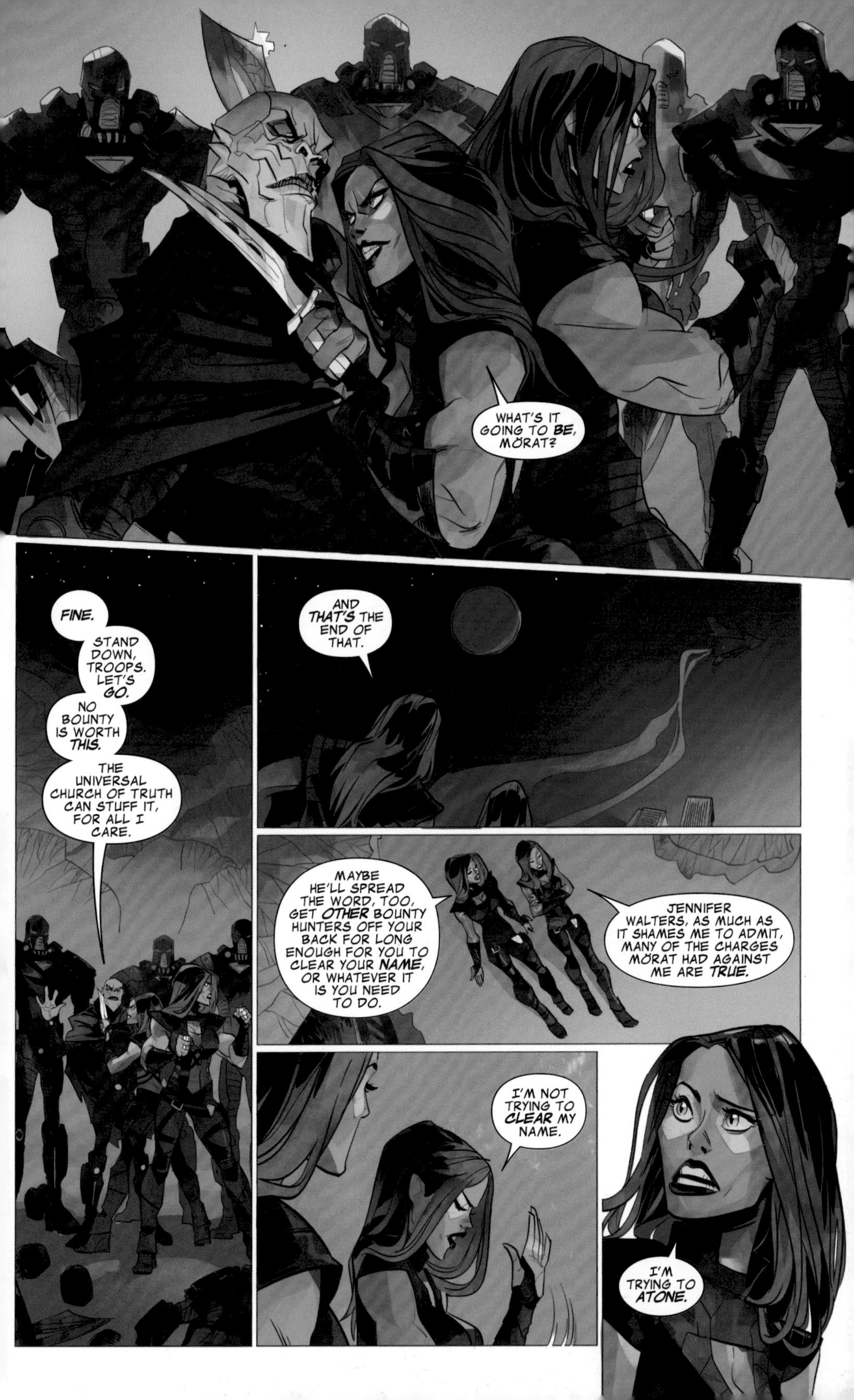
WHAT'S IT GOING TO BE, MÖRAT?
FINE.
STAND DOWN, TROOPS. LET'S GO.
NO BOUNTY IS WORTH THIS.
THE UNIVERSAL CHURCH OF TRUTH CAN STUFF IT, FOR ALL I CARE.
AND THAT'S THE END OF THAT.
MAYBE HE'LL SPREAD THE WORD, TOO, GET OTHER BOUNTY HUNTERS OFF YOUR BACK FOR LONG ENOUGH FOR YOU TO CLEAR YOUR NAME, OR WHATEVER IT IS YOU NEED TO DO.
JENNIFER WALTERS, AS MUCH AS IT SHAMES ME TO ADMIT, MANY OF THE CHARGES MÖRAT HAD AGAINST ME ARE TRUE.
I'M NOT TRYING TO CLEAR MY NAME.
I'M TRYING TO ATONE.

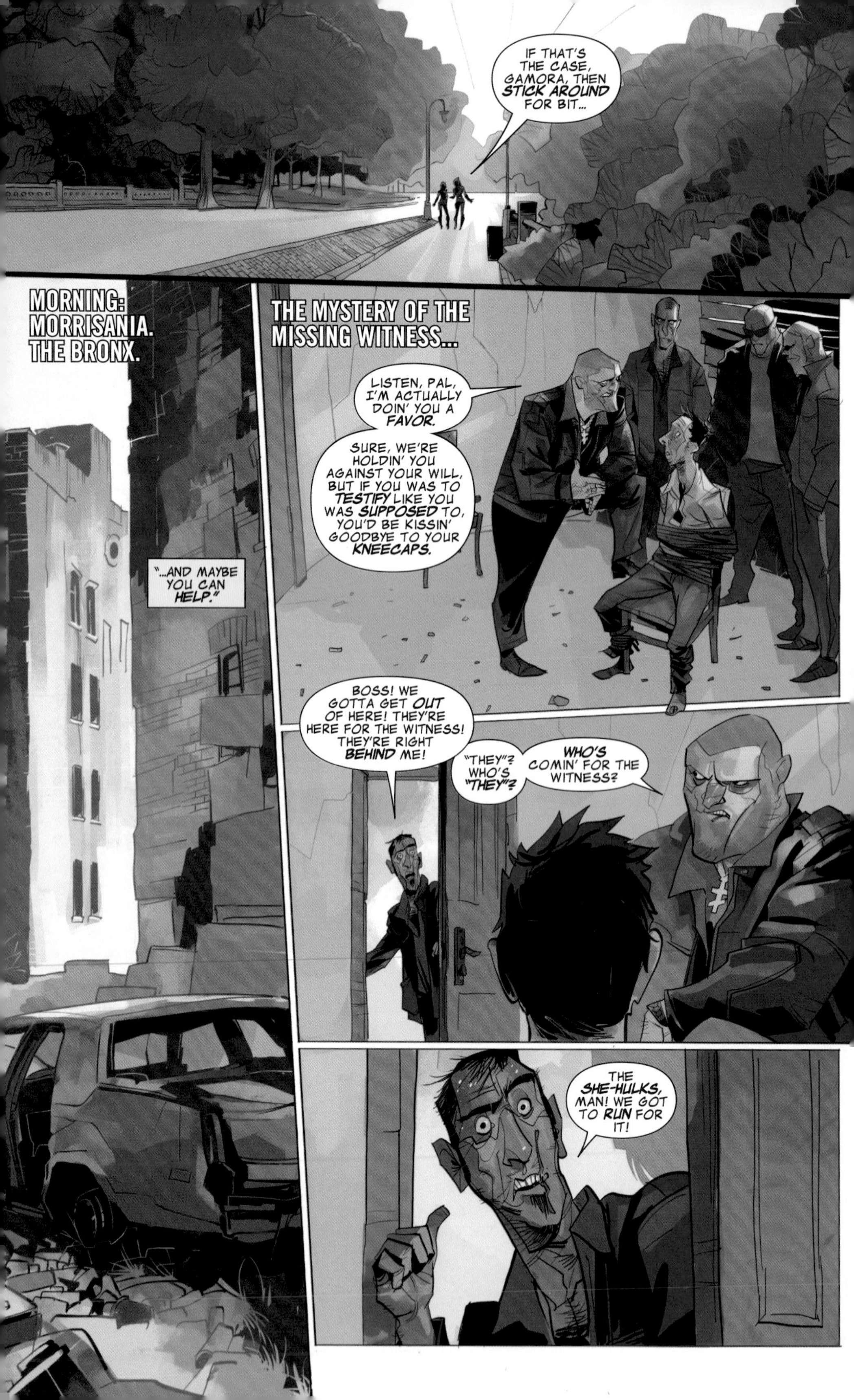
IF THAT'S THE CASE, GAMORA, THEN STICK AROUND FOR BIT...
MORNING: MORRISANIA. THE BRONX.
"...AND MAYBE YOU CAN HELP."
THE MYSTERY OF THE MISSING WITNESS...
LISTEN, PAL, I'M ACTUALLY DOIN' YOU A FAVOR.
SURE, WE'RE HOLDIN' YOU AGAINST YOUR WILL, BUT IF YOU WAS TO TESTIFY LIKE YOU WAS SUPPOSED TO, YOU'D BE KISSIN' GOODBYE TO YOUR KNEECAPS.
BOSS! WE GOTTA GET OUT OF HERE! THEY'RE HERE FOR THE WITNESS! THEY'RE RIGHT BEHIND ME!
"THEY"? WHO'S "THEY"?
WHO'S COMIN' FOR THE WITNESS?
THE SHE-HULKS, MAN! WE GOT TO RUN FOR IT!

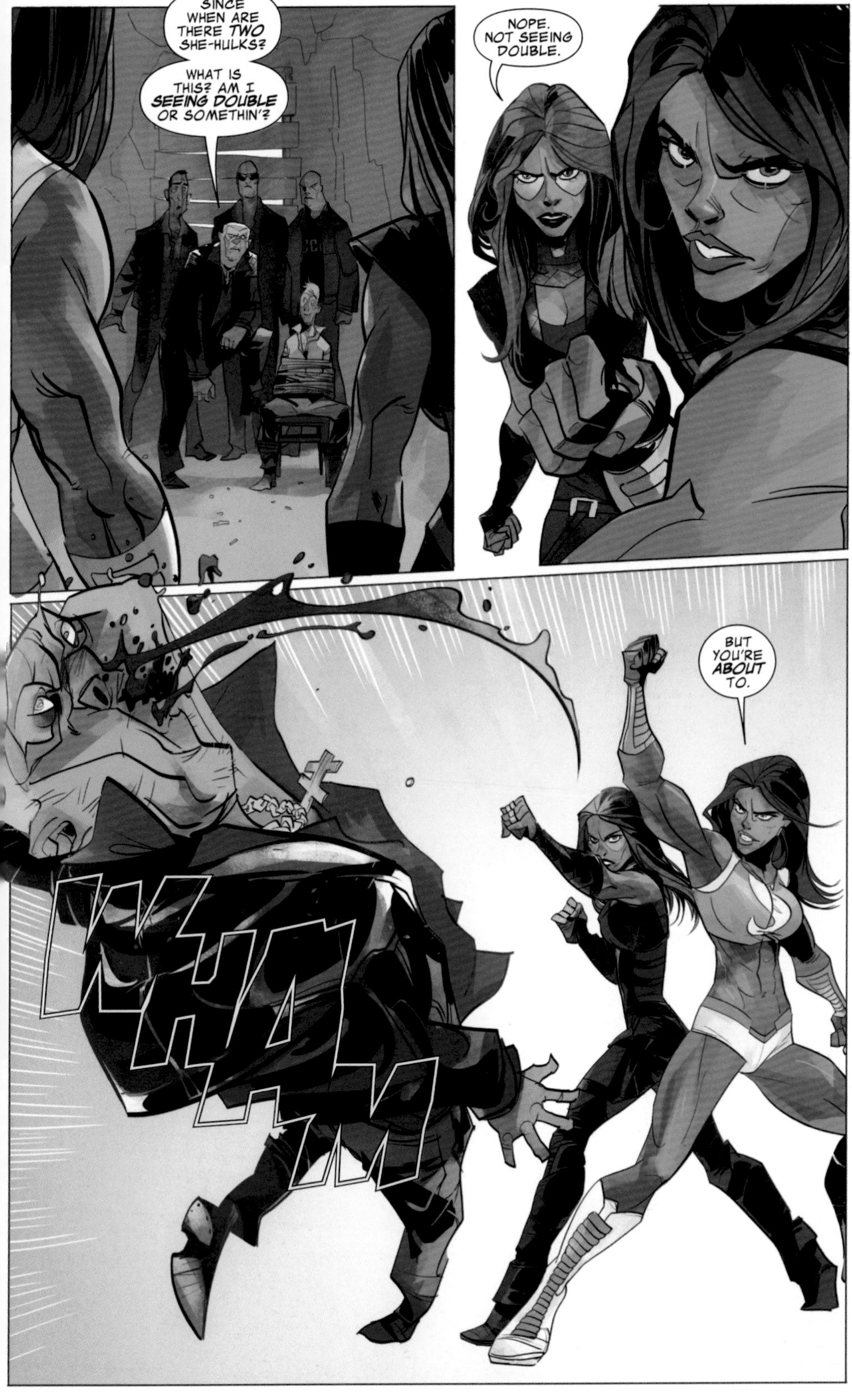
SINCE WHEN ARE THERE TWO SHE-HULKS?
WHAT IS THIS? AM I SEEING DOUBLE OR SOMETHIN'?
NOPE. NOT SEEING DOUBLE.
BUT YOU'RE ABOUT TO.
WHAM

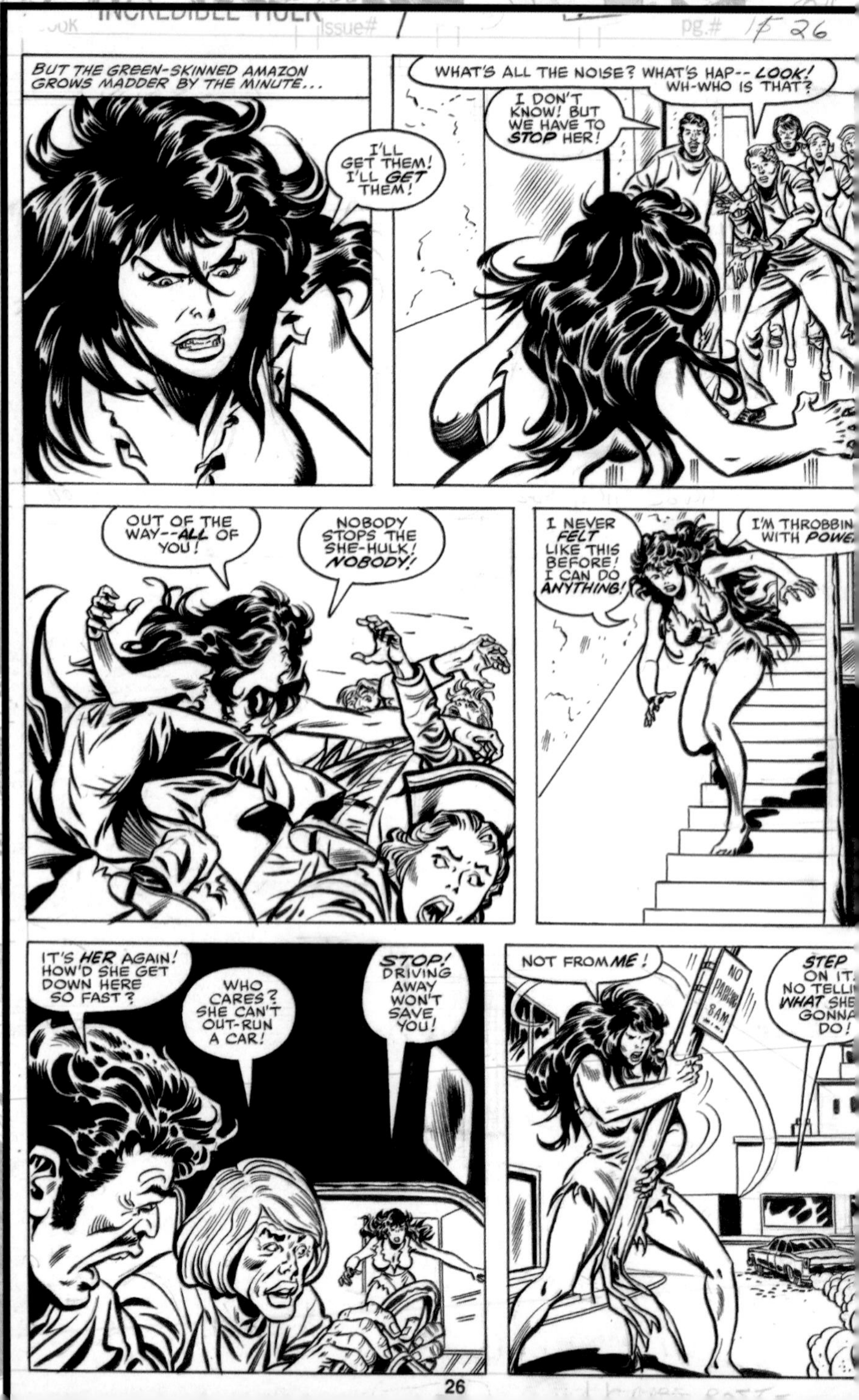
BUT THE GREEN-SKINNED AMAZON GROWS MADDER BY THE MINUTE...
I'LL GET THEM! I'LL GET THEM!
WHAT'S ALL THE NOISE? WHAT'S HAP-- LOOK! WH-WHO IS THAT?
I DON'T KNOW! BUT WE HAVE TO STOP HER!
OUT OF THE WAY--ALL OF YOU!
NOBODY STOPS THE SHE-HULK! NOBODY!
I NEVER FELT LIKE THIS BEFORE! I CAN DO ANYTHING!
I'M THROBBIN WITH POWE
IT'S HER AGAIN! HOW'D SHE GET DOWN HERE SO FAST?
WHO CARES? SHE CAN'T OUT-RUN A CAR!
STOP! DRIVING AWAY WON'T SAVE YOU!
NOT FROM ME!
NO PARKING 8AM
STEP ON IT NO TELLI WHAT SHE GONNA DO!

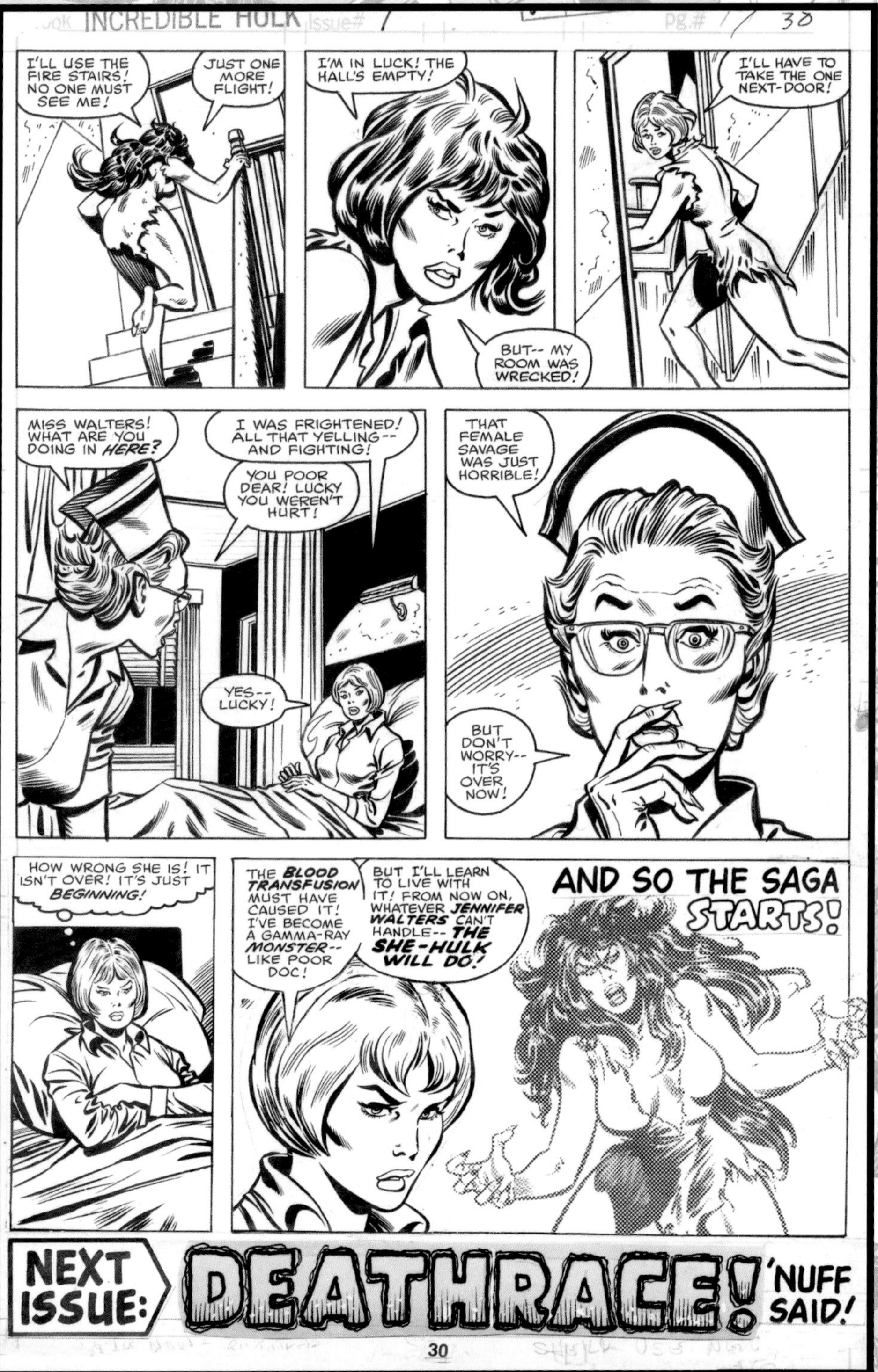
INCREDIBLE HULK
I'LL USE THE FIRE STAIRS! NO ONE MUST SEE ME!
JUST ONE MORE FLIGHT!
I'M IN LUCK! THE HALL'S EMPTY!
BUT-- MY ROOM WAS WRECKED!
I'LL HAVE TO TAKE THE ONE NEXT-DOOR!
MISS WALTERS! WHAT ARE YOU DOING IN HERE?
I WAS FRIGHTENED! ALL THAT YELLING-- AND FIGHTING!
YOU POOR DEAR! LUCKY YOU WEREN'T HURT!
YES-- LUCKY!
THAT FEMALE SAVAGE WAS JUST HORRIBLE!
BUT DON'T WORRY-- IT'S OVER NOW!
HOW WRONG SHE IS! IT ISN'T OVER! IT'S JUST BEGINNING!
THE BLOOD TRANSFUSION MUST HAVE CAUSED IT! I'VE BECOME A GAMMA-RAY MONSTER-- LIKE POOR DOC!
BUT I'LL LEARN TO LIVE WITH IT! FROM NOW ON, WHATEVER JENNIFER WALTERS CAN'T HANDLE-- THE SHE-HULK WILL DO!
AND SO THE SAGA STARTS!
NEXT ISSUE: DEATHRACE! 'NUFF SAID!
30

SAVAGE SHE-HULK #1

PAGE 17 ORIGINAL ART BY JOHN BUSCEMA & CHIC STONE
COURTESY OF HERITAGEAUCTIONS.COM

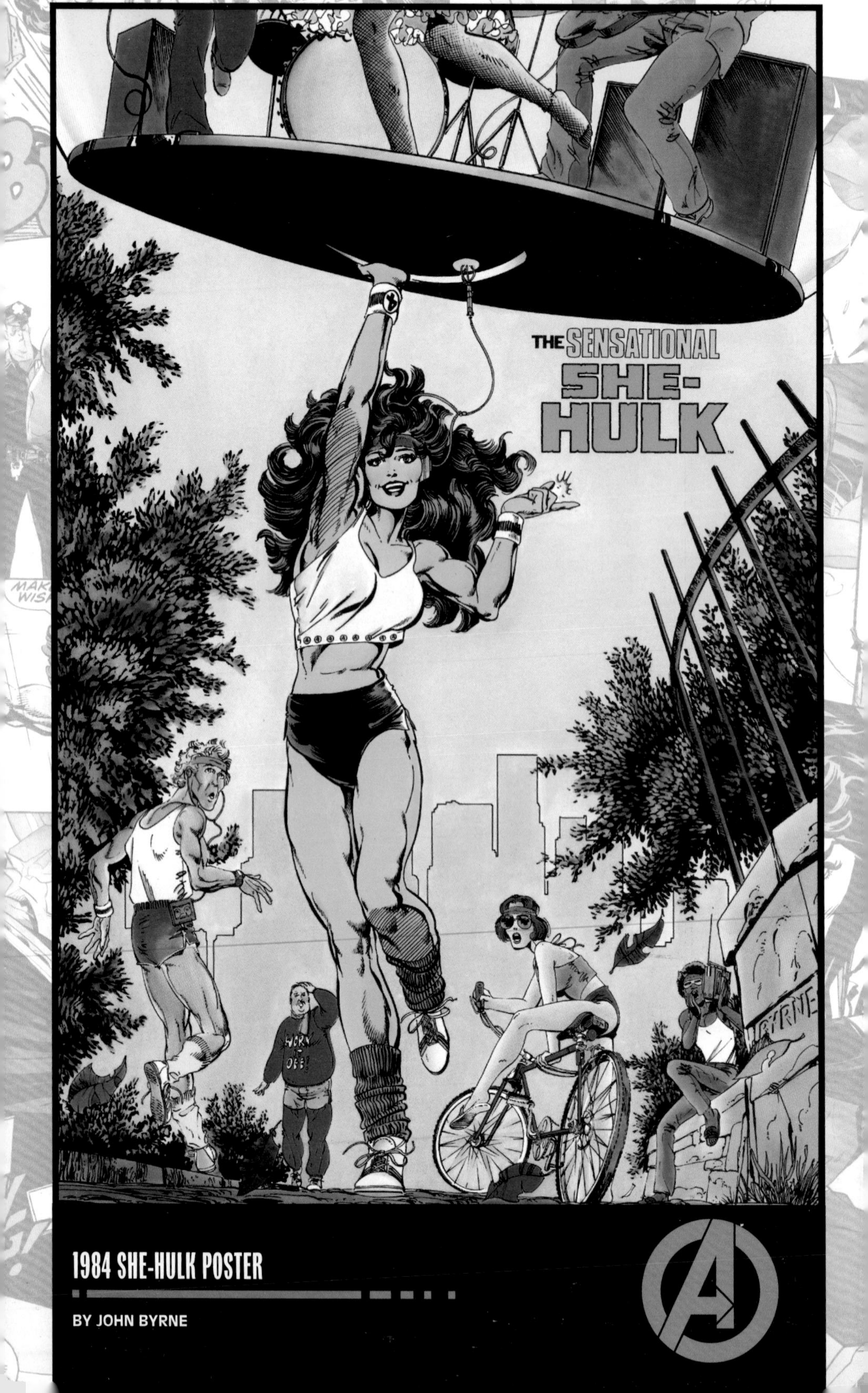
THE SENSATIONAL
SHE-HULK
WORK IT OFF!
BYRNE

1984 SHE-HULK POSTER

BY JOHN BYRNE